One thing that remains constant is excellent, emotionally charged storytelling. Ayashi no Ceres is as good as shojo gets.
—Anime News Network

Readers of the manga version of Ceres will not be disappointed. In short, Ceres is beautiful, deep, and enjoyable—a top notch supernatural work of art.
—John Robinson, NeedCoffee.com

Yu Watase's character designs are nothing short of spectacular. [She] is not only an amazing artist, but an amazing storyteller as well. Such depth is rarely found in any form of entertainment, but with Yu Watase at the helm of the project, it was guaranteed to be good.
—Louis Bedigian, DarkStation.com

The Ceres series is a great one, drama, action and suspense fill the plot and keep the pace moving while also keeping the continuing series interesting.
—John Stanley, DVDAnswerman.com

VIZ GRAPHIC NOVEL

CERES™
Celestial Legend
VOL. 3: SUZUMI

Story and Art by
YÛ WATASE

Aya
A boisterous, modern high-school girl.

Aki
Aya's nice-guy twin brother.

Toya
A handsome but mysterious stranger.

Grandpa
The head of the Mikage household and chairman of a vast corporation.

Kagami
The mastermind behind Mikage International's C-Project.

Suzumi
A Japanese dance teacher with a connection to Aya.

Yuhi
Suzumi's martial artist/cook brother-in-law.

Ceres
A legendary tennyo, a celestial maiden.

On the day of their sixteenth birthday, boisterous Aya Mikage and her twin brother Aki are led to a ceremony at their grandfather's mansion. A mummified hand is placed before them and Aya feels a power welling within her, while multiple lacerations appear out of nowhere on Aki's body. As a result of this ceremony, Aya's grandfather declares that Aki is to be taken into protective seclusion as the heir to the Mikage empire, and Aya must die!

Aya escapes the clutches of the murderous Mikage family with the help of a mysterious man named Tôya. She finds refuge with the traditional Japanese dance instructor Suzumi Aogiri and her brother-in-law, the cook/martial-artist, Yûhi Aogiri. Suzumi explains that Aya is directly descended from a celestial maiden (tennyo)—a character out of ancient Japanese legends.

Targeted for death by her own family, Aya discovers that in times of stress she loses consciousness and physically transforms into Ceres, a tennyo with sublime celestial powers. Long ago, the founder of the Mikage clan stole Ceres' celestial robes (hagoromo), preventing Ceres from returning to the heavens. He then forced himself on her, beginning the Mikage family line. Ceres wants the hagoromo back and is obsessed with getting revenge against the Mikage Family.

The handsome, enigmatic Tôya has the ability to withstand Ceres' attacks. However he has no idea who he is or where his power comes from. Tôya suffers from amnesia, and he works for the Mikage with the hopes that their advanced technology can help him get his memory back. Despite his employers plans, Tôya always feels compelled to help Aya out of dangerous situations. Aya is instantly attracted to Tôya, but he is an employee of her mortal enemies—can romance survive?

Aya, Tôya, and Aki, are all pawns in Mikage International's C-Project—a nefarious plan to use the power of the descendents of tennyo for the greater glory of the Mikage.

As Aya attempts to make some sense out of the chaos, she tries to make the best out of her dire situation, and she tries to get used to her new life in the Aogiri household. On the way to school, Aya has visions of a girl enveloped in flames. Guided by this vision, Aya and Yûhi discover classmate, Yûki Urakawa, passed out on the street. They take her to the school infirmary where they discover that Tôya has been planted as the school doctor to spy on Aya...

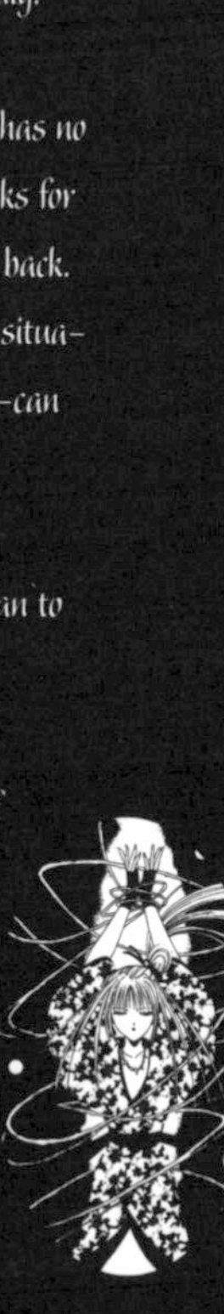

CERES™
Celestial Legend
VOL. 3: Suzumi

This volume contains the CERES: CELESTIAL LEGEND installments from
Part 3, issue 1 through Part 3, issue 4 in their entirety.

STORY & ART BY YÛ WATASE

English Adaptation/Gary Leach

Translaton/Lillian Olsen
Touch-Up Art & Lettering/Bill Schuch
Cover Design/Hidemi Sahara
Graphic Design/Carolina Ugalde
Editor/Andy Nakatani

Managing Editor/Annette Roman
Vice President of Sales & Marketing/Rick Bauer
Vice President of Editoral/Hyoe Narita
Publisher/Seiji Horibuchi

Printed in Canada

Published by Viz, LLC.
P.O. Box 77010 • San Francisco, CA 94107

10 9 8 7 6 5 4 3 2 1
First printing, January 2003

store.viz.com

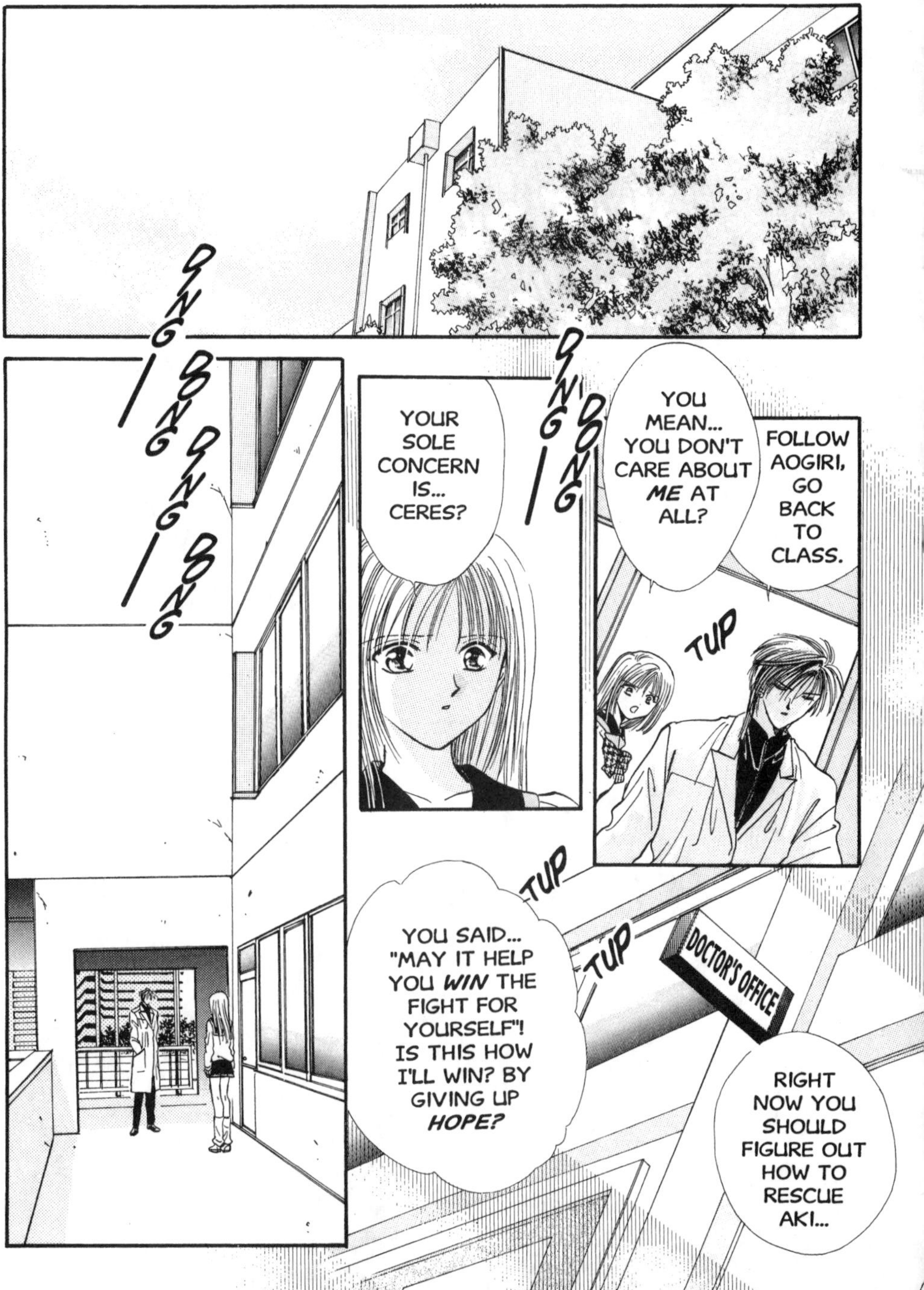
DING-DONG DING-DONG
YOUR SOLE CONCERN IS... CERES?
DING-DONG
YOU MEAN... YOU DON'T CARE ABOUT *ME* AT ALL?
FOLLOW AOGIRI, GO BACK TO CLASS.
TUP
TUP
TUP
YOU SAID... "MAY IT HELP YOU *WIN* THE FIGHT FOR YOURSELF"! IS THIS HOW I'LL WIN? BY GIVING UP *HOPE?*
DOCTOR'S OFFICE
RIGHT NOW YOU SHOULD FIGURE OUT HOW TO RESCUE AKI...

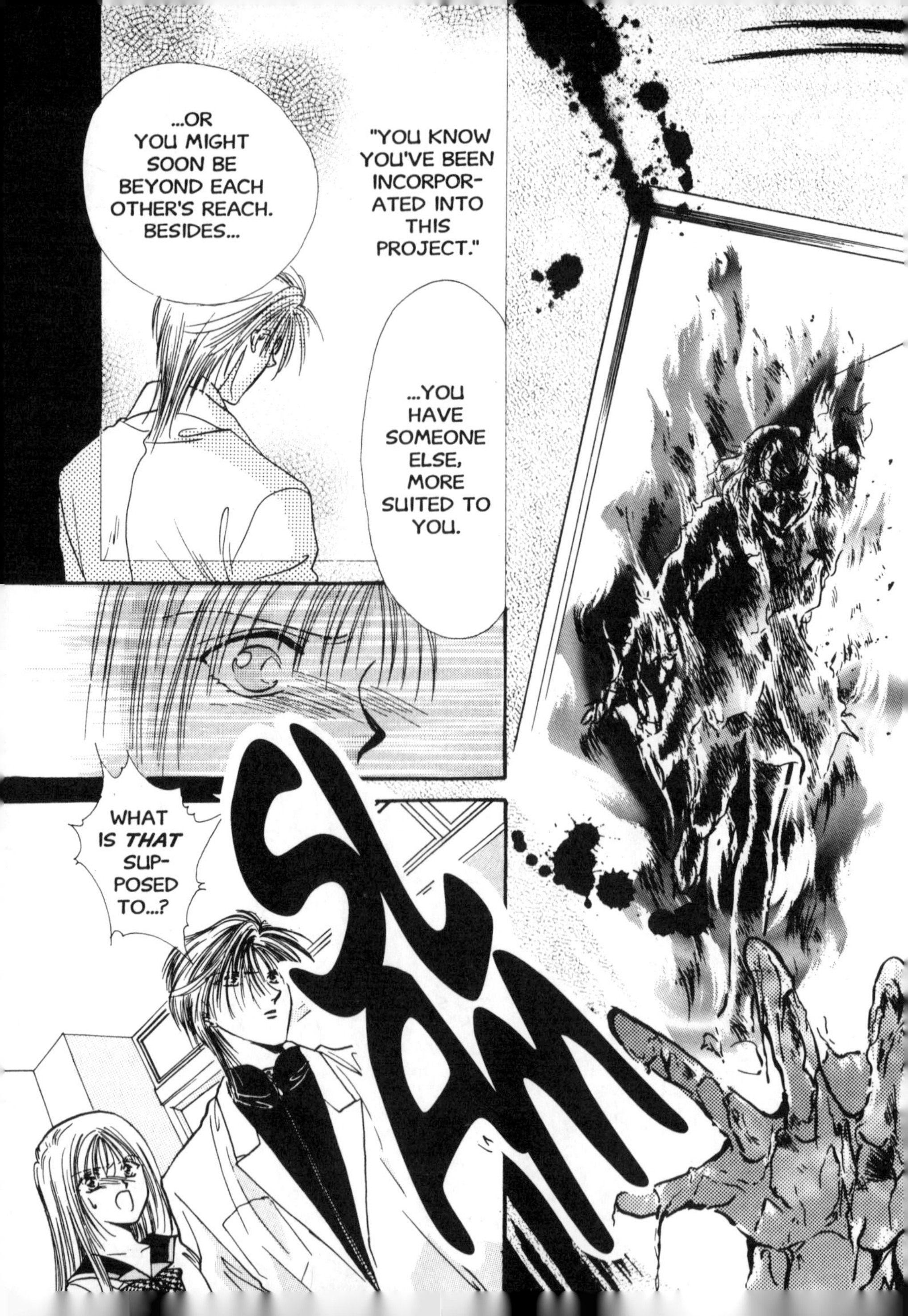
...OR YOU MIGHT SOON BE BEYOND EACH OTHER'S REACH. BESIDES...
"YOU KNOW YOU'VE BEEN INCORPORATED INTO THIS PROJECT."
...YOU HAVE SOMEONE ELSE, MORE SUITED TO YOU.
WHAT IS *THAT* SUPPOSED TO...?
SLAM

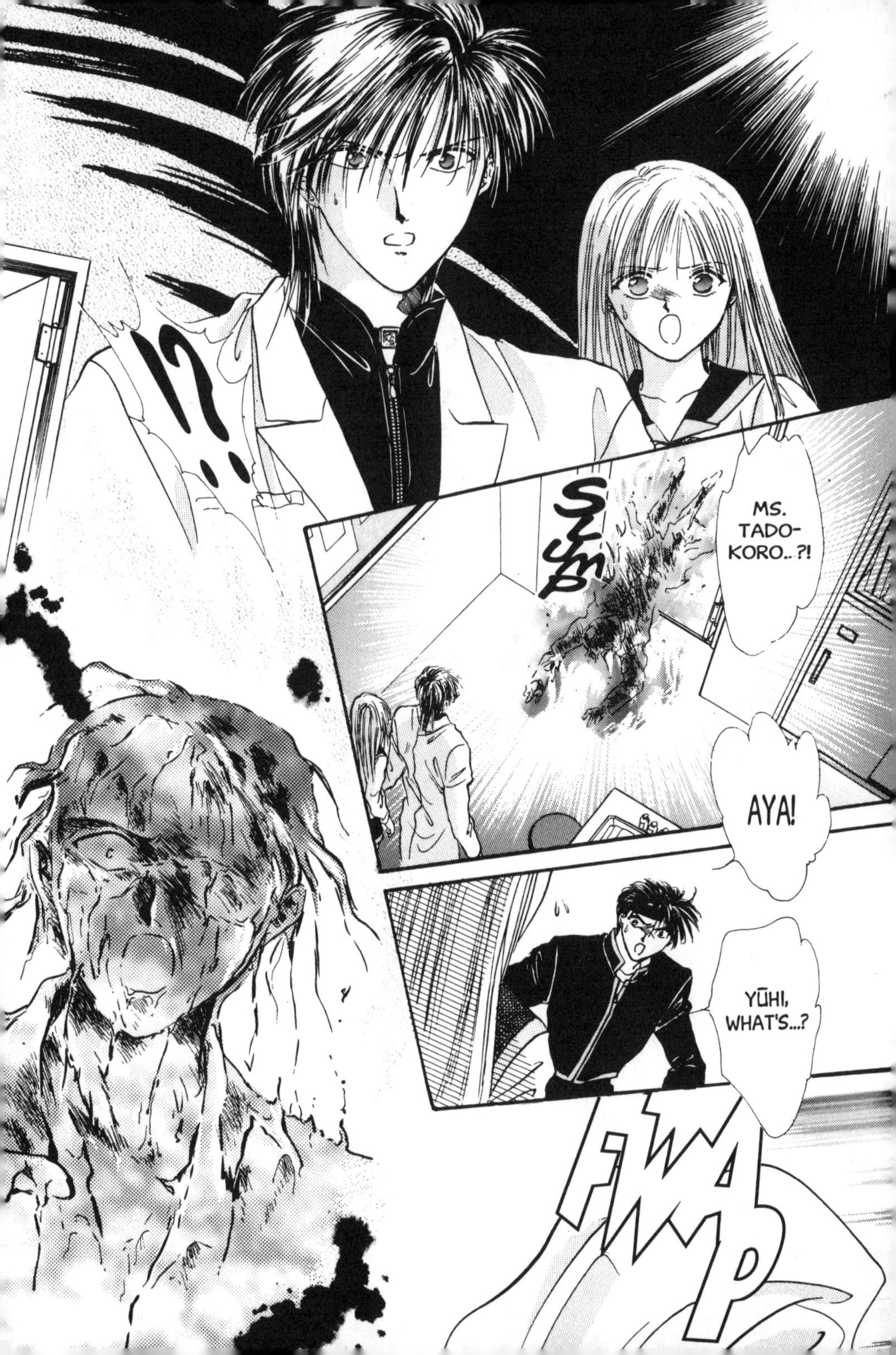
!?..
SLUMP
MS. TADO-KORO..?!
AYA!
YŪHI, WHAT'S...?
FWAMP

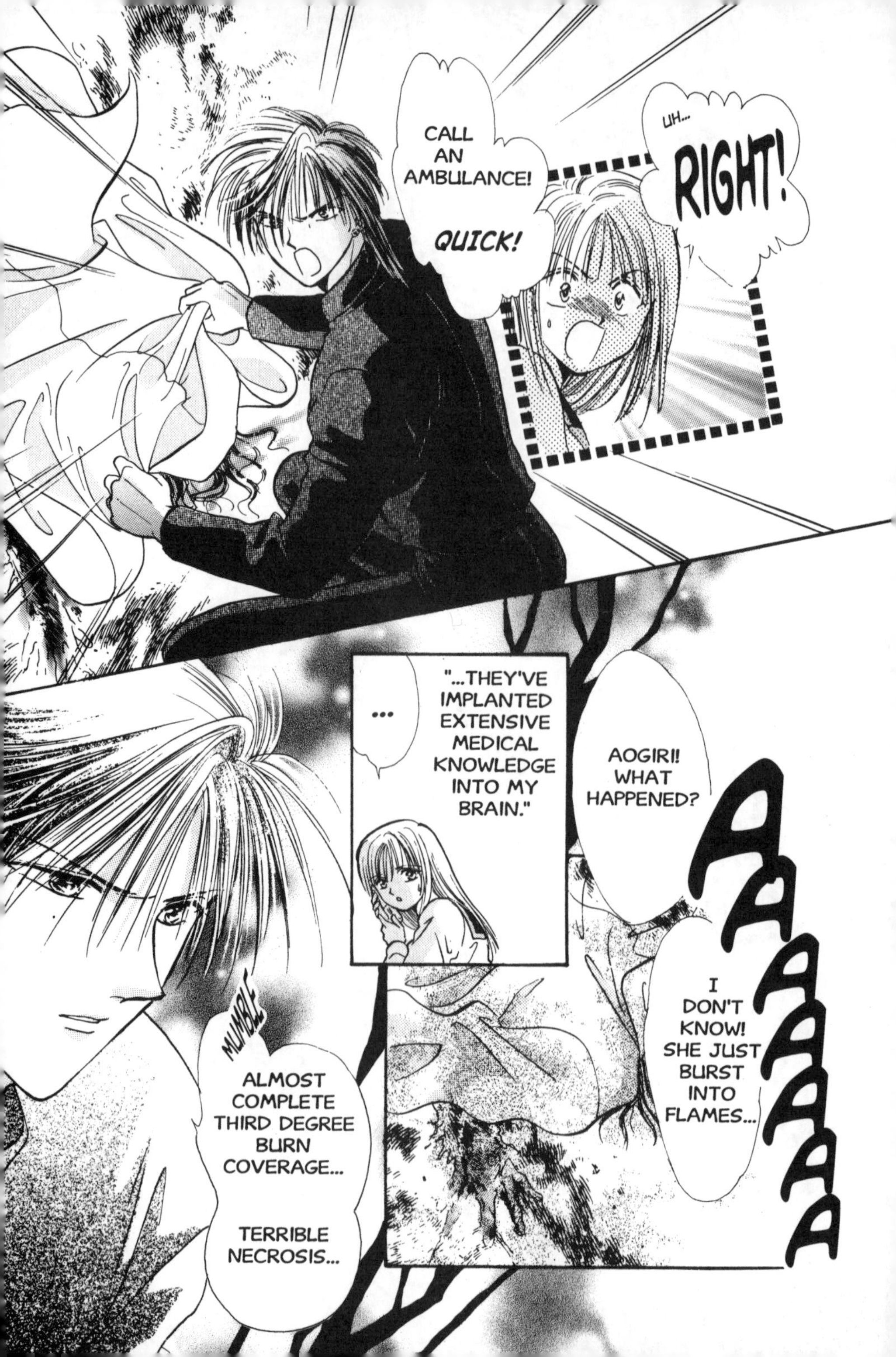
CALL AN AMBULANCE!
QUICK!
UH...
RIGHT!
MUMBLE
ALMOST COMPLETE THIRD DEGREE BURN COVERAGE...
TERRIBLE NECROSIS...
...
"...THEY'VE IMPLANTED EXTENSIVE MEDICAL KNOWLEDGE INTO MY BRAIN."
AOGIRI! WHAT HAPPENED?
I DON'T KNOW! SHE JUST BURST INTO FLAMES...
AAAAAAA

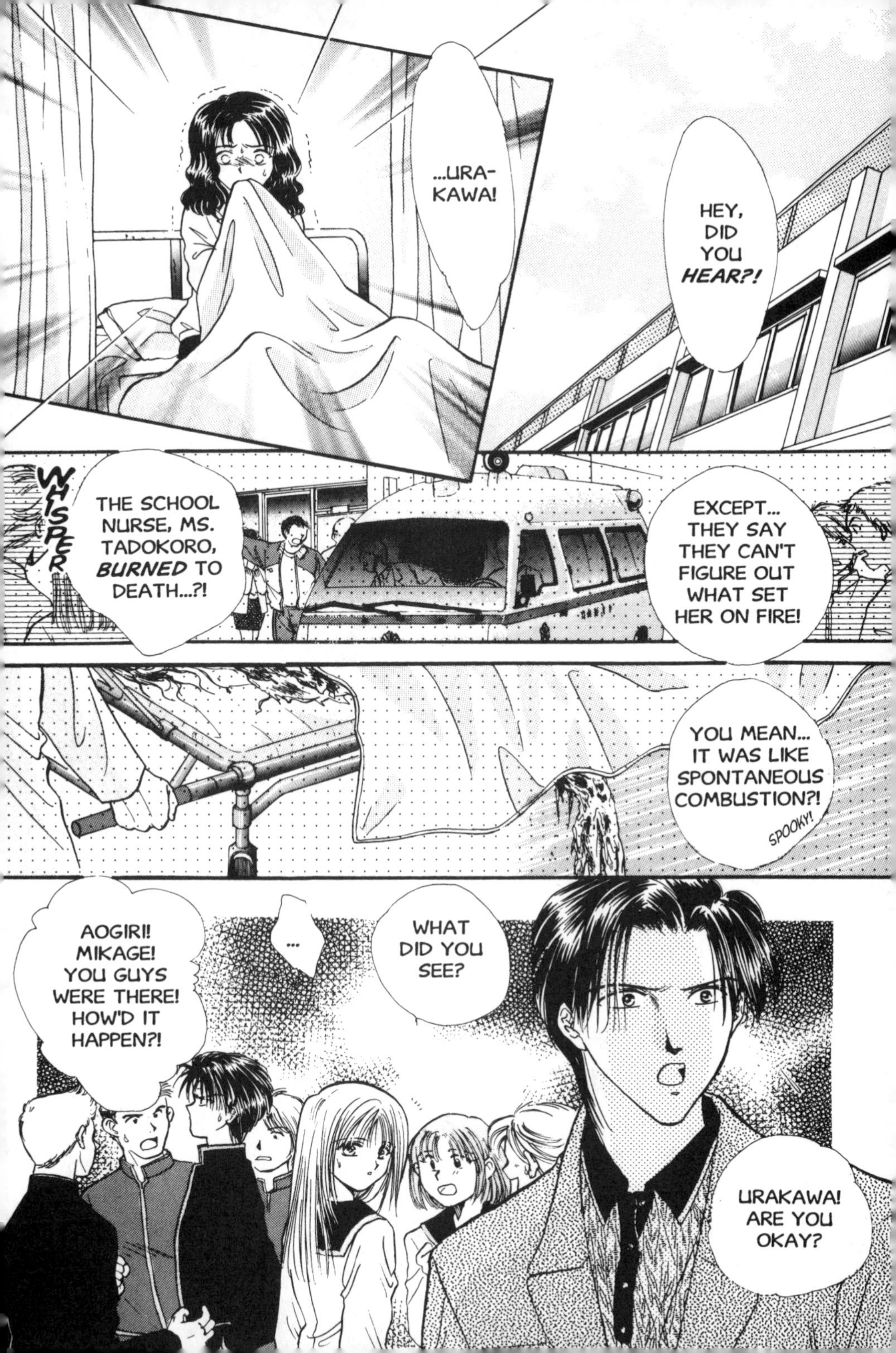
...URA-KAWA!
HEY, DID YOU *HEAR?!*
WHISPER
THE SCHOOL NURSE, MS. TADOKORO, *BURNED* TO DEATH...?!
EXCEPT... THEY SAY THEY CAN'T FIGURE OUT WHAT SET HER ON FIRE!
YOU MEAN... IT WAS LIKE SPONTANEOUS COMBUSTION?!
SPOOKY!
AOGIRI! MIKAGE! YOU GUYS WERE THERE! HOW'D IT HAPPEN?!
...
WHAT DID YOU SEE?
URAKAWA! ARE YOU OKAY?

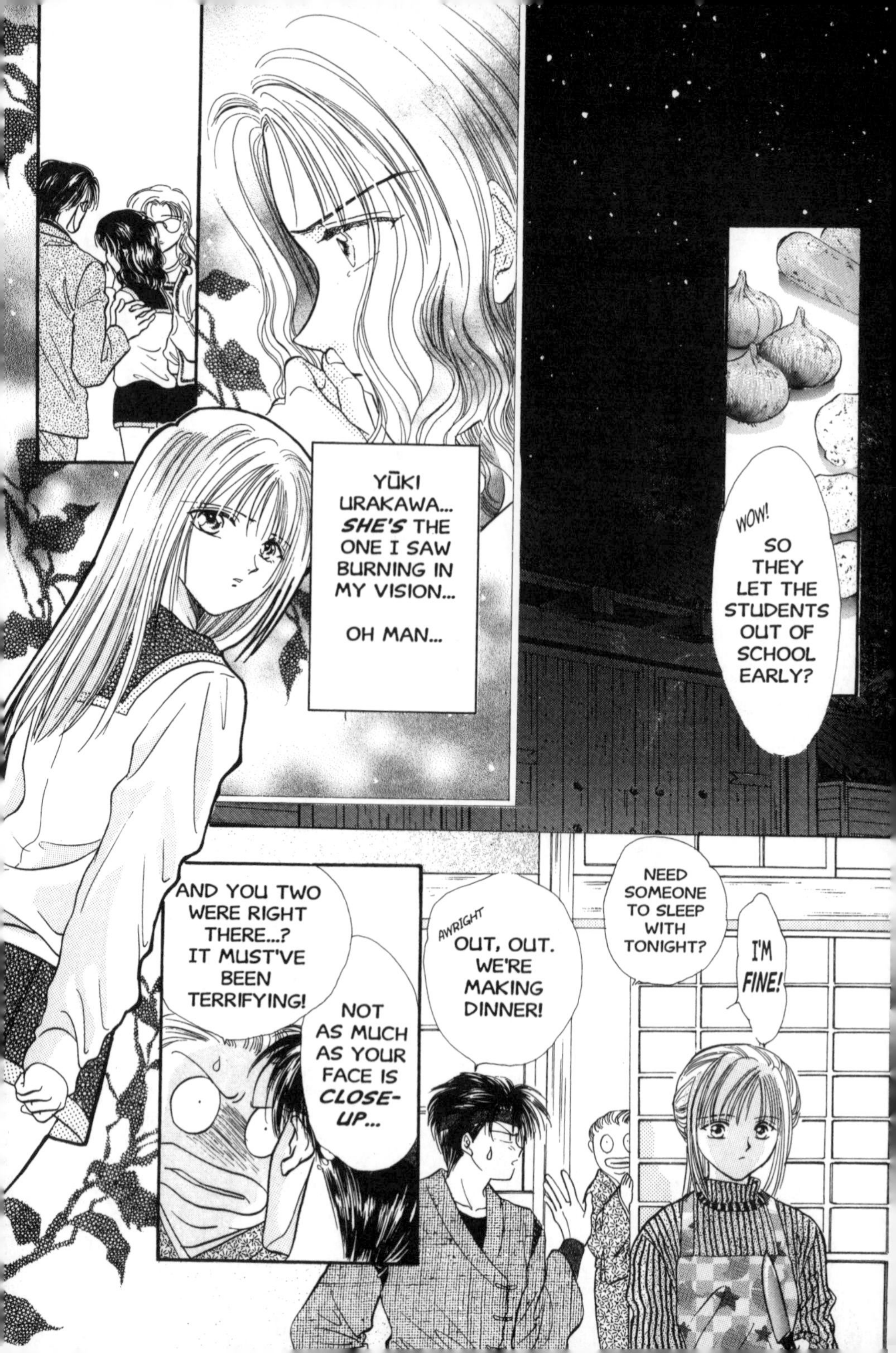
YŪKI URAKAWA... SHE'S THE ONE I SAW BURNING IN MY VISION...
OH MAN...
WOW!
SO THEY LET THE STUDENTS OUT OF SCHOOL EARLY?
AND YOU TWO WERE RIGHT THERE...? IT MUST'VE BEEN TERRIFYING!
NOT AS MUCH AS YOUR FACE IS CLOSE-UP...
AWRIGHT
OUT, OUT. WE'RE MAKING DINNER!
NEED SOMEONE TO SLEEP WITH TONIGHT?
I'M FINE!

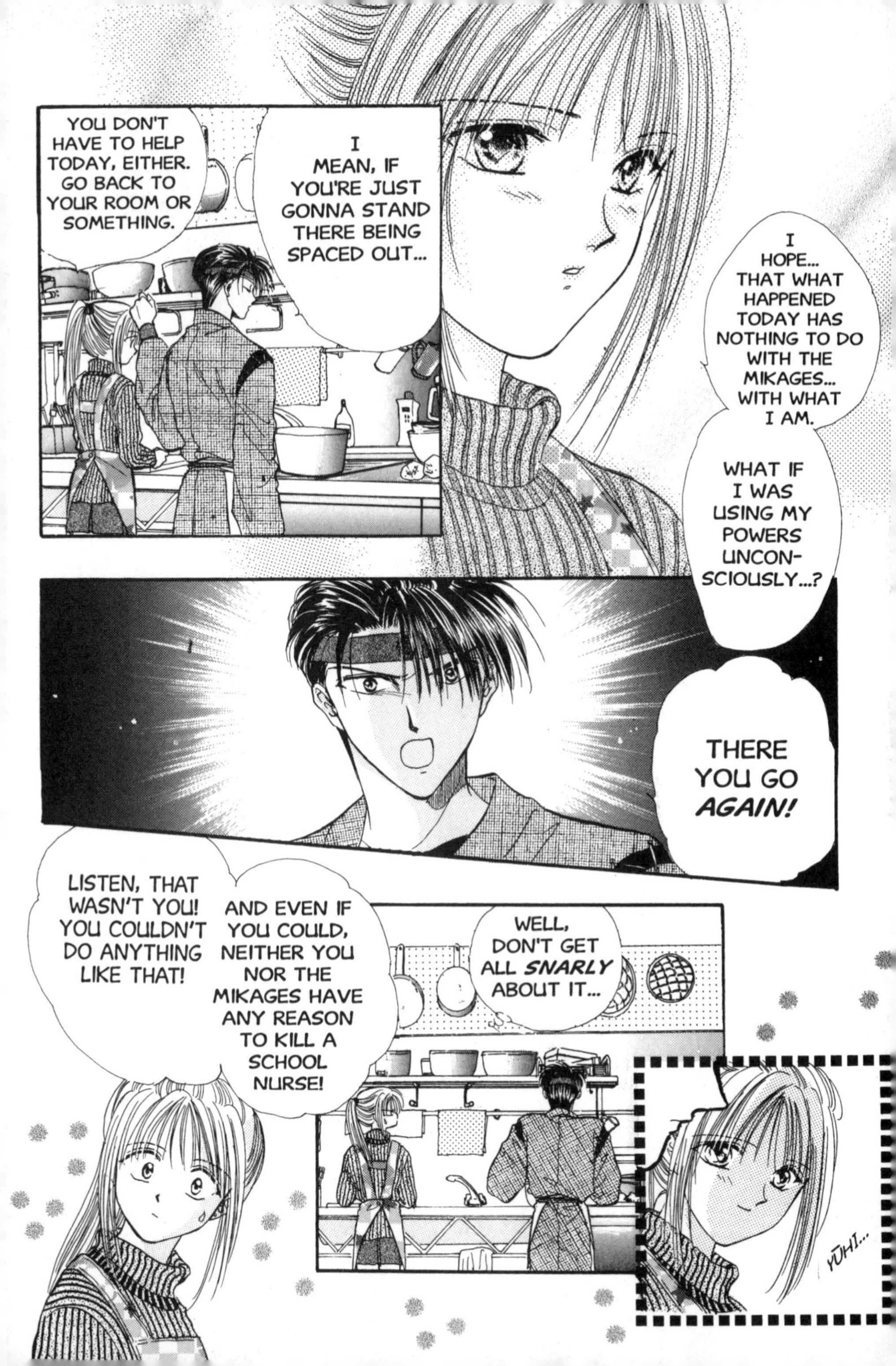
YOU DON'T HAVE TO HELP TODAY, EITHER. GO BACK TO YOUR ROOM OR SOMETHING.
I MEAN, IF YOU'RE JUST GONNA STAND THERE BEING SPACED OUT...
I HOPE... THAT WHAT HAPPENED TODAY HAS NOTHING TO DO WITH THE MIKAGES... WITH WHAT I AM.
WHAT IF I WAS USING MY POWERS UNCONSCIOUSLY...?
THERE YOU GO *AGAIN!*
LISTEN, THAT WASN'T YOU! YOU COULDN'T DO ANYTHING LIKE THAT!
AND EVEN IF YOU COULD, NEITHER YOU NOR THE MIKAGES HAVE ANY REASON TO KILL A SCHOOL NURSE!
WELL, DON'T GET ALL *SNARLY* ABOUT IT...
YUHI...

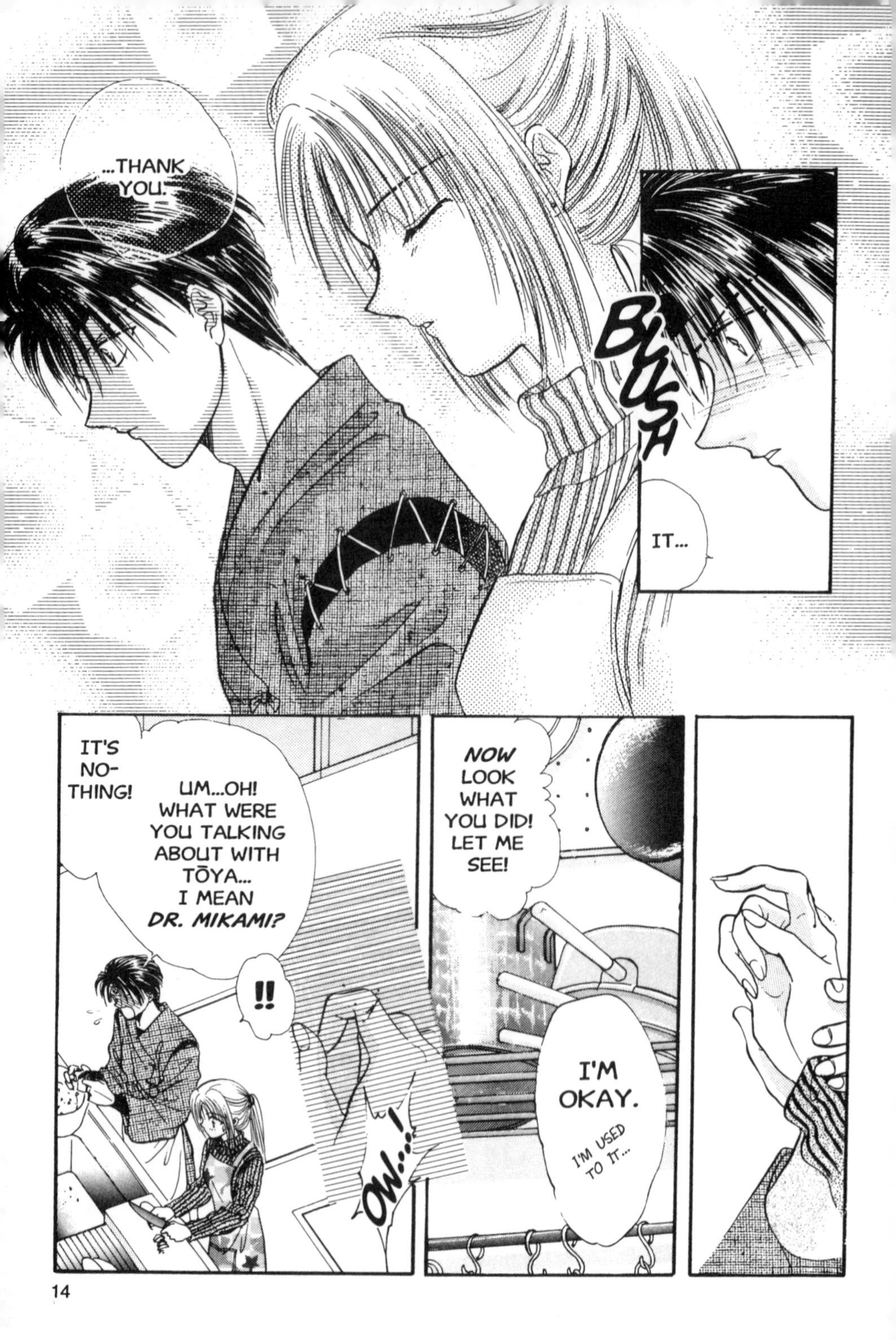
...THANK YOU.
BLUSH
IT...
IT'S NO-THING!
UM...OH! WHAT WERE YOU TALKING ABOUT WITH TŌYA... I MEAN *DR. MIKAMI?*
!!
OW...!
NOW LOOK WHAT YOU DID! LET ME SEE!
I'M OKAY.
I'M USED TO IT...

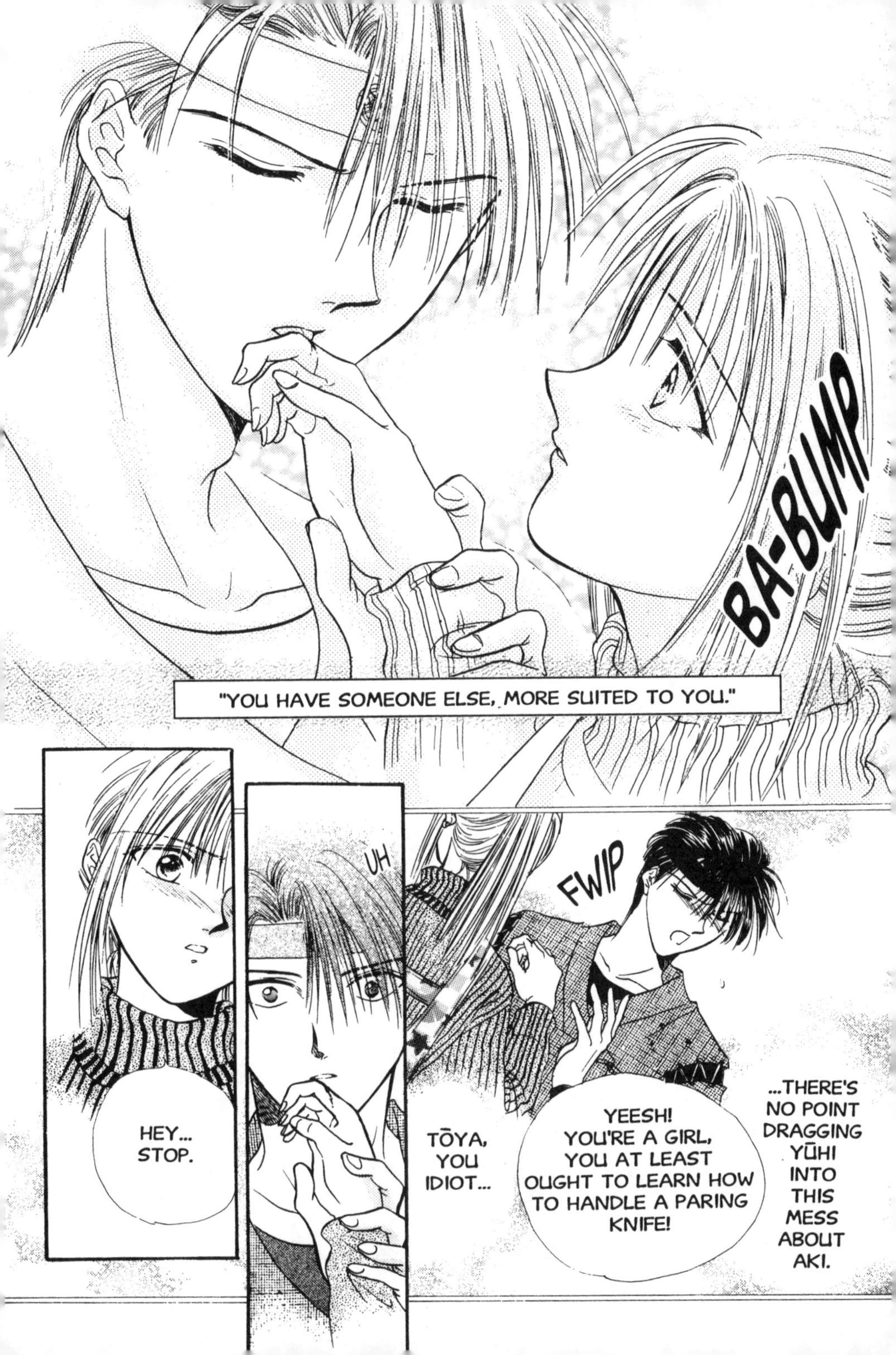
BA-BUMP
"YOU HAVE SOMEONE ELSE, MORE SUITED TO YOU."
HEY... STOP.
UH
FWIP
TŌYA, YOU IDIOT...
YEESH! YOU'RE A GIRL, YOU AT LEAST OUGHT TO LEARN HOW TO HANDLE A PARING KNIFE!
...THERE'S NO POINT DRAGGING YŪHI INTO THIS MESS ABOUT AKI.

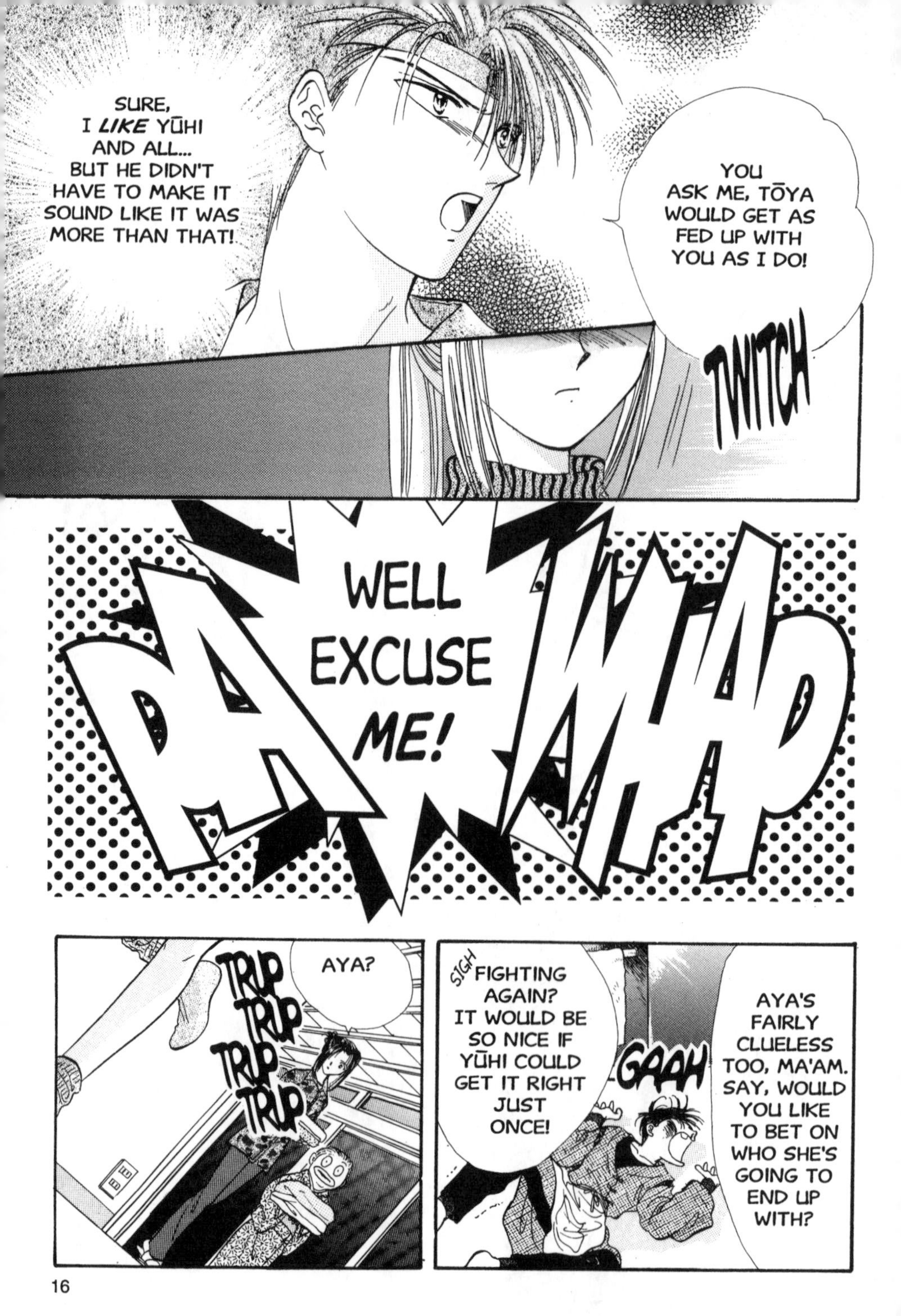
SURE, I *LIKE* YŪHI AND ALL... BUT HE DIDN'T HAVE TO MAKE IT SOUND LIKE IT WAS MORE THAN THAT!
YOU ASK ME, TŌYA WOULD GET AS FED UP WITH YOU AS I DO!
TWITCH
WELL EXCUSE *ME!*
PAWHAP
TRUP TRUP TRUP TRUP
AYA?
SIGH
FIGHTING AGAIN? IT WOULD BE SO NICE IF YŪHI COULD GET IT RIGHT JUST ONCE!
-GRAAH
AYA'S FAIRLY CLUELESS TOO, MA'AM. SAY, WOULD YOU LIKE TO BET ON WHO SHE'S GOING TO END UP WITH?

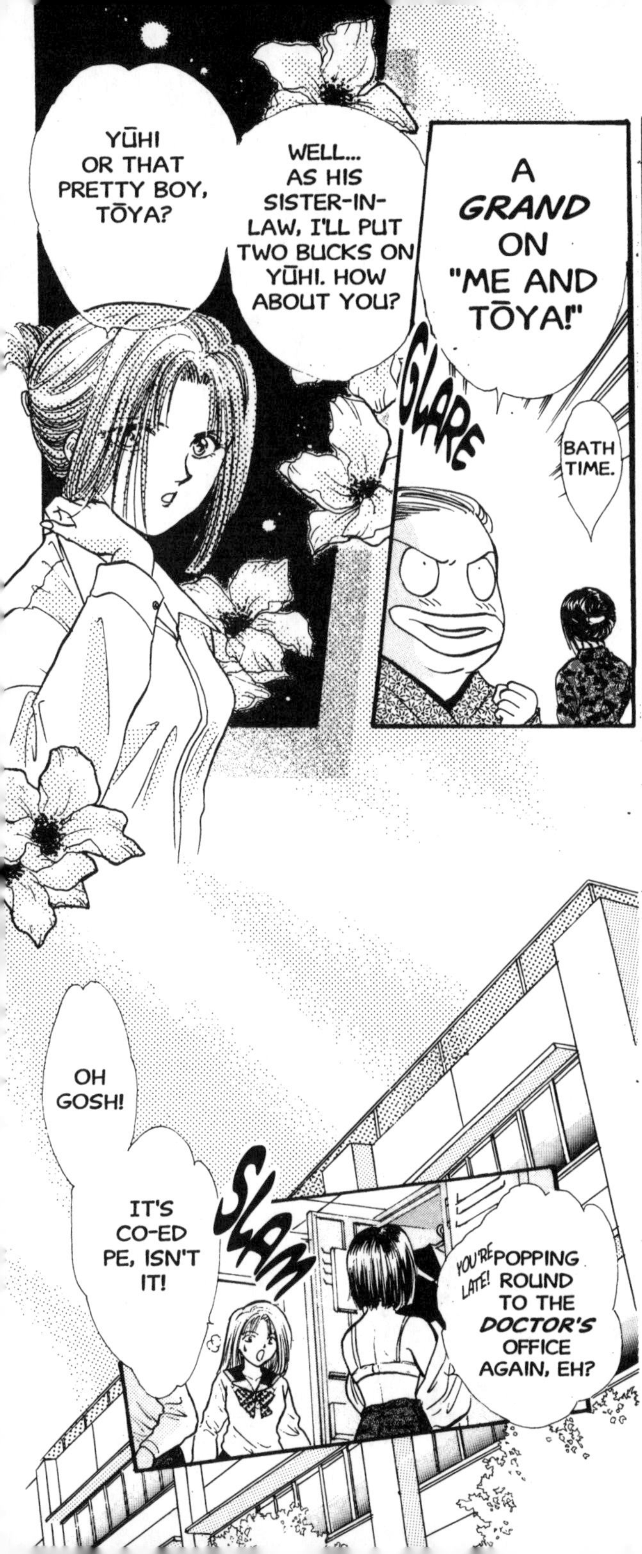
YŪHI OR THAT PRETTY BOY, TŌYA?
WELL... AS HIS SISTER-IN-LAW, I'LL PUT TWO BUCKS ON YŪHI. HOW ABOUT YOU?
A *GRAND* ON "ME AND TŌYA!"
GLARE
BATH TIME.
OH GOSH!
IT'S CO-ED PE, ISN'T IT!
SLAM
YOU'RE LATE!
POPPING ROUND TO THE *DOCTOR'S* OFFICE AGAIN, EH?

✦ Suzumi ✦

Phew... (I'm starving already)
We're in the third volume already. Time flies! Thank you all for keeping up with the story. Somebody please think up the rest of the storyline. ☺
No really, I **am** putting a lot of thought into it.
Manga that's based on someone else's story sounds so easy to do. Somebody else has already created the story for you. But I guess when it comes down to it, I might not like doing it, precisely **because** it's not really mine. ☺
And it might be tough to put someone else's idea's down on paper. (I wouldn't know since I've never done it.) There really is no such thing as an easy job.
...Hmm, we're off to a whiny start; or rather, my fatigue is showing through. Why? Because I only got 3 hours of sleep! I'm sooo sleepy! **Z** sniff
Wake up. I have no time. Right now, all you aspiring manga artists out there might be saying "All-nighters don't bother me," but that's only because you don't know how it really is! Yes... Before I went pro, I knew that it was going to be tough, but I hadn't actually experienced it yet; and I naively thought, "once I turn pro, I'm going to draw this and that, and do whatever story I want!" Boy, was I wrong! ☺
There is no job where you can do whatever you want. Your ego gets ripped to shreds, and you'll be humbled before you can ever feel proud of yourself; but then after a few years, some people will be flying high in the sky. ...What the heck am I talking about?

Looks like I'm too hungry and sleepy...

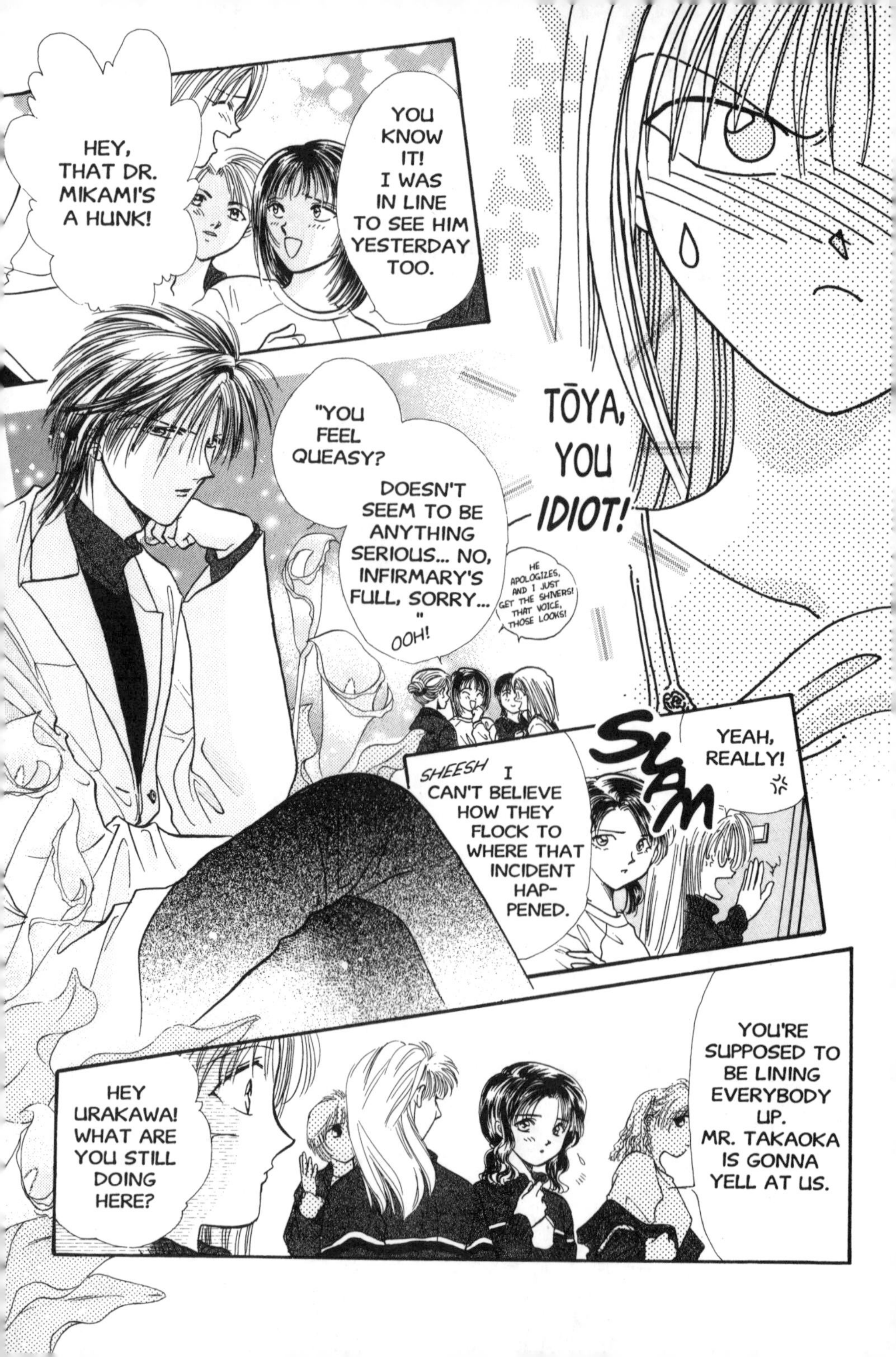
HEY, THAT DR. MIKAMI'S A HUNK!
YOU KNOW IT! I WAS IN LINE TO SEE HIM YESTERDAY TOO.
TŌYA, YOU IDIOT!
"YOU FEEL QUEASY? DOESN'T SEEM TO BE ANYTHING SERIOUS... NO, INFIRMARY'S FULL, SORRY..."
OOH!
HE APOLOGIZES, AND I JUST GET THE SHIVERS! THAT VOICE, THOSE LOOKS!
SHEESH
I CAN'T BELIEVE HOW THEY FLOCK TO WHERE THAT INCIDENT HAP-PENED.
SLAM
YEAH, REALLY!
HEY URAKAWA! WHAT ARE YOU STILL DOING HERE?
YOU'RE SUPPOSED TO BE LINING EVERYBODY UP. MR. TAKAOKA IS GONNA YELL AT US.

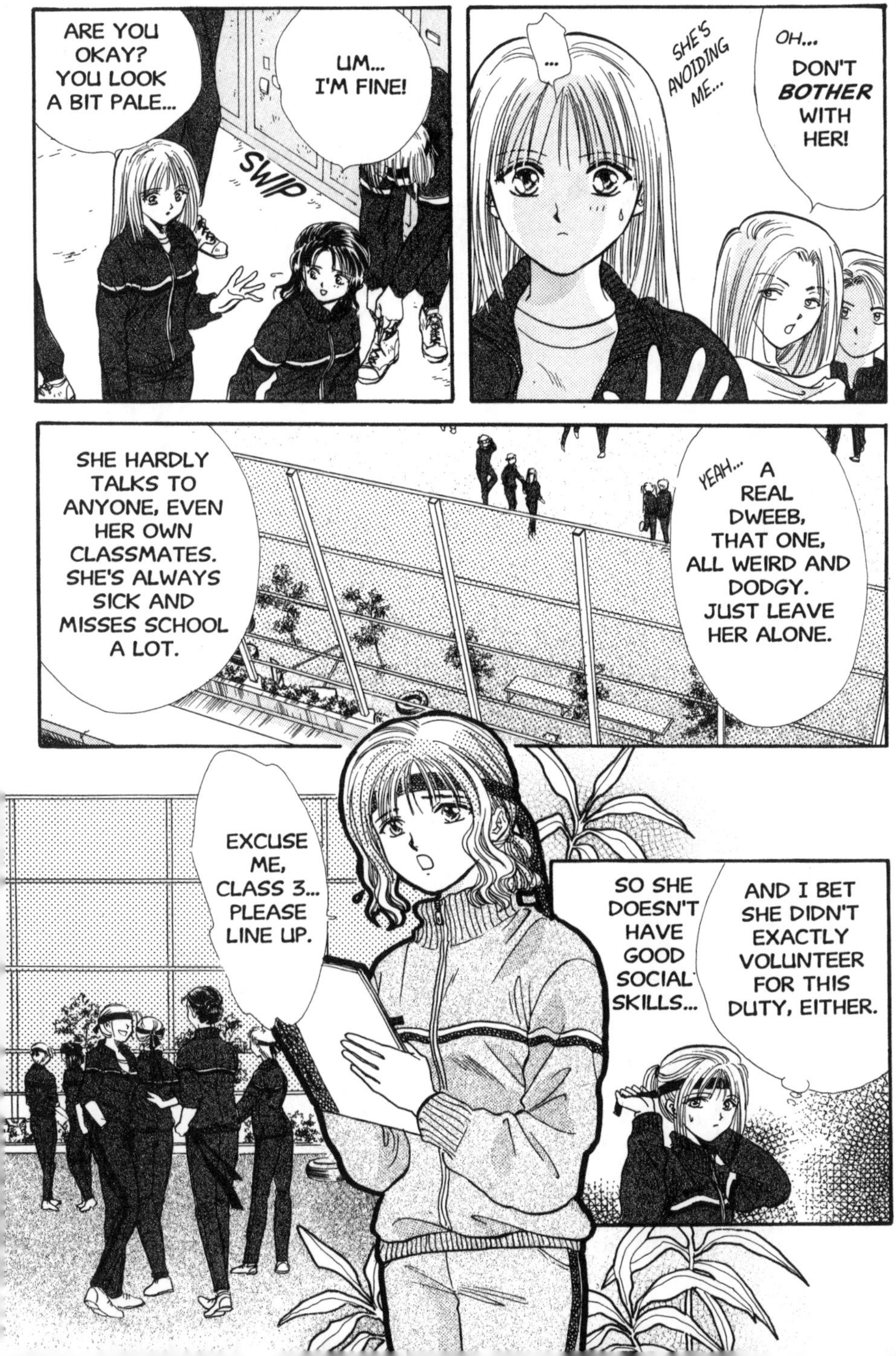
ARE YOU OKAY? YOU LOOK A BIT PALE...
UM... I'M FINE!
SWIP
...
SHE'S AVOIDING ME...
OH... DON'T BOTHER WITH HER!
SHE HARDLY TALKS TO ANYONE, EVEN HER OWN CLASSMATES. SHE'S ALWAYS SICK AND MISSES SCHOOL A LOT.
YEAH... A REAL DWEEB, THAT ONE, ALL WEIRD AND DODGY. JUST LEAVE HER ALONE.
EXCUSE ME, CLASS 3... PLEASE LINE UP.
SO SHE DOESN'T HAVE GOOD SOCIAL SKILLS...
AND I BET SHE DIDN'T EXACTLY VOLUNTEER FOR THIS DUTY, EITHER.

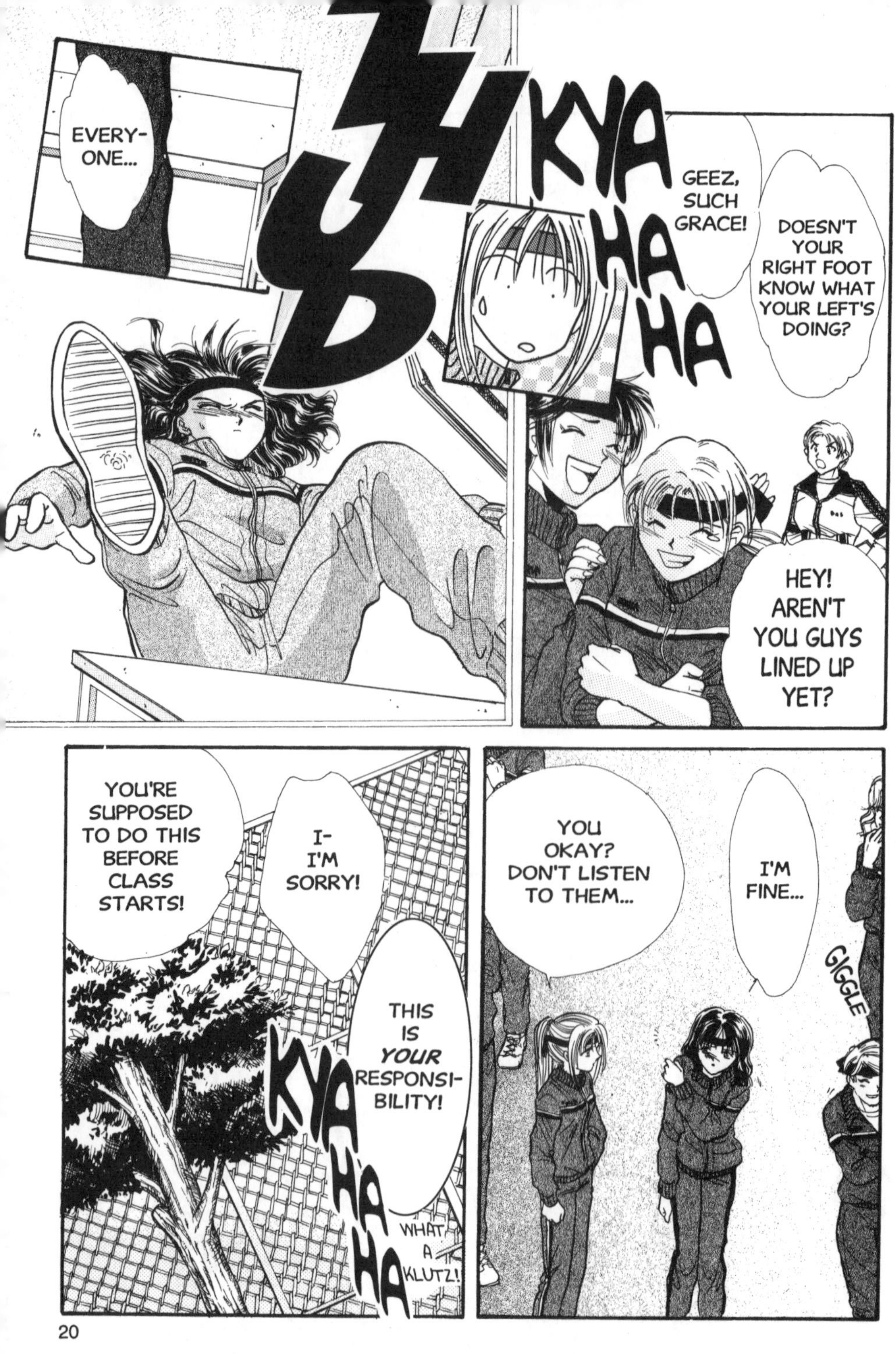
EVERY-ONE...
THUD
KYA HA HA HA
GEEZ, SUCH GRACE!
DOESN'T YOUR RIGHT FOOT KNOW WHAT YOUR LEFT'S DOING?
HEY! AREN'T YOU GUYS LINED UP YET?
YOU'RE SUPPOSED TO DO THIS BEFORE CLASS STARTS!
I- I'M SORRY!
THIS IS *YOUR* RESPONSI-BILITY!
KYA HA HA HA
WHAT A KLUTZ!
YOU OKAY? DON'T LISTEN TO THEM...
I'M FINE...
GIGGLE

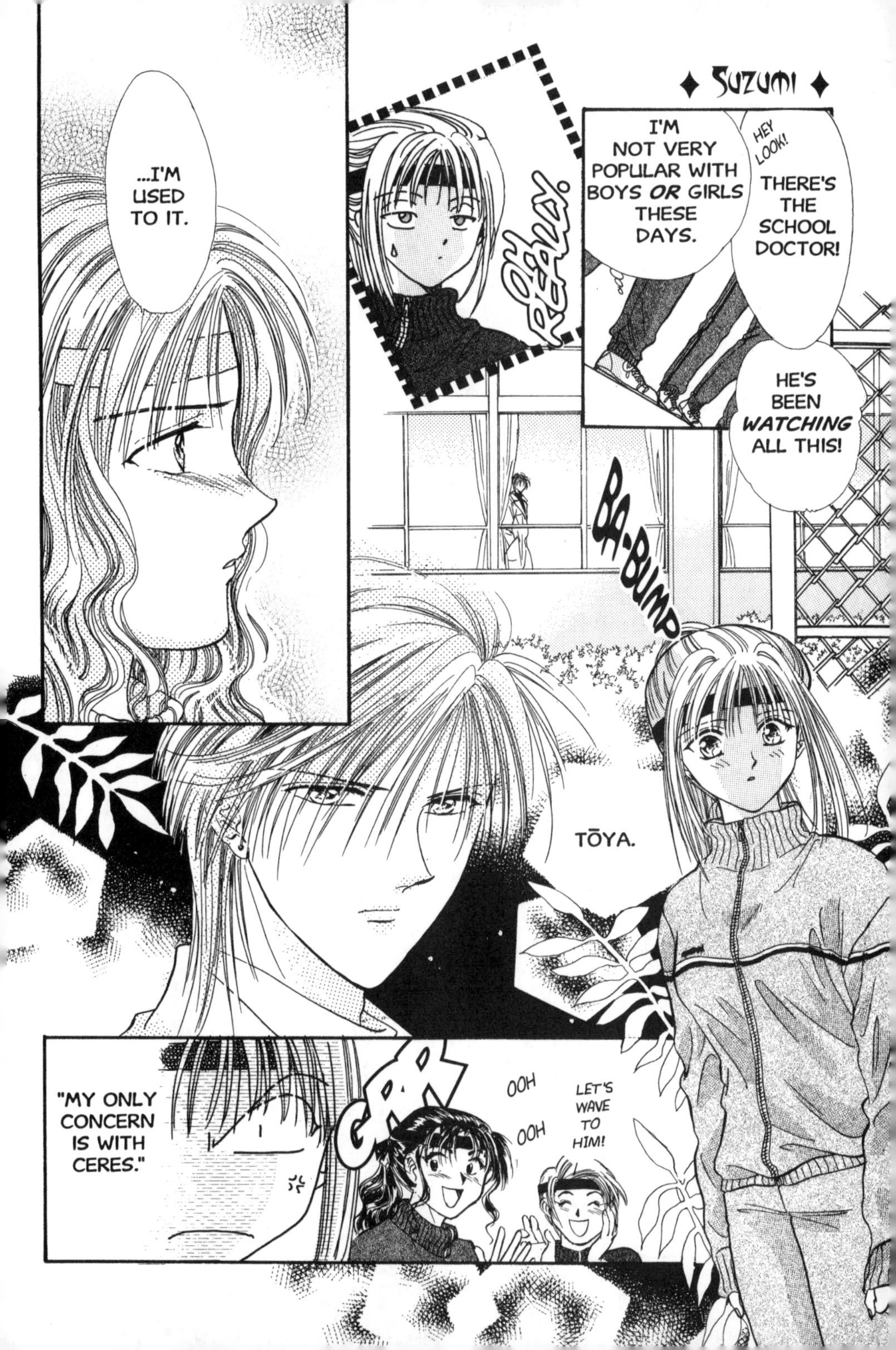

...I'M USED TO IT.
♦ SUZUMI ♦
Oh really.
I'M NOT VERY POPULAR WITH BOYS *OR* GIRLS THESE DAYS.
HEY LOOK!
THERE'S THE SCHOOL DOCTOR!
HE'S BEEN *WATCHING* ALL THIS!
BA-BUMP
TŌYA.
"MY ONLY CONCERN IS WITH CERES."
GRR
OOH
OOH
LET'S WAVE TO HIM!

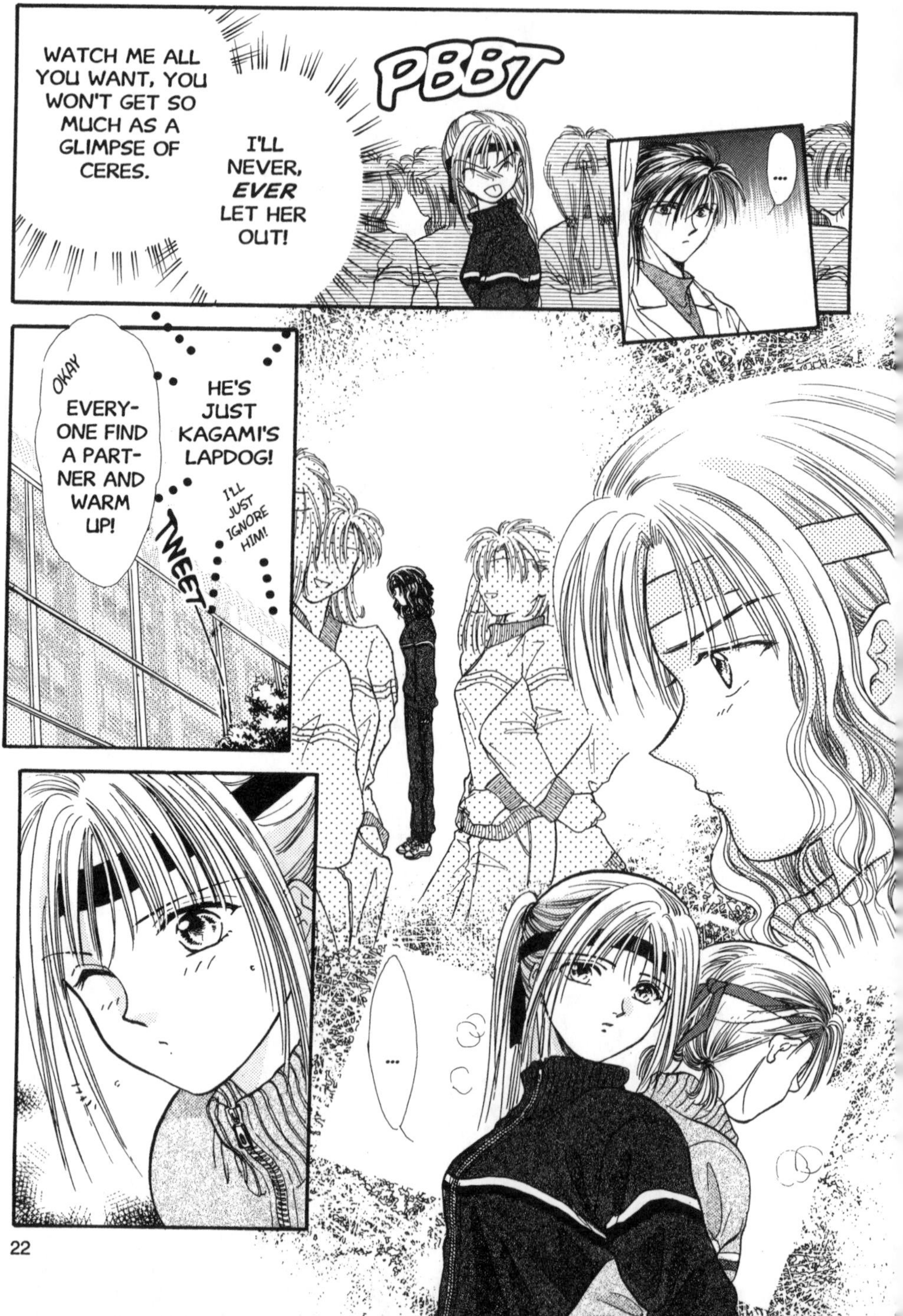
WATCH ME ALL YOU WANT, YOU WON'T GET SO MUCH AS A GLIMPSE OF CERES.
I'LL NEVER, *EVER* LET HER OUT!
PBBT
...
OKAY
EVERY-ONE FIND A PART-NER AND WARM UP!
TWEET
HE'S JUST KAGAMI'S LAPDOG!
I'LL JUST IGNORE HIM!
...

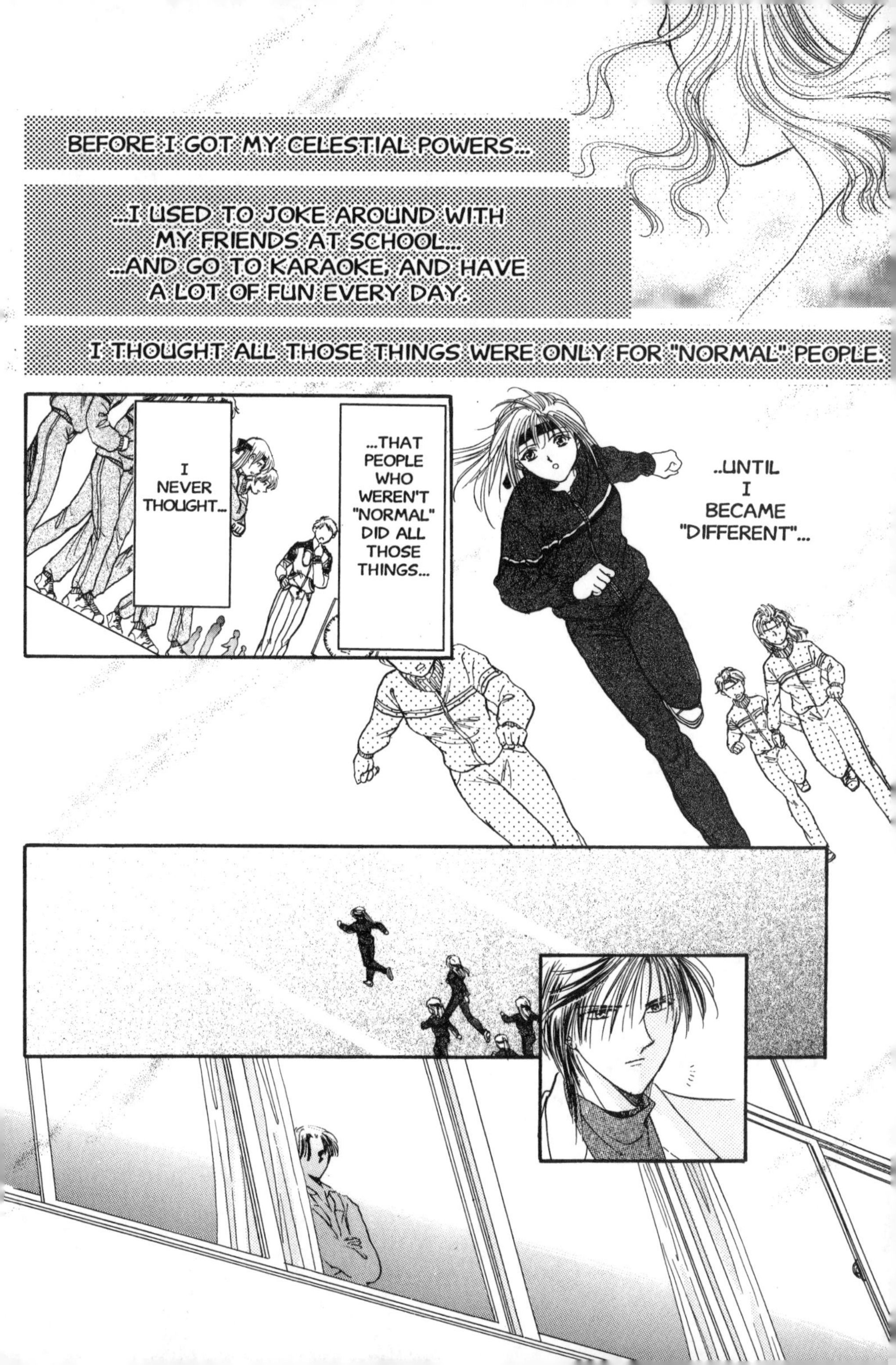
BEFORE I GOT MY CELESTIAL POWERS...
...I USED TO JOKE AROUND WITH MY FRIENDS AT SCHOOL... ...AND GO TO KARAOKE, AND HAVE A LOT OF FUN EVERY DAY.
I THOUGHT ALL THOSE THINGS WERE ONLY FOR "NORMAL" PEOPLE.
I NEVER THOUGHT...
...THAT PEOPLE WHO WEREN'T "NORMAL" DID ALL THOSE THINGS...
..UNTIL I BECAME "DIFFERENT"...

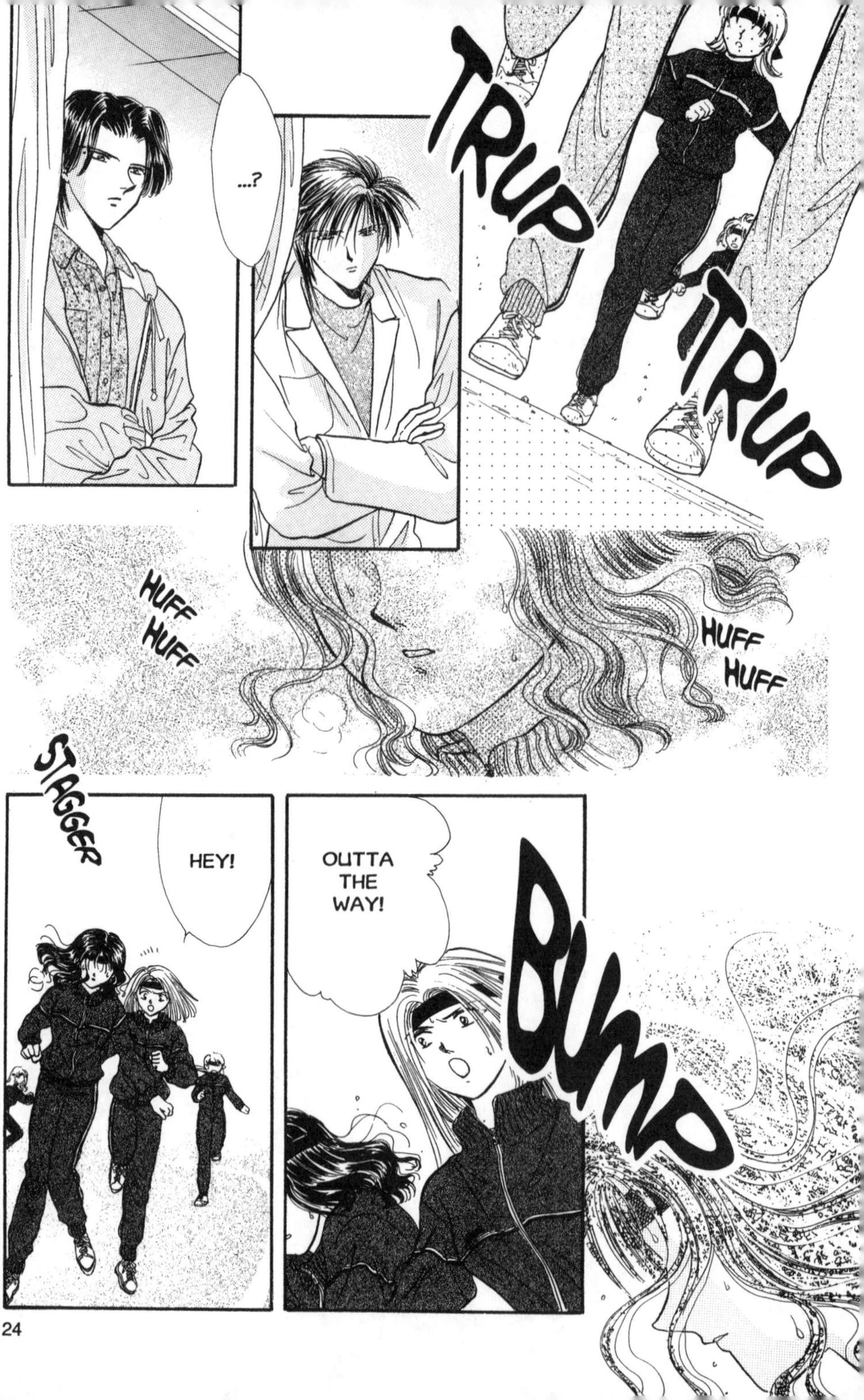
...?
TRUP
TRUP
HUFF
HUFF
HUFF
HUFF
STAGGER
HEY!
OUTTA THE WAY!
BUMP

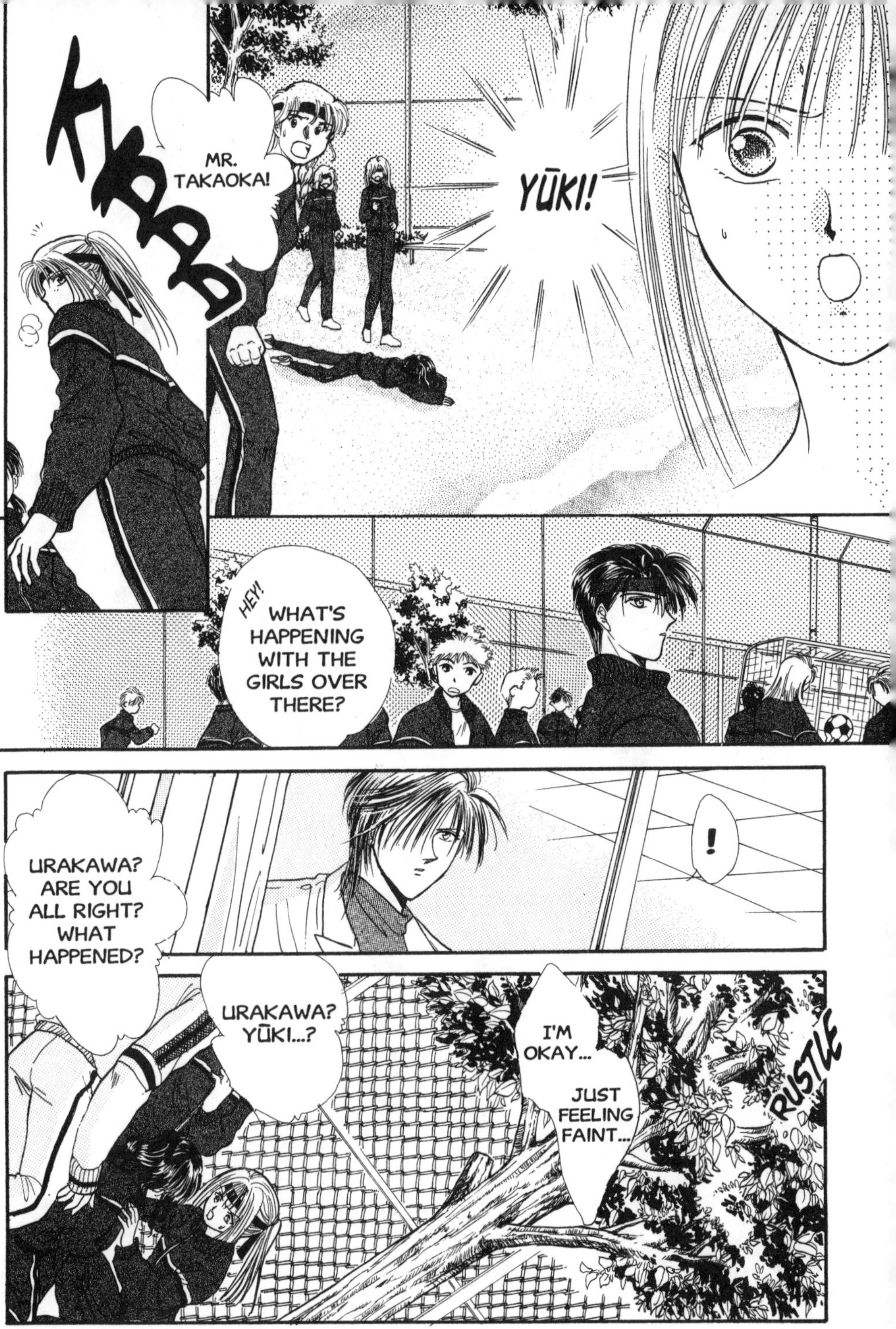
KYAAA
MR. TAKAOKA!
YŪKI!
HEY!
WHAT'S HAPPENING WITH THE GIRLS OVER THERE?
URAKAWA? ARE YOU ALL RIGHT? WHAT HAPPENED?
!
URAKAWA? YŪKI...?
I'M OKAY...
JUST FEELING FAINT...
RUSTLE

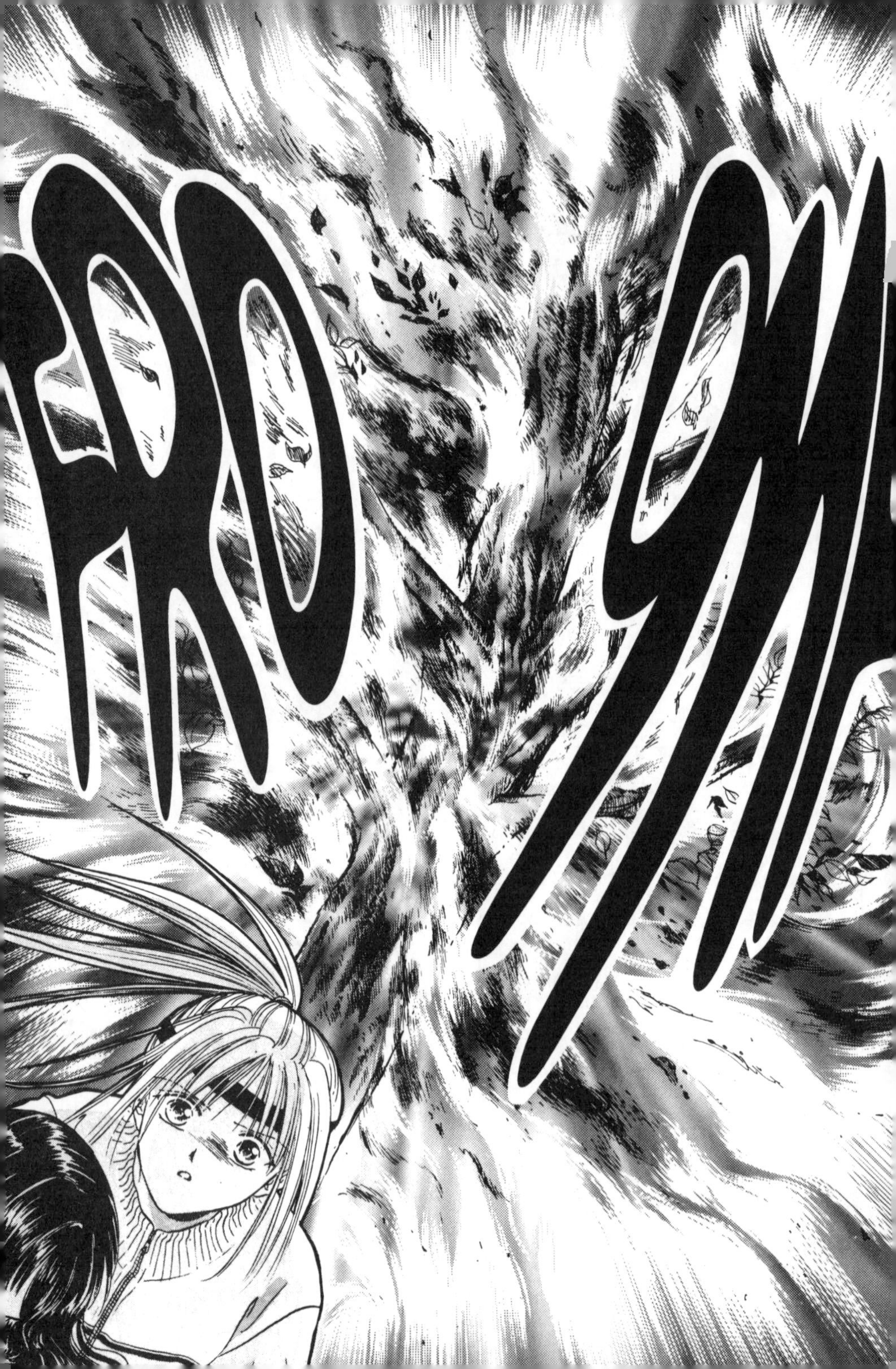
FROSH

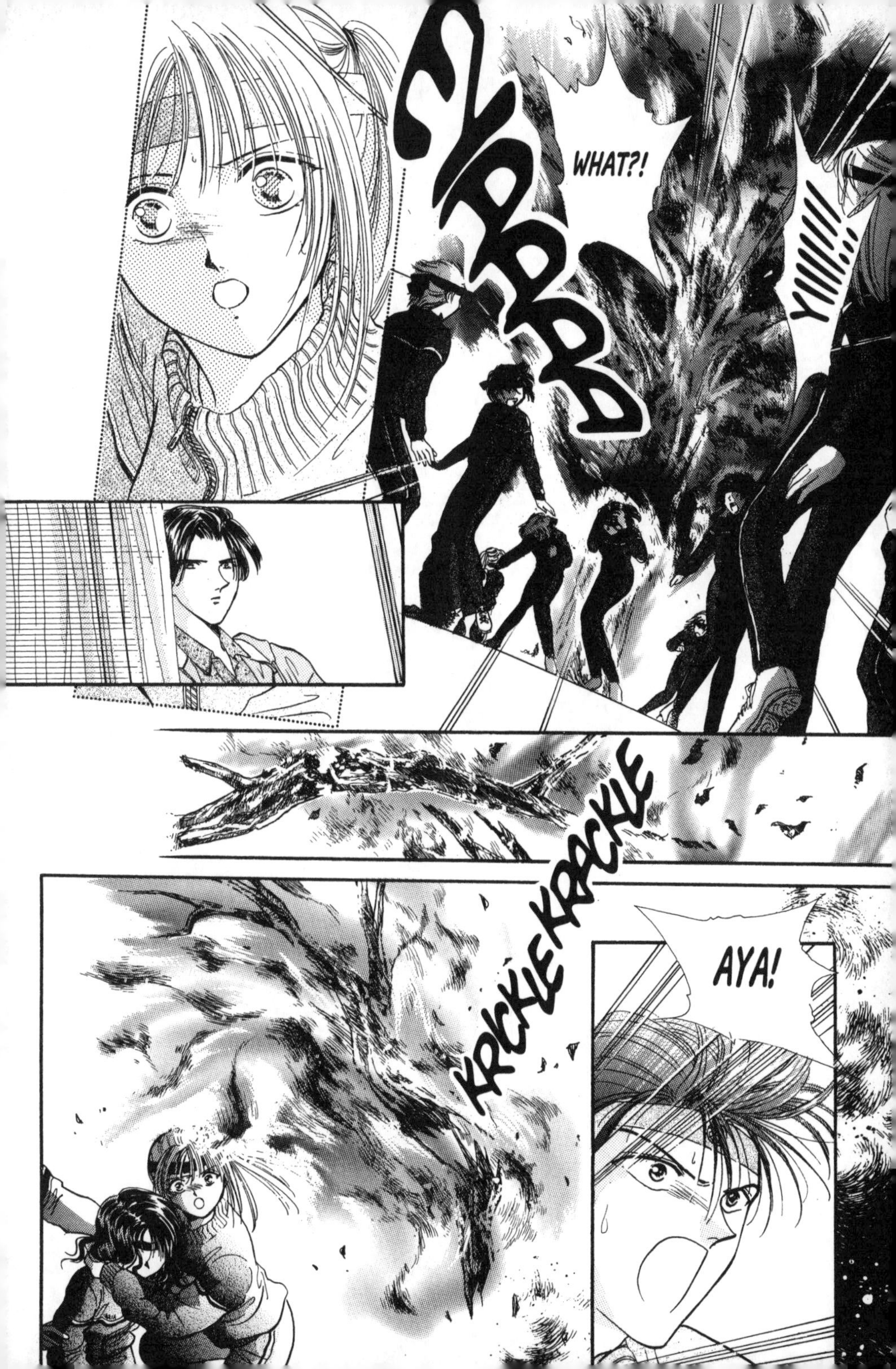
WHAT?!
YIIII!!!
KRICKLE KRACKLE
AYA!

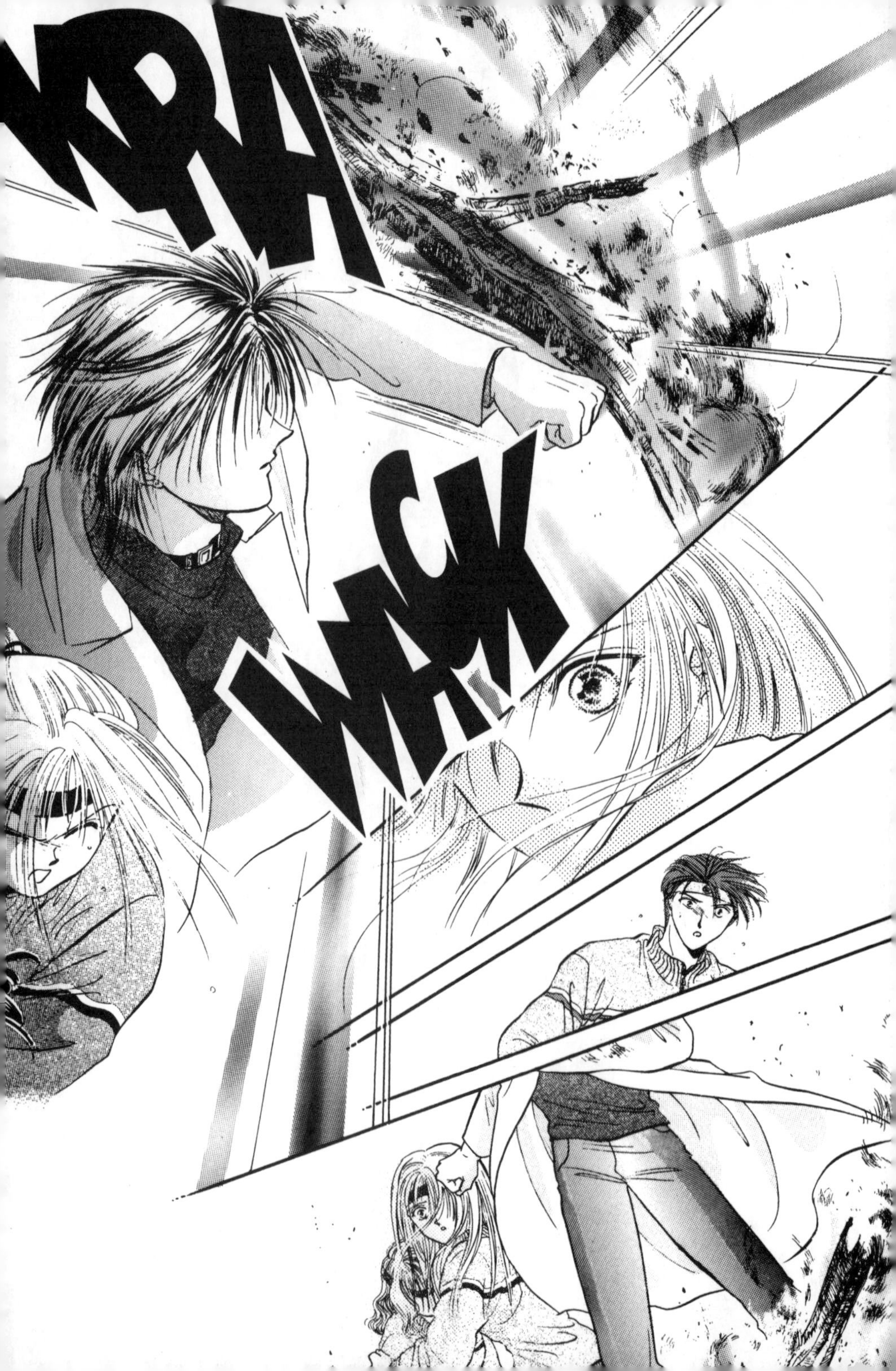
KRA
WHACK

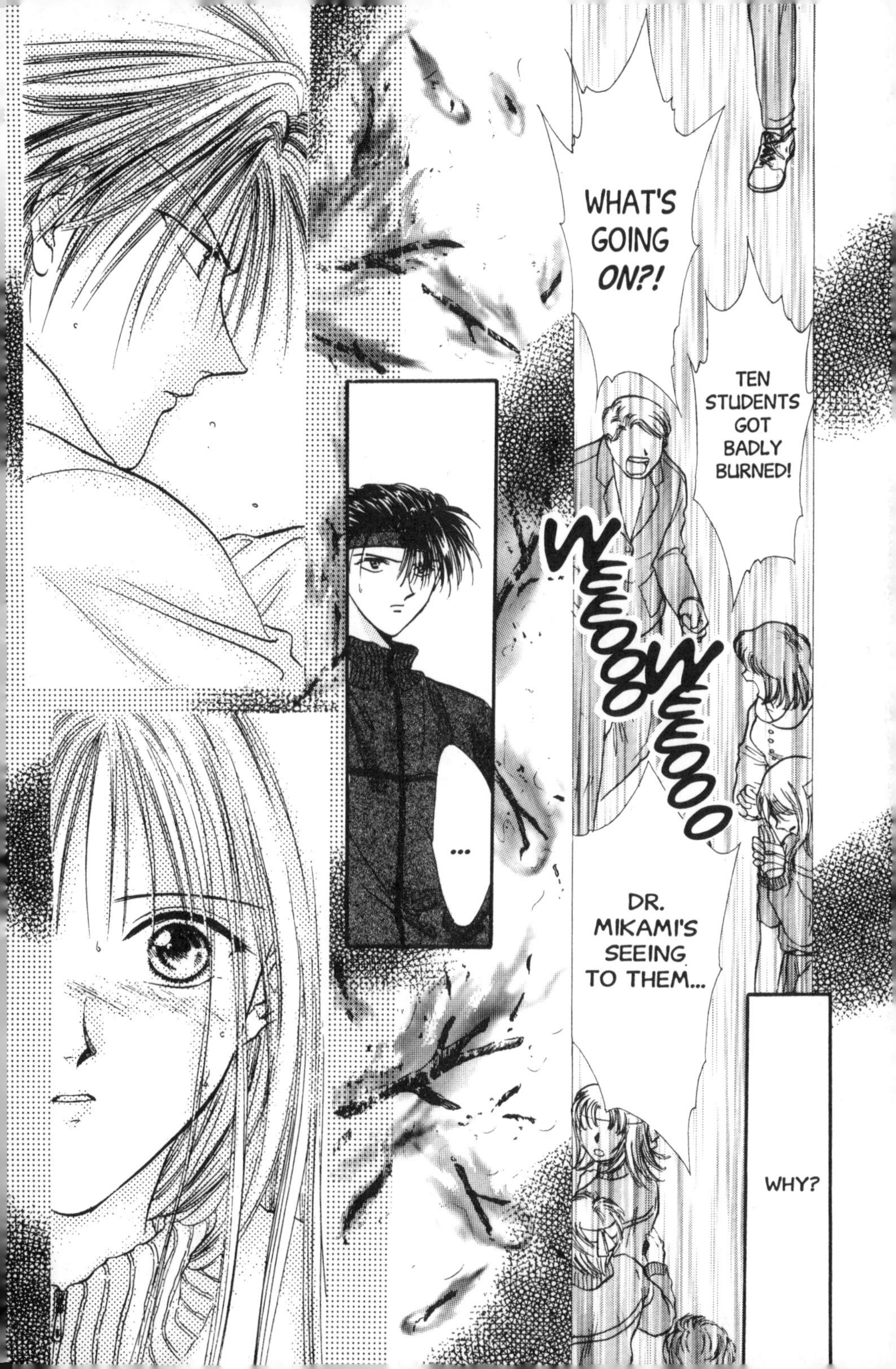
...
WHAT'S GOING ON?!
TEN STUDENTS GOT BADLY BURNED!
WEEOOWEEOOOO
DR. MIKAMI'S SEEING TO THEM...
WHY?

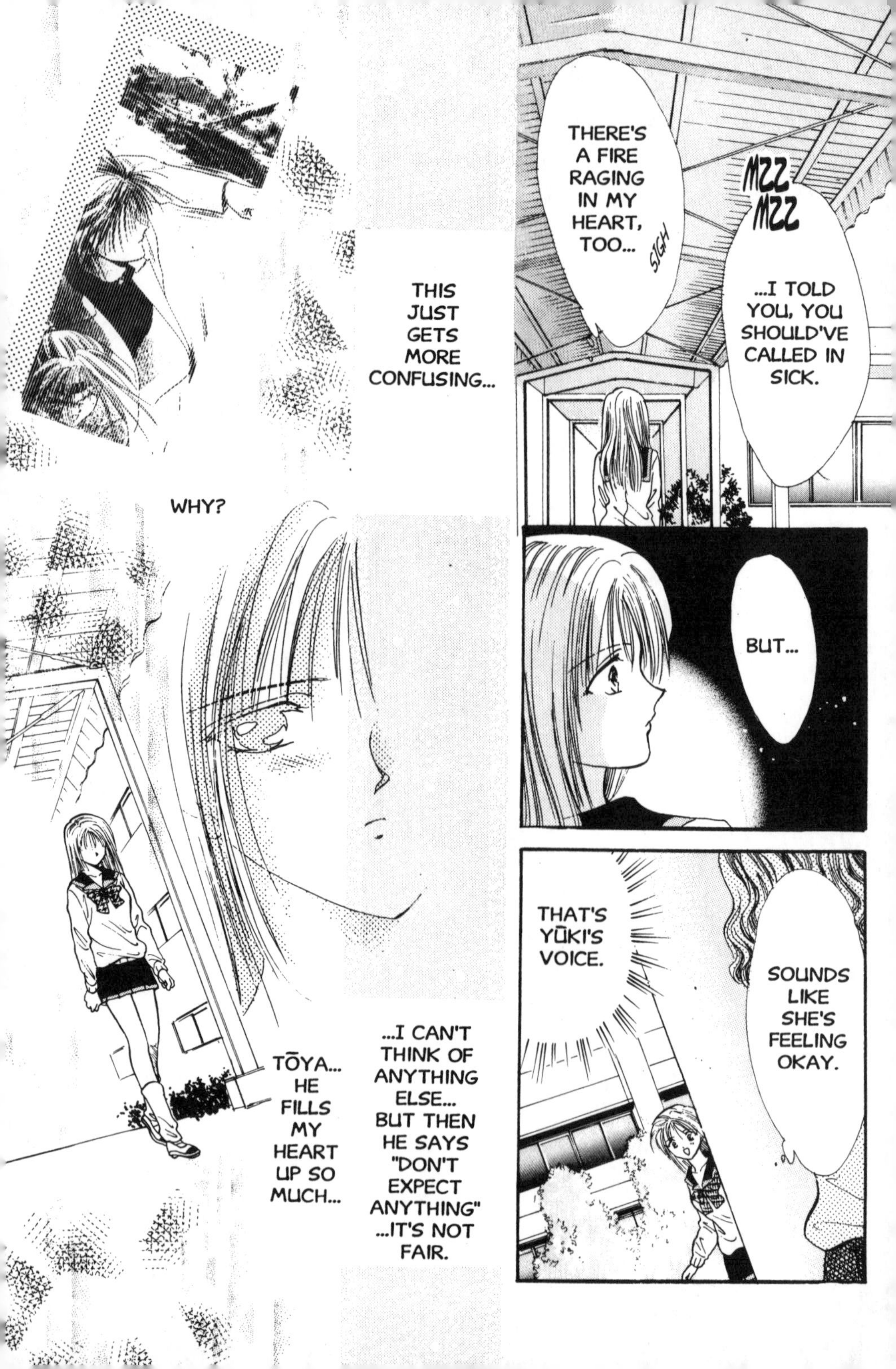
THIS JUST GETS MORE CONFUSING...
WHY?
TŌYA... HE FILLS MY HEART UP SO MUCH...
...I CAN'T THINK OF ANYTHING ELSE... BUT THEN HE SAYS "DON'T EXPECT ANYTHING" ...IT'S NOT FAIR.
THERE'S A FIRE RAGING IN MY HEART, TOO...
SIGH
MZZ MZZ
...I TOLD YOU, YOU SHOULD'VE CALLED IN SICK.
BUT...
THAT'S YŪKI'S VOICE.
SOUNDS LIKE SHE'S FEELING OKAY.

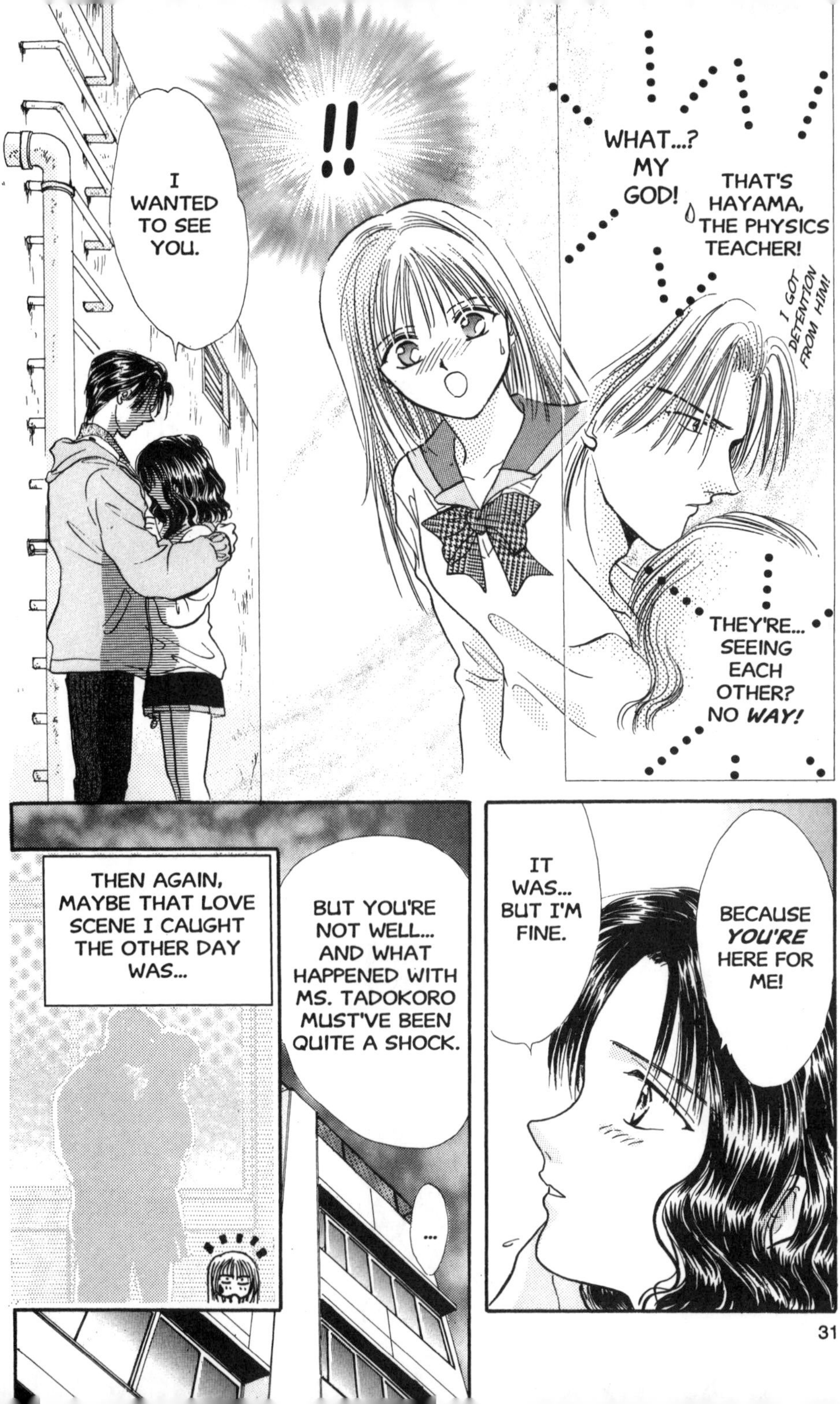
I WANTED TO SEE YOU.
!!
WHAT...? MY GOD!
THAT'S HAYAMA, THE PHYSICS TEACHER!
I GOT DETENTION FROM HIM!
THEY'RE... SEEING EACH OTHER? NO *WAY!*
THEN AGAIN, MAYBE THAT LOVE SCENE I CAUGHT THE OTHER DAY WAS...
BUT YOU'RE NOT WELL... AND WHAT HAPPENED WITH MS. TADOKORO MUST'VE BEEN QUITE A SHOCK.
...
IT WAS... BUT I'M FINE.
BECAUSE *YOU'RE* HERE FOR ME!

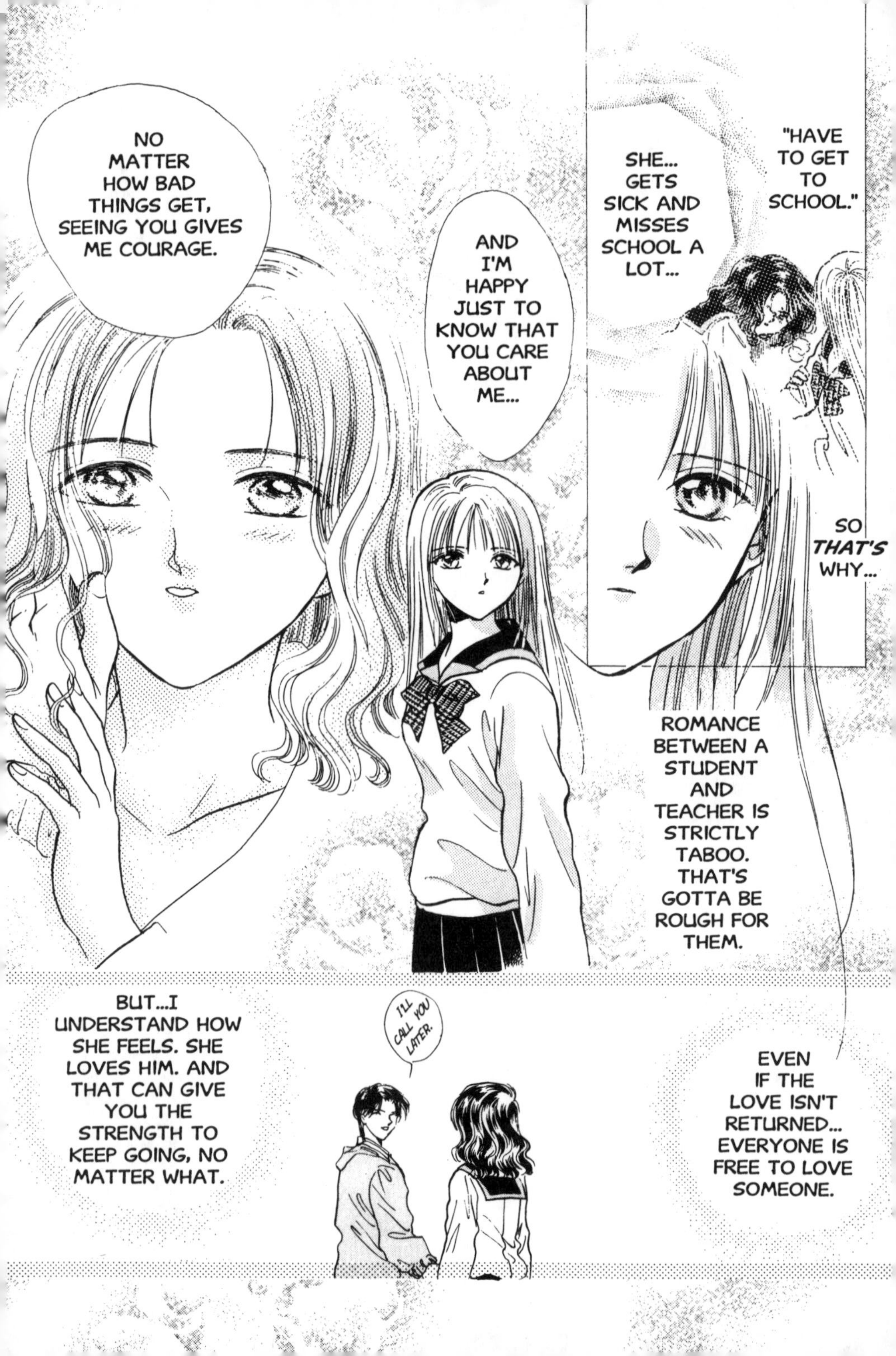

NO MATTER HOW BAD THINGS GET, SEEING YOU GIVES ME COURAGE.
AND I'M HAPPY JUST TO KNOW THAT YOU CARE ABOUT ME...
SHE... GETS SICK AND MISSES SCHOOL A LOT...
"HAVE TO GET TO SCHOOL."
SO *THAT'S* WHY...
ROMANCE BETWEEN A STUDENT AND TEACHER IS STRICTLY TABOO. THAT'S GOTTA BE ROUGH FOR THEM.
BUT...I UNDERSTAND HOW SHE FEELS. SHE LOVES HIM. AND THAT CAN GIVE YOU THE STRENGTH TO KEEP GOING, NO MATTER WHAT.
I'LL CALL YOU LATER.
EVEN IF THE LOVE ISN'T RETURNED... EVERYONE IS FREE TO LOVE SOMEONE.

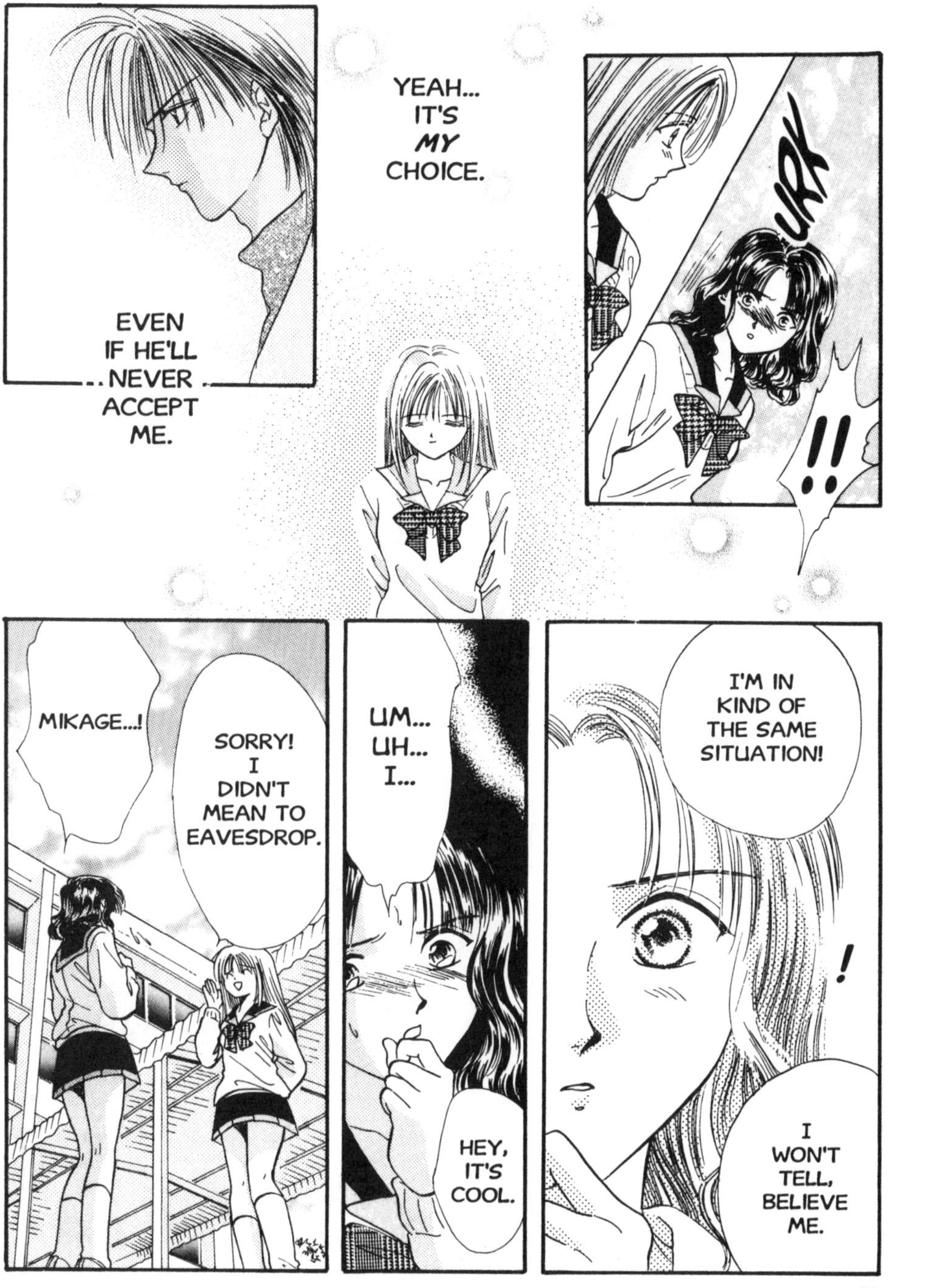
EVEN IF HE'LL NEVER ACCEPT ME.
YEAH... IT'S *MY* CHOICE.
URK
!!
MIKAGE...!
SORRY! I DIDN'T MEAN TO EAVESDROP.
UM... UH... I...
HEY, IT'S COOL.
I'M IN KIND OF THE SAME SITUATION!
!
I WON'T TELL, BELIEVE ME.

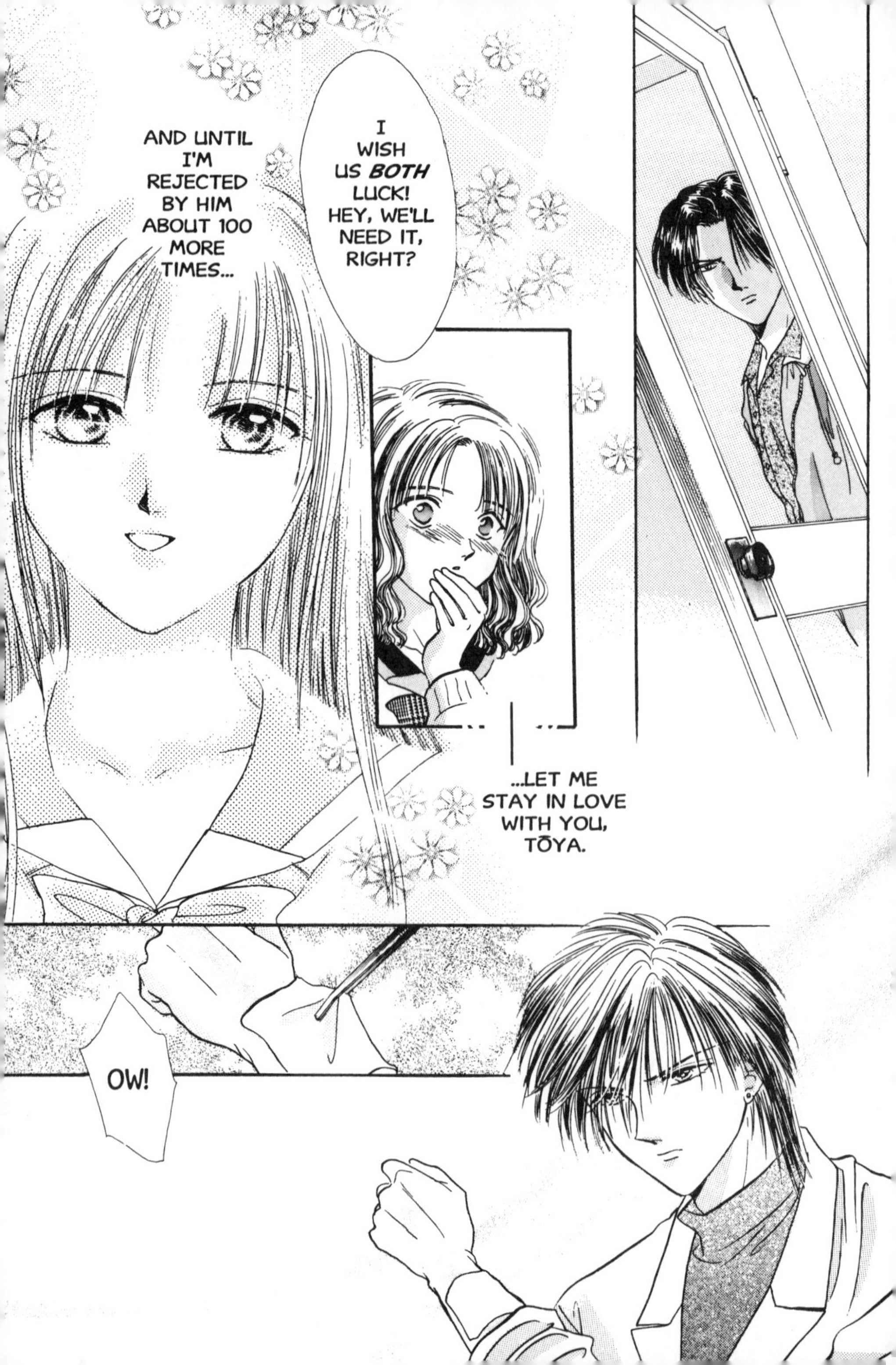
AND UNTIL I'M REJECTED BY HIM ABOUT 100 MORE TIMES...
I WISH US BOTH LUCK! HEY, WE'LL NEED IT, RIGHT?
...LET ME STAY IN LOVE WITH YOU, TŌYA.
OW!

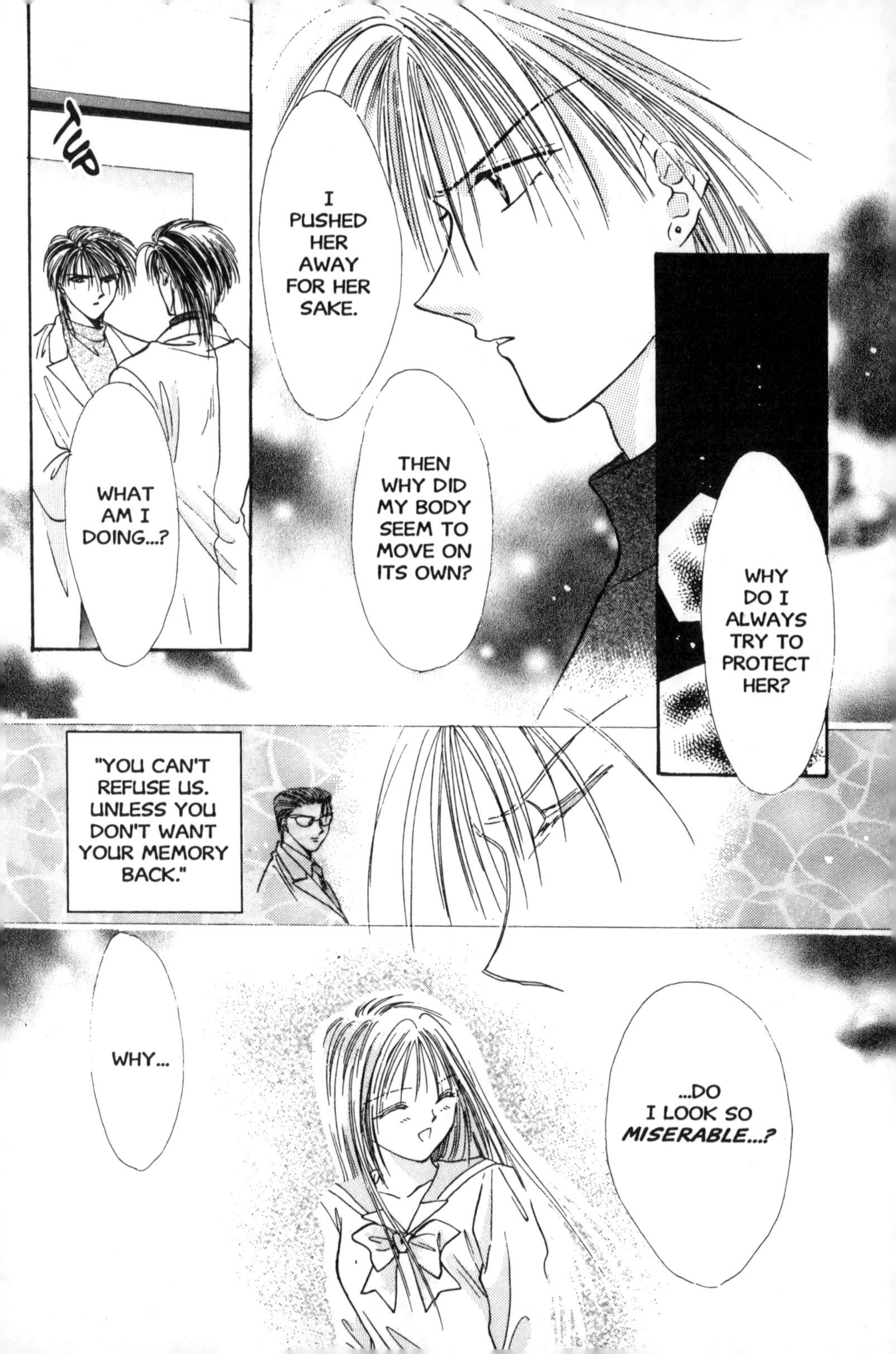
TUP
WHAT AM I DOING...?
I PUSHED HER AWAY FOR HER SAKE.
THEN WHY DID MY BODY SEEM TO MOVE ON ITS OWN?
WHY DO I ALWAYS TRY TO PROTECT HER?
"YOU CAN'T REFUSE US. UNLESS YOU DON'T WANT YOUR MEMORY BACK."
WHY...
...DO I LOOK SO *MISERABLE...?*

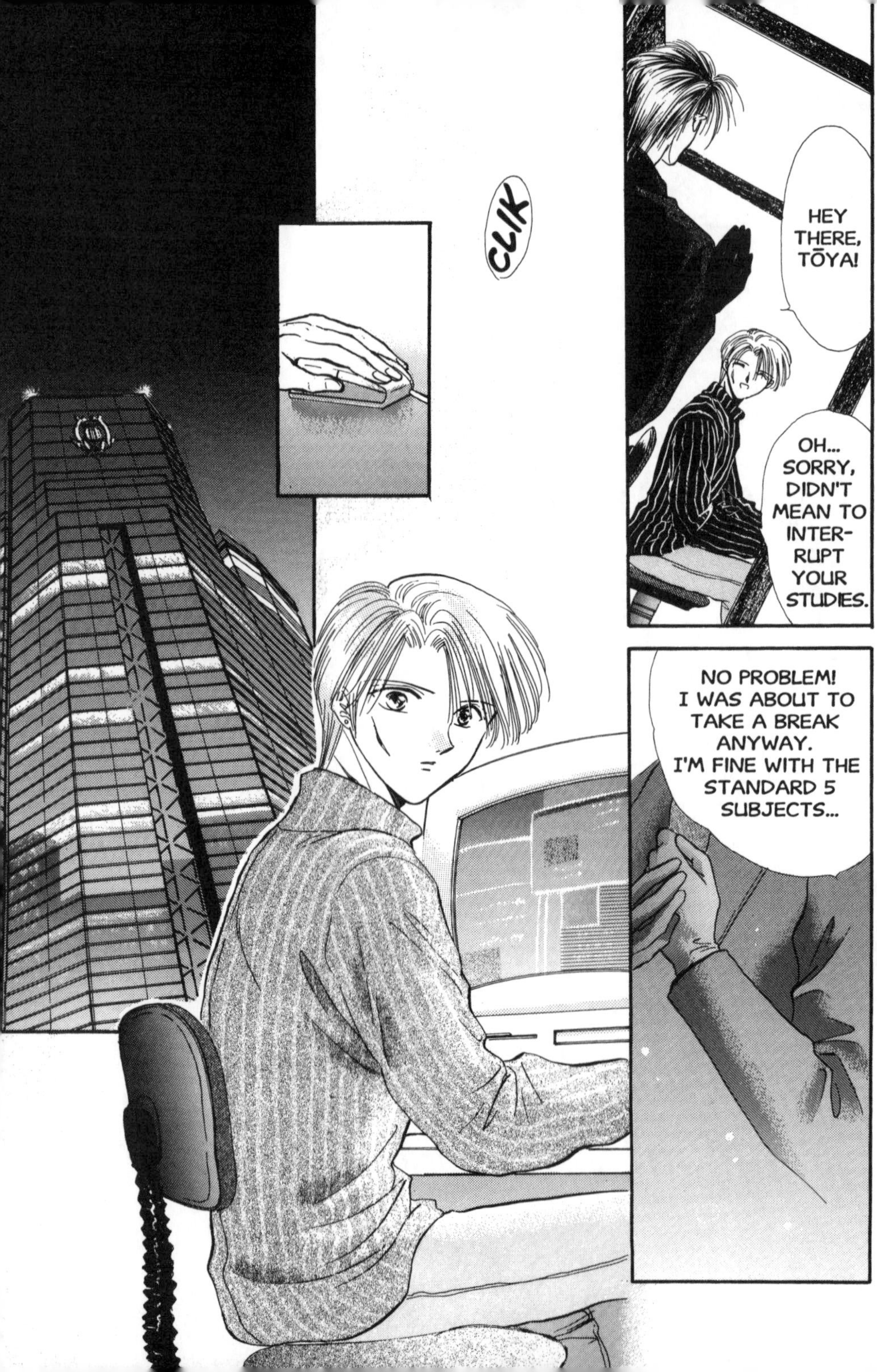
CLIK
HEY THERE, TŌYA!
OH... SORRY, DIDN'T MEAN TO INTER-RUPT YOUR STUDIES.
NO PROBLEM! I WAS ABOUT TO TAKE A BREAK ANYWAY. I'M FINE WITH THE STANDARD 5 SUBJECTS...

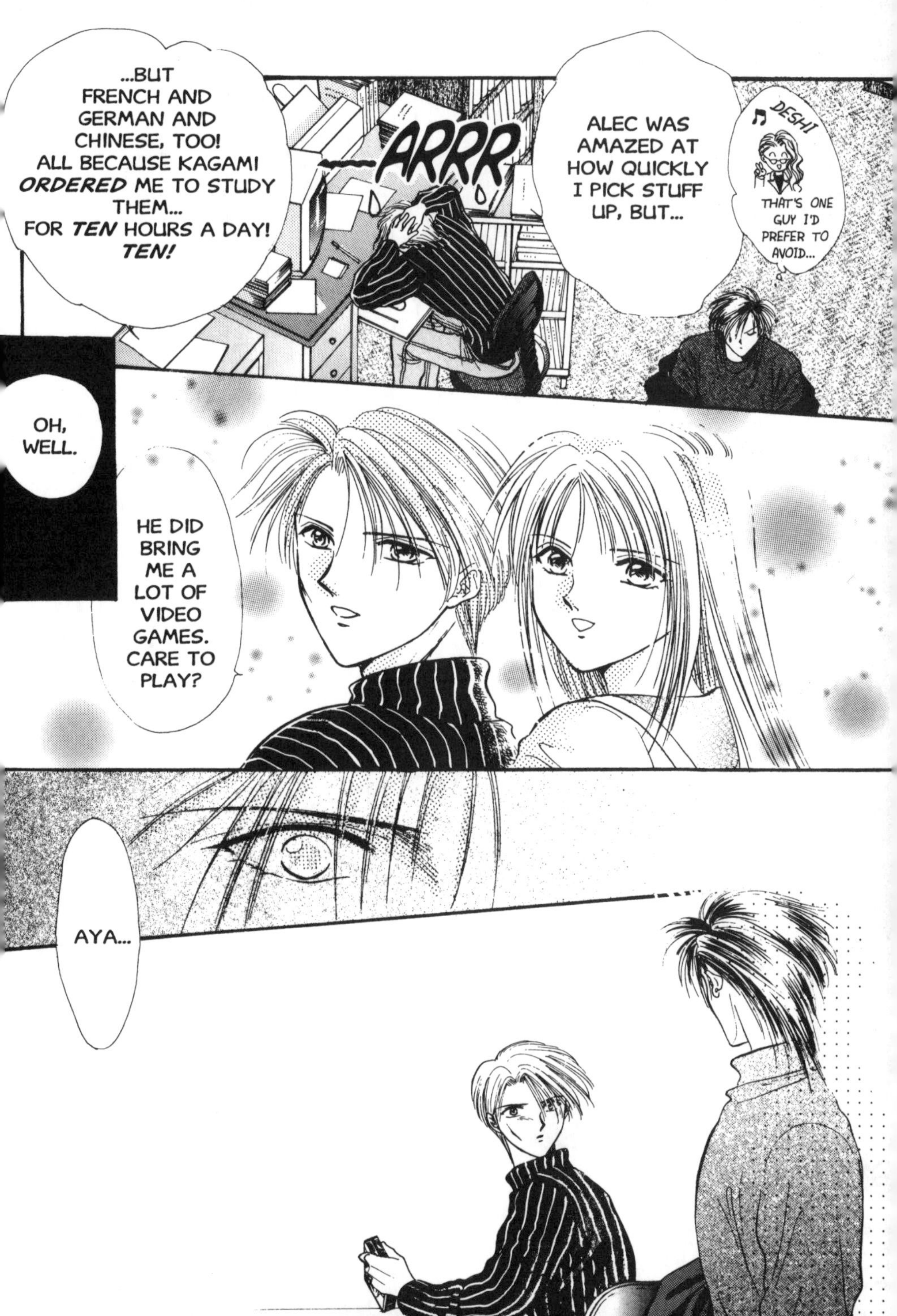
...BUT FRENCH AND GERMAN AND CHINESE, TOO! ALL BECAUSE KAGAMI *ORDERED* ME TO STUDY THEM... FOR *TEN* HOURS A DAY! *TEN!*
ARRR
ALEC WAS AMAZED AT HOW QUICKLY I PICK STUFF UP, BUT...
DESHI
THAT'S ONE GUY I'D PREFER TO AVOID...
OH, WELL.
HE DID BRING ME A LOT OF VIDEO GAMES. CARE TO PLAY?
AYA...

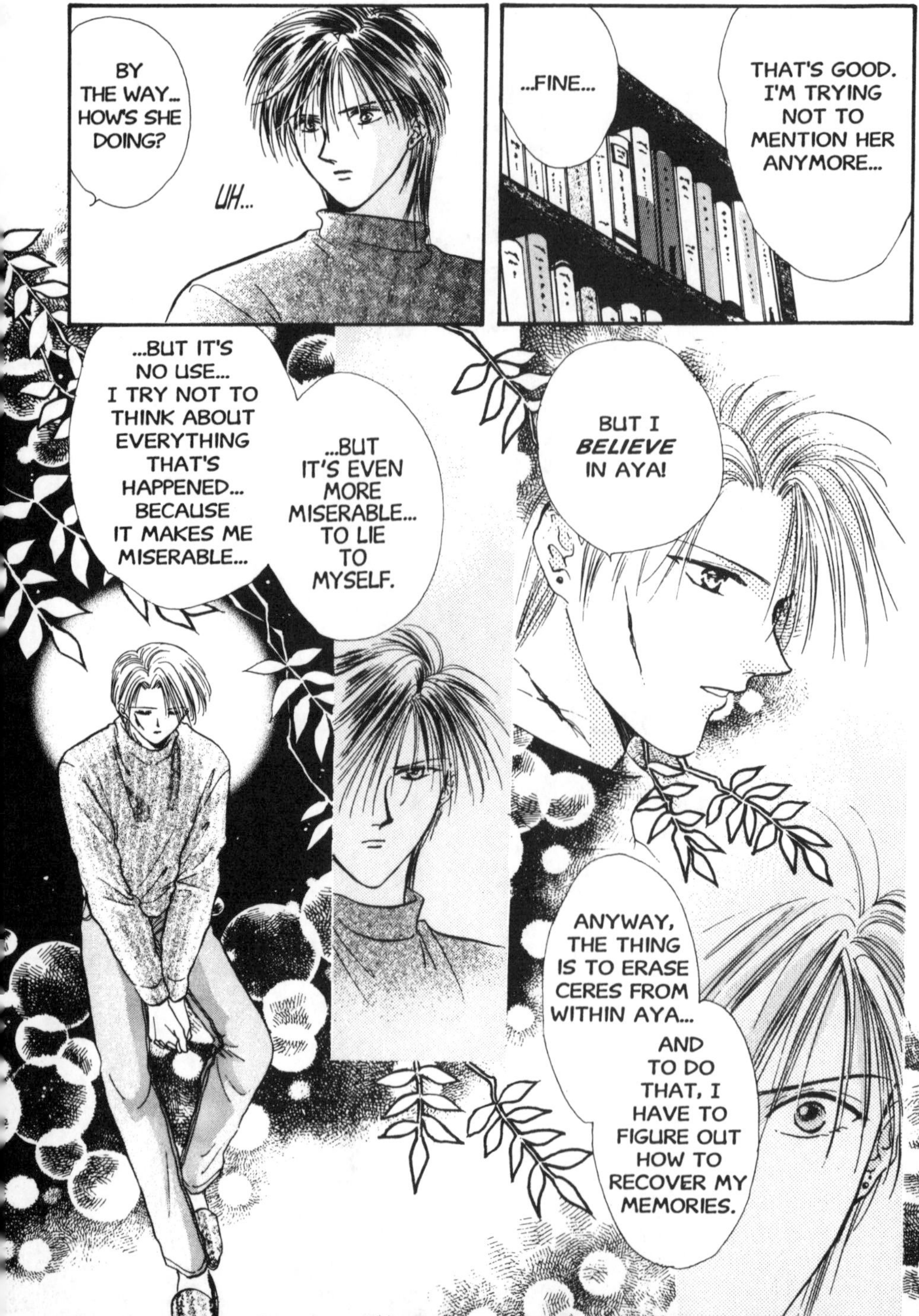
BY THE WAY... HOW'S SHE DOING?
UH...
...FINE...
THAT'S GOOD. I'M TRYING NOT TO MENTION HER ANYMORE...
...BUT IT'S NO USE... I TRY NOT TO THINK ABOUT EVERYTHING THAT'S HAPPENED... BECAUSE IT MAKES ME MISERABLE...
...BUT IT'S EVEN MORE MISERABLE... TO LIE TO MYSELF.
BUT I *BELIEVE* IN AYA!
ANYWAY, THE THING IS TO ERASE CERES FROM WITHIN AYA...
AND TO DO THAT, I HAVE TO FIGURE OUT HOW TO RECOVER MY MEMORIES.

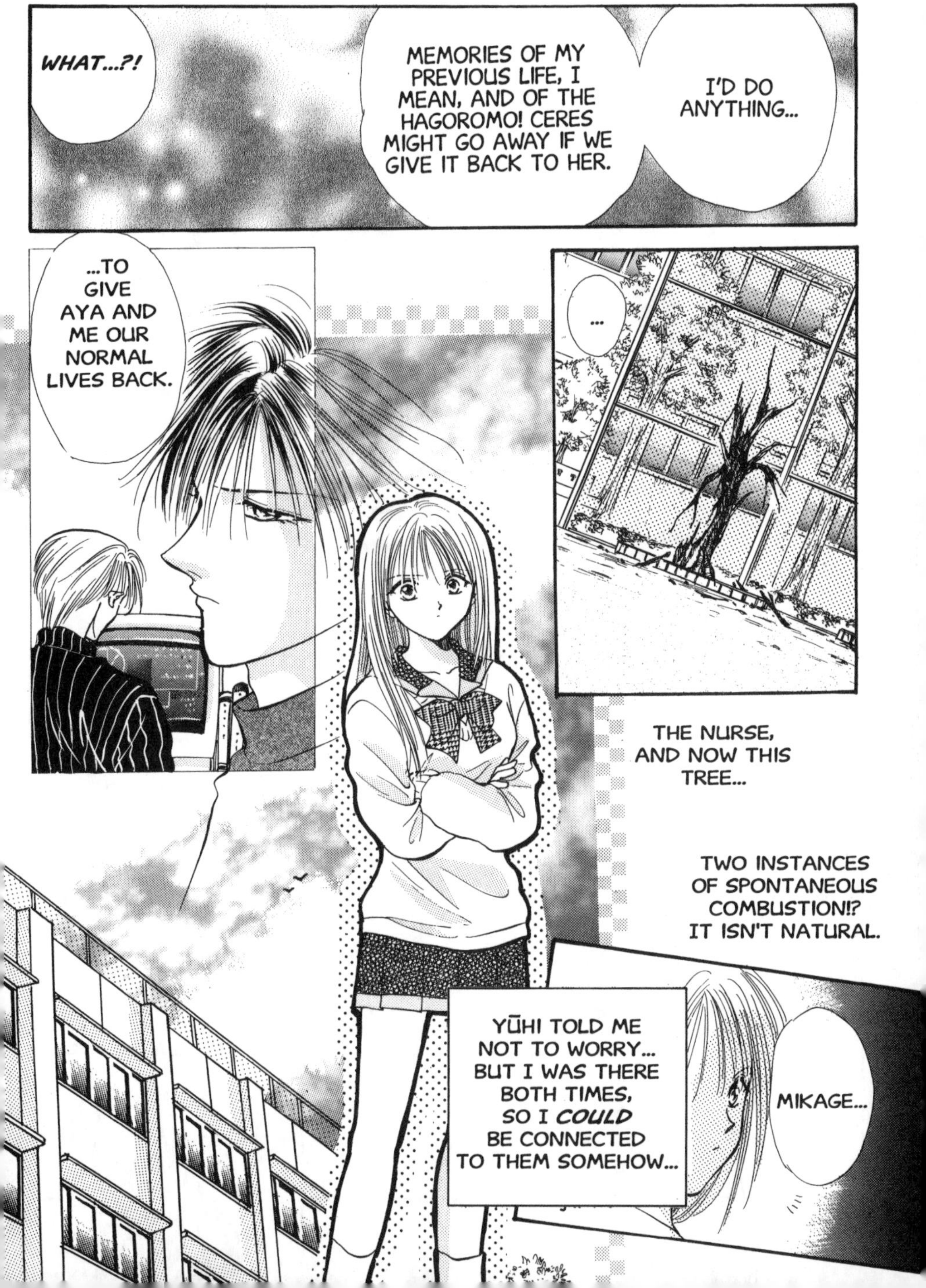
WHAT...?!
MEMORIES OF MY PREVIOUS LIFE, I MEAN, AND OF THE HAGOROMO! CERES MIGHT GO AWAY IF WE GIVE IT BACK TO HER.
I'D DO ANYTHING...
...TO GIVE AYA AND ME OUR NORMAL LIVES BACK.
...
THE NURSE, AND NOW THIS TREE...
TWO INSTANCES OF SPONTANEOUS COMBUSTION!? IT ISN'T NATURAL.
YŪHI TOLD ME NOT TO WORRY... BUT I WAS THERE BOTH TIMES, SO I *COULD* BE CONNECTED TO THEM SOMEHOW...
MIKAGE...

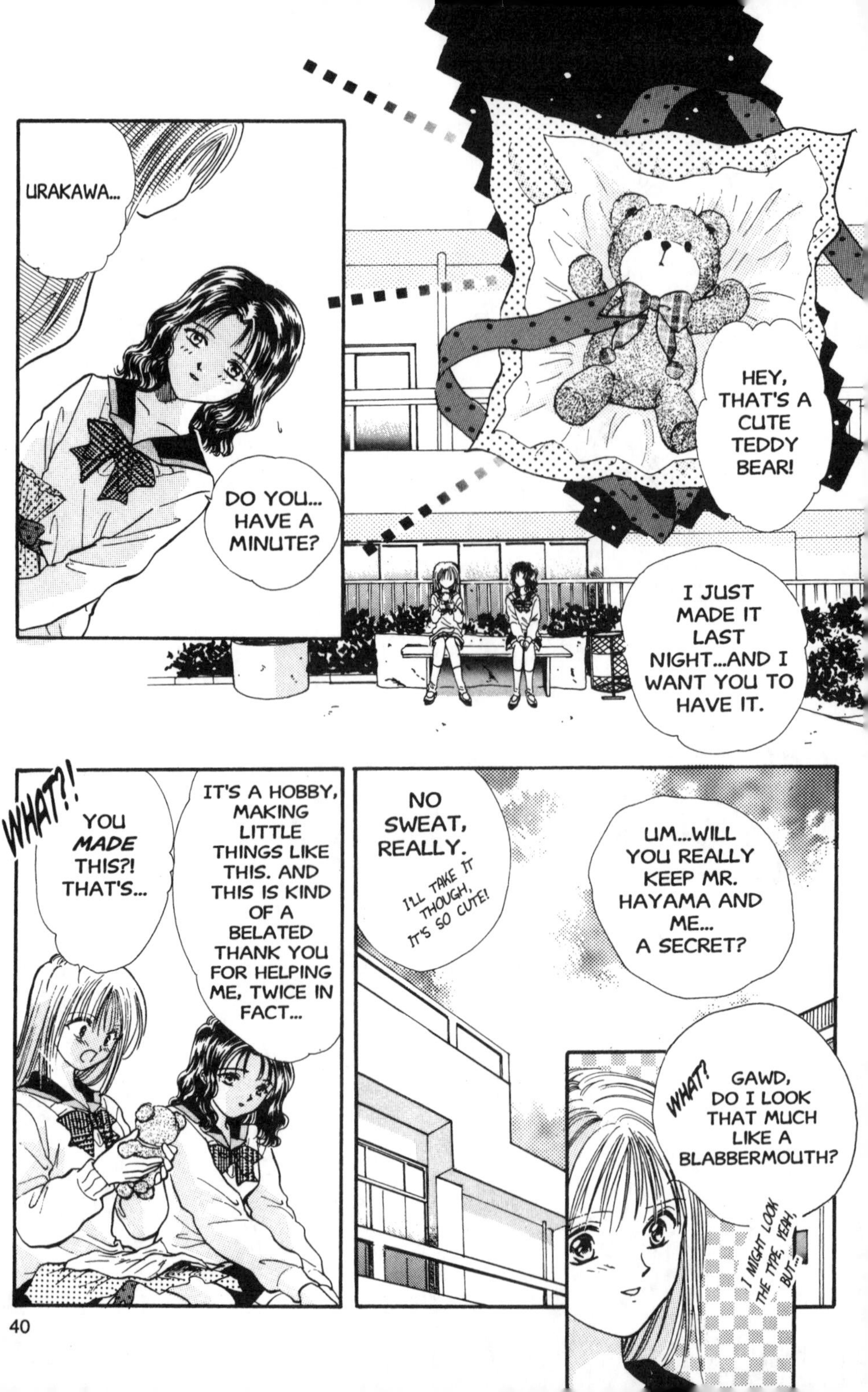
URAKAWA...
DO YOU... HAVE A MINUTE?
HEY, THAT'S A CUTE TEDDY BEAR!
I JUST MADE IT LAST NIGHT...AND I WANT YOU TO HAVE IT.
WHAT?!
YOU *MADE* THIS?! THAT'S...
IT'S A HOBBY, MAKING LITTLE THINGS LIKE THIS. AND THIS IS KIND OF A BELATED THANK YOU FOR HELPING ME, TWICE IN FACT...
NO SWEAT, REALLY.
I'LL TAKE IT THOUGH, IT'S SO CUTE!
UM...WILL YOU REALLY KEEP MR. HAYAMA AND ME... A SECRET?
WHAT?
GAWD, DO I LOOK THAT MUCH LIKE A BLABBERMOUTH?
I MIGHT LOOK THE TYPE, YEAH, BUT...

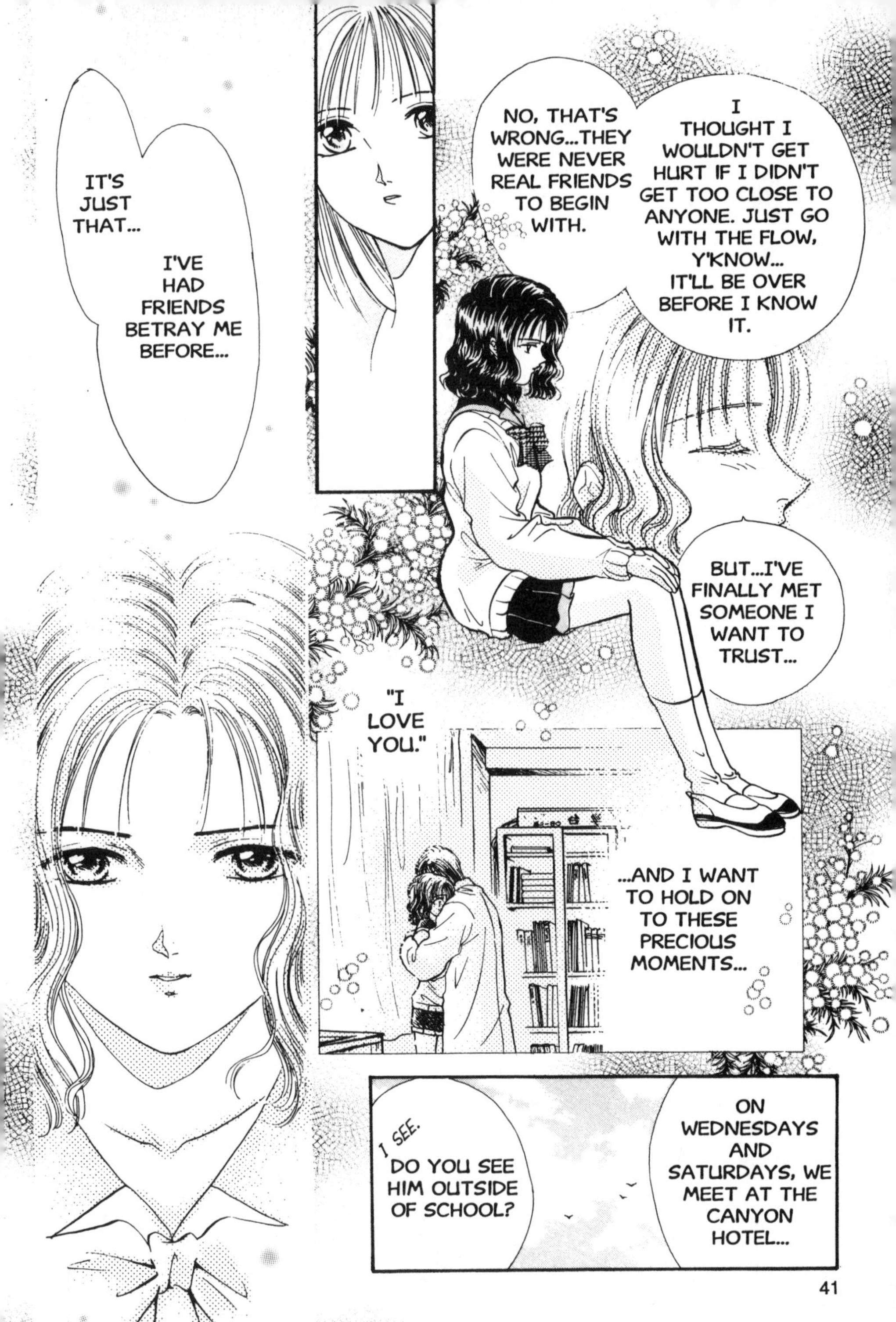
IT'S JUST THAT...
I'VE HAD FRIENDS BETRAY ME BEFORE...
NO, THAT'S WRONG...THEY WERE NEVER REAL FRIENDS TO BEGIN WITH.
I THOUGHT I WOULDN'T GET HURT IF I DIDN'T GET TOO CLOSE TO ANYONE. JUST GO WITH THE FLOW, Y'KNOW... IT'LL BE OVER BEFORE I KNOW IT.
BUT...I'VE FINALLY MET SOMEONE I WANT TO TRUST...
"I LOVE YOU."
...AND I WANT TO HOLD ON TO THESE PRECIOUS MOMENTS...
I SEE.
DO YOU SEE HIM OUTSIDE OF SCHOOL?
ON WEDNESDAYS AND SATURDAYS, WE MEET AT THE CANYON HOTEL...

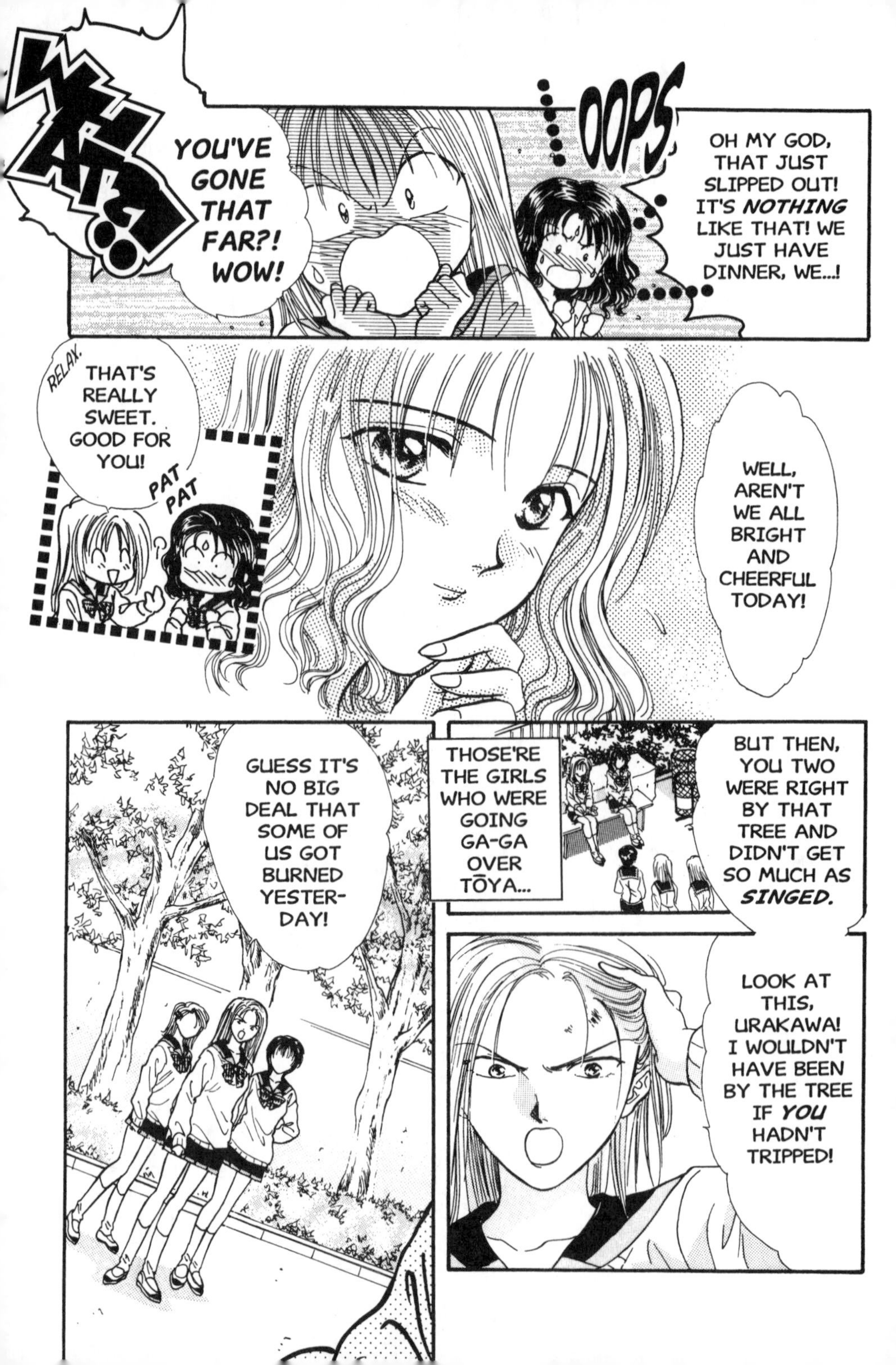
YOU'VE GONE THAT FAR?! WOW!
OOPS
OH MY GOD, THAT JUST SLIPPED OUT! IT'S *NOTHING* LIKE THAT! WE JUST HAVE DINNER, WE...!
RELAX.
THAT'S REALLY SWEET. GOOD FOR YOU!
PAT PAT
WELL, AREN'T WE ALL BRIGHT AND CHEERFUL TODAY!
GUESS IT'S NO BIG DEAL THAT SOME OF US GOT BURNED YESTER-DAY!
THOSE'RE THE GIRLS WHO WERE GOING GA-GA OVER TŌYA...
BUT THEN, YOU TWO WERE RIGHT BY THAT TREE AND DIDN'T GET SO MUCH AS ***SINGED.***
LOOK AT THIS, URAKAWA! I WOULDN'T HAVE BEEN BY THE TREE IF *YOU* HADN'T TRIPPED!

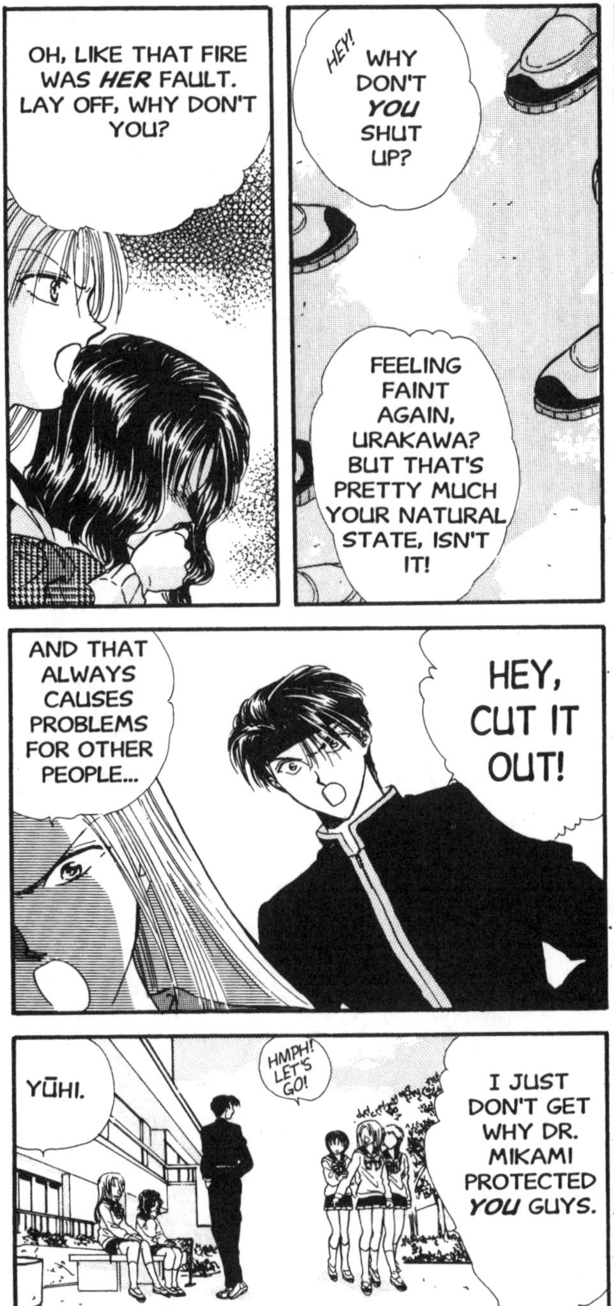
OH, LIKE THAT FIRE WAS *HER* FAULT. LAY OFF, WHY DON'T YOU?
HEY!
WHY DON'T *YOU* SHUT UP?
FEELING FAINT AGAIN, URAKAWA? BUT THAT'S PRETTY MUCH YOUR NATURAL STATE, ISN'T IT!
AND THAT ALWAYS CAUSES PROBLEMS FOR OTHER PEOPLE...
HEY, CUT IT OUT!
YŪHI.
HMPH! LET'S GO!
I JUST DON'T GET WHY DR. MIKAMI PROTECTED *YOU* GUYS.

I just had dinner! Phew. Now I can write with more coherence. But I'm still sleepy ♫ Oh, the first volume of the OAV for **FY part 2** is now on sale! (as of June '97) Please take a look at it! ♫ Vol.2 won't be out for a while, though... I really like the new opening and ending theme songs. ♥
So check out the CDs too! Come to think of it, they gave out CD singles as a free gift for readers in the April issue of Animedia. And speaking of CD singles, I participated (half hesitatingly) in the recording on the bonus CD that comes with buying all 3 volumes of the first OAV series. I always act for fun with my assistants, but I fell apart when I actually got up to the mike! I was so nervous. If someone was doing it for me, and I was demonstrating, "this is how you do it," I could've been more relaxed. *Darnit.*

Actually... on another note, I think in China, there's a pop group called "Ceres: Chinese Sugar Girls" (*I think? Maybe I'm wrong.*). ☺ There are 5 girls, and the group's name is Ceres! What a coincidence -I had to laugh. I've heard of them before, but they just recently came out with a photo book. I wonder how they decided on the name "Ceres"? Actually, Toyota had a car called "Ceres" too. I wonder if they were named for the same reasons.

Oh, about the question "why does the tennyo from a Japanese legend have an English name?" I mean, she's from heaven. She's not Japanese.
...It sounds pretty too.
So what if it's English?

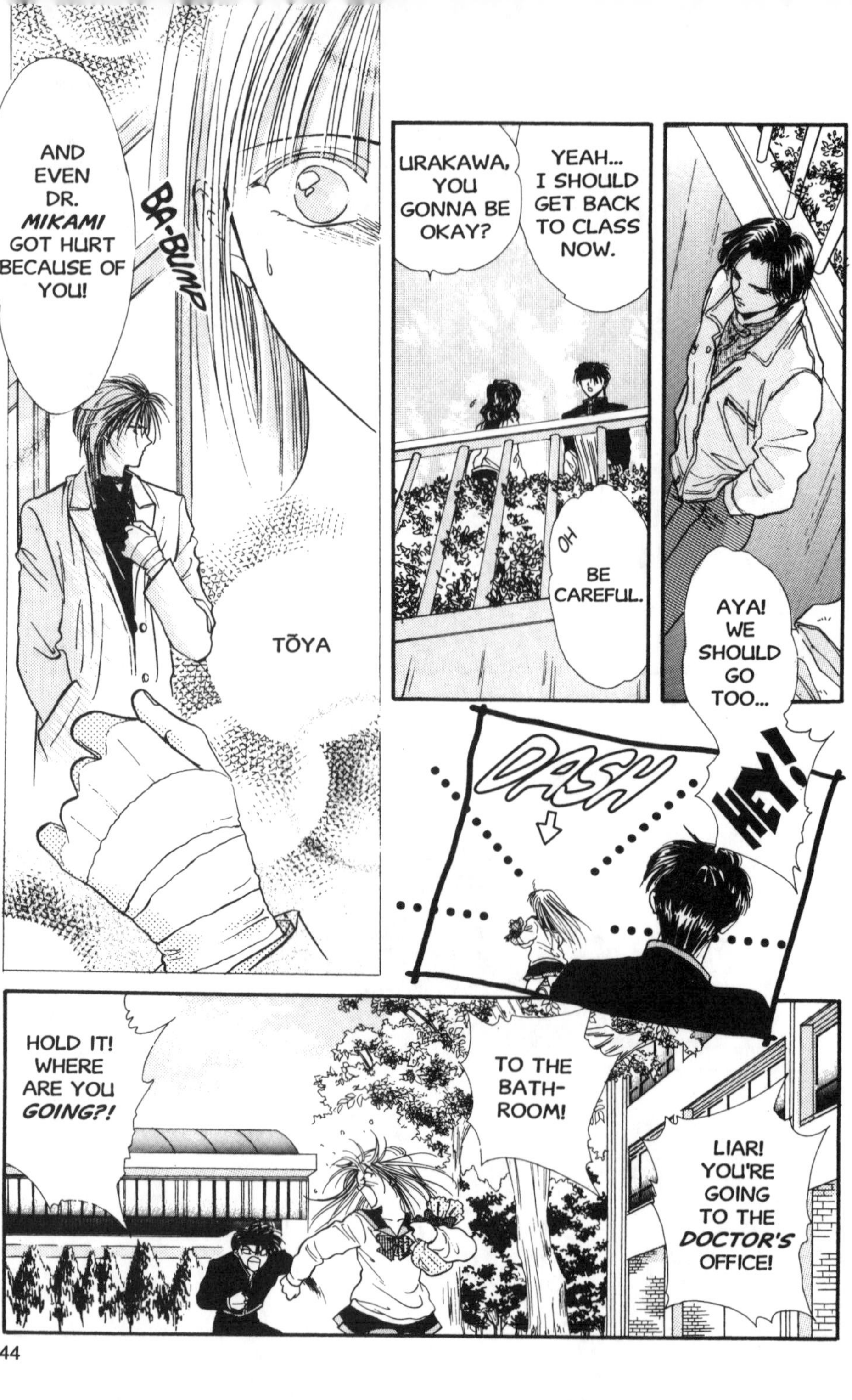
AND EVEN DR. *MIKAMI* GOT HURT BECAUSE OF YOU!
BA-BUMP
TŌYA
URAKAWA, YOU GONNA BE OKAY?
YEAH... I SHOULD GET BACK TO CLASS NOW.
OH
BE CAREFUL.
AYA! WE SHOULD GO TOO...
DASH
HEY!
HOLD IT! WHERE ARE YOU *GOING?!*
TO THE BATH-ROOM!
LIAR! YOU'RE GOING TO THE *DOCTOR'S* OFFICE!

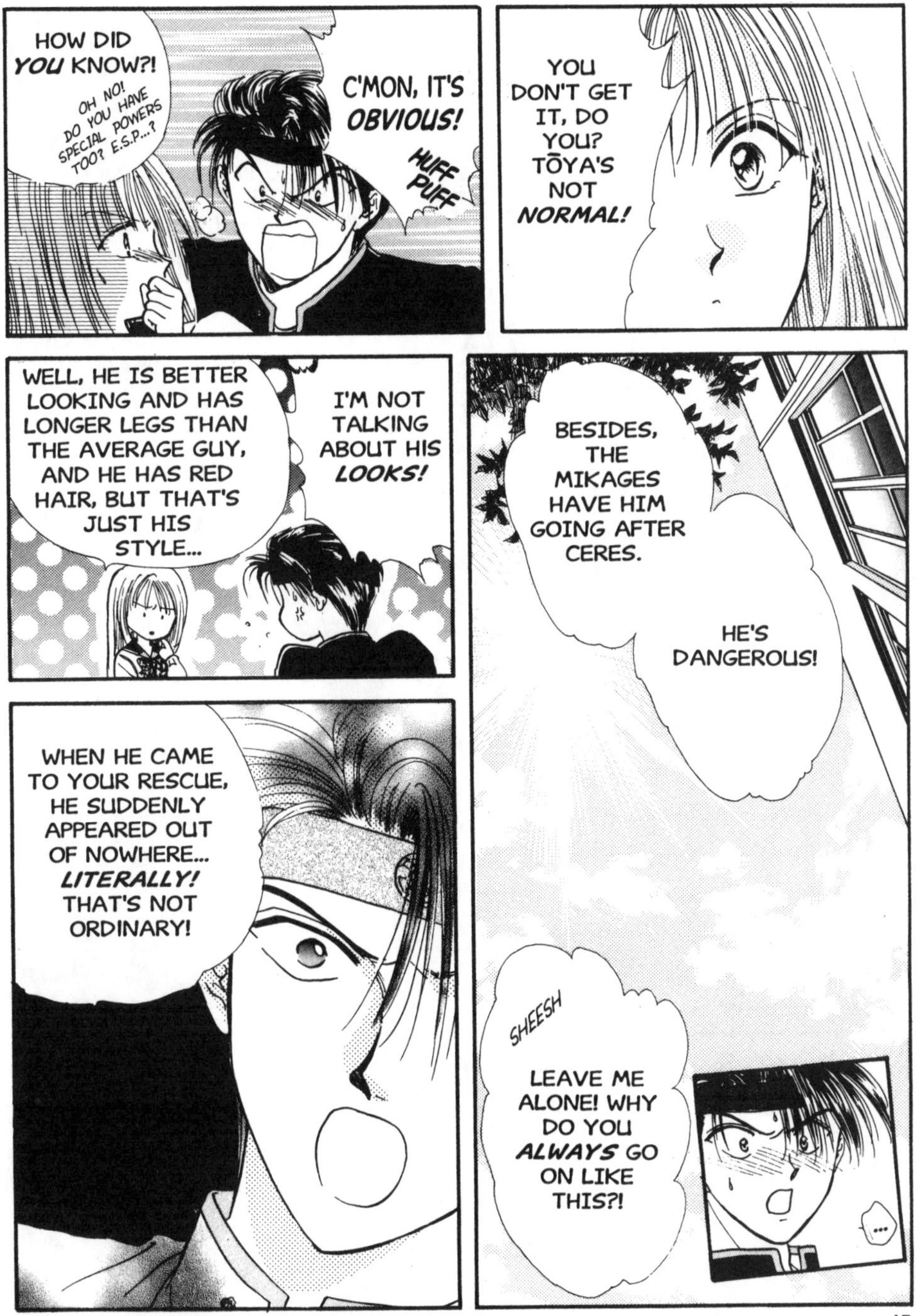
HOW DID *YOU* KNOW?!
OH NO! DO YOU HAVE SPECIAL POWERS TOO? E.S.P...?
C'MON, IT'S *OBVIOUS!*
HUFF PUFF
YOU DON'T GET IT, DO YOU? TŌYA'S NOT *NORMAL!*
WELL, HE IS BETTER LOOKING AND HAS LONGER LEGS THAN THE AVERAGE GUY, AND HE HAS RED HAIR, BUT THAT'S JUST HIS STYLE...
I'M NOT TALKING ABOUT HIS *LOOKS!*
WHEN HE CAME TO YOUR RESCUE, HE SUDDENLY APPEARED OUT OF NOWHERE... *LITERALLY!* THAT'S NOT ORDINARY!
BESIDES, THE MIKAGES HAVE HIM GOING AFTER CERES.
HE'S DANGEROUS!
SHEESH
LEAVE ME ALONE! WHY DO YOU *ALWAYS* GO ON LIKE THIS?!
...

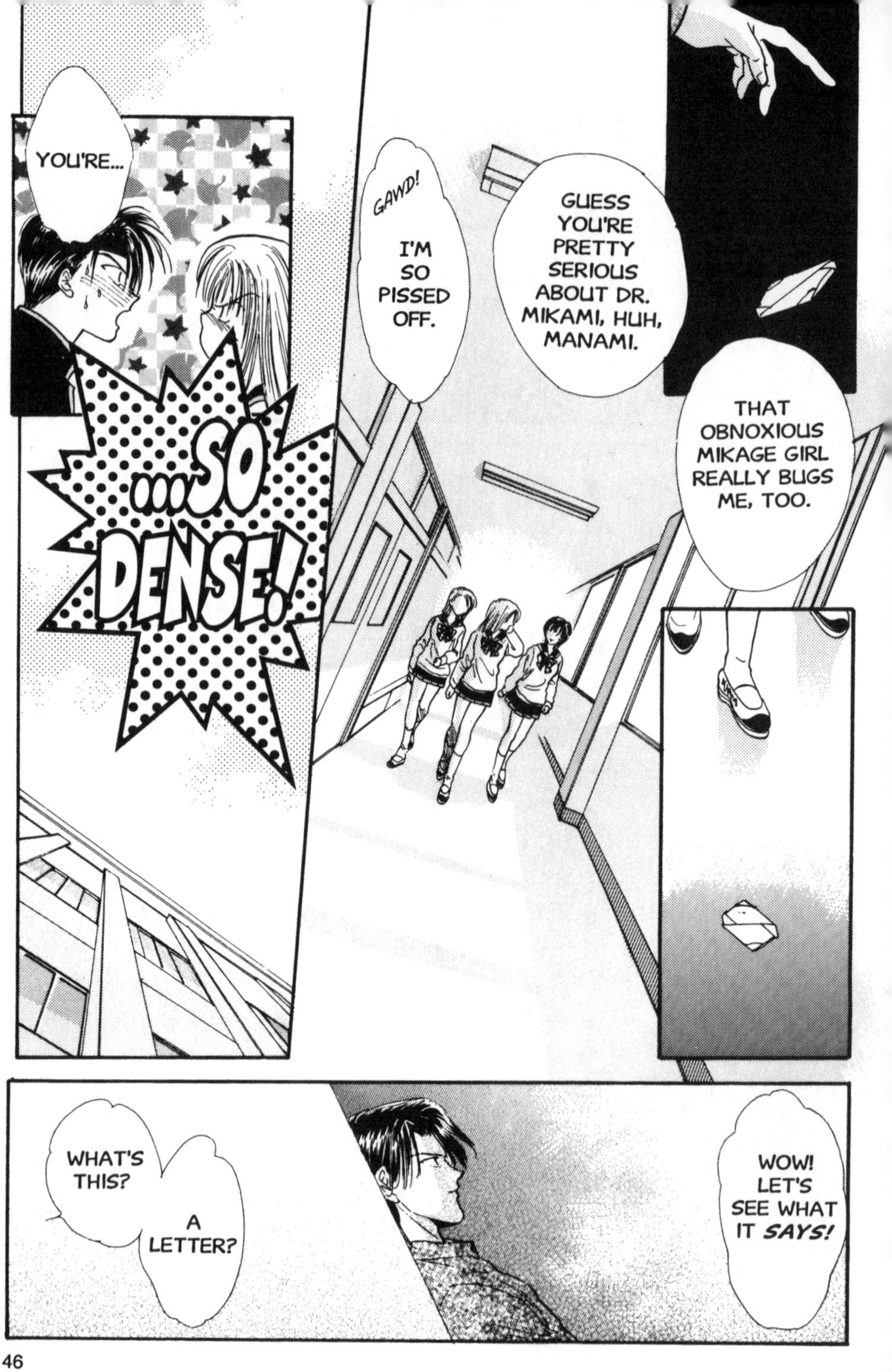
YOU'RE...
...SO DENSE!
GAWD!
I'M SO PISSED OFF.
GUESS YOU'RE PRETTY SERIOUS ABOUT DR. MIKAMI, HUH, MANAMI.
THAT OBNOXIOUS MIKAGE GIRL REALLY BUGS ME, TOO.
WHAT'S THIS?
A LETTER?
WOW! LET'S SEE WHAT IT *SAYS!*

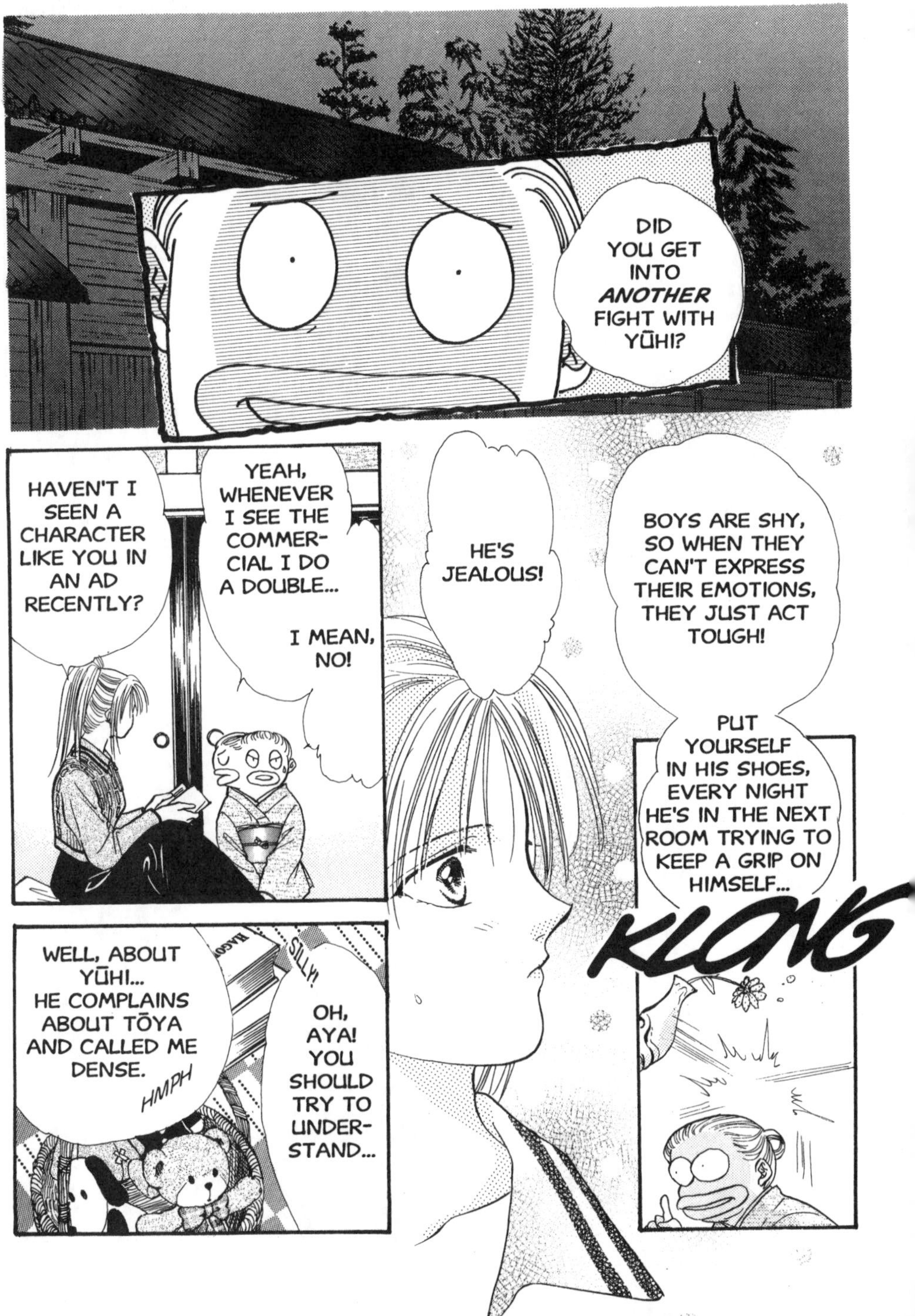

DID YOU GET INTO ANOTHER FIGHT WITH YŪHI?
HAVEN'T I SEEN A CHARACTER LIKE YOU IN AN AD RECENTLY?
YEAH, WHENEVER I SEE THE COMMERCIAL I DO A DOUBLE...
I MEAN, NO!
HE'S JEALOUS!
BOYS ARE SHY, SO WHEN THEY CAN'T EXPRESS THEIR EMOTIONS, THEY JUST ACT TOUGH!
PUT YOURSELF IN HIS SHOES, EVERY NIGHT HE'S IN THE NEXT ROOM TRYING TO KEEP A GRIP ON HIMSELF...
KLONG
WELL, ABOUT YŪHI... HE COMPLAINS ABOUT TŌYA AND CALLED ME DENSE.
HMPH
SILLY!
OH, AYA! YOU SHOULD TRY TO UNDERSTAND...

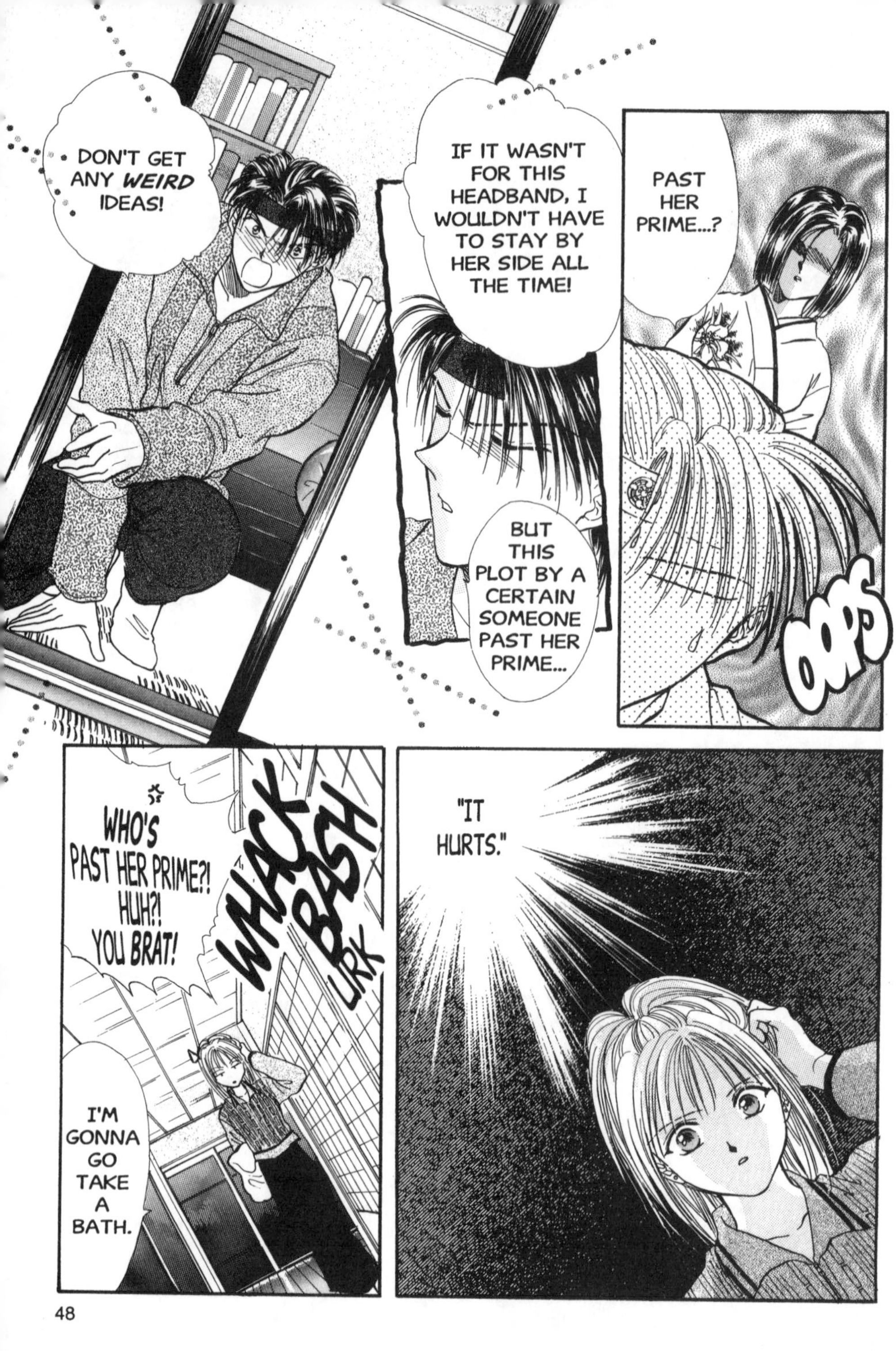
DON'T GET ANY WEIRD IDEAS!
IF IT WASN'T FOR THIS HEADBAND, I WOULDN'T HAVE TO STAY BY HER SIDE ALL THE TIME!
BUT THIS PLOT BY A CERTAIN SOMEONE PAST HER PRIME...
PAST HER PRIME...?
OOPS
WHO'S PAST HER PRIME?! HUH?! YOU BRAT!
WHACK
BASH
URK
I'M GONNA GO TAKE A BATH.
"IT HURTS."

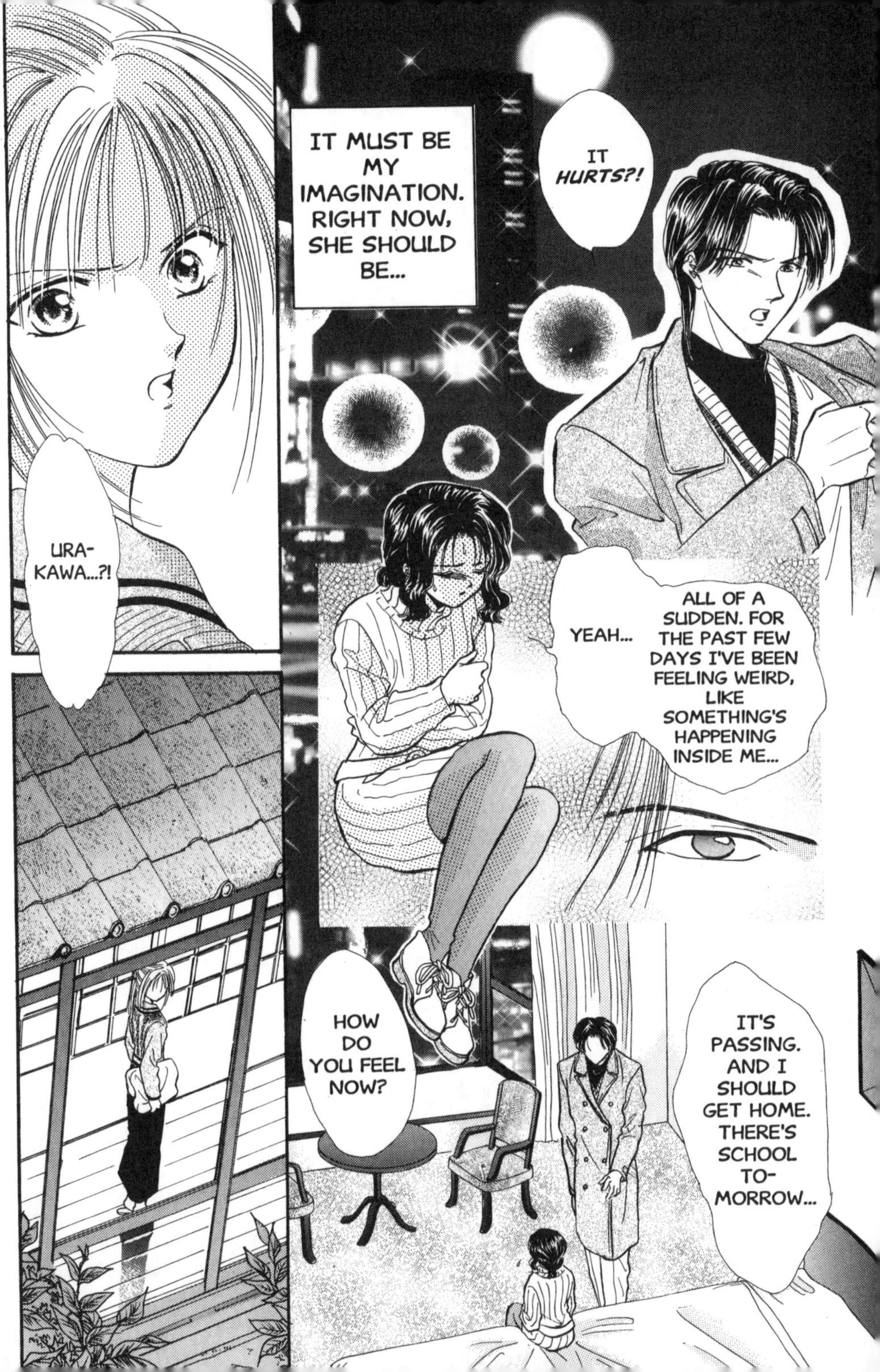
URA-KAWA...?!
IT MUST BE MY IMAGINATION. RIGHT NOW, SHE SHOULD BE...
IT *HURTS?!*
YEAH...
ALL OF A SUDDEN. FOR THE PAST FEW DAYS I'VE BEEN FEELING WEIRD, LIKE SOMETHING'S HAPPENING INSIDE ME...
HOW DO YOU FEEL NOW?
IT'S PASSING. AND I SHOULD GET HOME. THERE'S SCHOOL TO-MORROW...

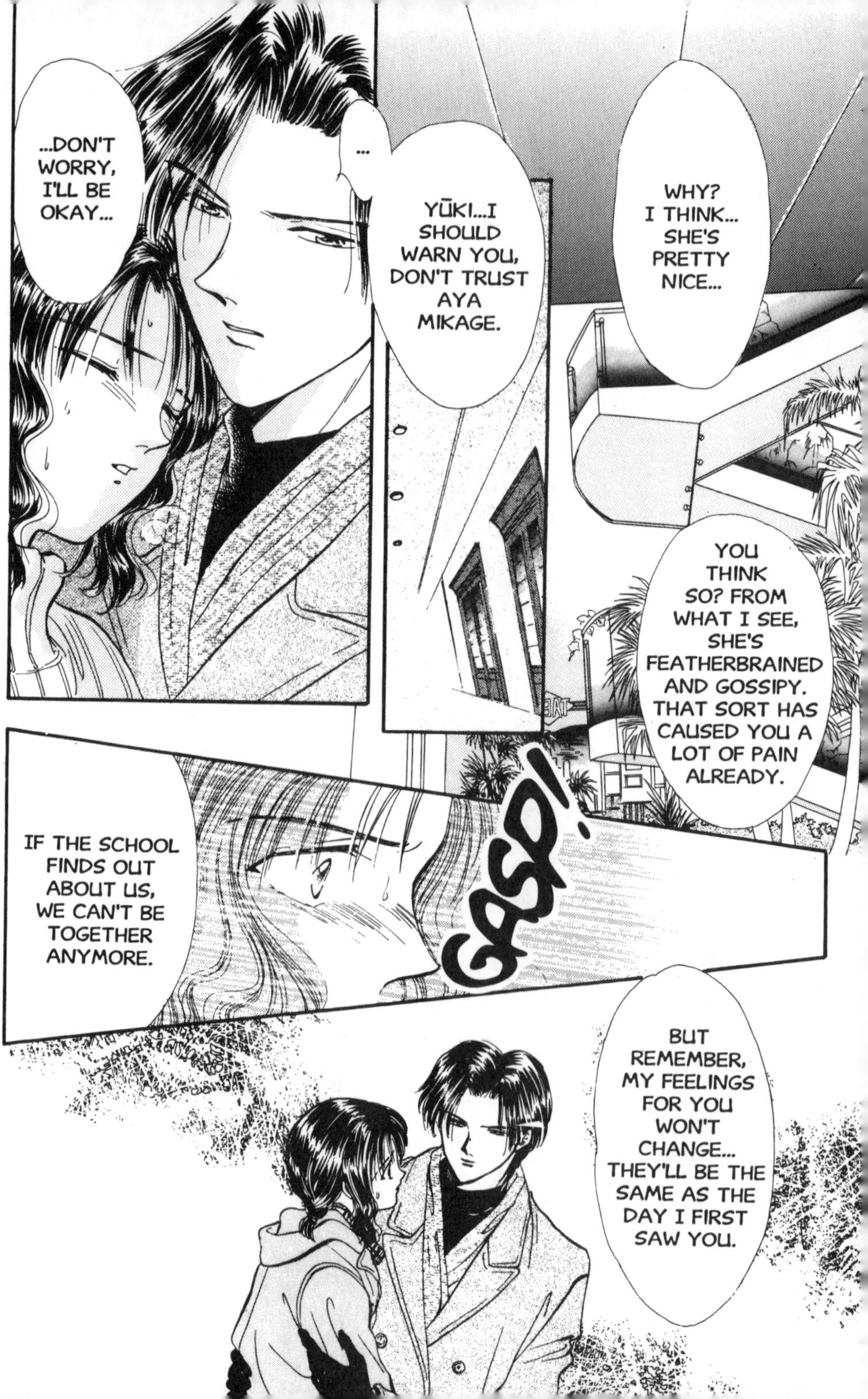
...DON'T WORRY, I'LL BE OKAY...
...
YŪKI...I SHOULD WARN YOU, DON'T TRUST AYA MIKAGE.
WHY? I THINK... SHE'S PRETTY NICE...
YOU THINK SO? FROM WHAT I SEE, SHE'S FEATHERBRAINED AND GOSSIPY. THAT SORT HAS CAUSED YOU A LOT OF PAIN ALREADY.
IF THE SCHOOL FINDS OUT ABOUT US, WE CAN'T BE TOGETHER ANYMORE.
GASP!
BUT REMEMBER, MY FEELINGS FOR YOU WON'T CHANGE... THEY'LL BE THE SAME AS THE DAY I FIRST SAW YOU.

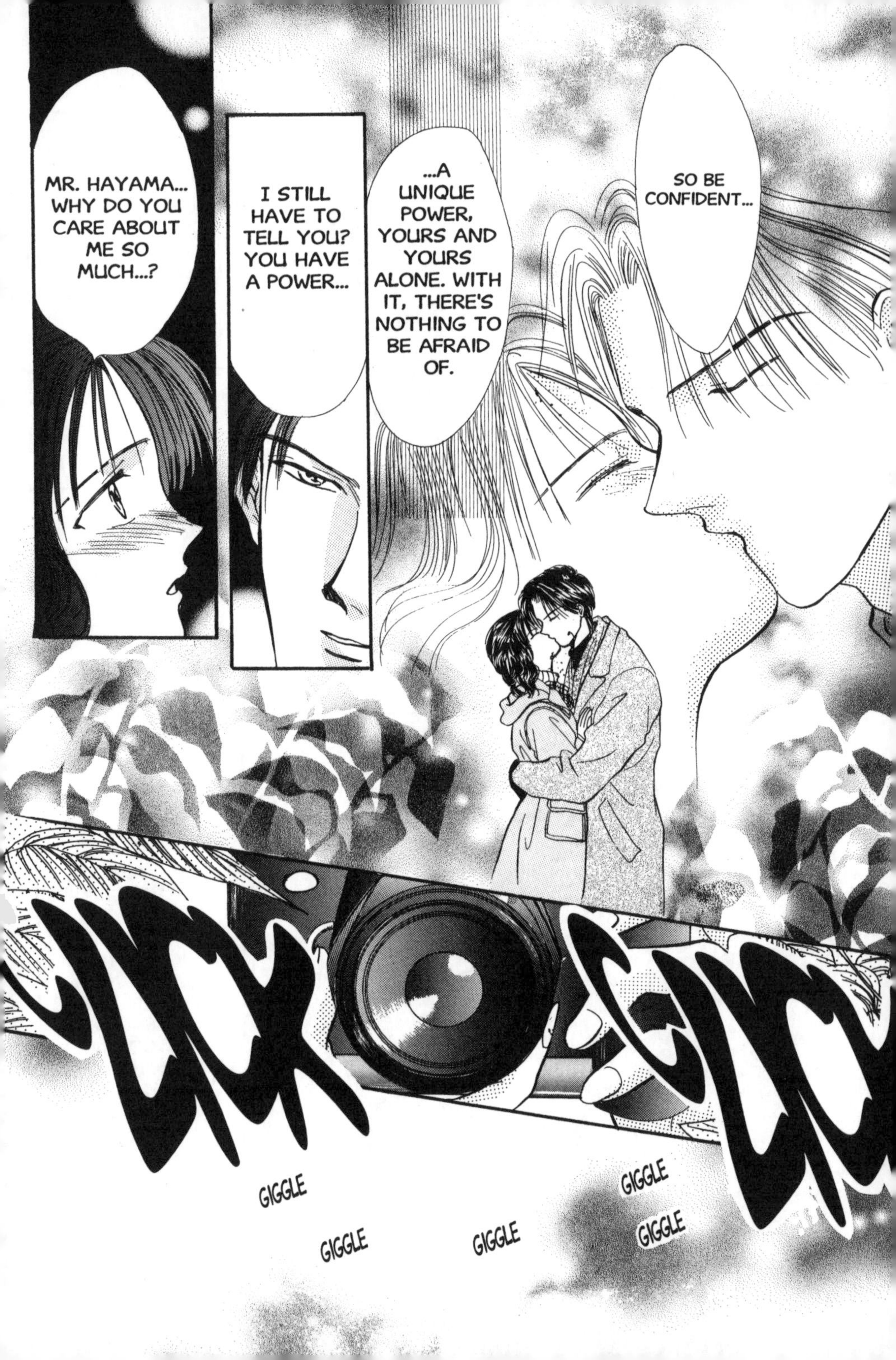
MR. HAYAMA... WHY DO YOU CARE ABOUT ME SO MUCH...?
I STILL HAVE TO TELL YOU? YOU HAVE A POWER...
...A UNIQUE POWER, YOURS AND YOURS ALONE. WITH IT, THERE'S NOTHING TO BE AFRAID OF.
SO BE CONFIDENT...
CLICK
CLICK
GIGGLE
GIGGLE
GIGGLE
GIGGLE
GIGGLE

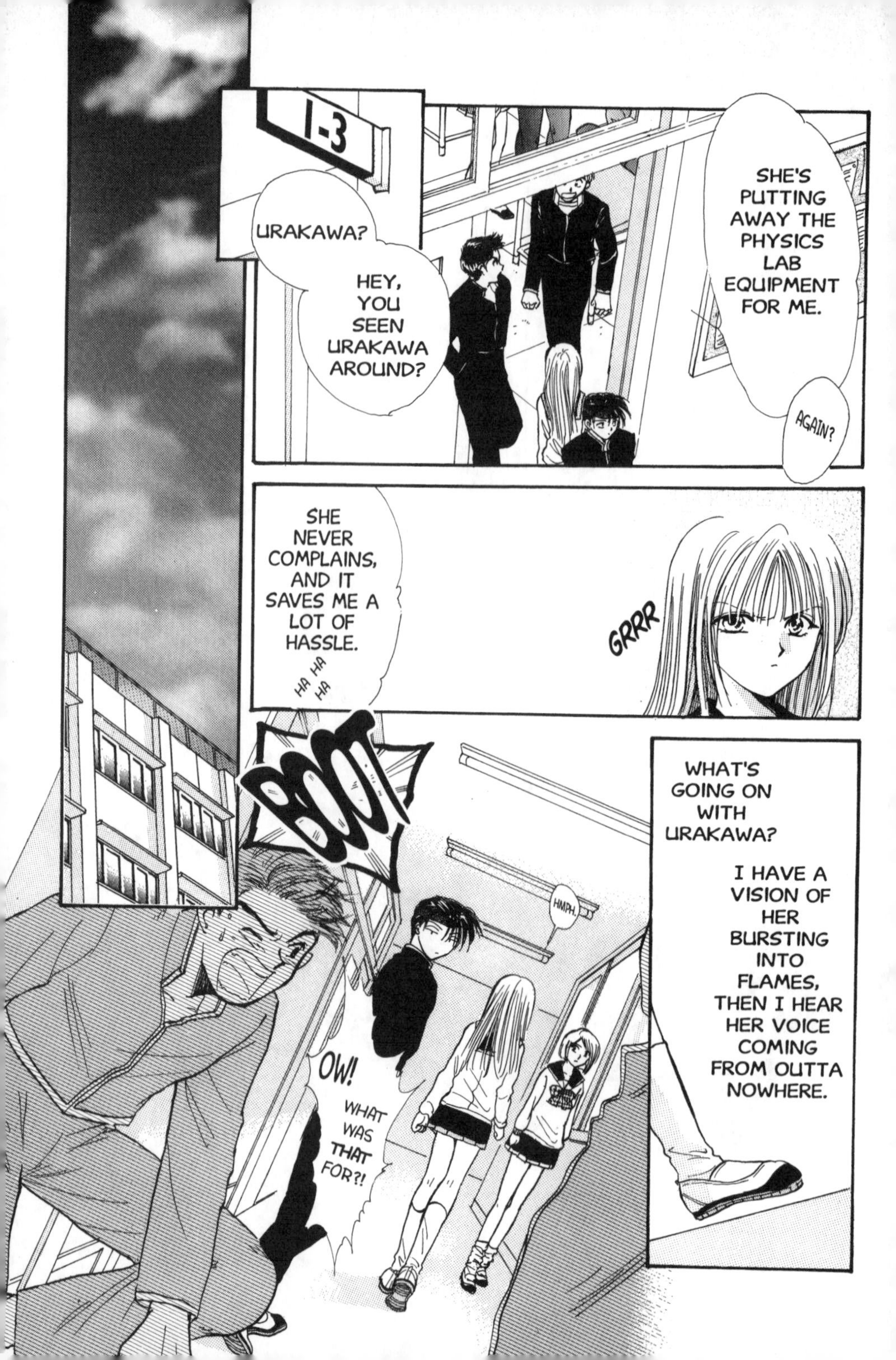
1-3
URAKAWA?
HEY, YOU SEEN URAKAWA AROUND?
SHE'S PUTTING AWAY THE PHYSICS LAB EQUIPMENT FOR ME.
AGAIN?
SHE NEVER COMPLAINS, AND IT SAVES ME A LOT OF HASSLE.
HA HA HA
GRRR
BOOT
OW!
WHAT WAS THAT FOR?!
HMPH.
WHAT'S GOING ON WITH URAKAWA?
I HAVE A VISION OF HER BURSTING INTO FLAMES, THEN I HEAR HER VOICE COMING FROM OUTTA NOWHERE.

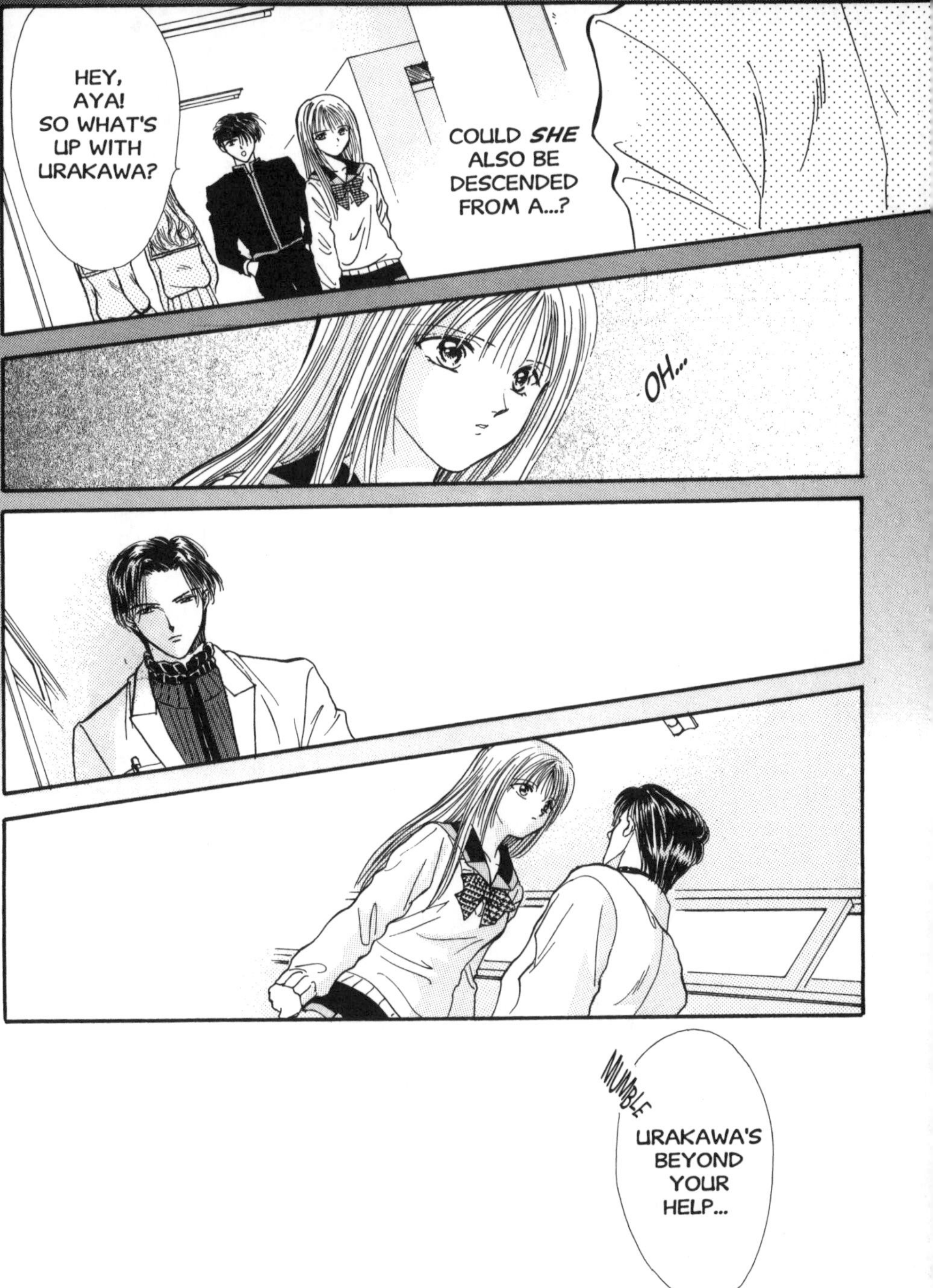
HEY, AYA! SO WHAT'S UP WITH URAKAWA?
COULD SHE ALSO BE DESCENDED FROM A...?
OH...
MUMBLE
URAKAWA'S BEYOND YOUR HELP...

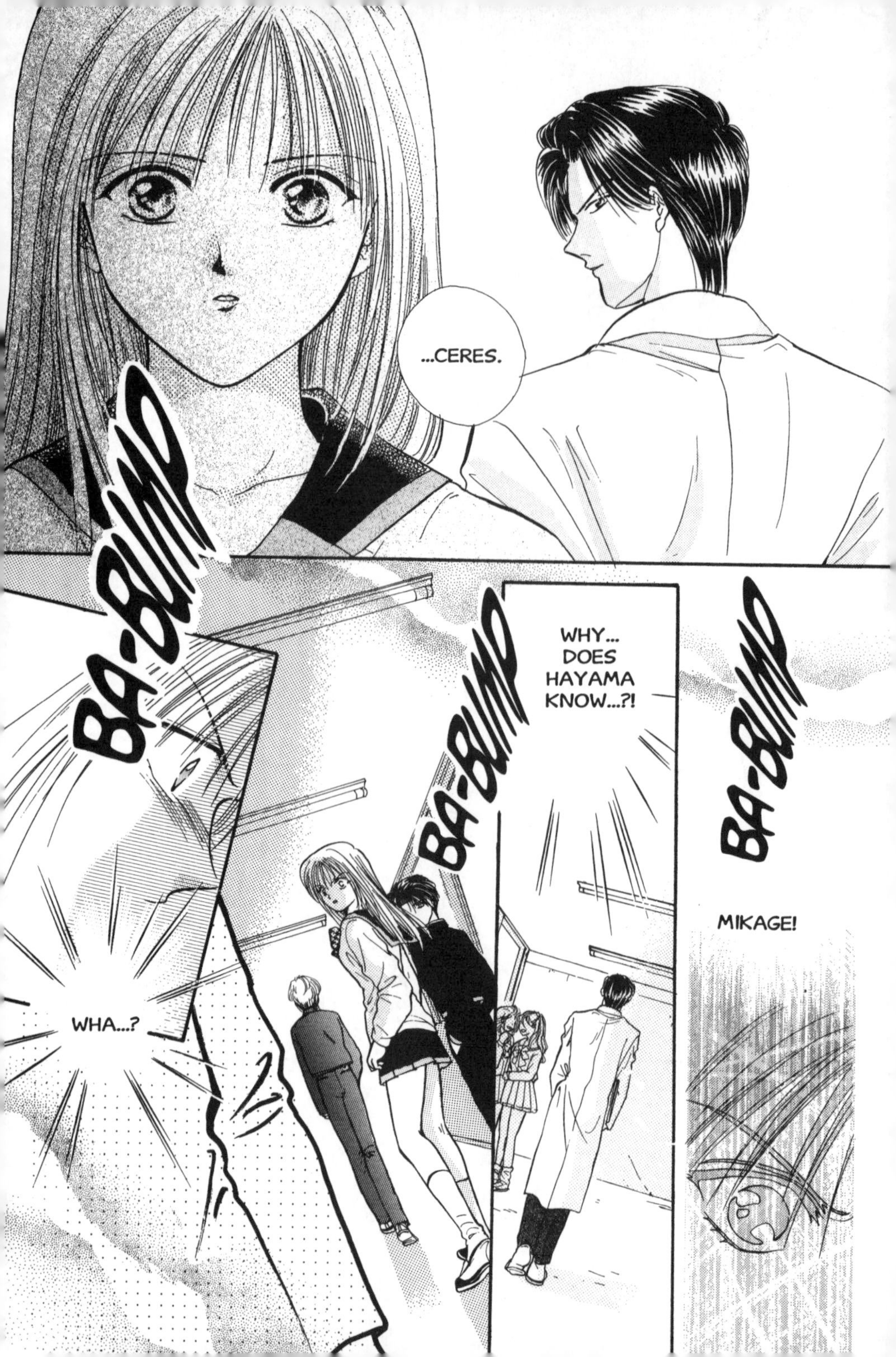

...CERES.
BA-BUMP
WHA...?
BA-BUMP
WHY... DOES HAYAMA KNOW...?!
BA-BUMP
MIKAGE!

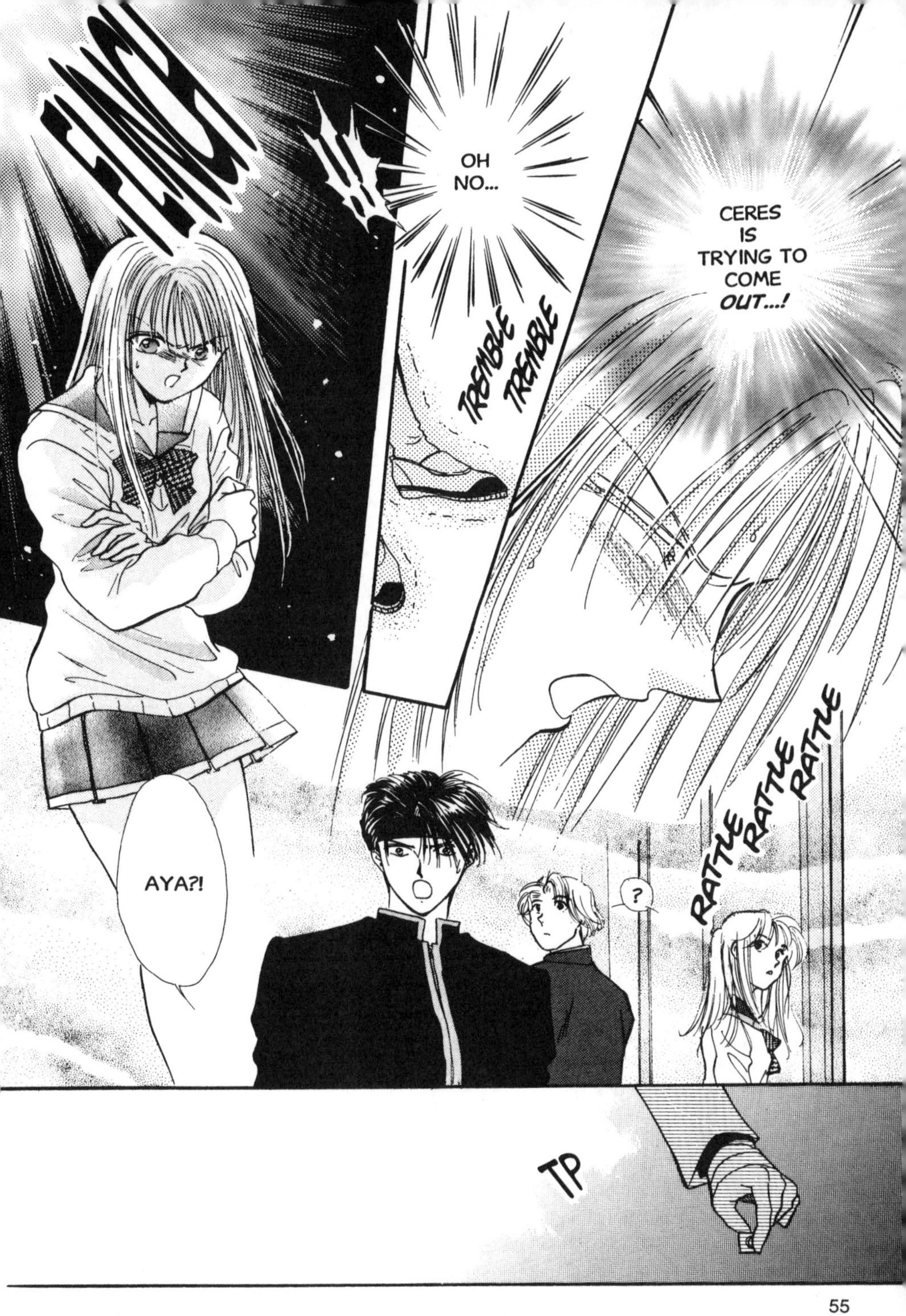
FING!!
OH NO...
TREMBLE TREMBLE
CERES IS TRYING TO COME OUT...!
AYA?!
?
RATTLE RATTLE RATTLE
TP

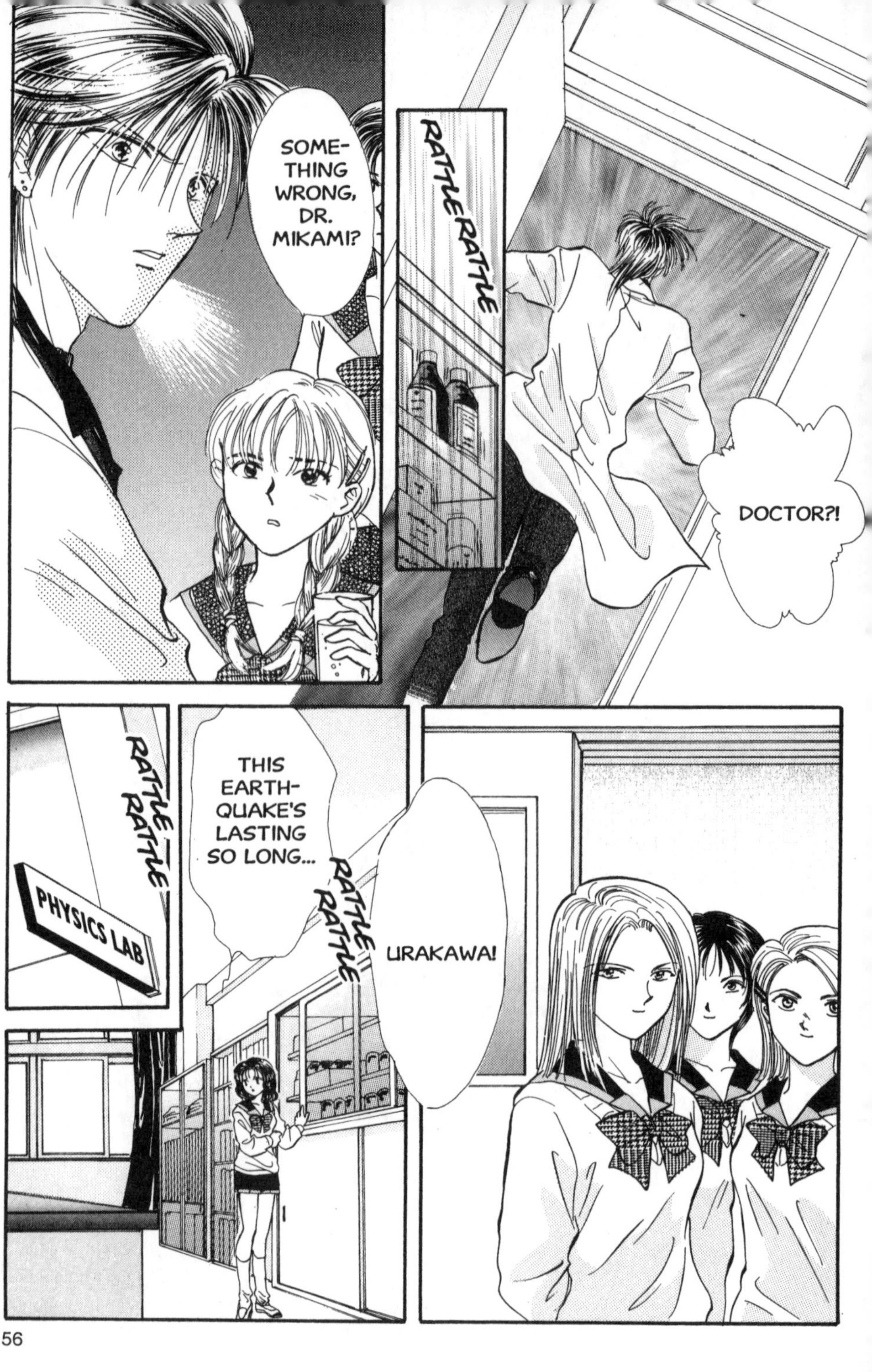
SOMETHING WRONG, DR. MIKAMI?
RATTLE RATTLE
DOCTOR?!
RATTLE RATTLE
PHYSICS LAB
THIS EARTHQUAKE'S LASTING SO LONG...
RATTLE RATTLE
URAKAWA!

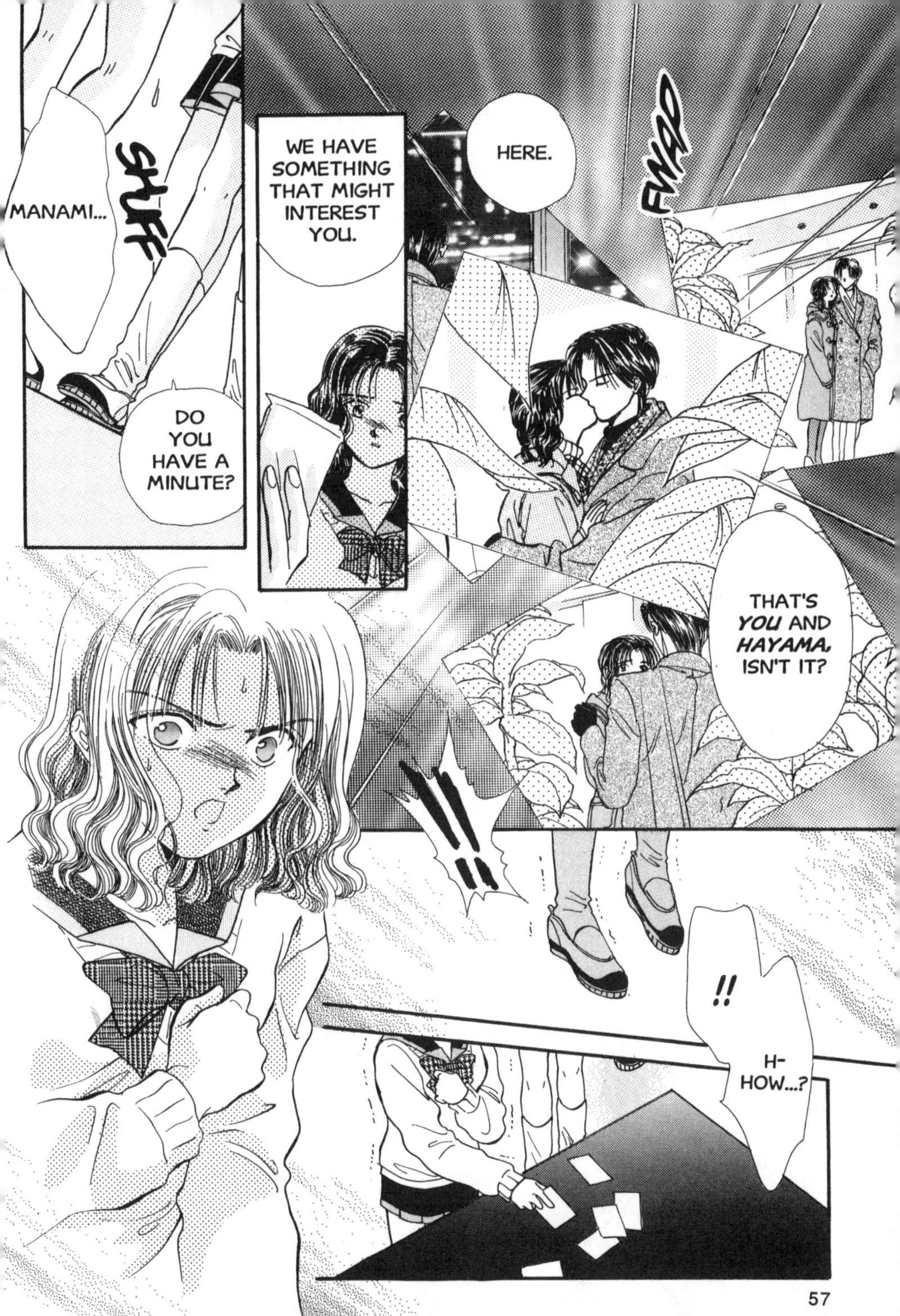

SHUFF
MANAMI...
DO YOU HAVE A MINUTE?
WE HAVE SOMETHING THAT MIGHT INTEREST YOU.
HERE.
FWAP
THAT'S *YOU* AND *HAYAMA,* ISN'T IT?
!!
H- HOW...?

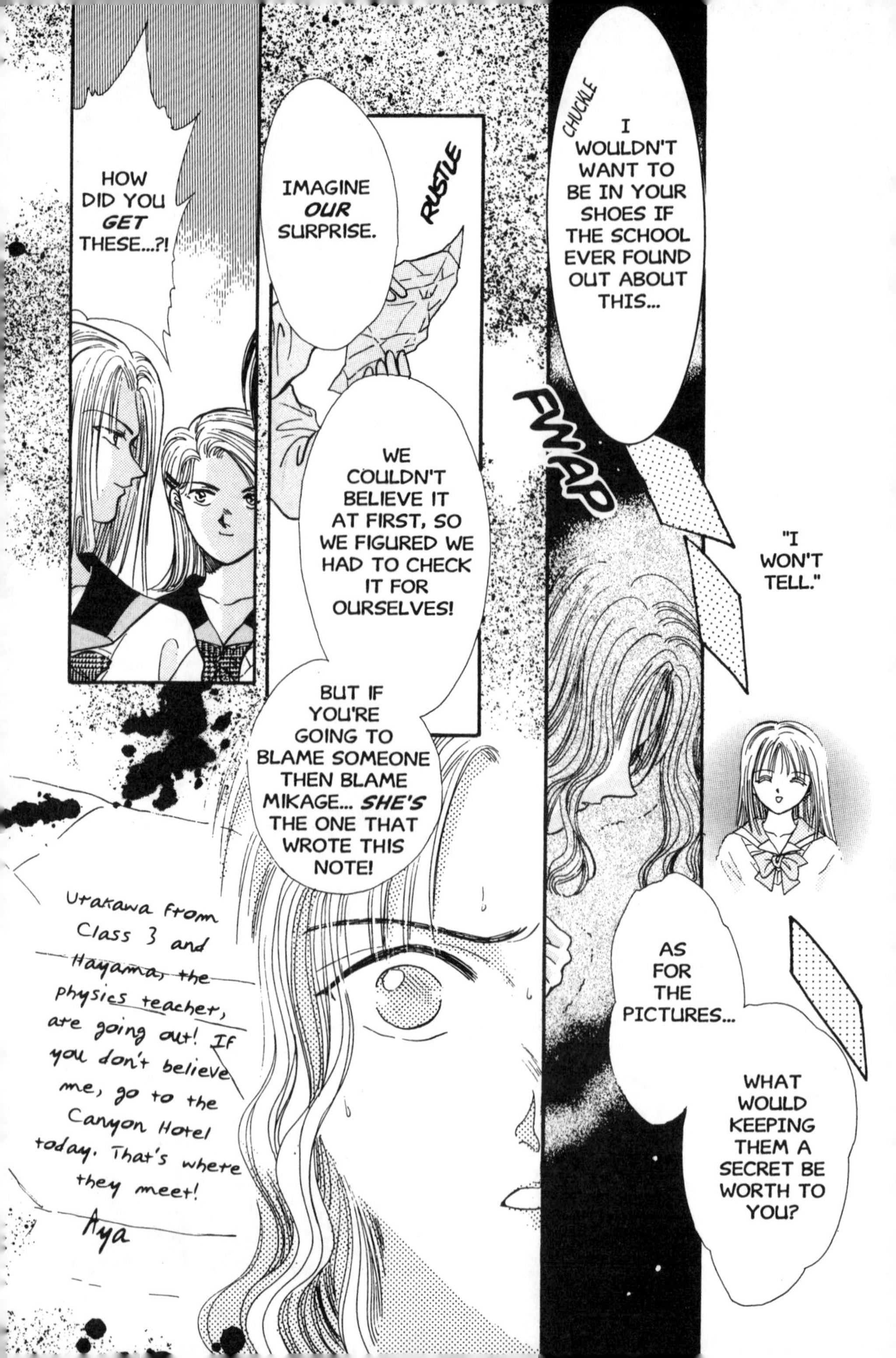
HOW DID YOU *GET* THESE...?!
IMAGINE *OUR* SURPRISE.
RUSTLE
WE COULDN'T BELIEVE IT AT FIRST, SO WE FIGURED WE HAD TO CHECK IT FOR OURSELVES!
BUT IF YOU'RE GOING TO BLAME SOMEONE THEN BLAME MIKAGE... *SHE'S* THE ONE THAT WROTE THIS NOTE!
Utakawa from Class 3 and Hayama, the physics teacher, are going out! If you don't believe me, go to the Canyon Hotel today. That's where they meet!
Aya
CHUCKLE
I WOULDN'T WANT TO BE IN YOUR SHOES IF THE SCHOOL EVER FOUND OUT ABOUT THIS...
FWAP
"I WON'T TELL."
AS FOR THE PICTURES...
WHAT WOULD KEEPING THEM A SECRET BE WORTH TO YOU?

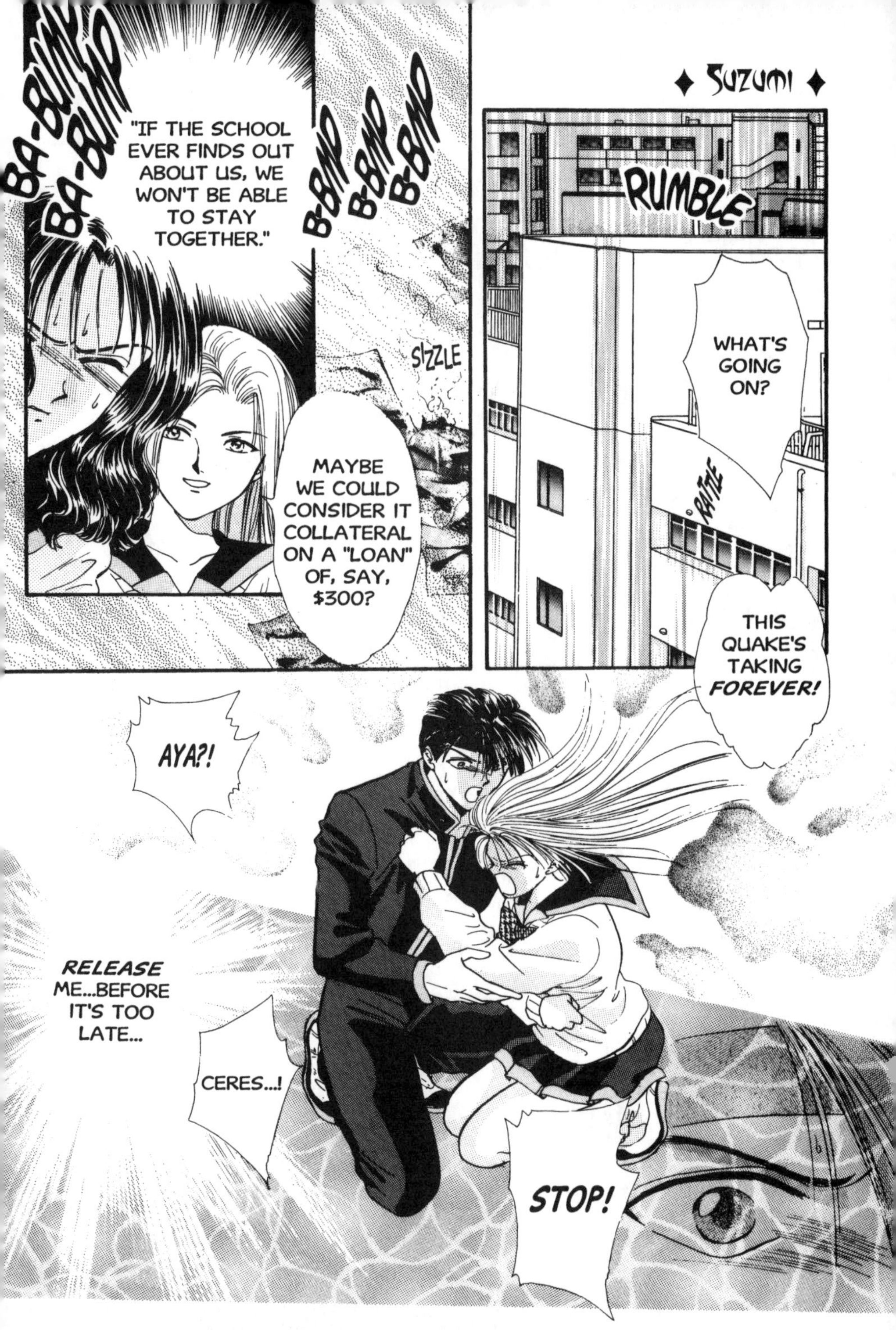
BA-BUMP BA-BUMP
"IF THE SCHOOL EVER FINDS OUT ABOUT US, WE WON'T BE ABLE TO STAY TOGETHER."
B-BMP B-BMP B-BMP
SIZZLE
MAYBE WE COULD CONSIDER IT COLLATERAL ON A "LOAN" OF, SAY, $300?
RUMBLE
WHAT'S GOING ON?
RATTLE
THIS QUAKE'S TAKING *FOREVER!*
AYA?!
RELEASE ME...BEFORE IT'S TOO LATE...
CERES...!
STOP!

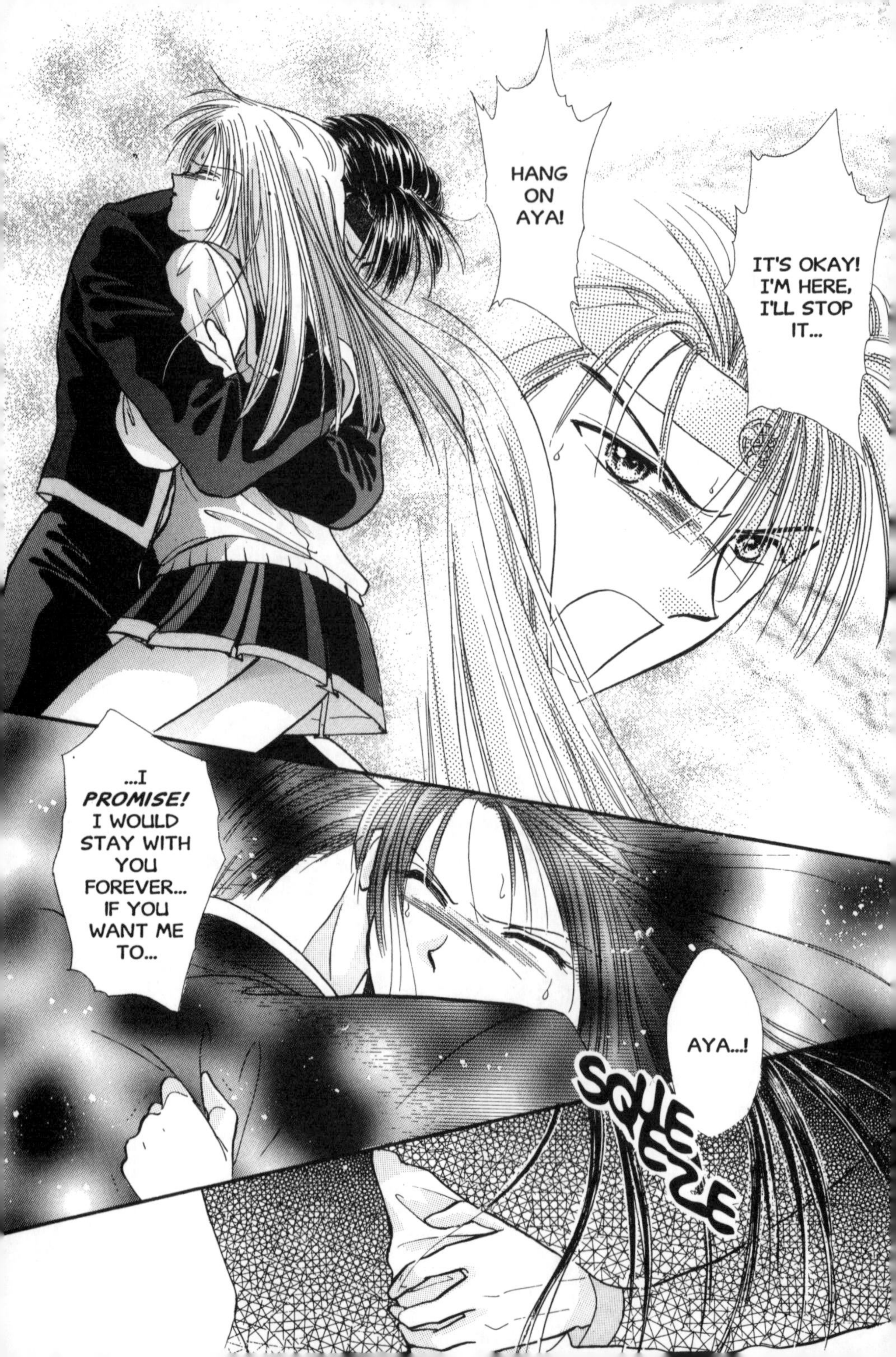
HANG ON AYA!
IT'S OKAY! I'M HERE, I'LL STOP IT...
...I *PROMISE!* I WOULD STAY WITH YOU FOREVER... IF YOU WANT ME TO...
AYA...!
SQUEEZE

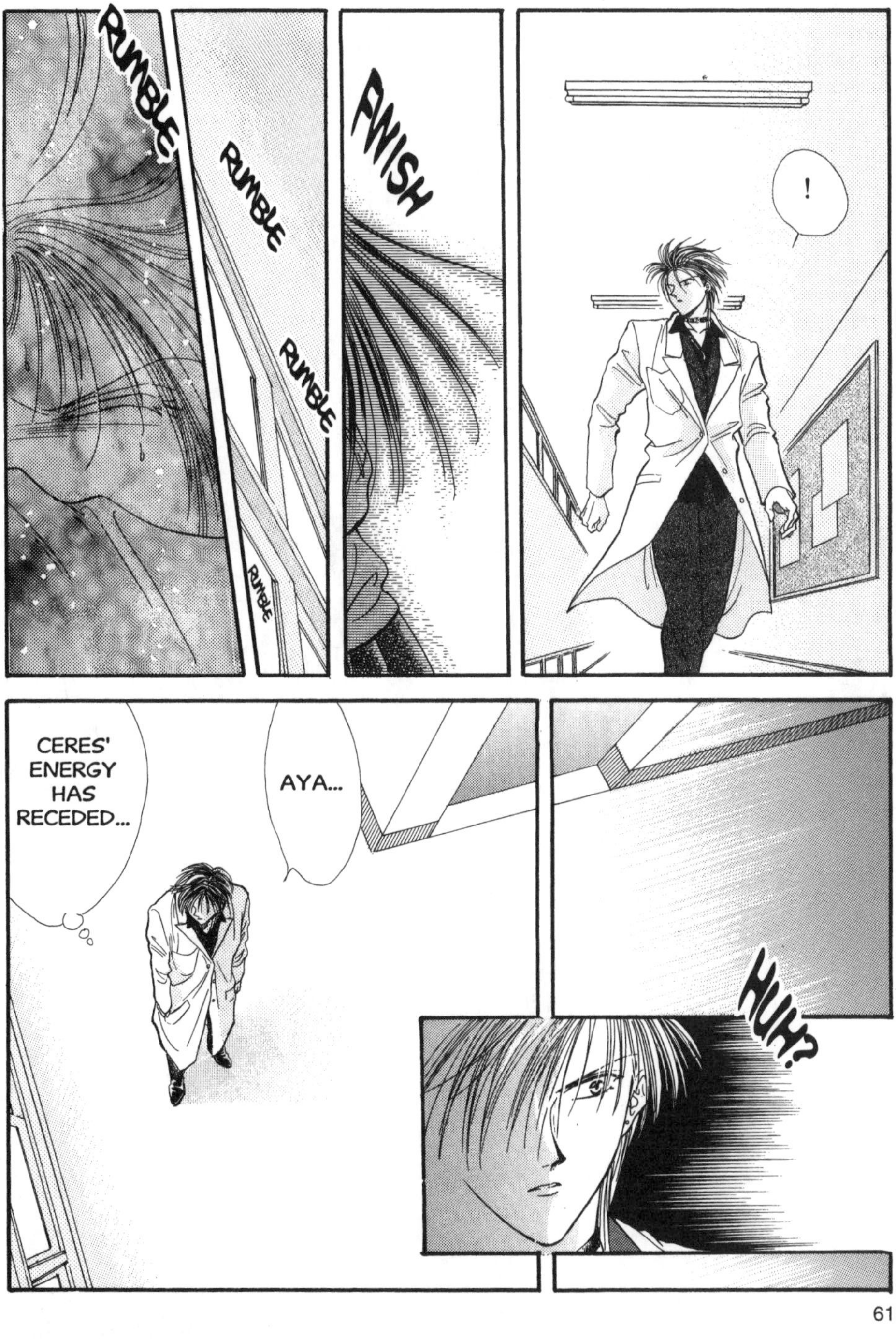
RUMBLE
RUMBLE
RUMBLE
RUMBLE
FWISH
!
CERES' ENERGY HAS RECEDED...
AYA...
HUH?

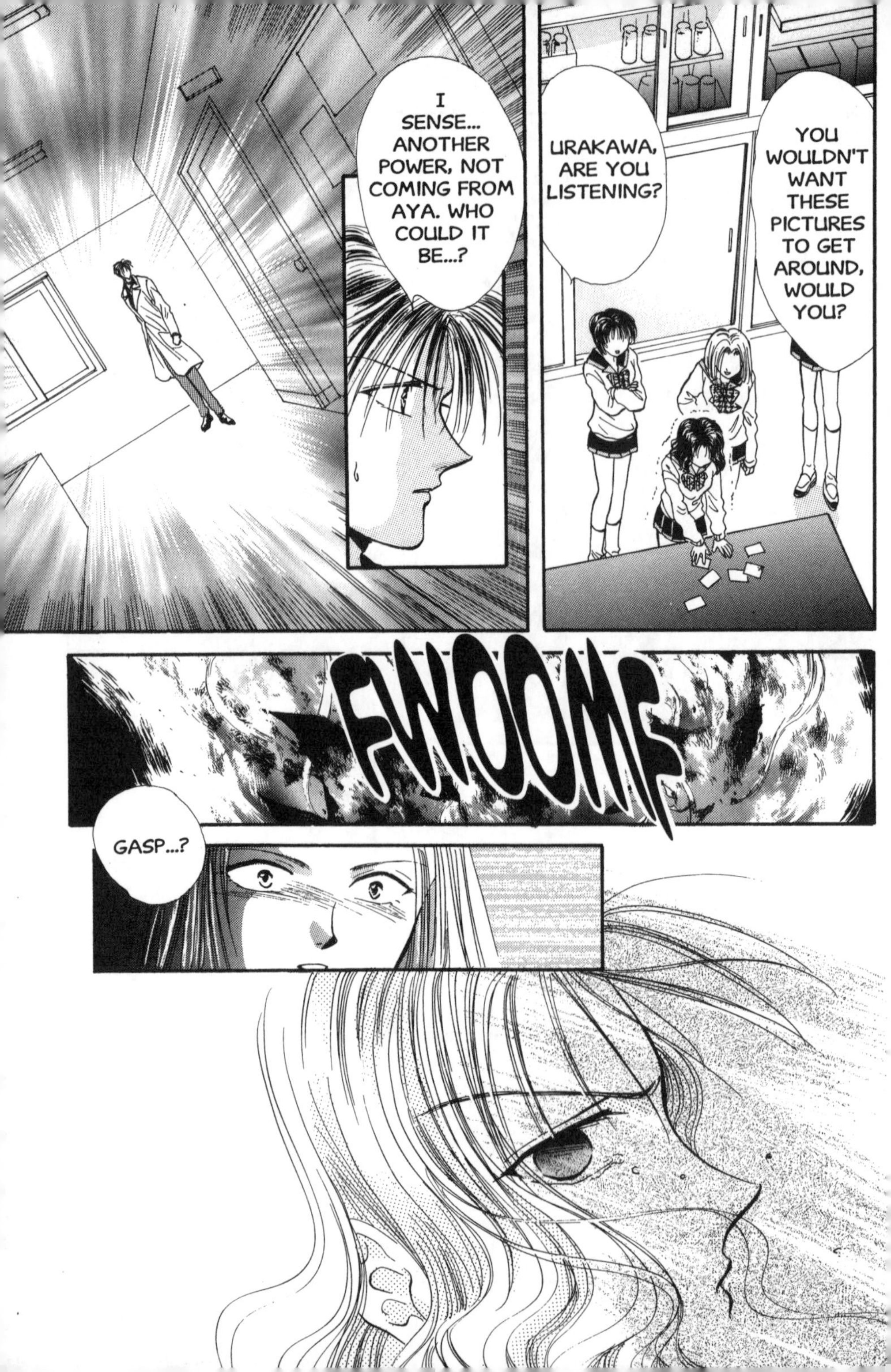
I SENSE... ANOTHER POWER, NOT COMING FROM AYA. WHO COULD IT BE...?
URAKAWA, ARE YOU LISTENING?
YOU WOULDN'T WANT THESE PICTURES TO GET AROUND, WOULD YOU?
FWOOMF
GASP...?

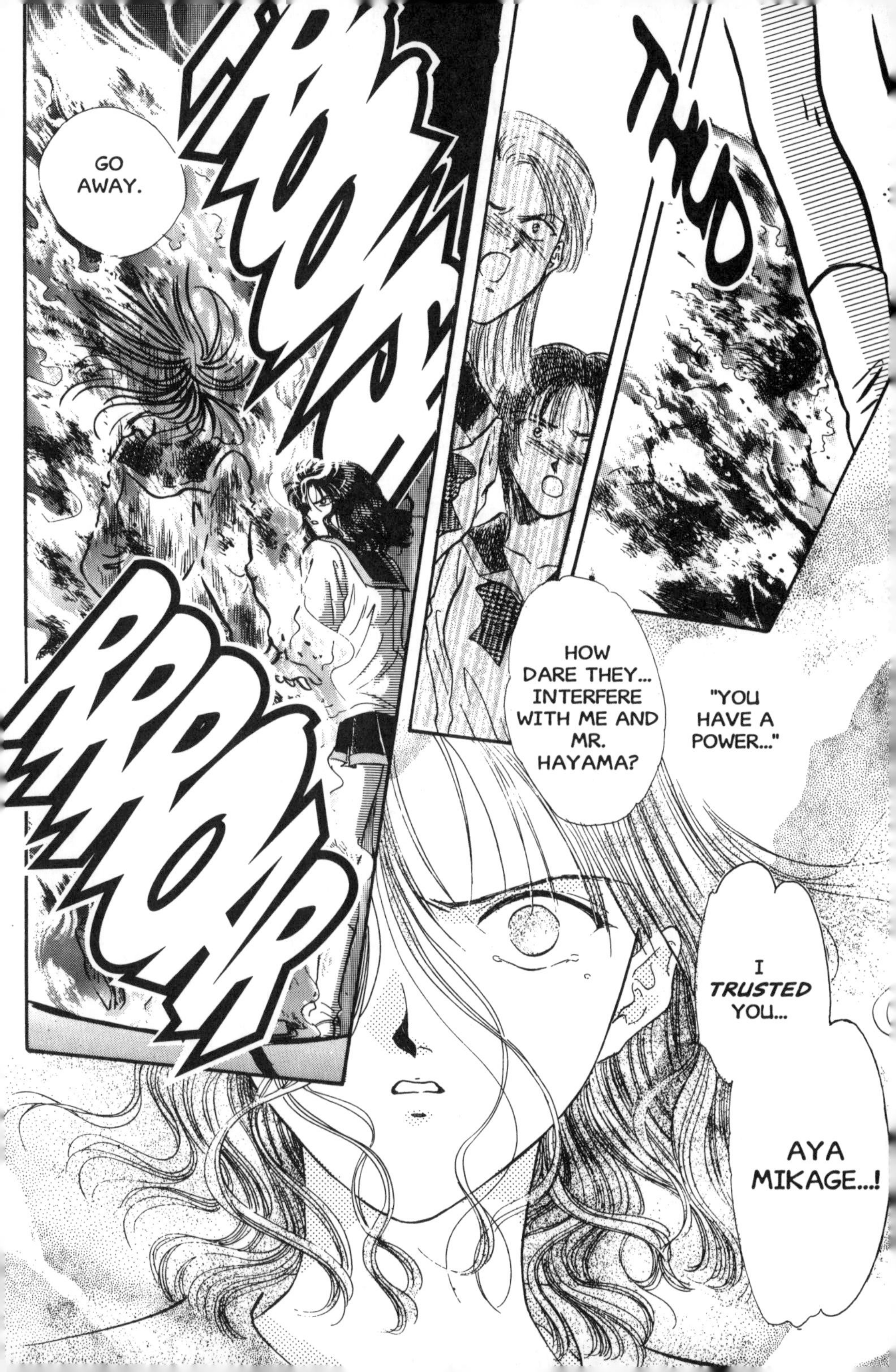
GO AWAY.
THUD
HOW DARE THEY... INTERFERE WITH ME AND MR. HAYAMA?
"YOU HAVE A POWER..."
I *TRUSTED* YOU...
AYA MIKAGE...!

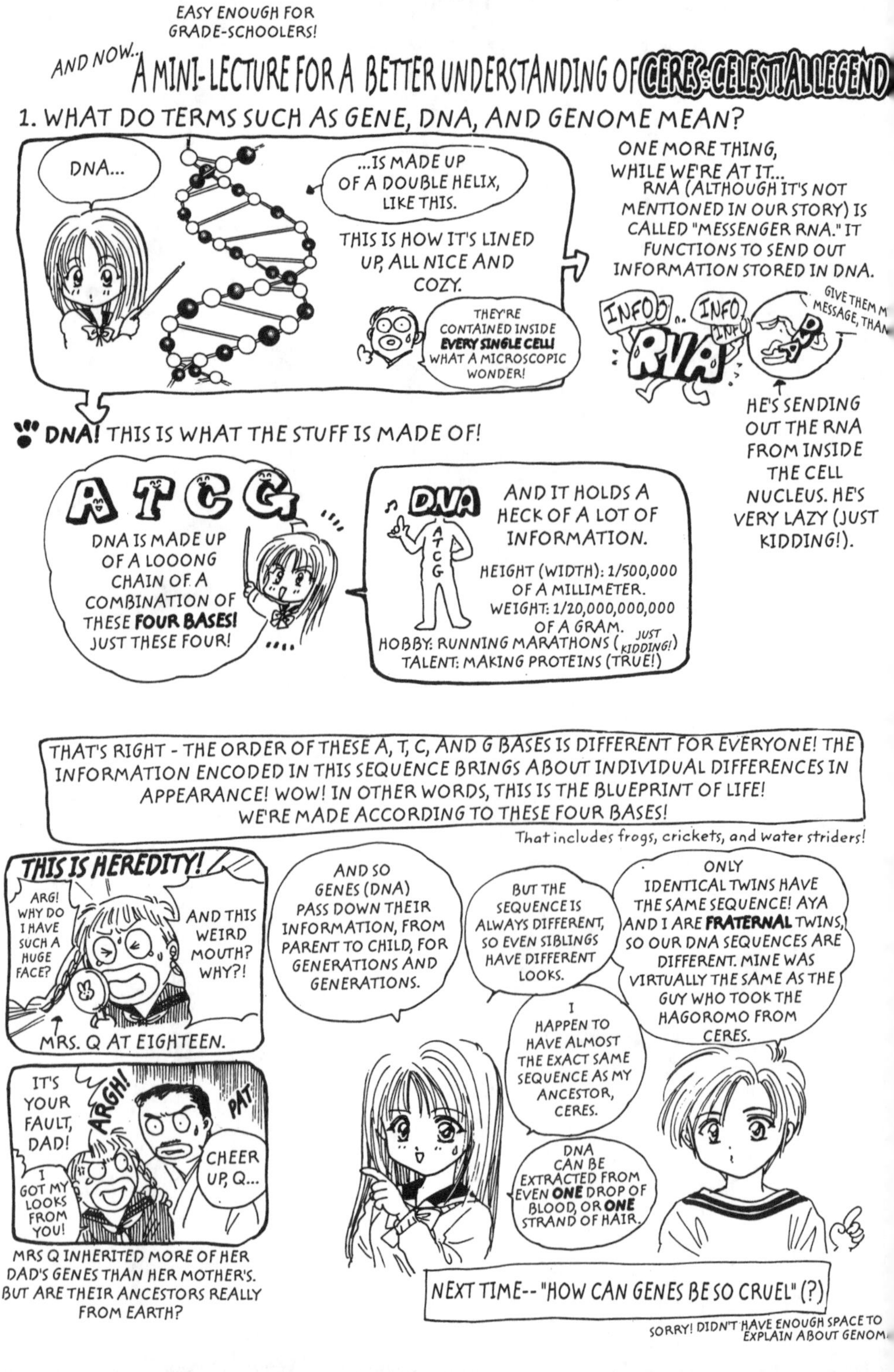

EASY ENOUGH FOR GRADE-SCHOOLERS!
AND NOW... A MINI-LECTURE FOR A BETTER UNDERSTANDING OF CERES: CELESTIAL LEGEND
1. WHAT DO TERMS SUCH AS GENE, DNA, AND GENOME MEAN?
DNA...
...IS MADE UP OF A DOUBLE HELIX, LIKE THIS.
THIS IS HOW IT'S LINED UP, ALL NICE AND COZY.
THEY'RE CONTAINED INSIDE EVERY SINGLE CELL! WHAT A MICROSCOPIC WONDER!
ONE MORE THING, WHILE WE'RE AT IT... RNA (ALTHOUGH IT'S NOT MENTIONED IN OUR STORY) IS CALLED "MESSENGER RNA." IT FUNCTIONS TO SEND OUT INFORMATION STORED IN DNA.
INFO
INFO
INFO
RNA
GIVE THEM M
MESSAGE, THAN
HE'S SENDING OUT THE RNA FROM INSIDE THE CELL NUCLEUS. HE'S VERY LAZY (JUST KIDDING!).
DNA! THIS IS WHAT THE STUFF IS MADE OF!
A T C G
DNA IS MADE UP OF A LOOONG CHAIN OF A COMBINATION OF THESE FOUR BASES! JUST THESE FOUR!
DNA
A T C G
AND IT HOLDS A HECK OF A LOT OF INFORMATION.
HEIGHT (WIDTH): 1/500,000 OF A MILLIMETER.
WEIGHT: 1/20,000,000,000 OF A GRAM.
HOBBY: RUNNING MARATHONS (JUST KIDDING!)
TALENT: MAKING PROTEINS (TRUE!)
THAT'S RIGHT - THE ORDER OF THESE A, T, C, AND G BASES IS DIFFERENT FOR EVERYONE! THE INFORMATION ENCODED IN THIS SEQUENCE BRINGS ABOUT INDIVIDUAL DIFFERENCES IN APPEARANCE! WOW! IN OTHER WORDS, THIS IS THE BLUEPRINT OF LIFE! WE'RE MADE ACCORDING TO THESE FOUR BASES!
That includes frogs, crickets, and water striders!
THIS IS HEREDITY!
ARG! WHY DO I HAVE SUCH A HUGE FACE?
AND THIS WEIRD MOUTH? WHY?!
MRS. Q AT EIGHTEEN.
IT'S YOUR FAULT, DAD!
ARGH!
I GOT MY LOOKS FROM YOU!
PAT
CHEER UP, Q...
MRS Q INHERITED MORE OF HER DAD'S GENES THAN HER MOTHER'S. BUT ARE THEIR ANCESTORS REALLY FROM EARTH?
AND SO GENES (DNA) PASS DOWN THEIR INFORMATION, FROM PARENT TO CHILD, FOR GENERATIONS AND GENERATIONS.
BUT THE SEQUENCE IS ALWAYS DIFFERENT, SO EVEN SIBLINGS HAVE DIFFERENT LOOKS.
ONLY IDENTICAL TWINS HAVE THE SAME SEQUENCE! AYA AND I ARE FRATERNAL TWINS, SO OUR DNA SEQUENCES ARE DIFFERENT. MINE WAS VIRTUALLY THE SAME AS THE GUY WHO TOOK THE HAGOROMO FROM CERES.
I HAPPEN TO HAVE ALMOST THE EXACT SAME SEQUENCE AS MY ANCESTOR, CERES.
DNA CAN BE EXTRACTED FROM EVEN ONE DROP OF BLOOD, OR ONE STRAND OF HAIR.
NEXT TIME-- "HOW CAN GENES BE SO CRUEL" (?)
SORRY! DIDN'T HAVE ENOUGH SPACE TO EXPLAIN ABOUT GENOM

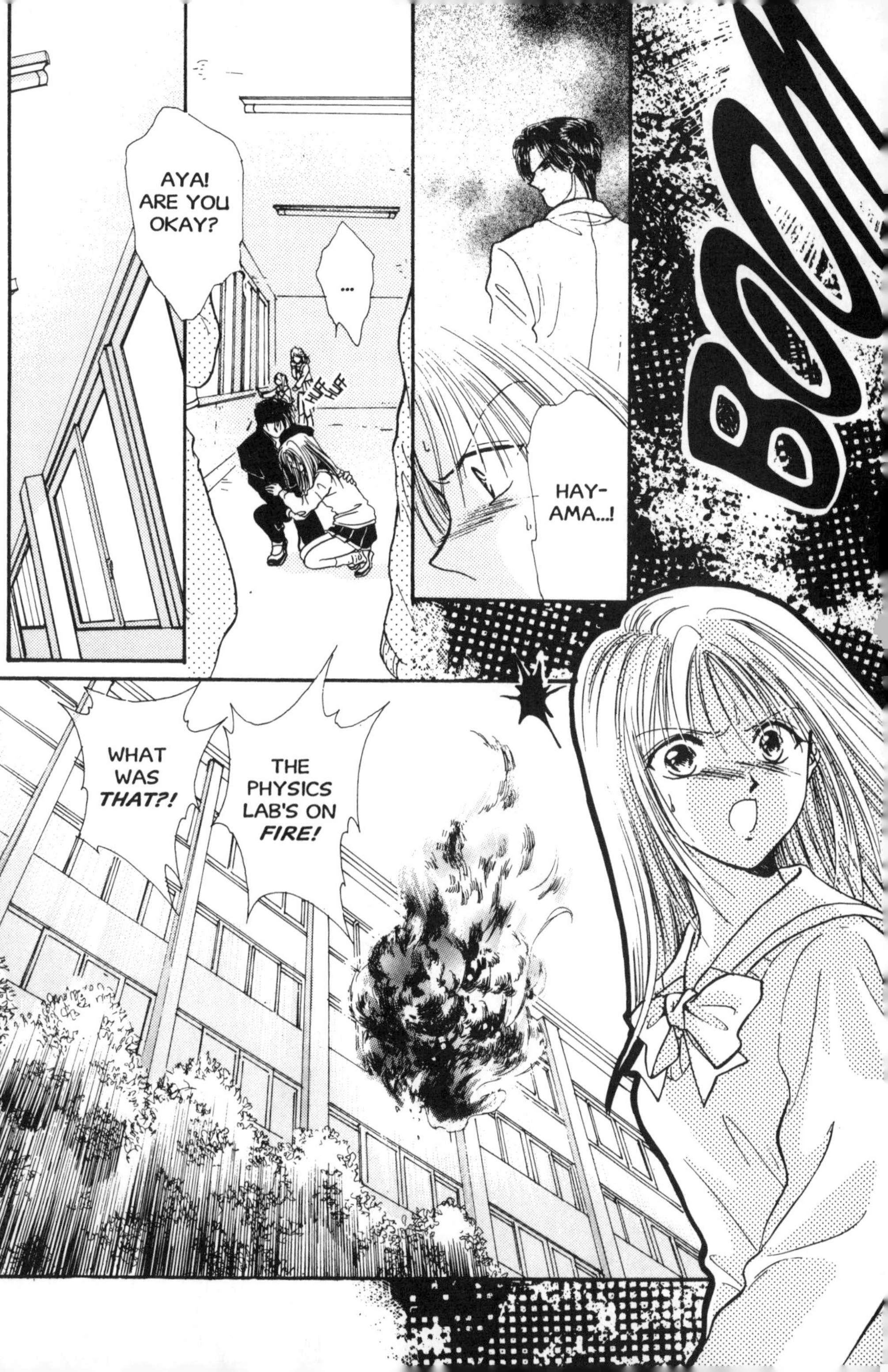
AYA! ARE YOU OKAY?
...
HUFF HUFF
HAY-AMA...!
BOOM
WHAT WAS *THAT?!*
THE PHYSICS LAB'S ON *FIRE!*

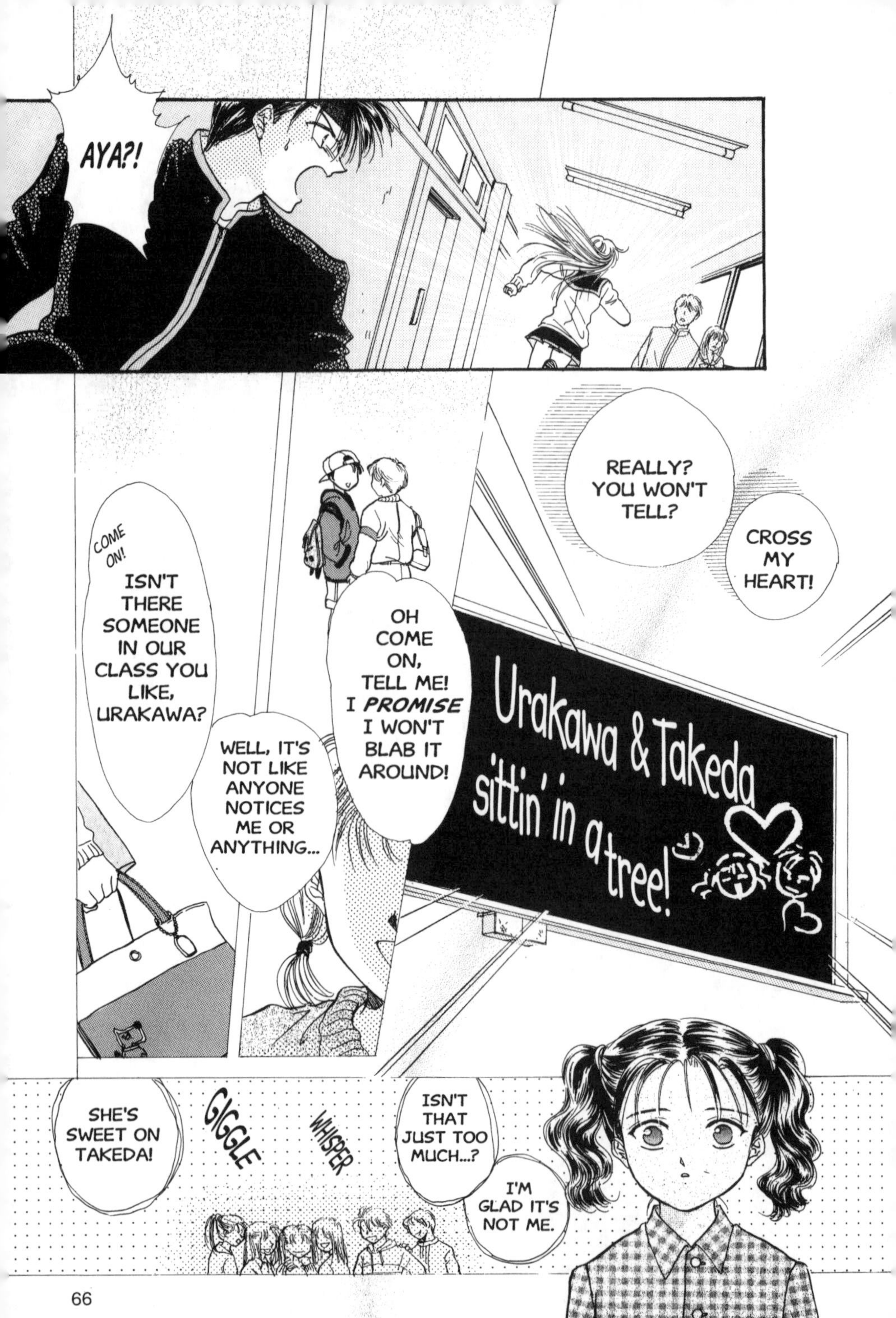
AYA?!
COME ON! ISN'T THERE SOMEONE IN OUR CLASS YOU LIKE, URAKAWA?
WELL, IT'S NOT LIKE ANYONE NOTICES ME OR ANYTHING...
OH COME ON, TELL ME! I *PROMISE* I WON'T BLAB IT AROUND!
REALLY? YOU WON'T TELL?
CROSS MY HEART!
Urakawa & Takeda sittin' in a tree!
SHE'S SWEET ON TAKEDA!
GIGGLE
WHISPER
ISN'T THAT JUST TOO MUCH...?
I'M GLAD IT'S NOT ME.

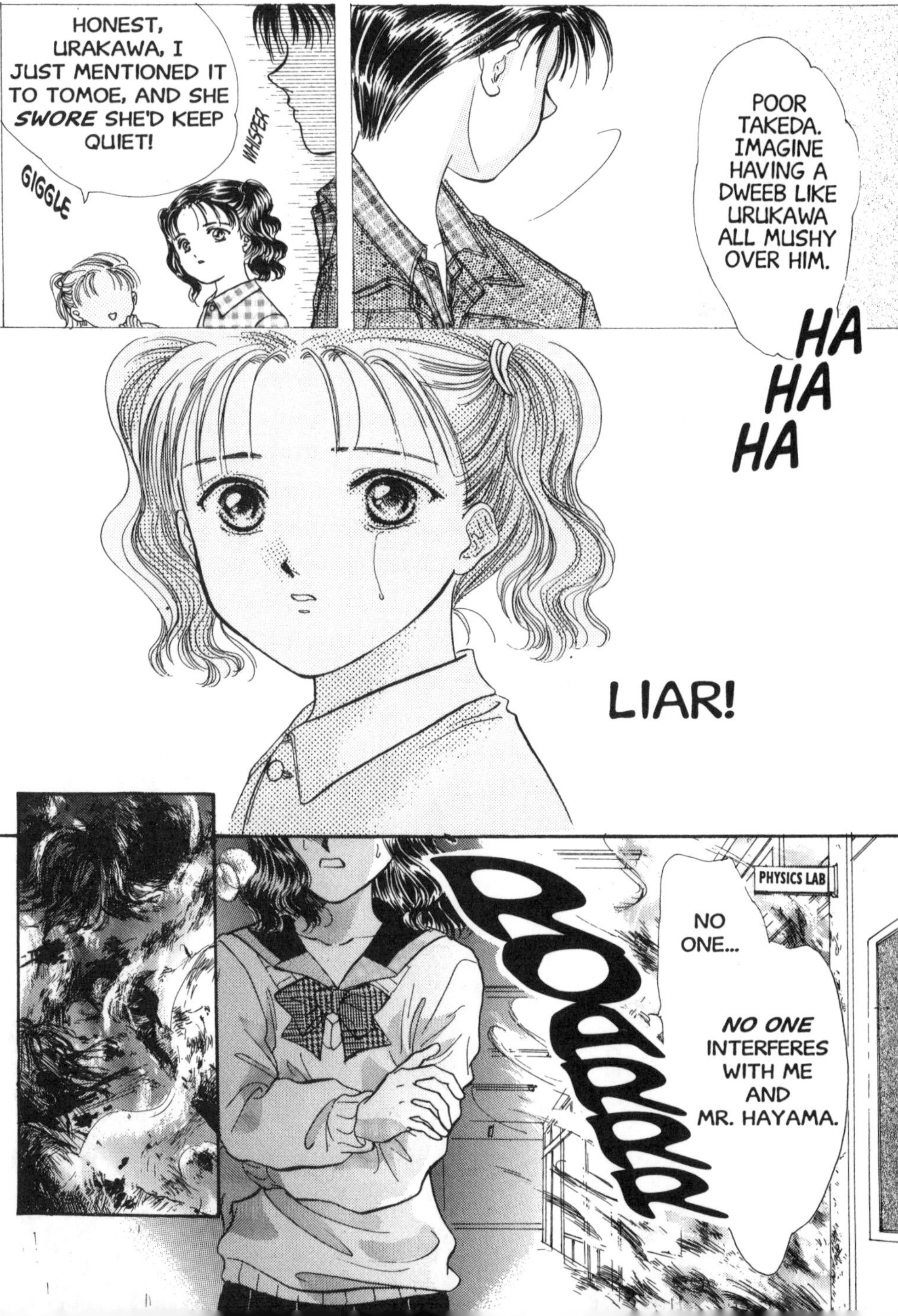
HONEST, URAKAWA, I JUST MENTIONED IT TO TOMOE, AND SHE *SWORE* SHE'D KEEP QUIET!
GIGGLE
WHISPER
POOR TAKEDA. IMAGINE HAVING A DWEEB LIKE URUKAWA ALL MUSHY OVER HIM.
HA HA HA
LIAR!
PHYSICS LAB
NO ONE...
NO ONE INTERFERES WITH ME AND MR. HAYAMA.

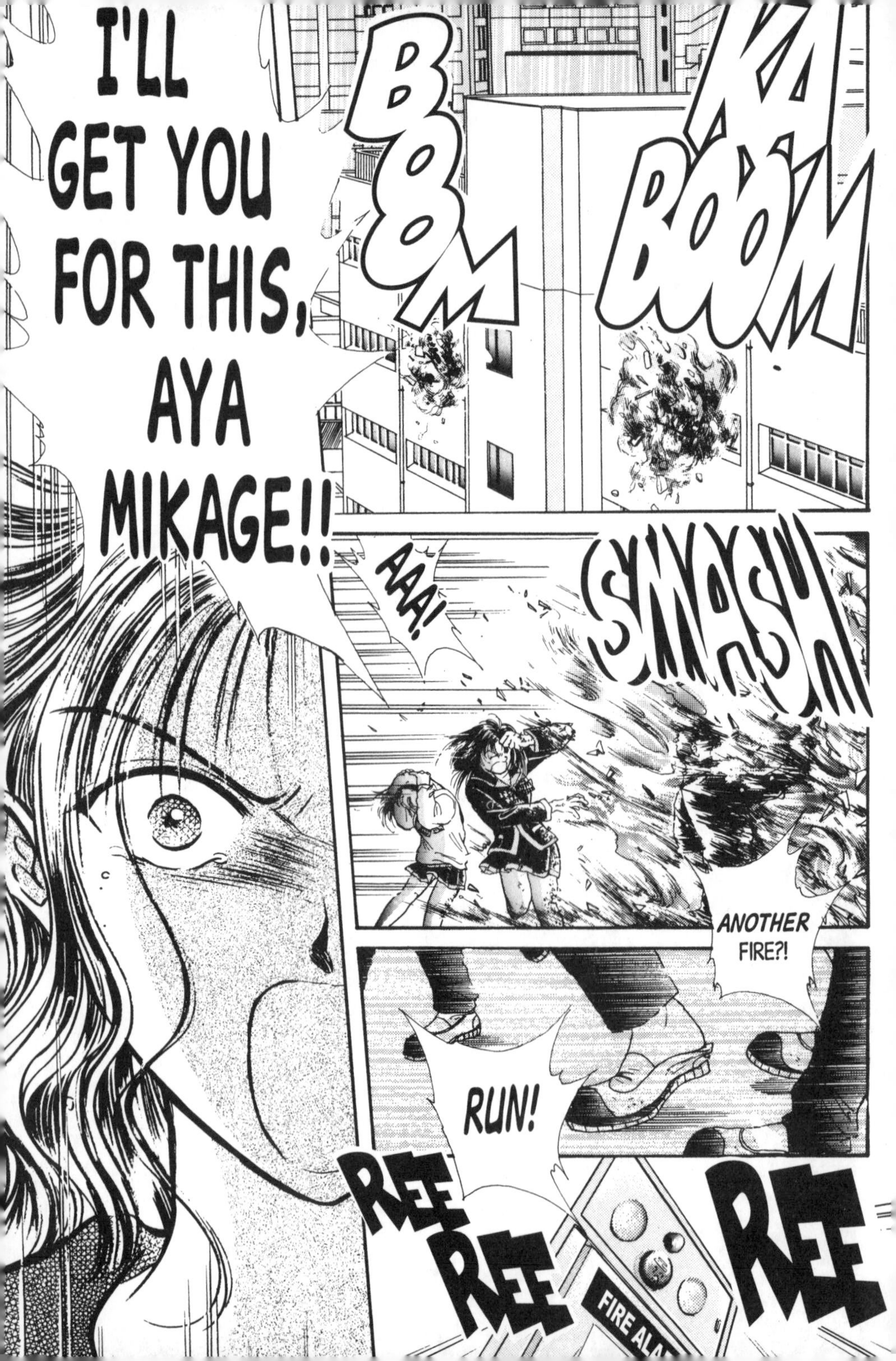
I'LL GET YOU FOR THIS, AYA MIKAGE!!
BOOM
KA BOOM
AAA!
SWASH
ANOTHER FIRE?!
RUN!
REE
REE
REE

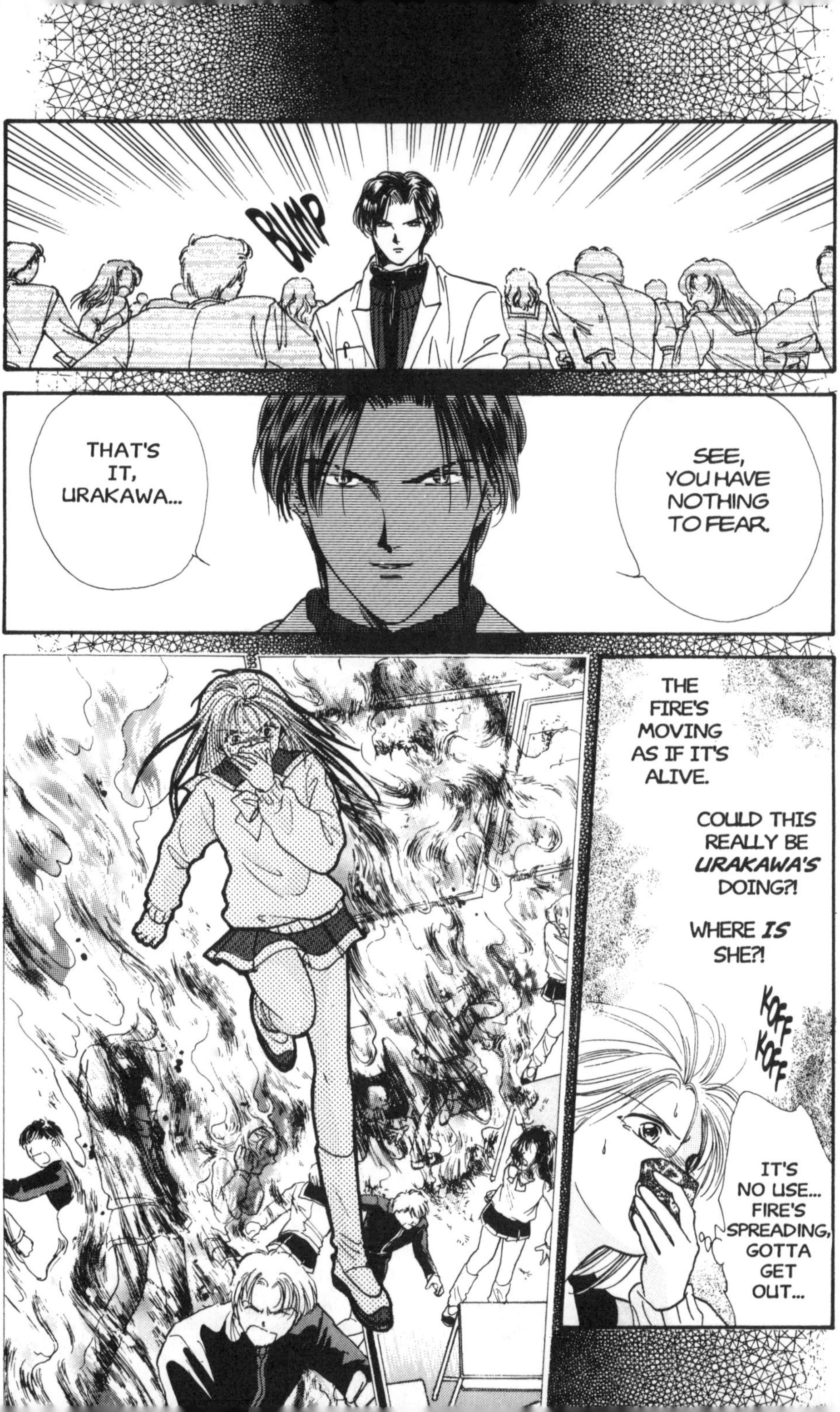
BUMP
THAT'S IT, URAKAWA...
SEE, YOU HAVE NOTHING TO FEAR.
THE FIRE'S MOVING AS IF IT'S ALIVE.
COULD THIS REALLY BE *URAKAWA'S* DOING?!
WHERE *IS* SHE?!
KOFF KOFF
IT'S NO USE... FIRE'S SPREADING, GOTTA GET OUT...

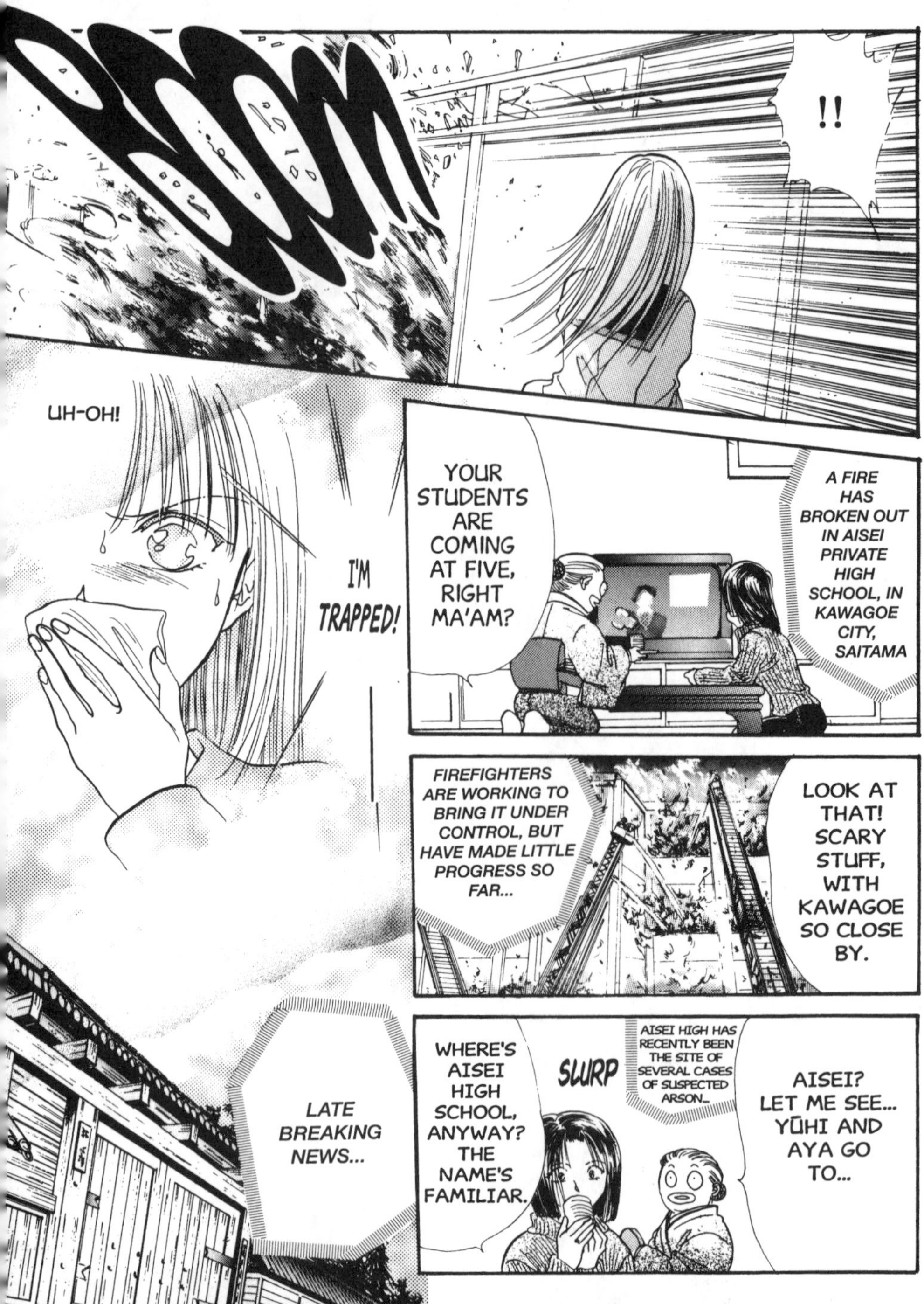
!!
UH-OH!
I'M TRAPPED!
LATE BREAKING NEWS...
YOUR STUDENTS ARE COMING AT FIVE, RIGHT MA'AM?
A FIRE HAS BROKEN OUT IN AISEI PRIVATE HIGH SCHOOL, IN KAWAGOE CITY, SAITAMA
FIREFIGHTERS ARE WORKING TO BRING IT UNDER CONTROL, BUT HAVE MADE LITTLE PROGRESS SO FAR...
LOOK AT THAT! SCARY STUFF, WITH KAWAGOE SO CLOSE BY.
WHERE'S AISEI HIGH SCHOOL, ANYWAY? THE NAME'S FAMILIAR.
SLURP
AISEI HIGH HAS RECENTLY BEEN THE SITE OF SEVERAL CASES OF SUSPECTED ARSON...
AISEI? LET ME SEE... YŪHI AND AYA GO TO...

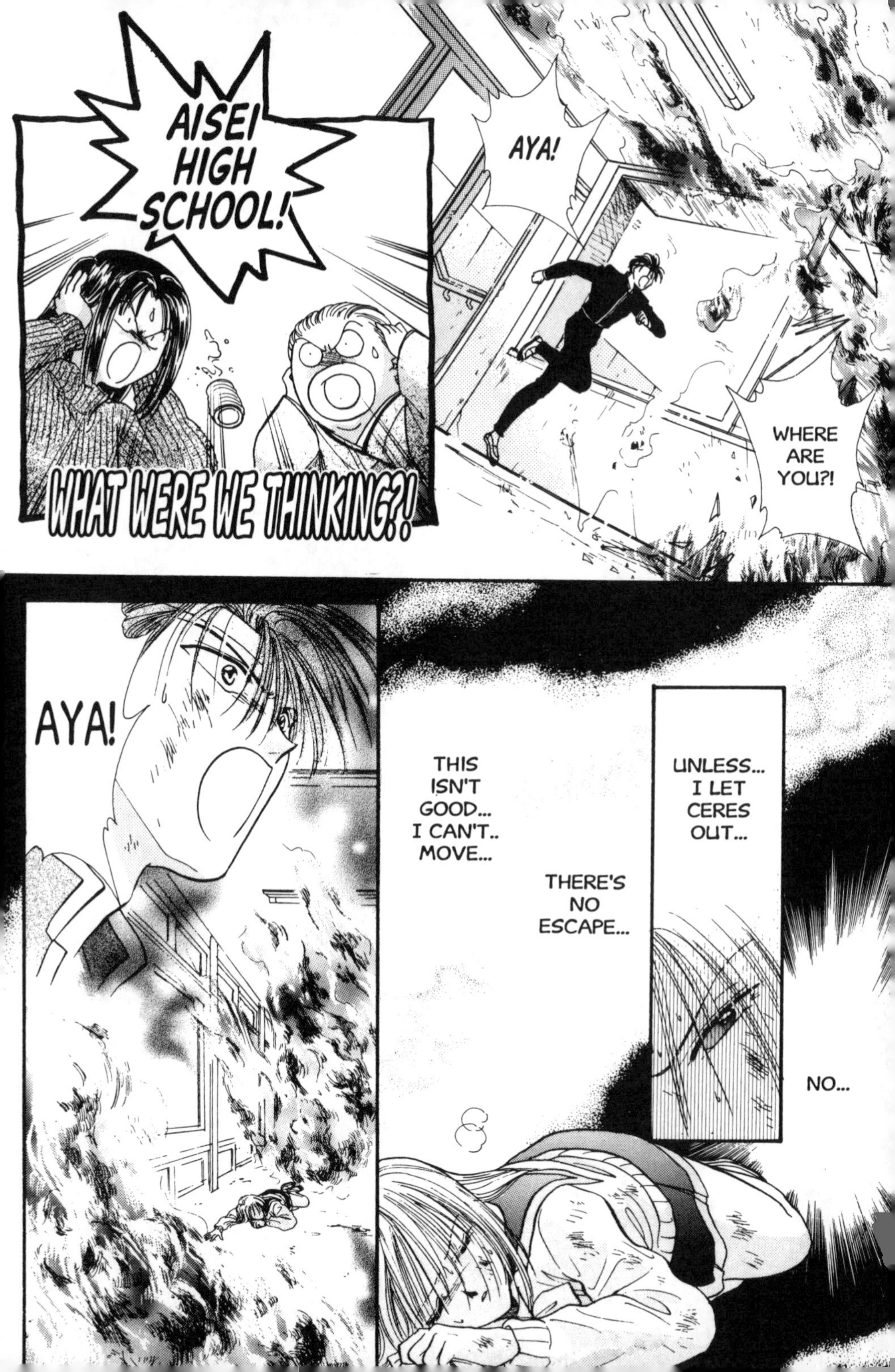
AISEI HIGH SCHOOL!
WHAT WERE WE THINKING?!
AYA!
WHERE ARE YOU?!
AYA!
THIS ISN'T GOOD... I CAN'T.. MOVE...
THERE'S NO ESCAPE...
UNLESS... I LET CERES OUT...
NO...

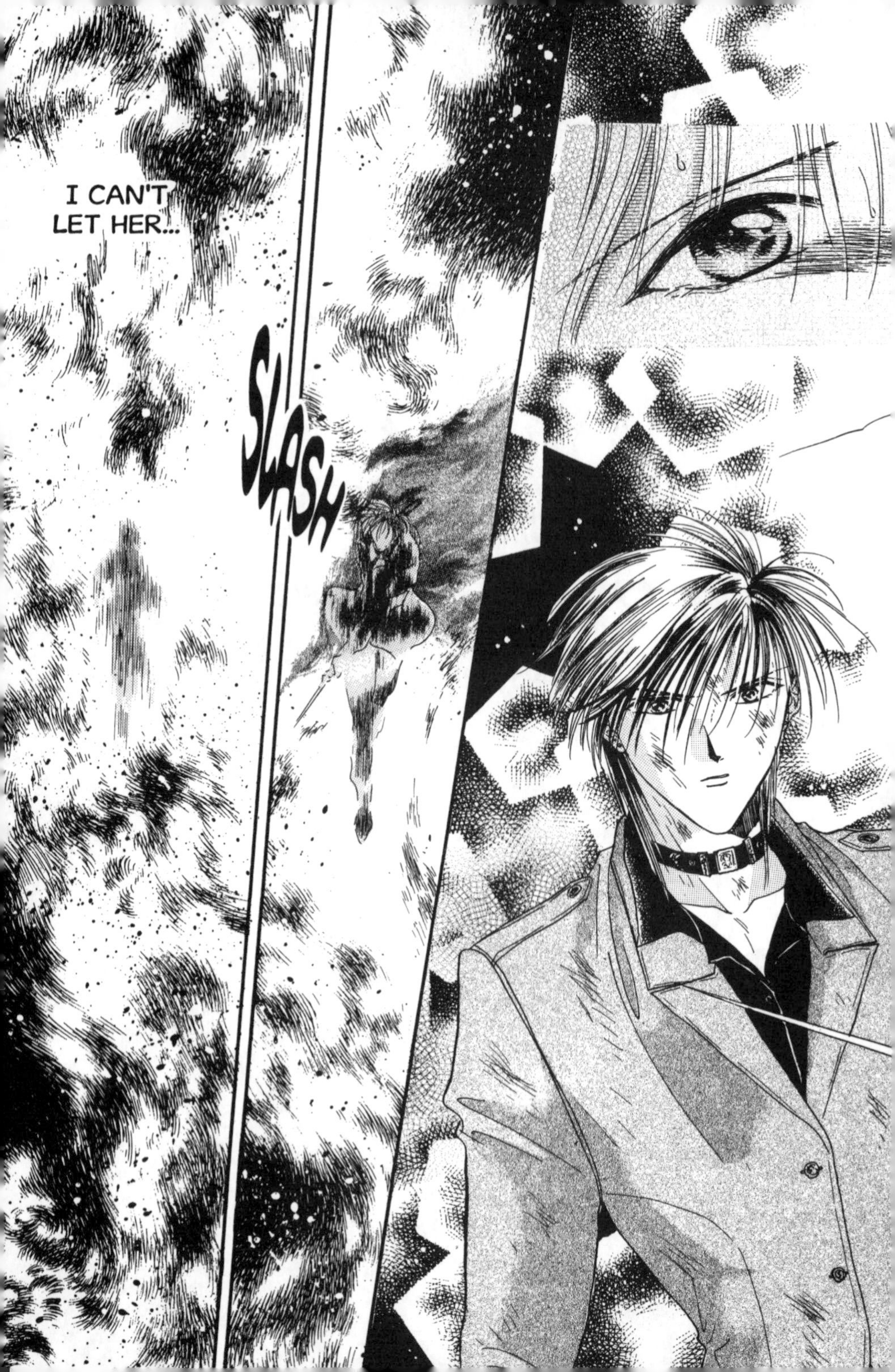
I CAN'T LET HER...
SLASH

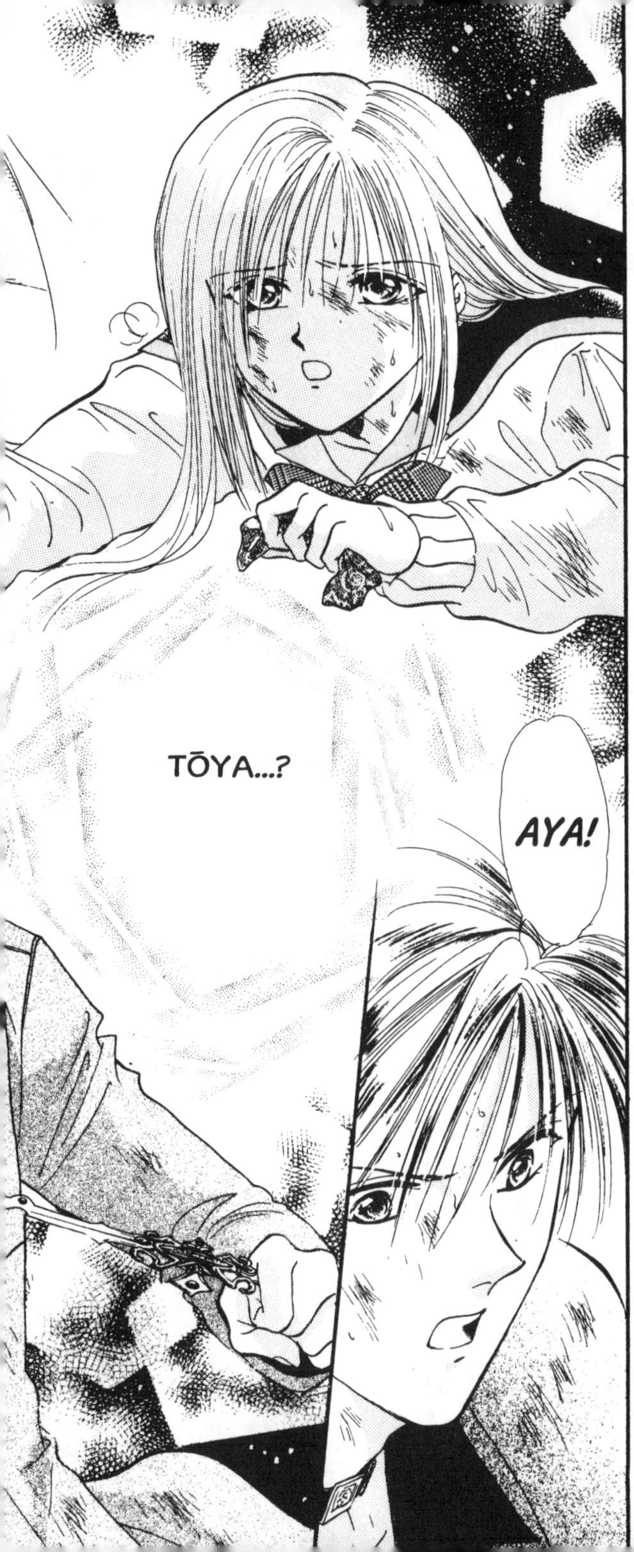
AYA!
TŌYA...?

Ceres: 3

By the way... My assistant H, my editor, and I went on a field trip. Where? *Heh heh...*"The Mitsubishi Chemical Research Laboratory"! I gained a lot of knowledge there, and I was able to feel smart for a few days after the visit. It's (supposedly) one of the top five labs in the world. I was nervous at first, but they were all very nice there, and answered all my silly questions. It was a great educational experience. Thank you so much. One of the researchers explained celestial maiden genetics for me, and even drew some diagrams on the chalkboard. It was great! And so, I've clarified (I think) whether or not the logistics I created for the story make scientific sense. Now at least half of Ceres has the official stamp of approval from scientists! (oh, really?!) *well, let's just say it does.* The rest is fictional. People tend to think that genetics and biology use a lot of special terminology and that makes them hard to understand, but when you get to know even a little bit about the subjects, they're very interesting fields. I actually hated all the memorizing we had to do in high school science, but I liked biology and astronomy. The labs were a pain, but it was fun to get to use a microscope. At the Mitsubishi lab they let me use their microscope to take a peek at some mouse sperm. I also checked out mouse genes. I took pictures in a room that was minus 22°F. The whole time I was screaming about how cold it was...This is just a manga, but I should at least know about the fundamentals of science.

They also taught me about cloning, which was really interesting. There's been a lot of books out recently that look at men and women from a biological perspective. This is an age when society's eyes are turned towards the mysticism of life.

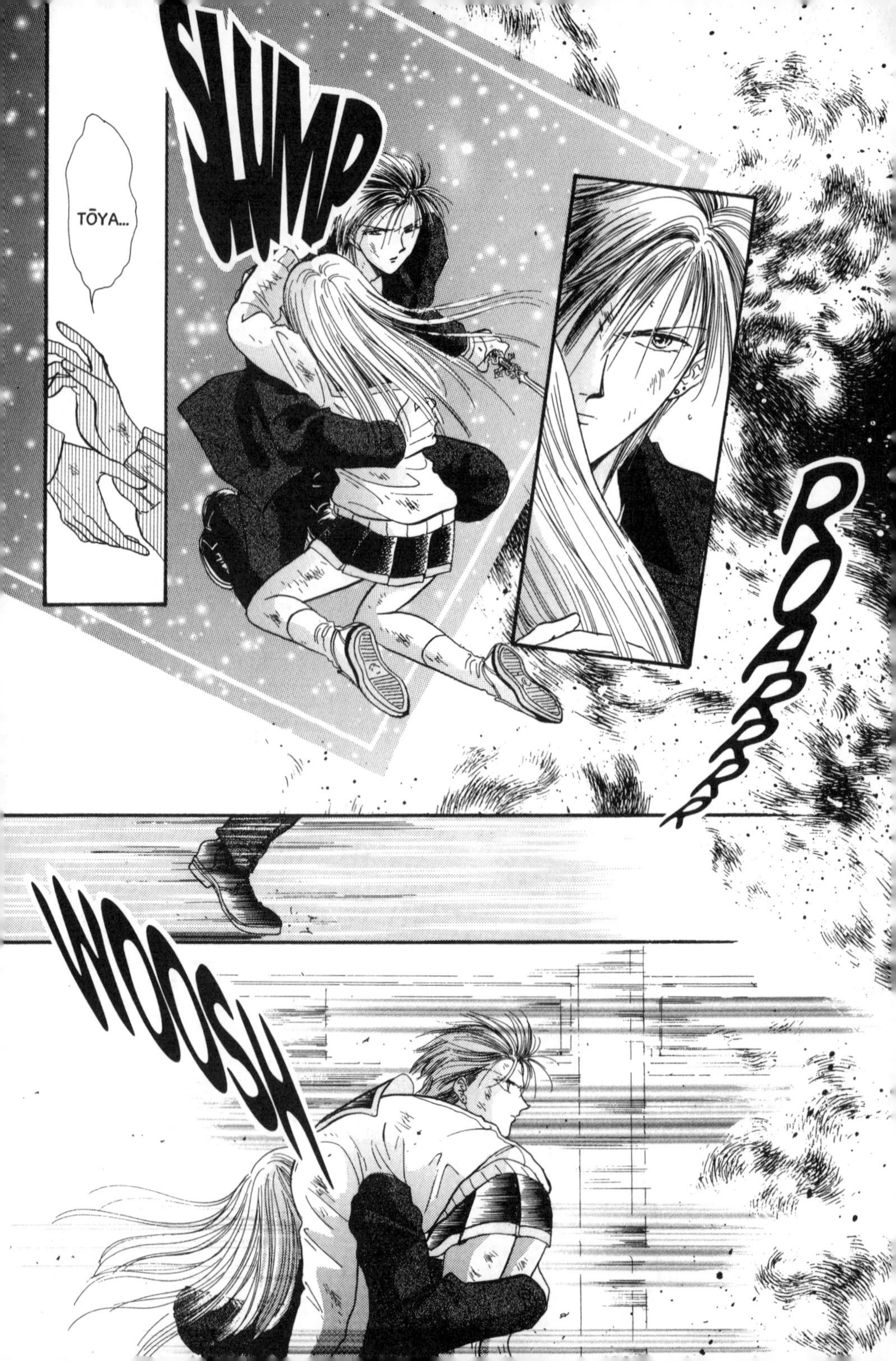
TŌYA...
SHUMP
ROARRRR
WOOSH

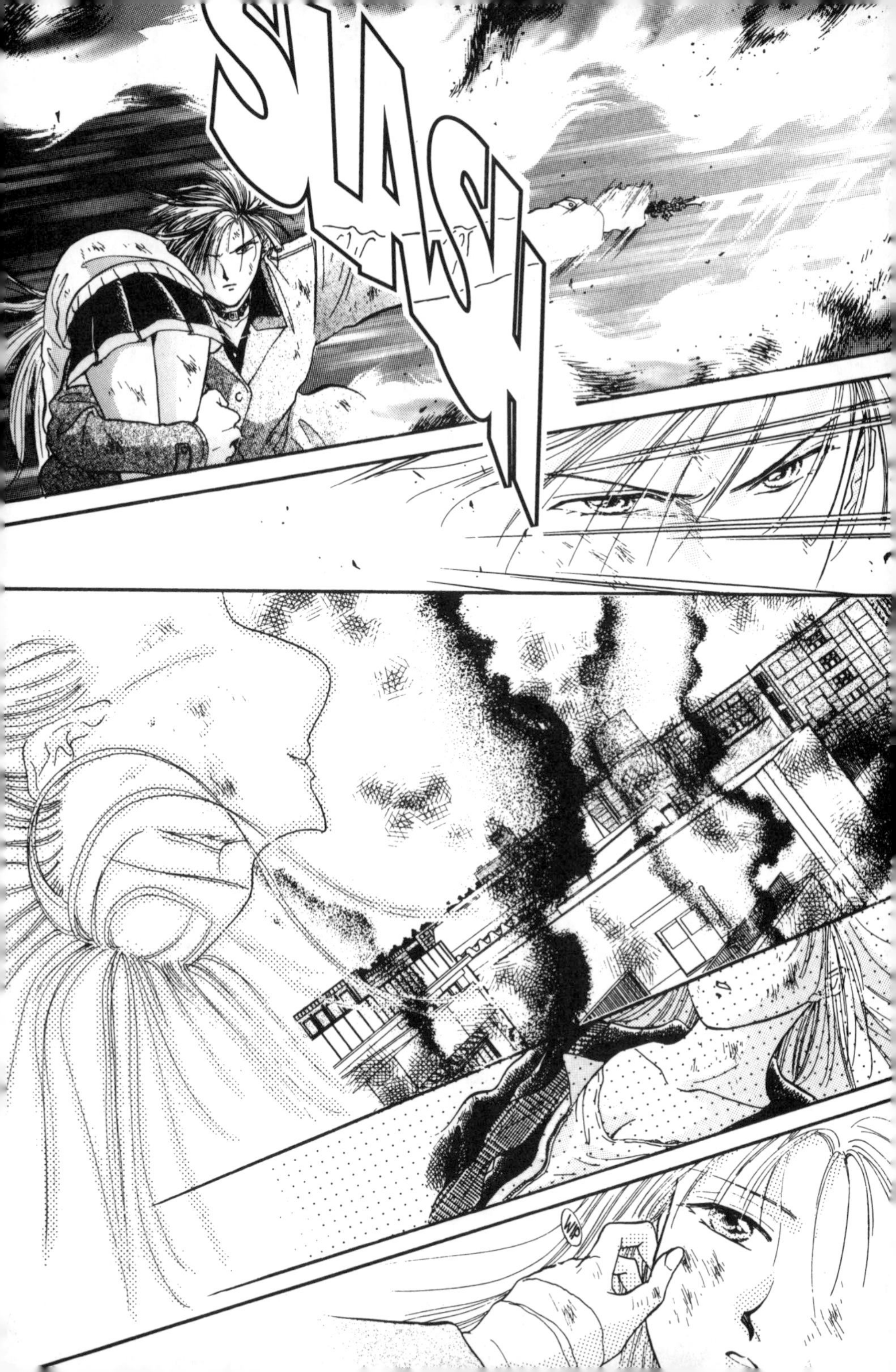
SLASH
WIP

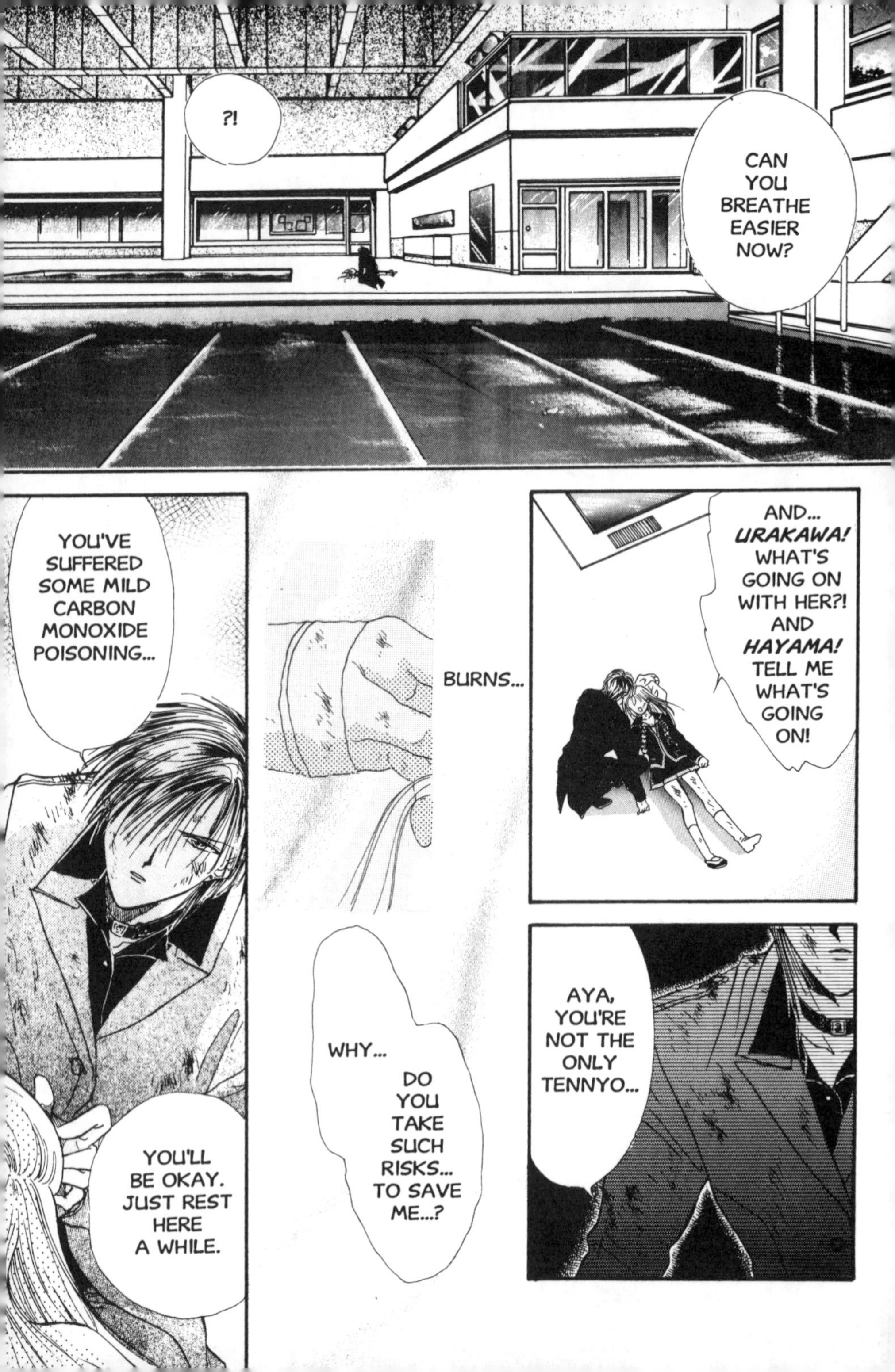
?!
CAN YOU BREATHE EASIER NOW?
YOU'VE SUFFERED SOME MILD CARBON MONOXIDE POISONING...
YOU'LL BE OKAY. JUST REST HERE A WHILE.
BURNS...
WHY... DO YOU TAKE SUCH RISKS... TO SAVE ME...?
AND... *URAKAWA!* WHAT'S GOING ON WITH HER?! AND *HAYAMA!* TELL ME WHAT'S GOING ON!
AYA, YOU'RE NOT THE ONLY TENNYO...

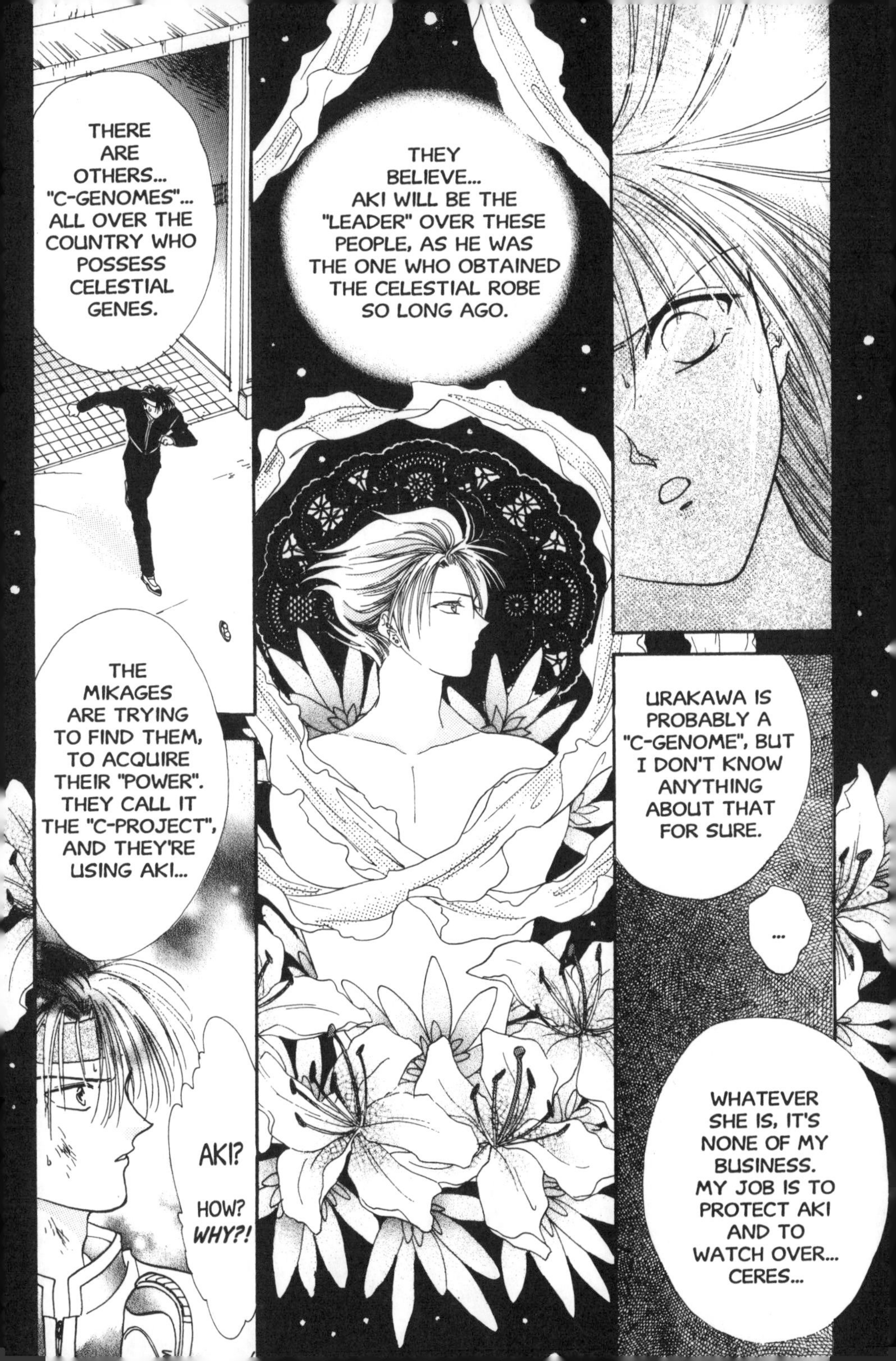
THERE ARE OTHERS... "C-GENOMES"... ALL OVER THE COUNTRY WHO POSSESS CELESTIAL GENES.
THE MIKAGES ARE TRYING TO FIND THEM, TO ACQUIRE THEIR "POWER". THEY CALL IT THE "C-PROJECT", AND THEY'RE USING AKI...
AKI?
HOW? WHY?!
THEY BELIEVE... AKI WILL BE THE "LEADER" OVER THESE PEOPLE, AS HE WAS THE ONE WHO OBTAINED THE CELESTIAL ROBE SO LONG AGO.
URAKAWA IS PROBABLY A "C-GENOME", BUT I DON'T KNOW ANYTHING ABOUT THAT FOR SURE.
...
WHATEVER SHE IS, IT'S NONE OF MY BUSINESS. MY JOB IS TO PROTECT AKI AND TO WATCH OVER... CERES...

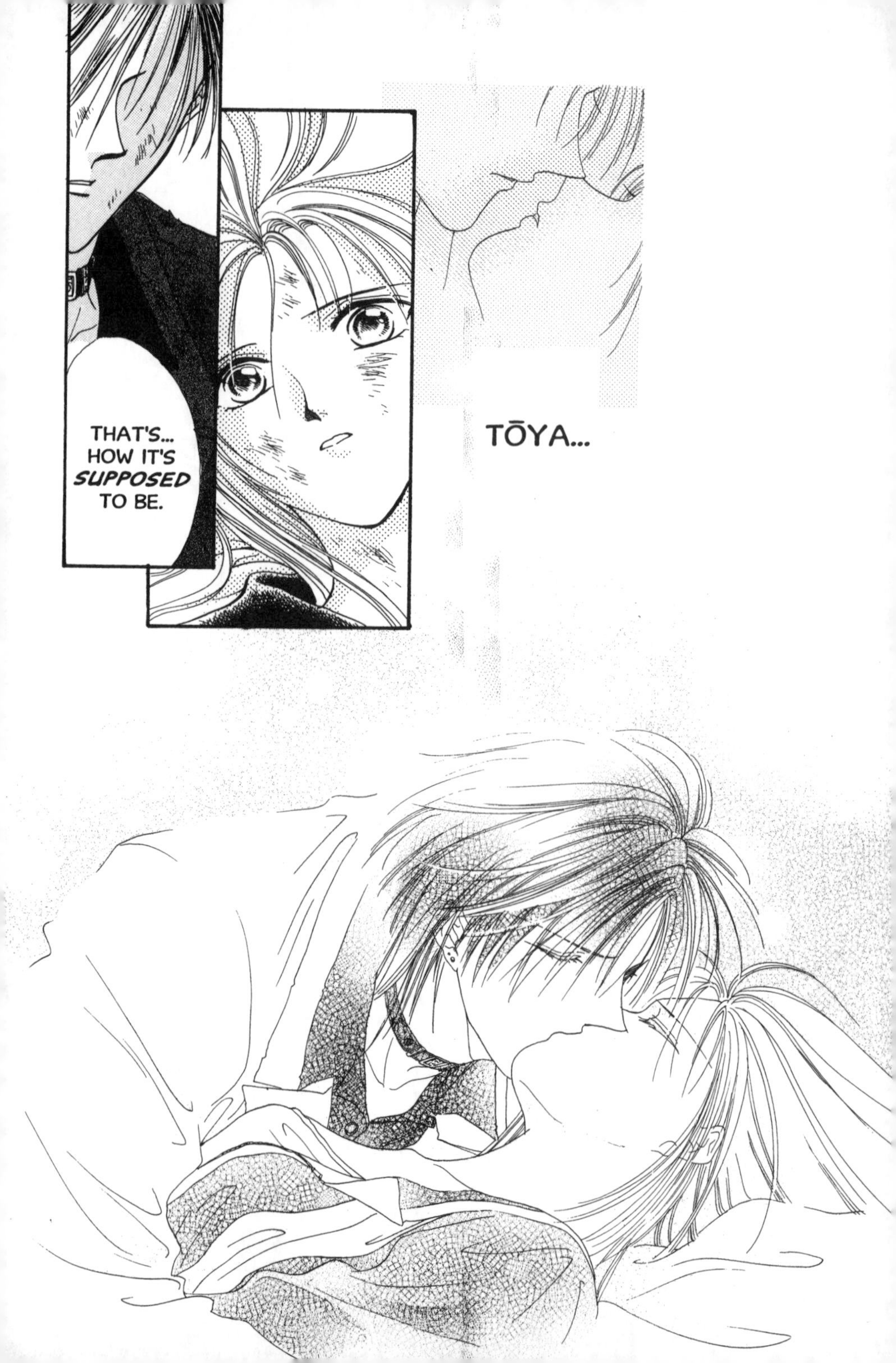
THAT'S... HOW IT'S *SUPPOSED* TO BE.
TŌYA...

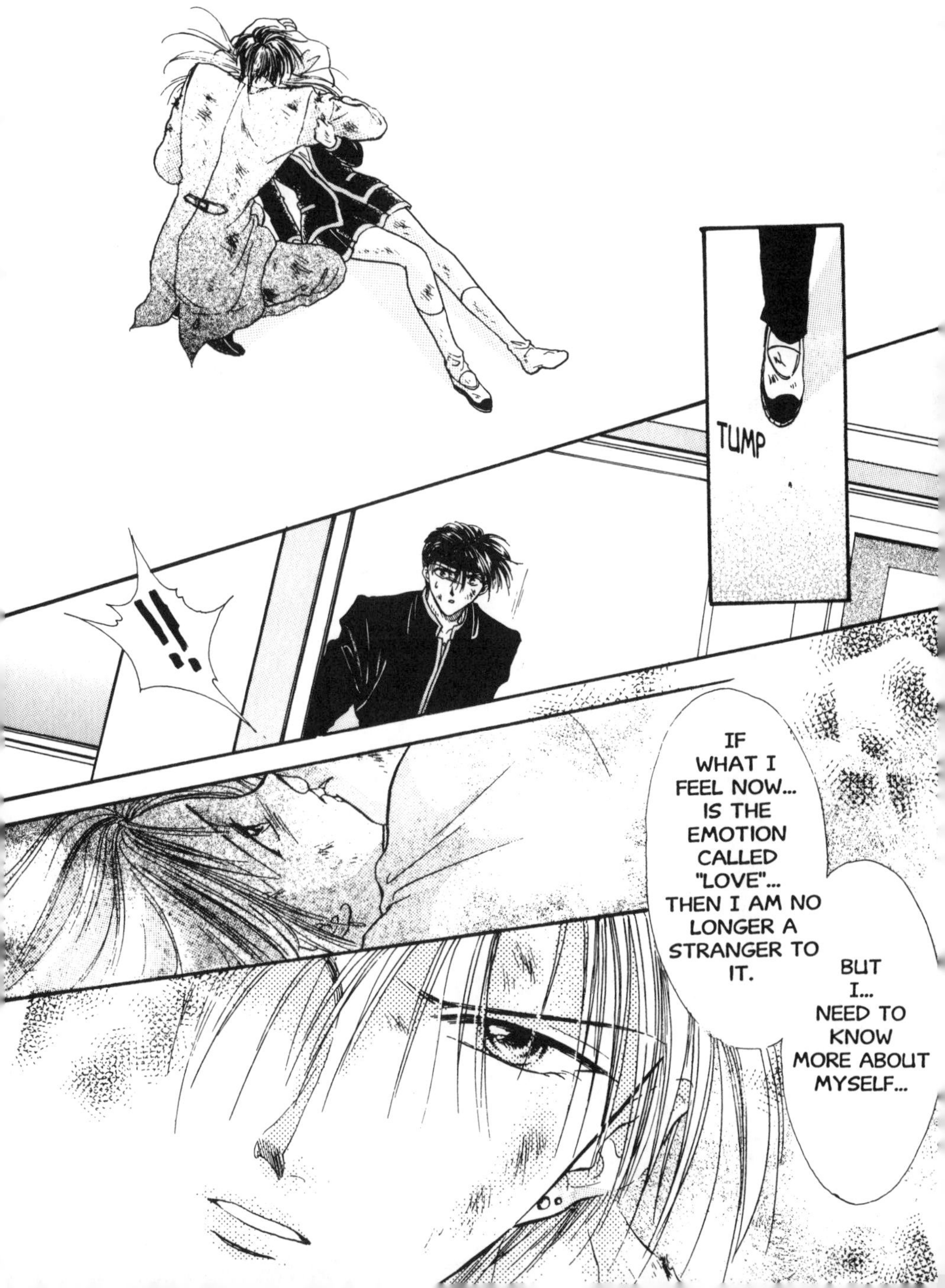
TUMP
!!..
IF WHAT I FEEL NOW... IS THE EMOTION CALLED "LOVE"... THEN I AM NO LONGER A STRANGER TO IT.
BUT I... NEED TO KNOW MORE ABOUT MYSELF...

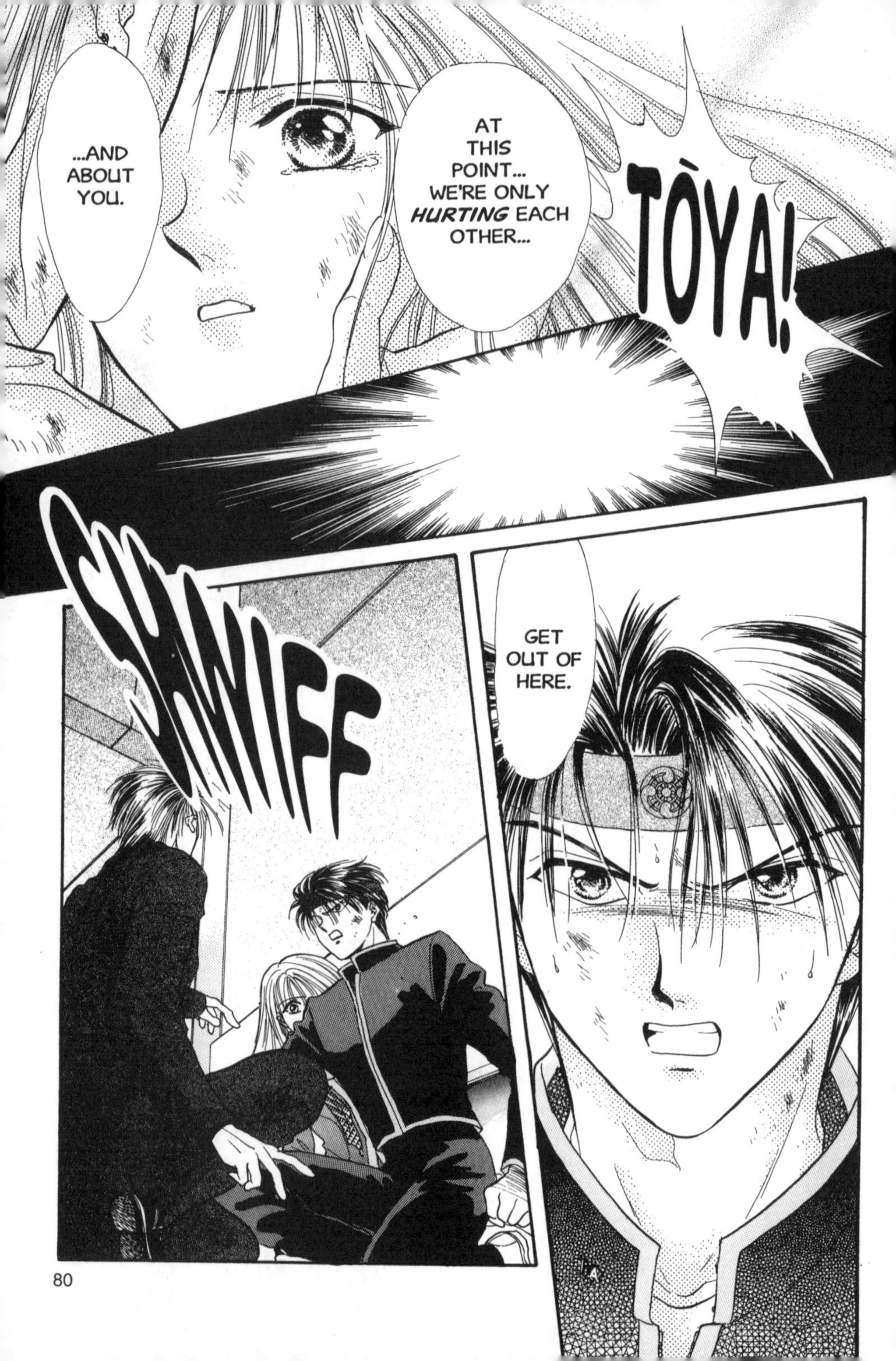
...AND ABOUT YOU.
AT THIS POINT... WE'RE ONLY *HURTING* EACH OTHER...
TÒYA!
SHWIFF
GET OUT OF HERE.

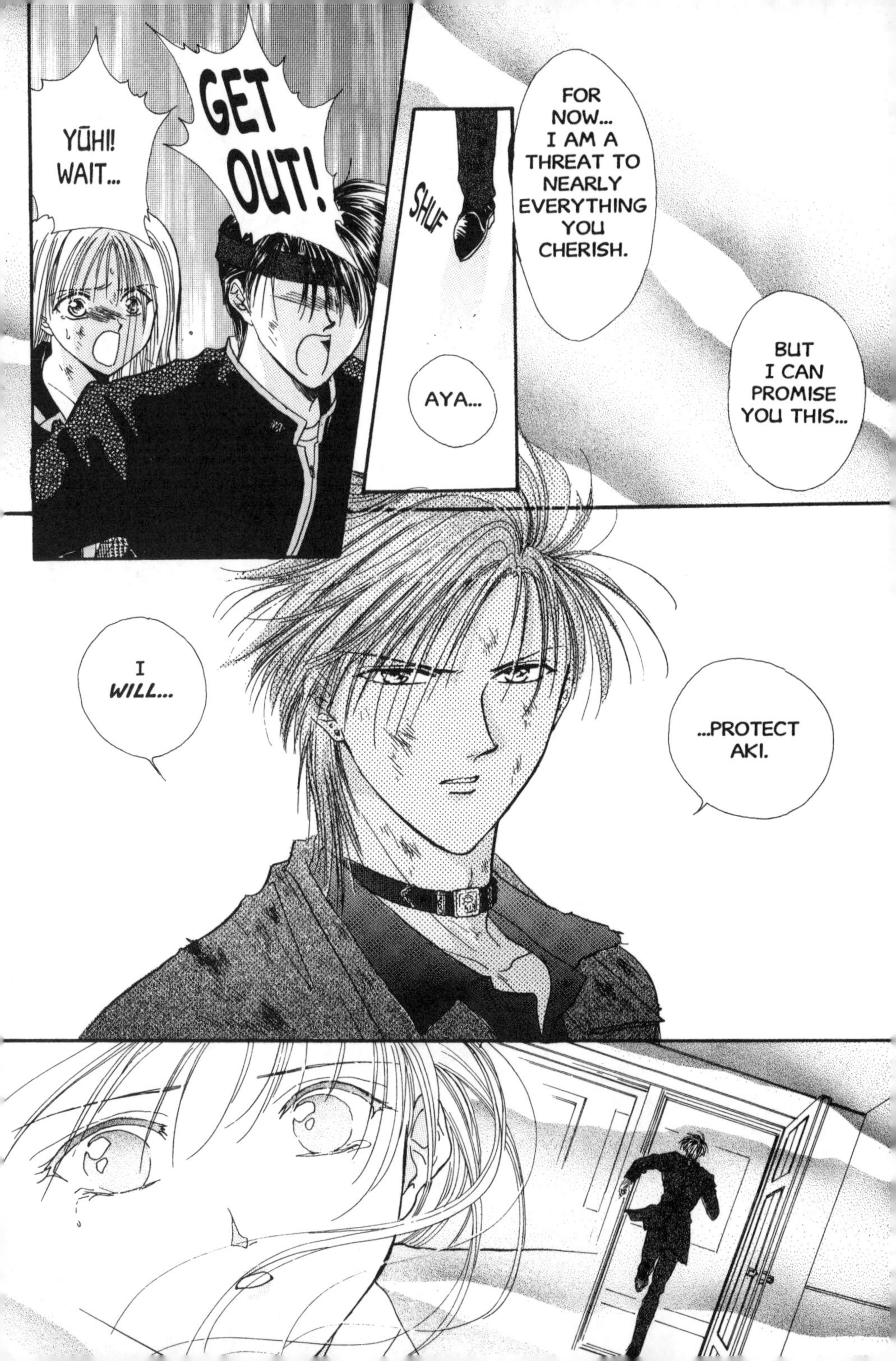
GET OUT!
YŪHI! WAIT...
SHUF
AYA...
FOR NOW... I AM A THREAT TO NEARLY EVERYTHING YOU CHERISH.
BUT I CAN PROMISE YOU THIS...
I WILL...
...PROTECT AKI.

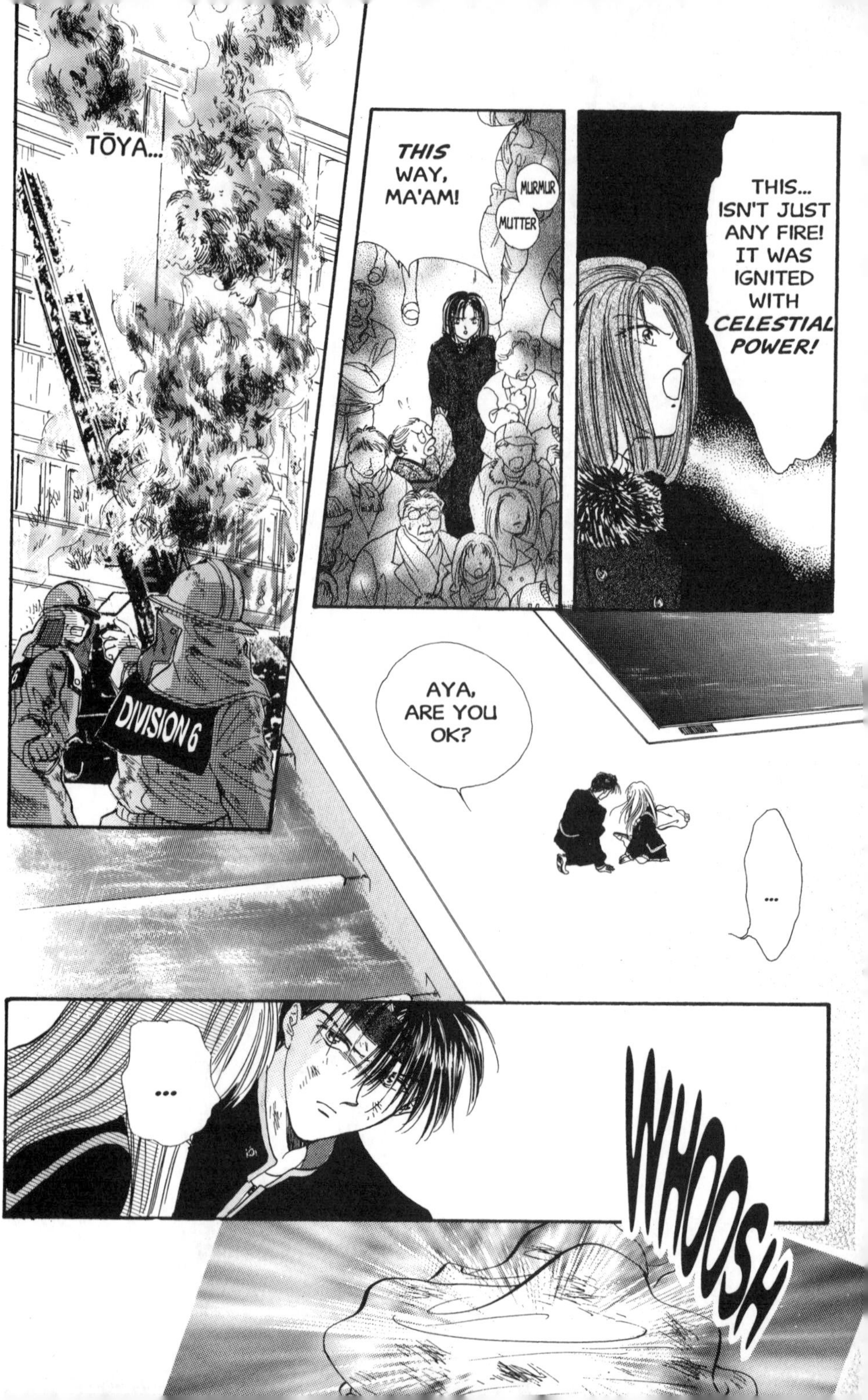
TŌYA...
DIVISION 6
THIS WAY, MA'AM!
MURMUR
MUTTER
THIS... ISN'T JUST ANY FIRE! IT WAS IGNITED WITH CELESTIAL POWER!
AYA, ARE YOU OK?
...
...
WHOOSH

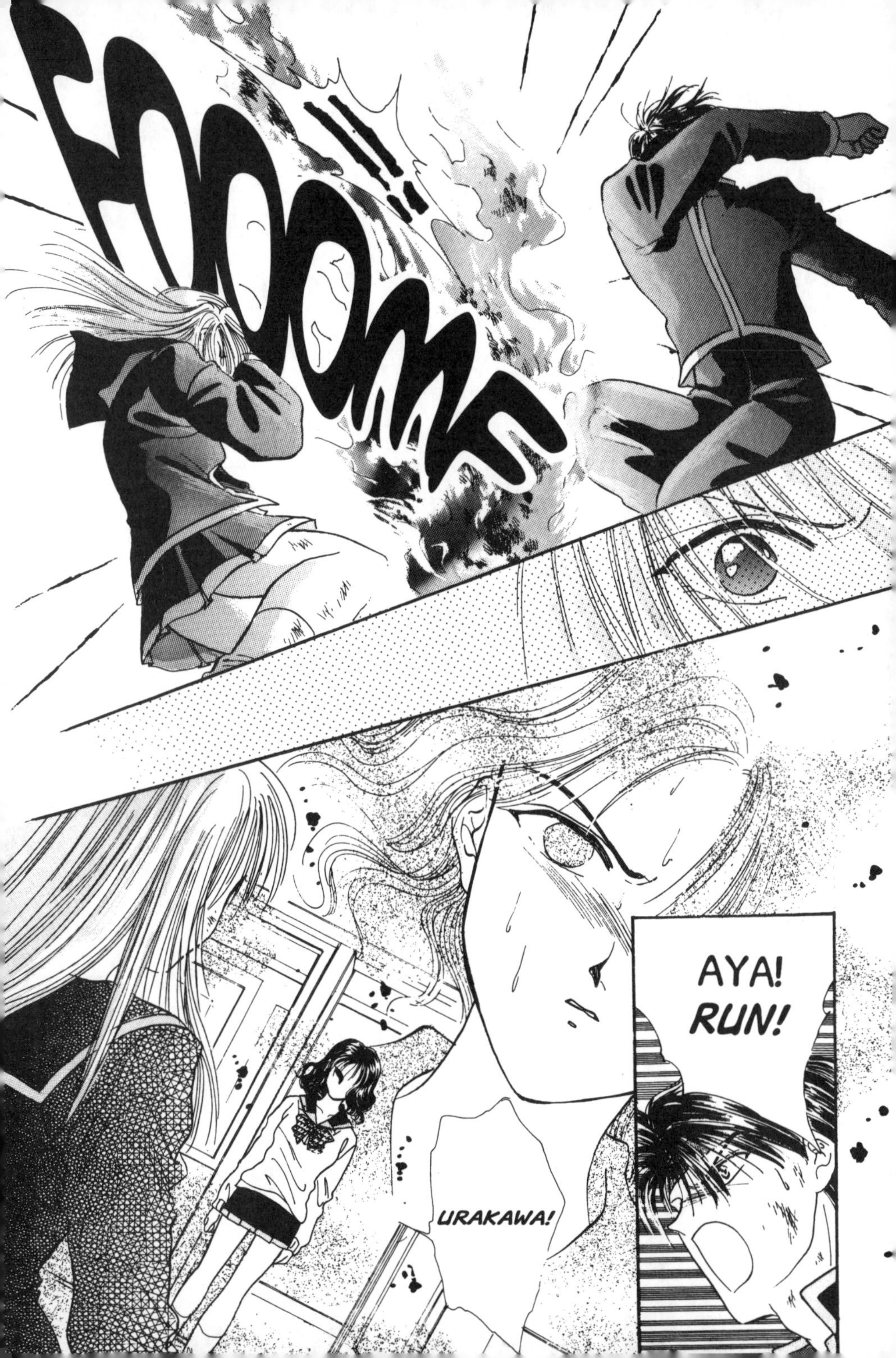
FOOOM!!
AYA! RUN!
URAKAWA!

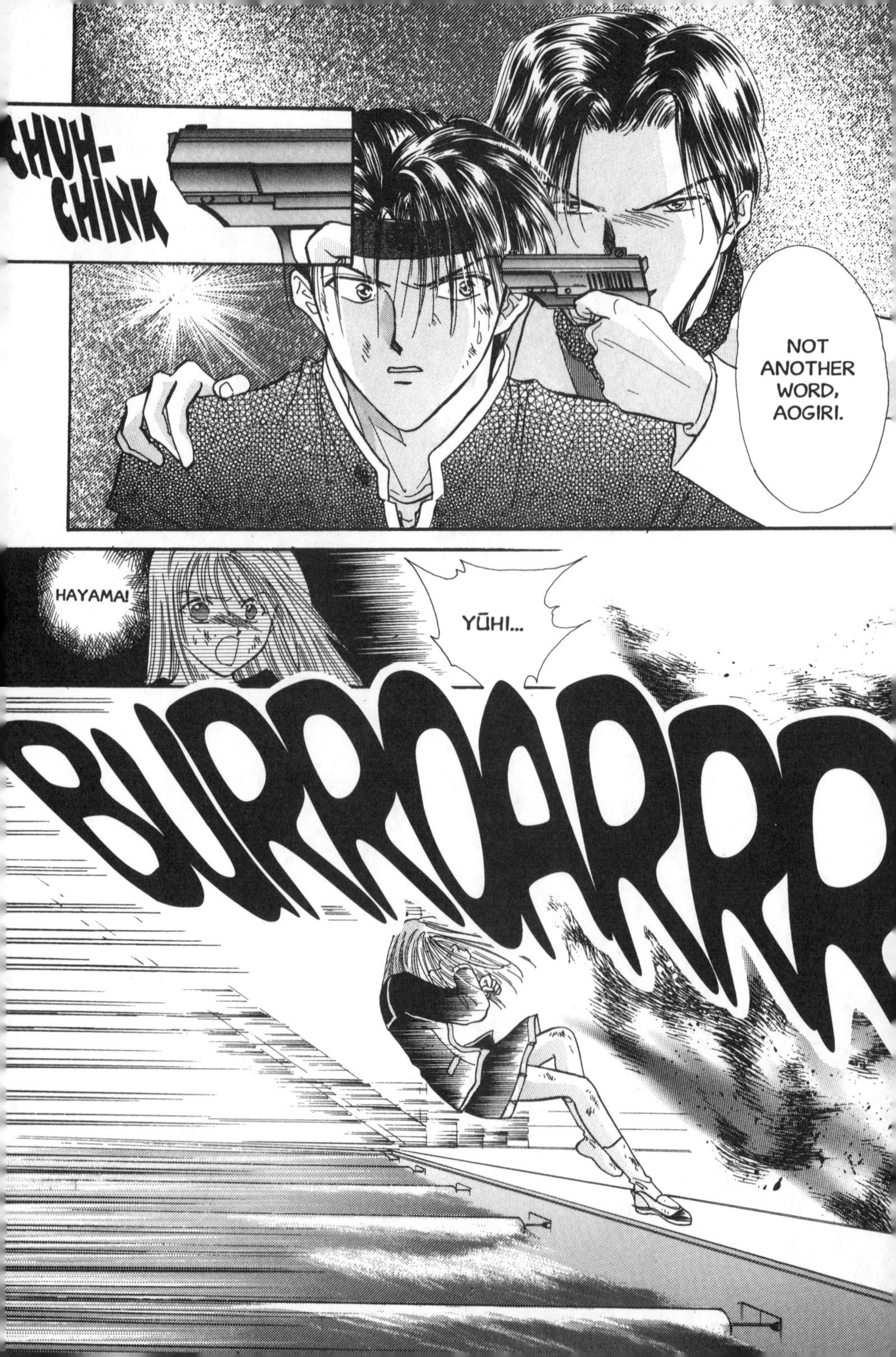
CHUH-CHINK
NOT ANOTHER WORD, AOGIRI.
HAYAMA!
YŪHI...
BUROOARRR

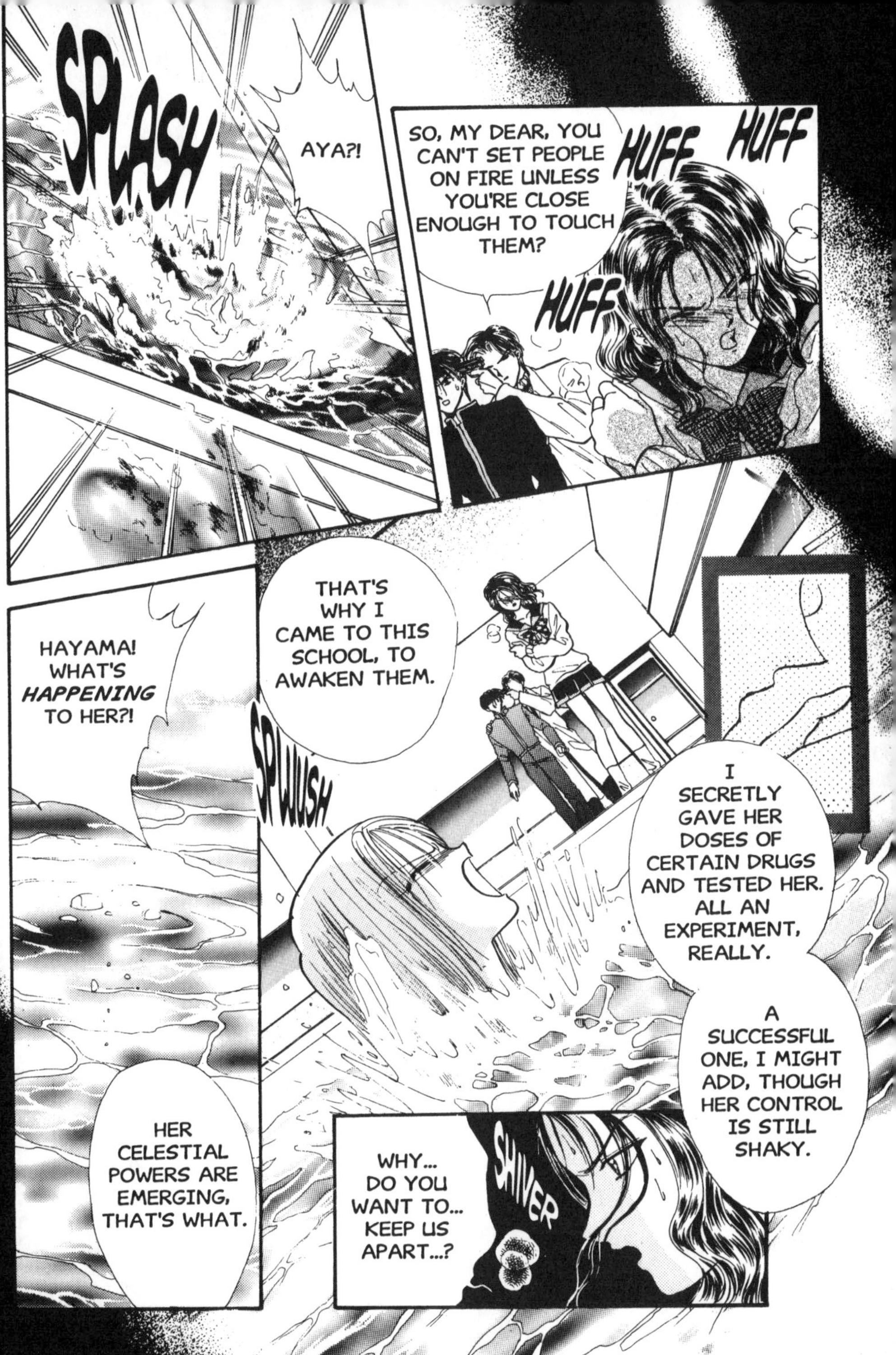
SPLASH
AYA?!
SO, MY DEAR, YOU CAN'T SET PEOPLE ON FIRE UNLESS YOU'RE CLOSE ENOUGH TO TOUCH THEM?
HUFF HUFF
HUFF
HAYAMA! WHAT'S *HAPPENING* TO HER?!
HER CELESTIAL POWERS ARE EMERGING, THAT'S WHAT.
THAT'S WHY I CAME TO THIS SCHOOL, TO AWAKEN THEM.
SPLJUSH
I SECRETLY GAVE HER DOSES OF CERTAIN DRUGS AND TESTED HER. ALL AN EXPERIMENT, REALLY.
A SUCCESSFUL ONE, I MIGHT ADD, THOUGH HER CONTROL IS STILL SHAKY.
WHY... DO YOU WANT TO... KEEP US APART...?
SHIVER

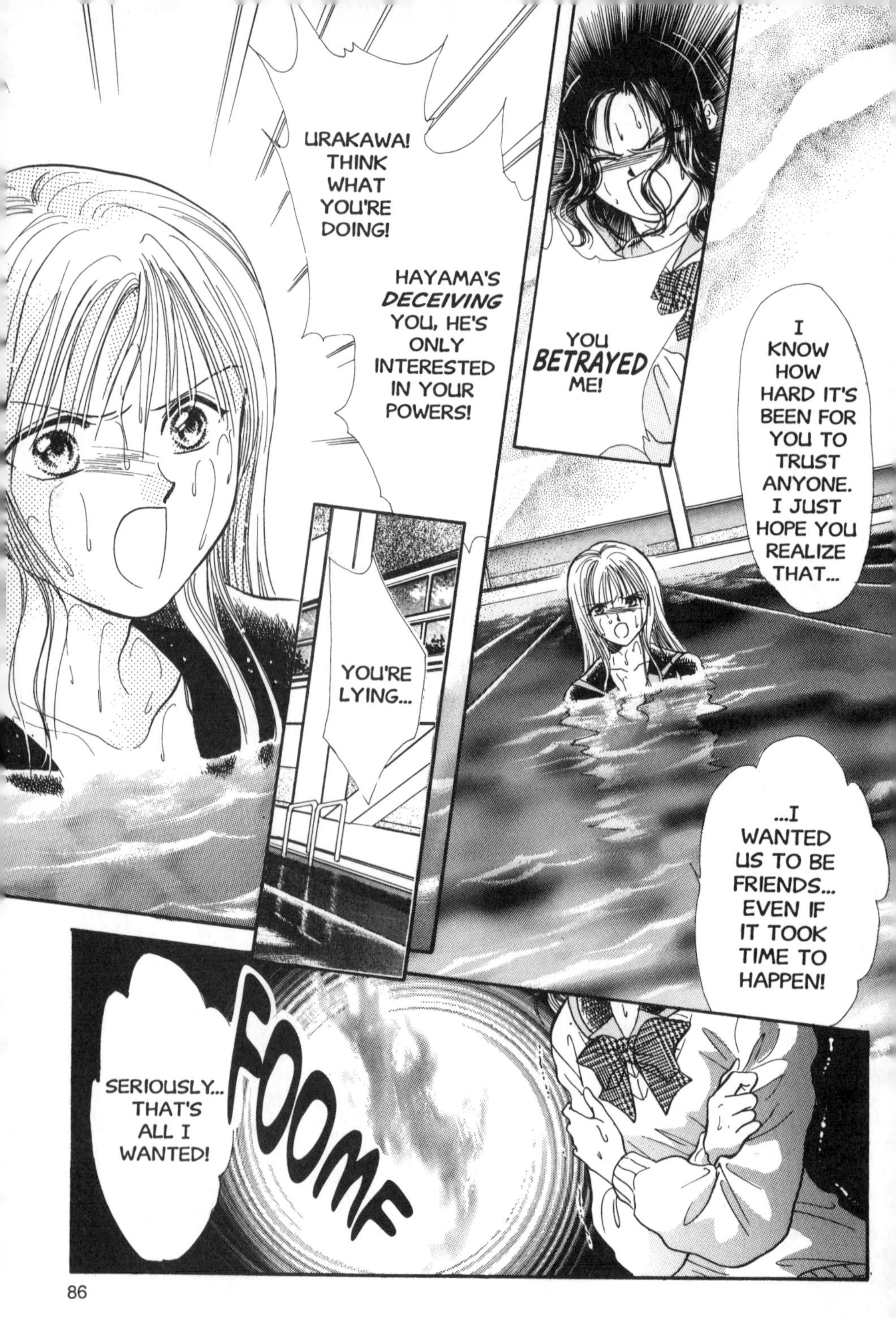
URAKAWA! THINK WHAT YOU'RE DOING!
HAYAMA'S *DECEIVING* YOU, HE'S ONLY INTERESTED IN YOUR POWERS!
YOU **BETRAYED** ME!
YOU'RE LYING...
I KNOW HOW HARD IT'S BEEN FOR YOU TO TRUST ANYONE. I JUST HOPE YOU REALIZE THAT...
...I WANTED US TO BE FRIENDS... EVEN IF IT TOOK TIME TO HAPPEN!
SERIOUSLY... THAT'S ALL I WANTED!
FOOMF

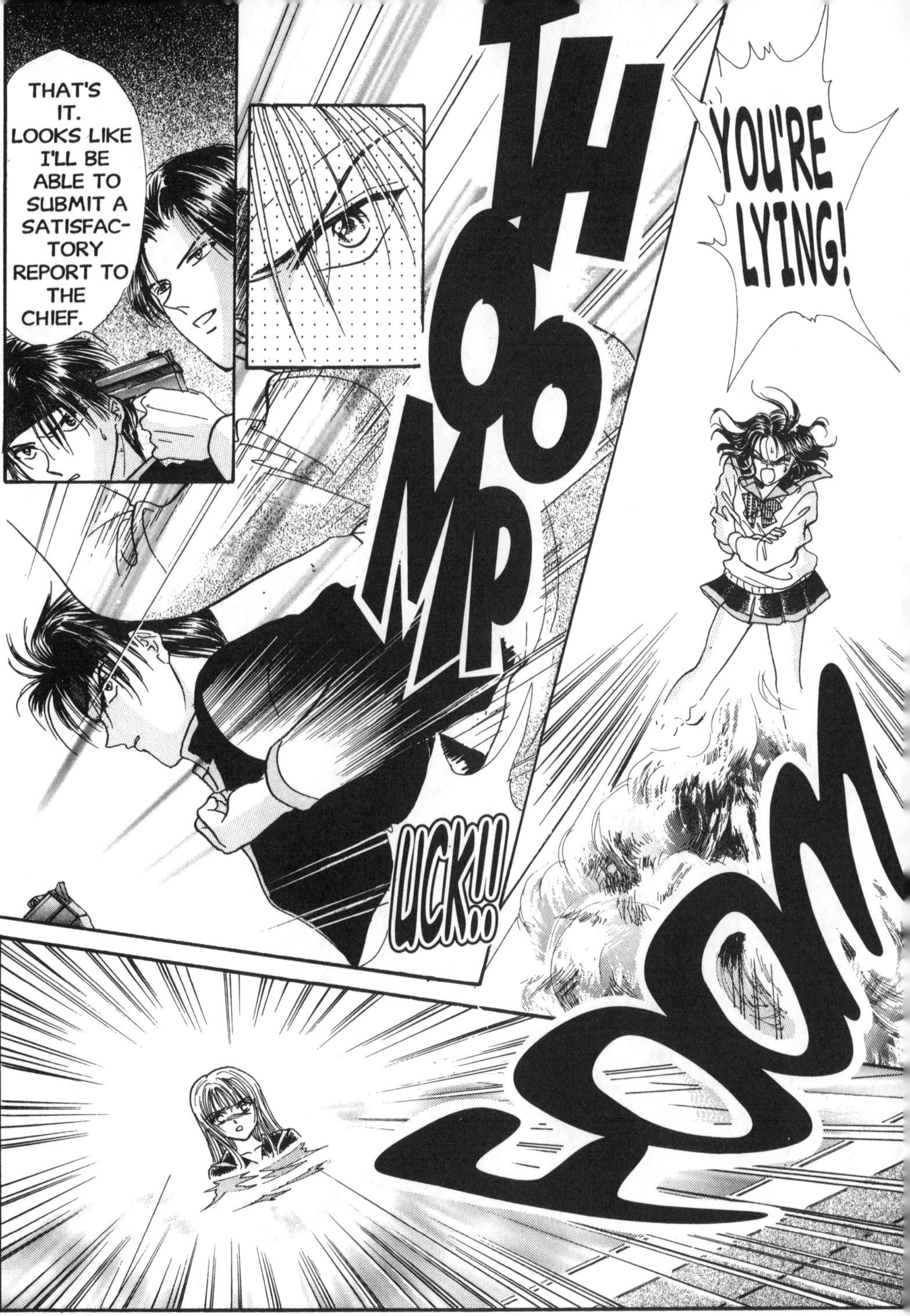
THAT'S IT. LOOKS LIKE I'LL BE ABLE TO SUBMIT A SATISFACTORY REPORT TO THE CHIEF.
THOOMP
LICK!!
YOU'RE LYING!

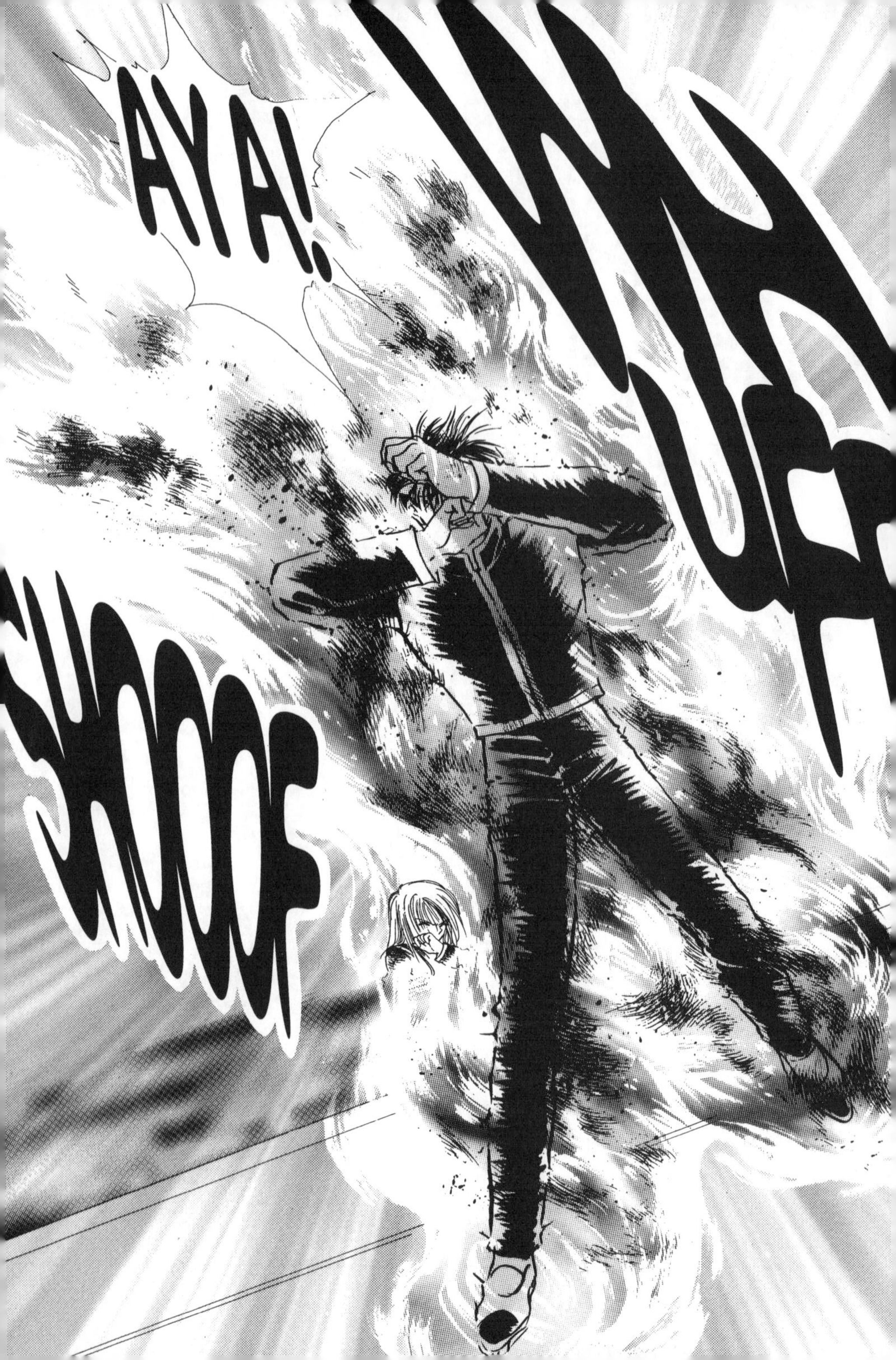
AYA!
WHOOF
SHOOOF

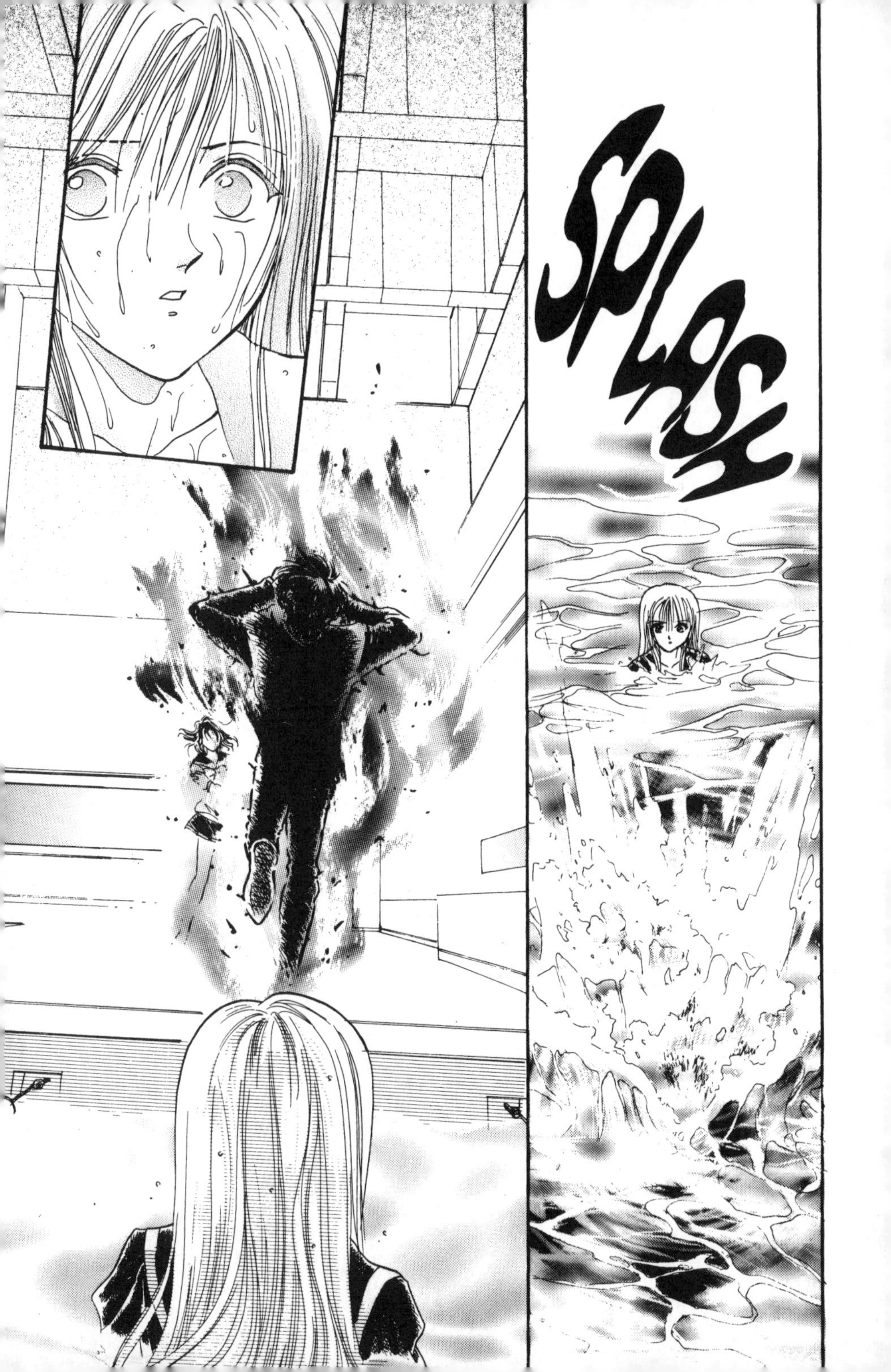
SPLASH

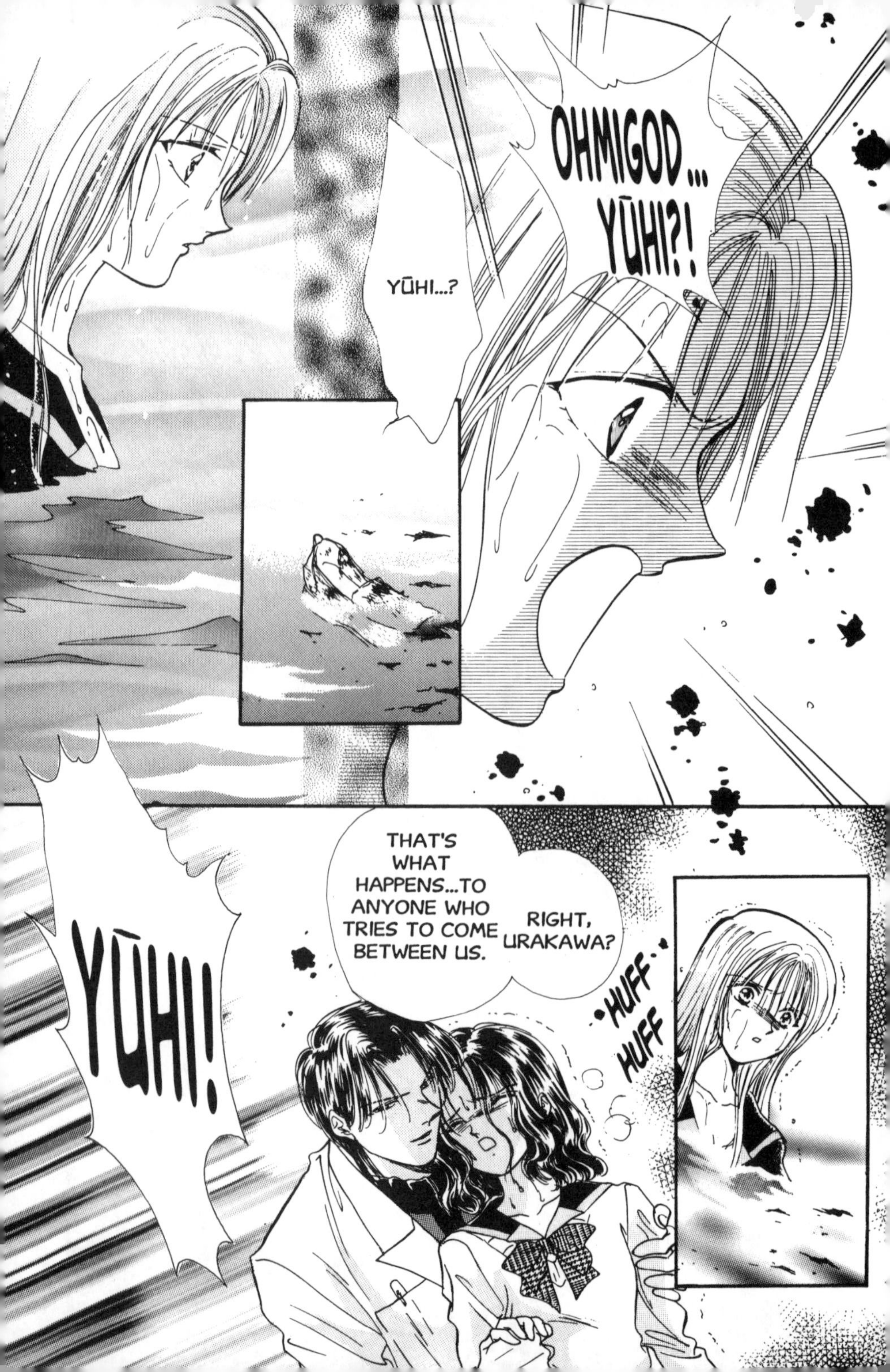
OHMIGOD... YŪHI?!
YŪHI...?
THAT'S WHAT HAPPENS...TO ANYONE WHO TRIES TO COME BETWEEN US.
RIGHT, URAKAWA?
HUFF HUFF
YŪHI!

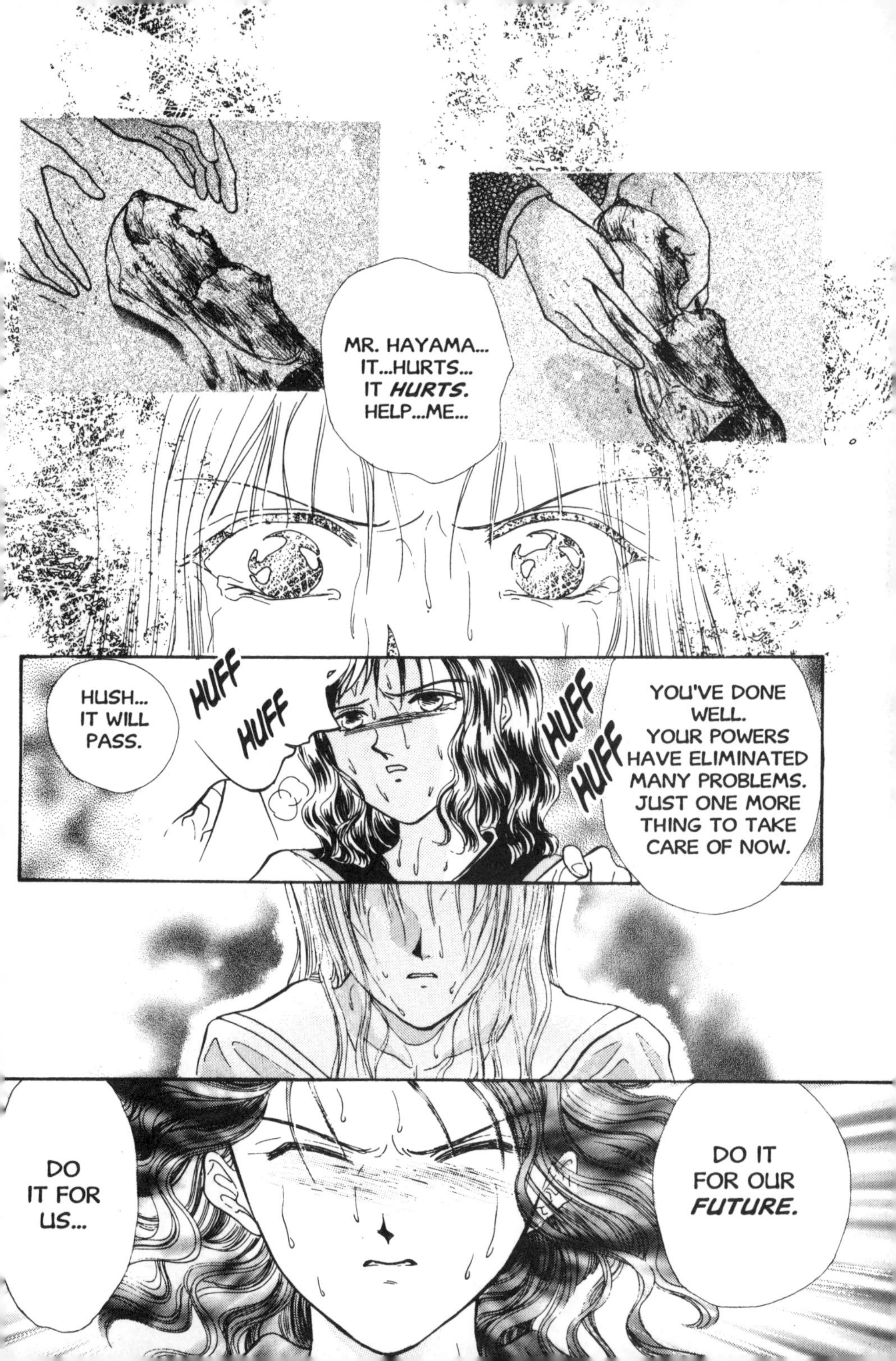
MR. HAYAMA... IT...HURTS... IT *HURTS.* HELP...ME...
HUSH... IT WILL PASS.
HUFF HUFF
HUFF HUFF
YOU'VE DONE WELL. YOUR POWERS HAVE ELIMINATED MANY PROBLEMS. JUST ONE MORE THING TO TAKE CARE OF NOW.
DO IT FOR US...
DO IT FOR OUR *FUTURE.*

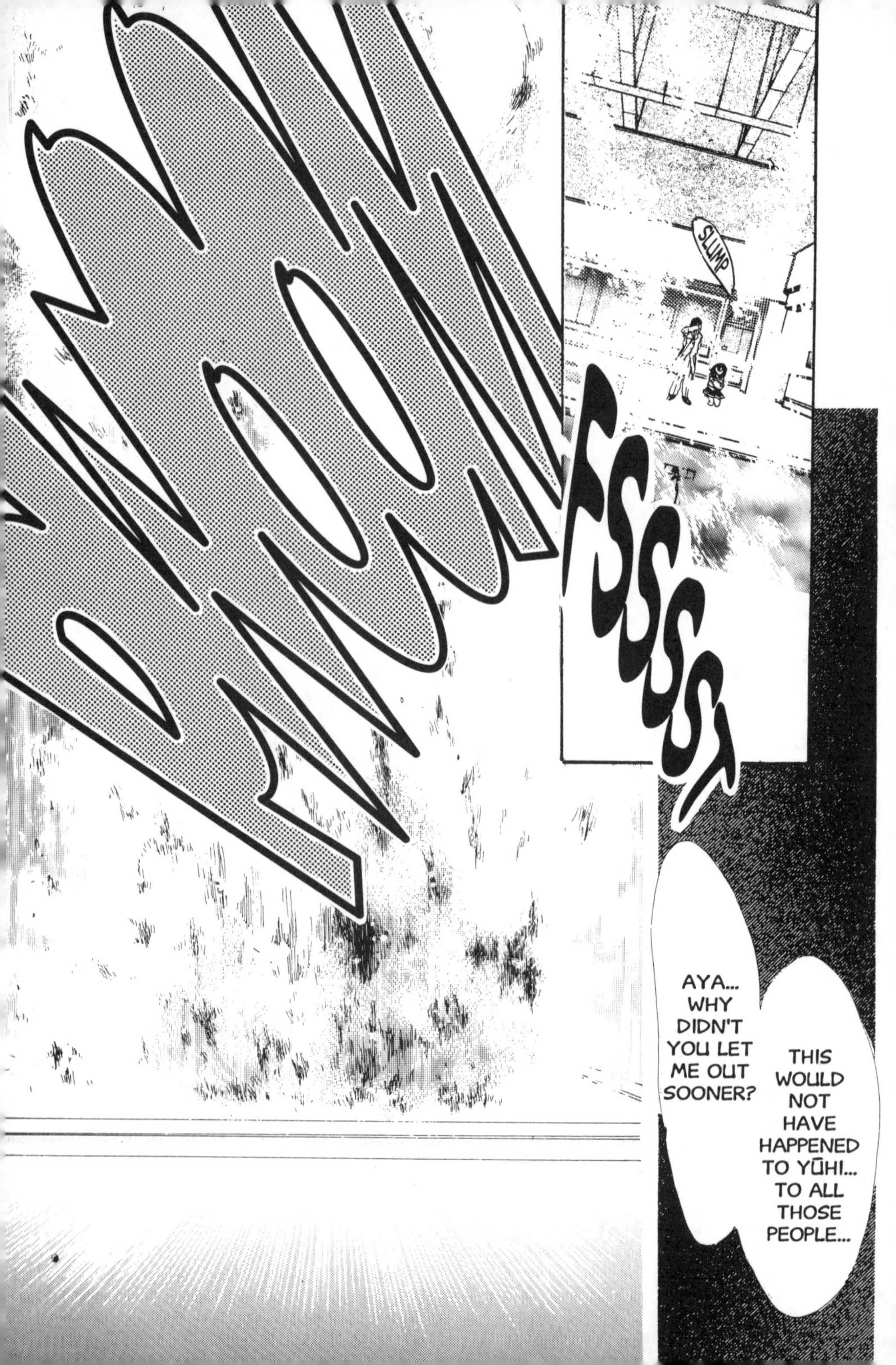
SLUMP
FSSSST
AYA... WHY DIDN'T YOU LET ME OUT SOONER?
THIS WOULD NOT HAVE HAPPENED TO YŪHI... TO ALL THOSE PEOPLE...

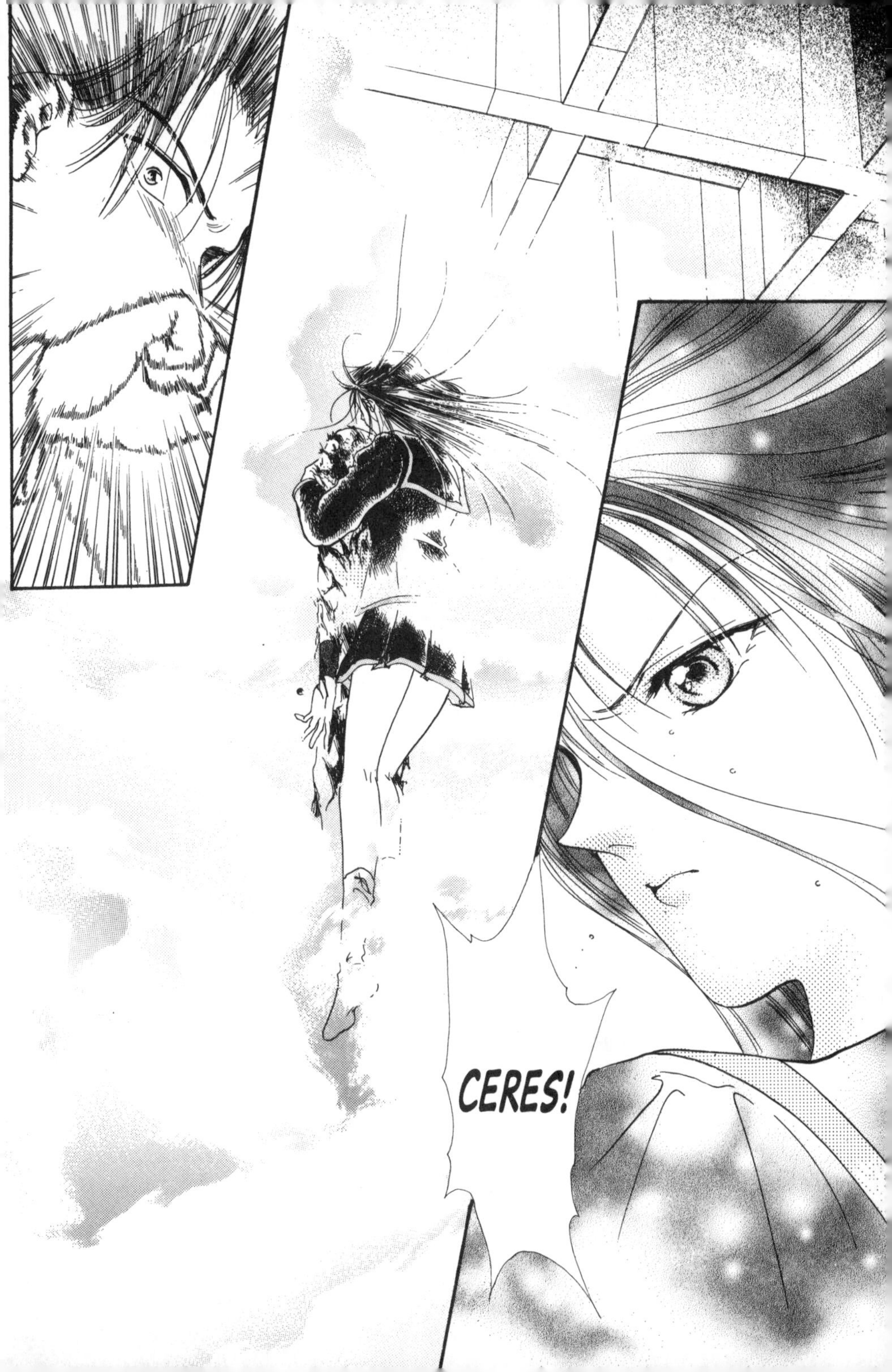
CERES!

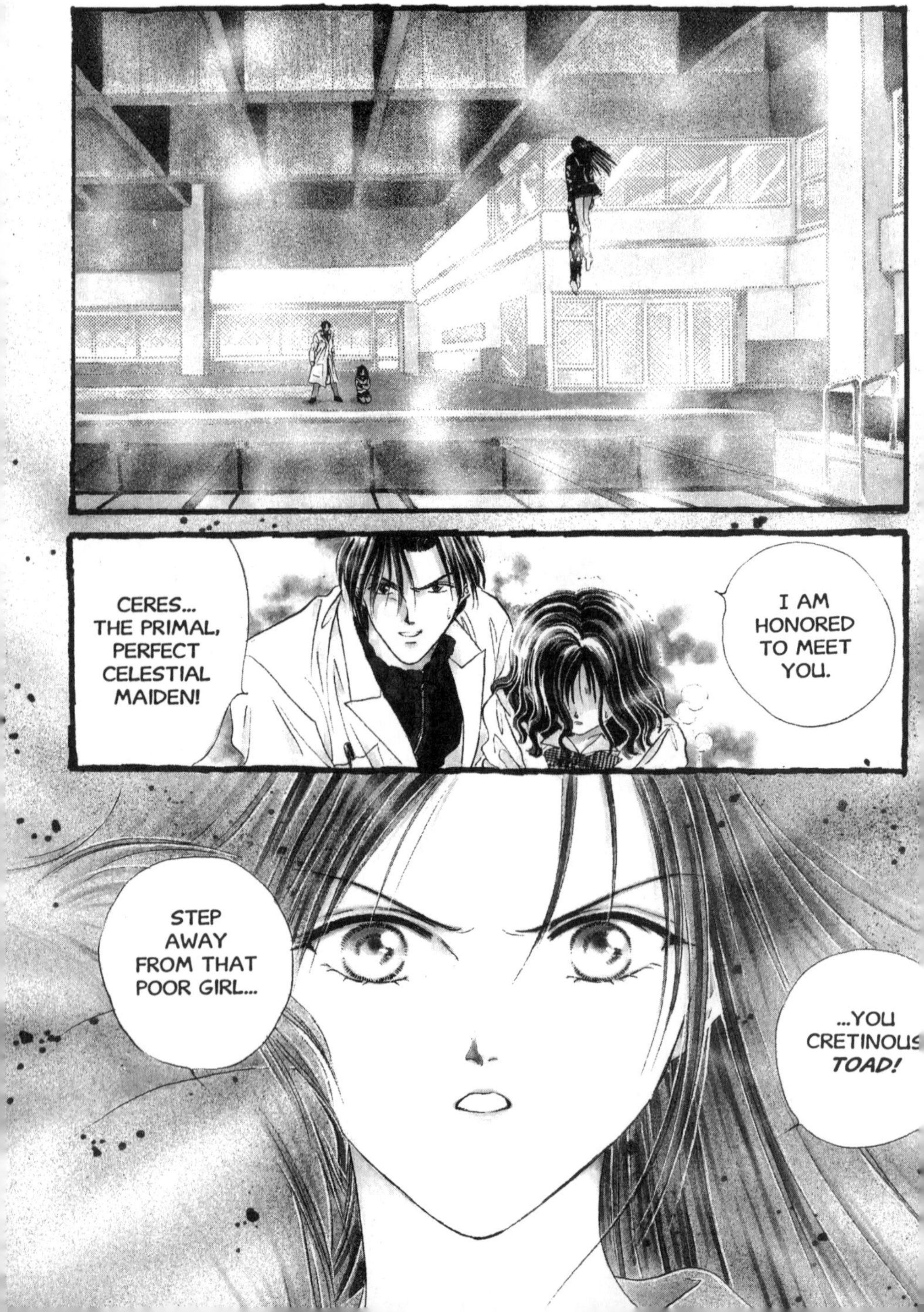

CERES... THE PRIMAL, PERFECT CELESTIAL MAIDEN!
I AM HONORED TO MEET YOU.
STEP AWAY FROM THAT POOR GIRL...
...YOU CRETINOUS *TOAD!*

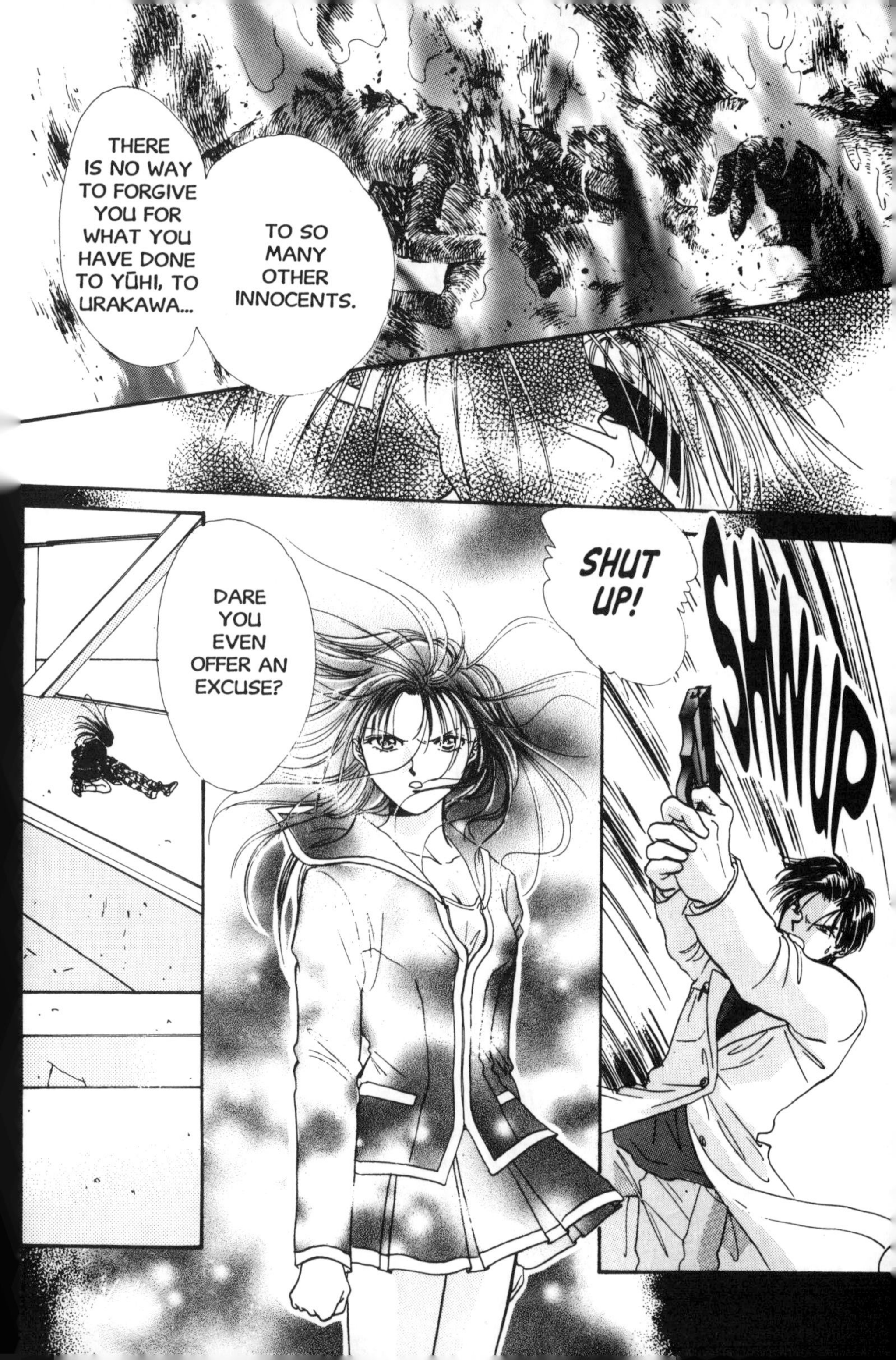
THERE IS NO WAY TO FORGIVE YOU FOR WHAT YOU HAVE DONE TO YŪHI, TO URAKAWA...
TO SO MANY OTHER INNOCENTS.
DARE YOU EVEN OFFER AN EXCUSE?
SHUT UP!
SHWUP

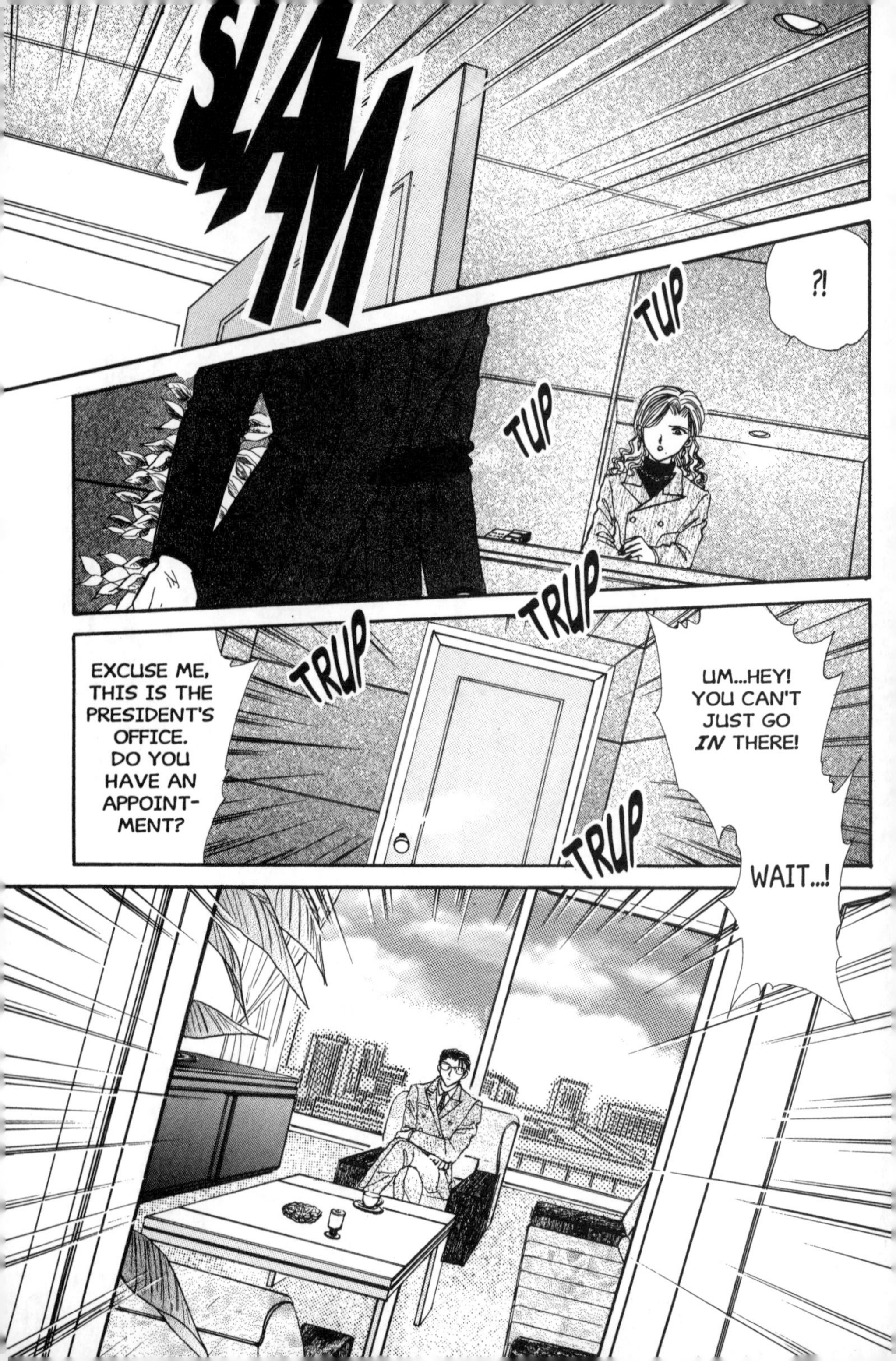
SLAM
TUP
TUP
?!
EXCUSE ME, THIS IS THE PRESIDENT'S OFFICE. DO YOU HAVE AN APPOINTMENT?
TRUP
TRUP
UM...HEY! YOU CAN'T JUST GO *IN* THERE!
TRUP
WAIT...!

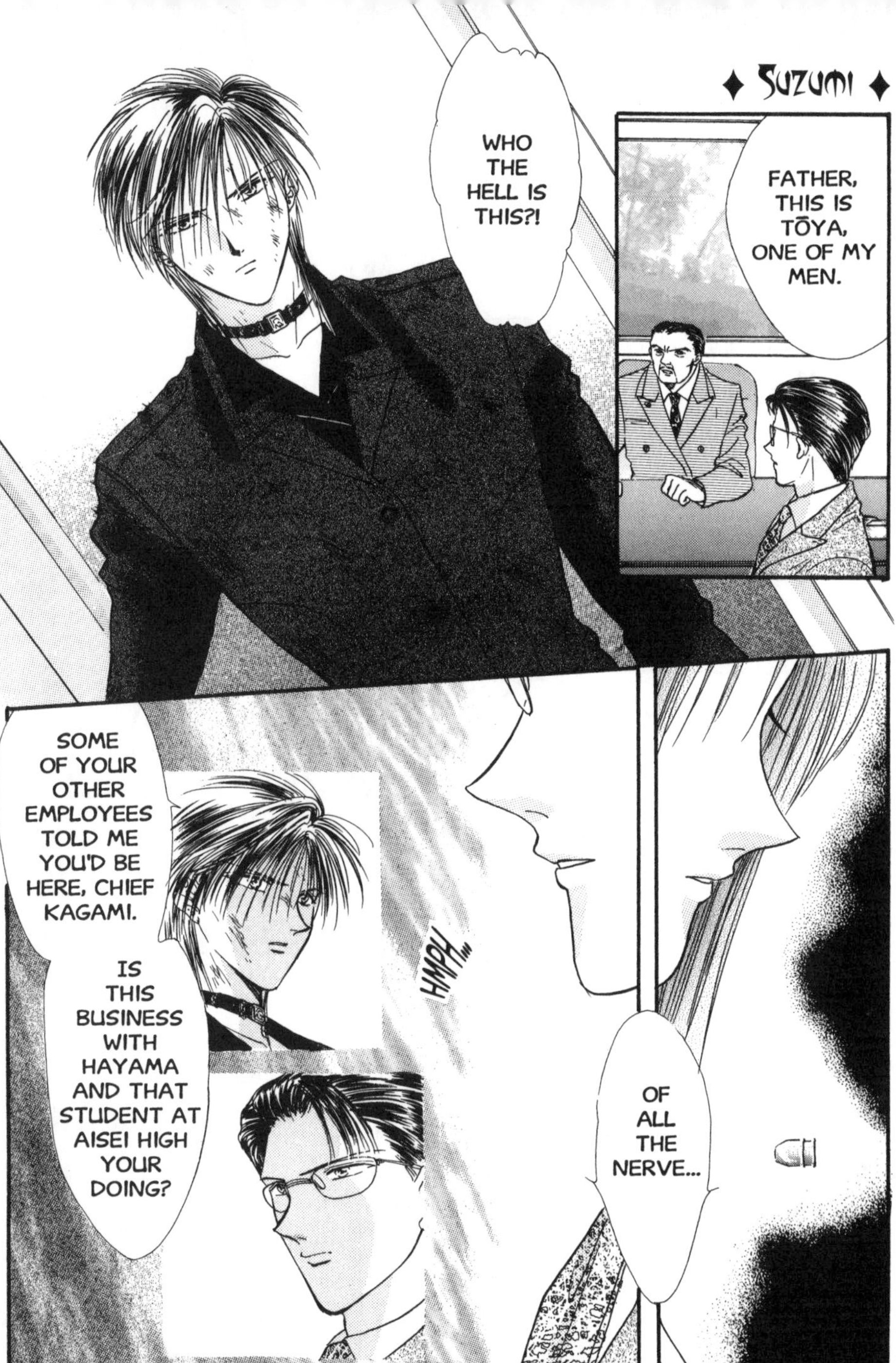
WHO THE HELL IS THIS?!
FATHER, THIS IS TŌYA, ONE OF MY MEN.
SOME OF YOUR OTHER EMPLOYEES TOLD ME YOU'D BE HERE, CHIEF KAGAMI.
IS THIS BUSINESS WITH HAYAMA AND THAT STUDENT AT AISEI HIGH YOUR DOING?
HMPH...
OF ALL THE NERVE...

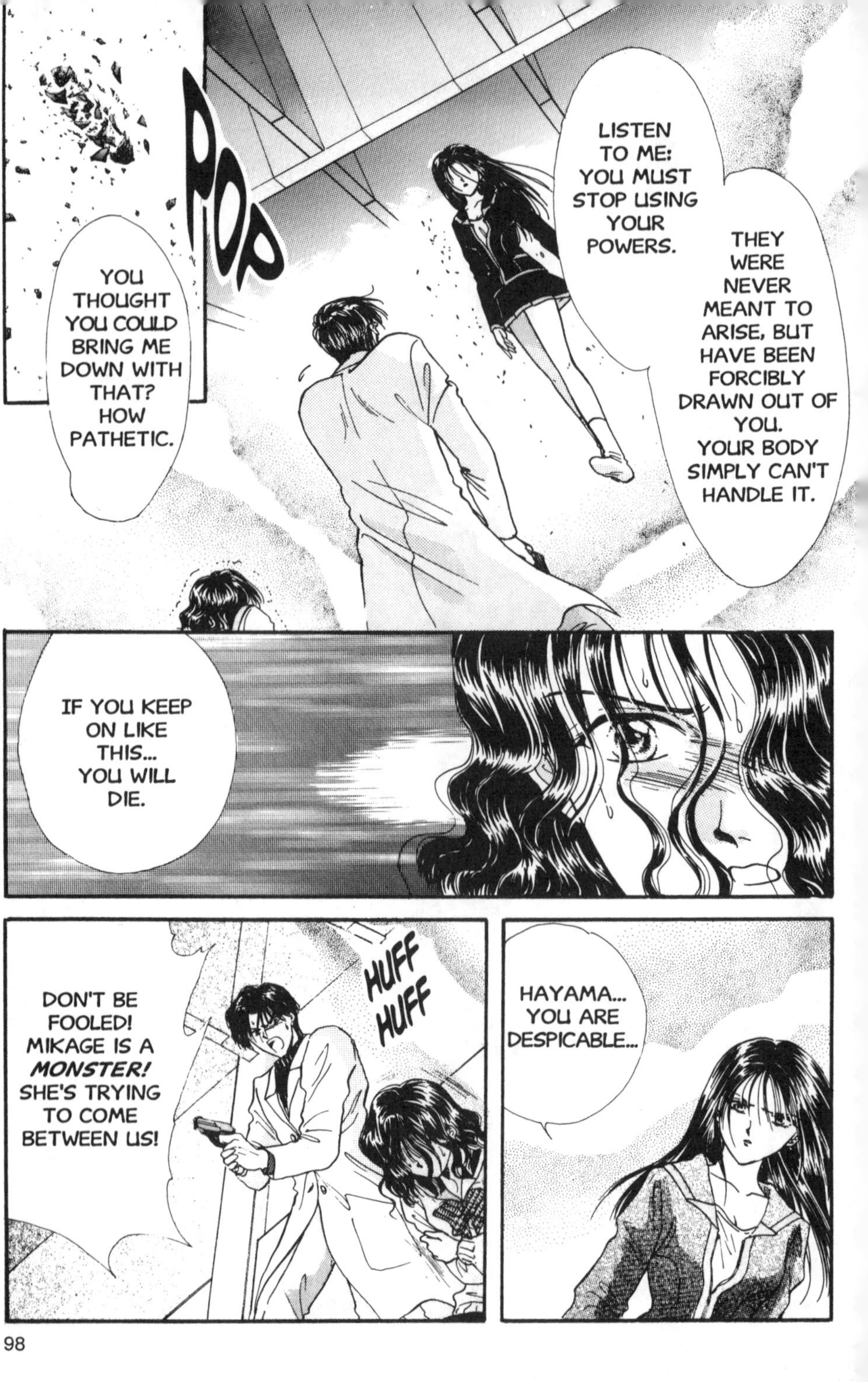
POP
YOU THOUGHT YOU COULD BRING ME DOWN WITH THAT? HOW PATHETIC.
LISTEN TO ME: YOU MUST STOP USING YOUR POWERS.
THEY WERE NEVER MEANT TO ARISE, BUT HAVE BEEN FORCIBLY DRAWN OUT OF YOU. YOUR BODY SIMPLY CAN'T HANDLE IT.
IF YOU KEEP ON LIKE THIS... YOU WILL DIE.
DON'T BE FOOLED! MIKAGE IS A *MONSTER!* SHE'S TRYING TO COME BETWEEN US!
HUFF HUFF
HAYAMA... YOU ARE DESPICABLE...

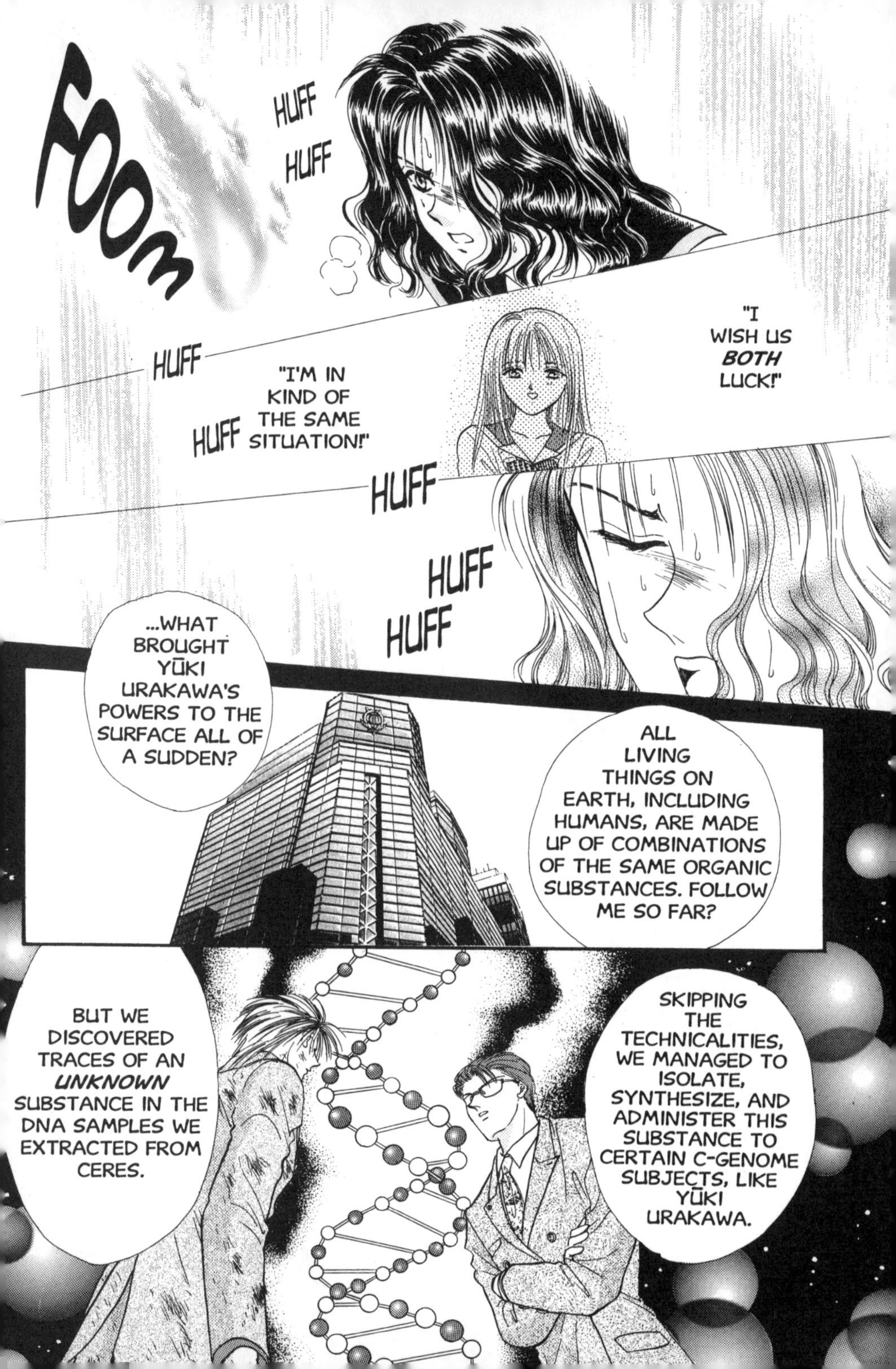
FOOM
HUFF
HUFF
HUFF
HUFF
"I'M IN KIND OF THE SAME SITUATION!"
"I WISH US *BOTH* LUCK!"
HUFF
HUFF
HUFF
...WHAT BROUGHT YŪKI URAKAWA'S POWERS TO THE SURFACE ALL OF A SUDDEN?
ALL LIVING THINGS ON EARTH, INCLUDING HUMANS, ARE MADE UP OF COMBINATIONS OF THE SAME ORGANIC SUBSTANCES. FOLLOW ME SO FAR?
BUT WE DISCOVERED TRACES OF AN *UNKNOWN* SUBSTANCE IN THE DNA SAMPLES WE EXTRACTED FROM CERES.
SKIPPING THE TECHNICALITIES, WE MANAGED TO ISOLATE, SYNTHESIZE, AND ADMINISTER THIS SUBSTANCE TO CERTAIN C-GENOME SUBJECTS, LIKE YŪKI URAKAWA.

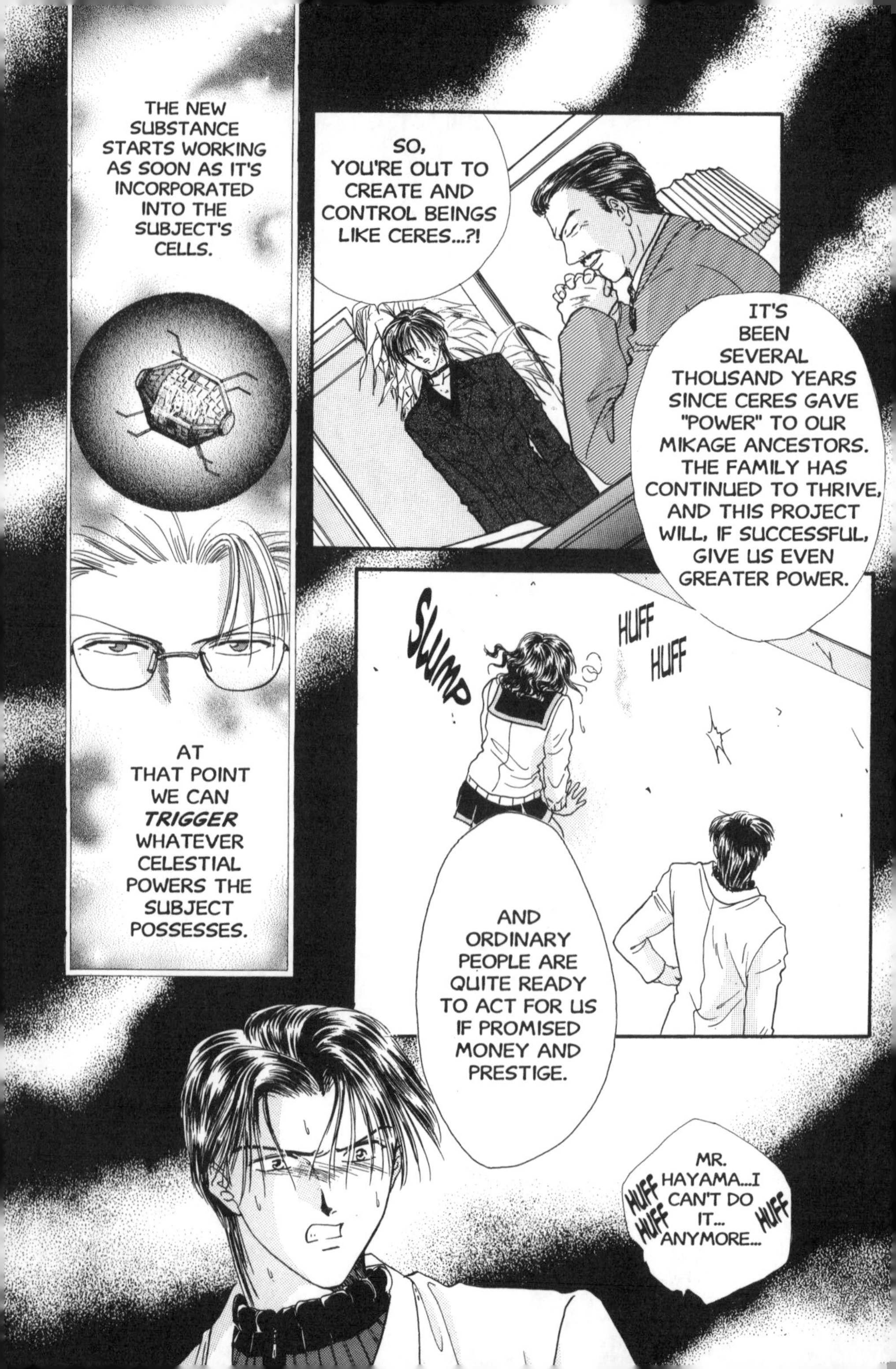
THE NEW SUBSTANCE STARTS WORKING AS SOON AS IT'S INCORPORATED INTO THE SUBJECT'S CELLS.
AT THAT POINT WE CAN *TRIGGER* WHATEVER CELESTIAL POWERS THE SUBJECT POSSESSES.
SO, YOU'RE OUT TO CREATE AND CONTROL BEINGS LIKE CERES...?!
IT'S BEEN SEVERAL THOUSAND YEARS SINCE CERES GAVE "POWER" TO OUR MIKAGE ANCESTORS. THE FAMILY HAS CONTINUED TO THRIVE, AND THIS PROJECT WILL, IF SUCCESSFUL, GIVE US EVEN GREATER POWER.
SLUMP
HUFF HUFF
AND ORDINARY PEOPLE ARE QUITE READY TO ACT FOR US IF PROMISED MONEY AND PRESTIGE.
HUFF HUFF
MR. HAYAMA...I CAN'T DO IT... ANYMORE...
HUFF

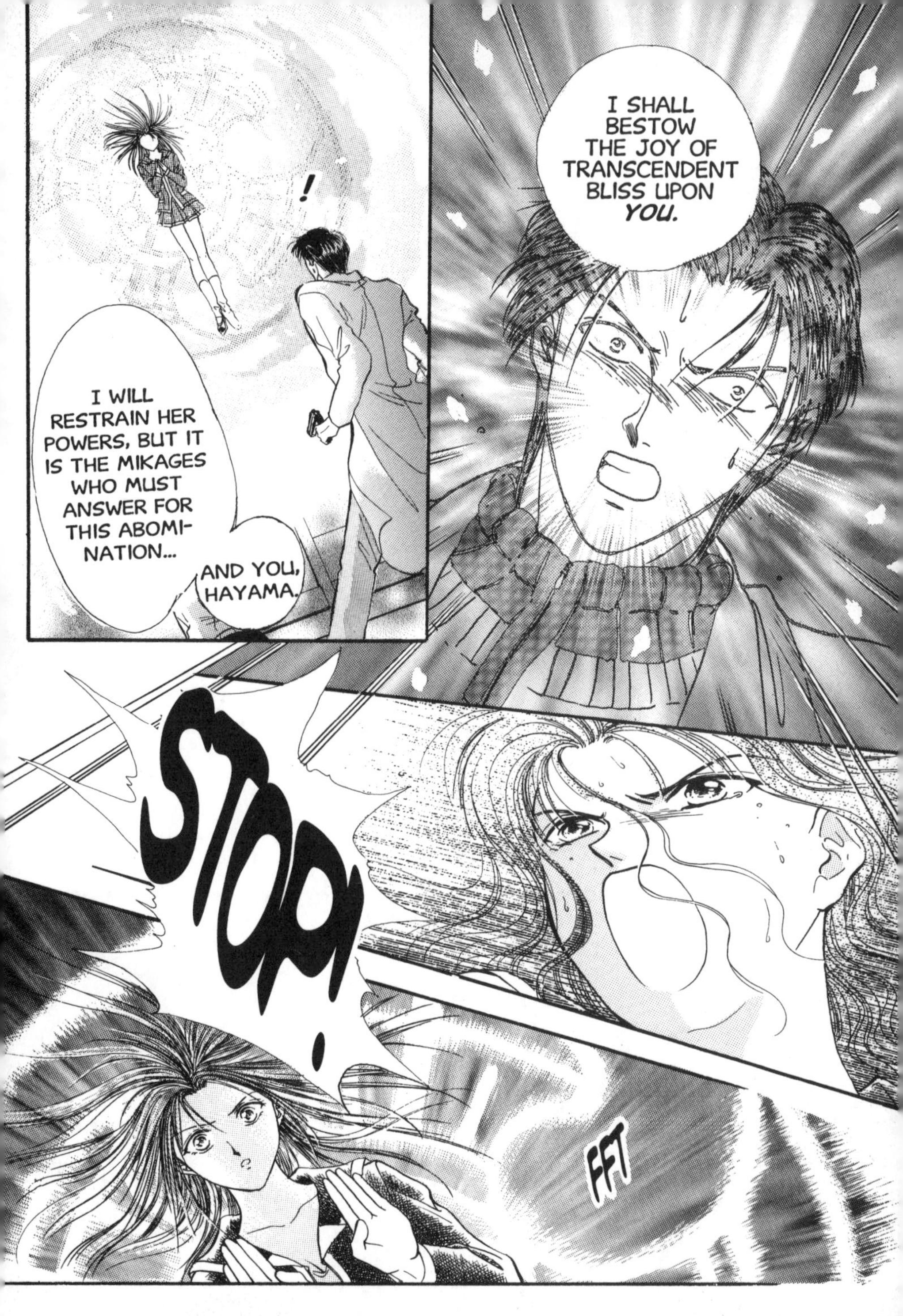
!
I WILL RESTRAIN HER POWERS, BUT IT IS THE MIKAGES WHO MUST ANSWER FOR THIS ABOMINATION...
AND YOU, HAYAMA.
I SHALL BESTOW THE JOY OF TRANSCENDENT BLISS UPON *YOU.*
STOP!
FFT

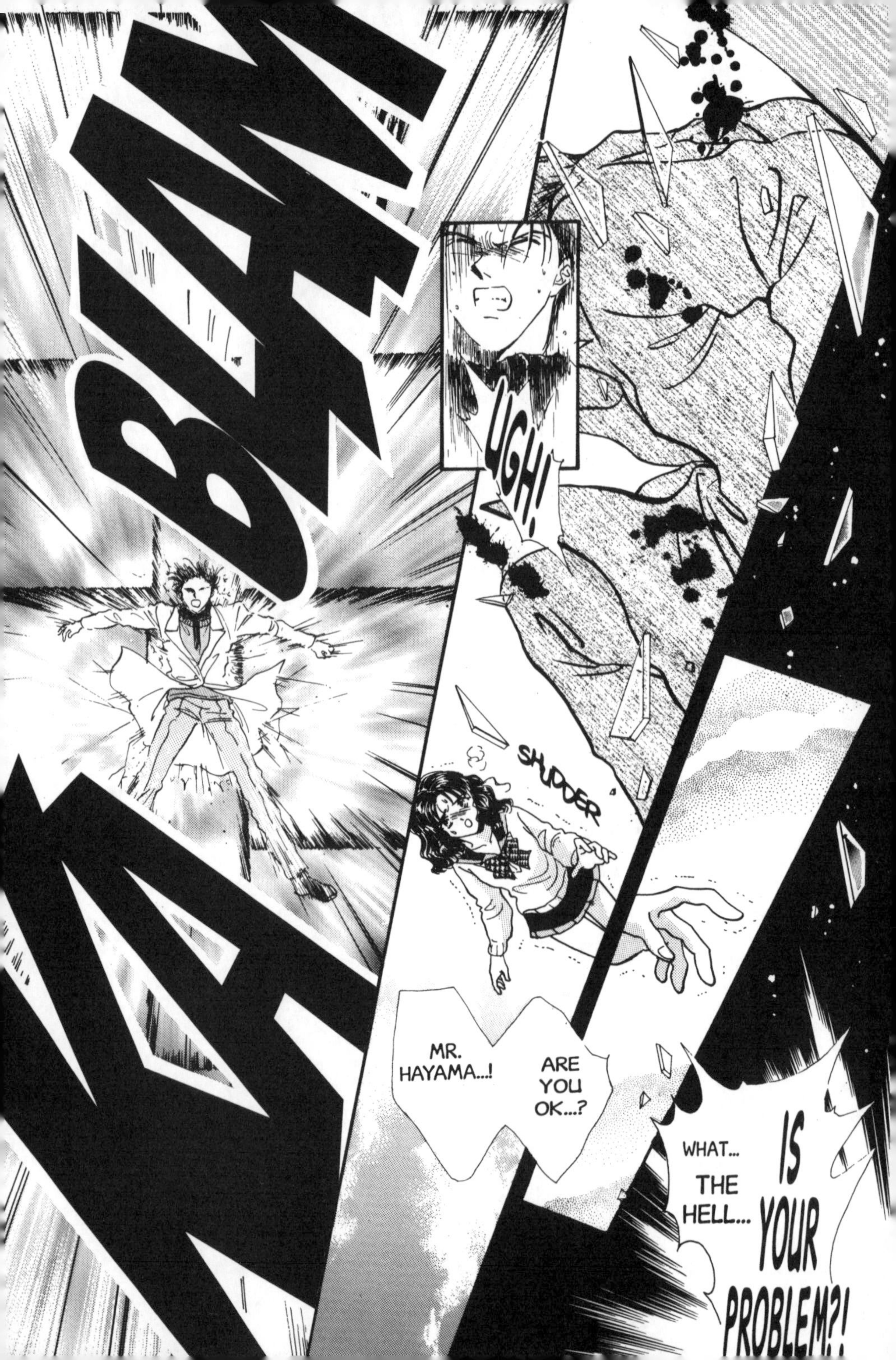

KA-BLAM!
UGH!
SHUDDER
MR. HAYAMA...!
ARE YOU OK...?
WHAT... THE HELL... IS YOUR PROBLEM?!

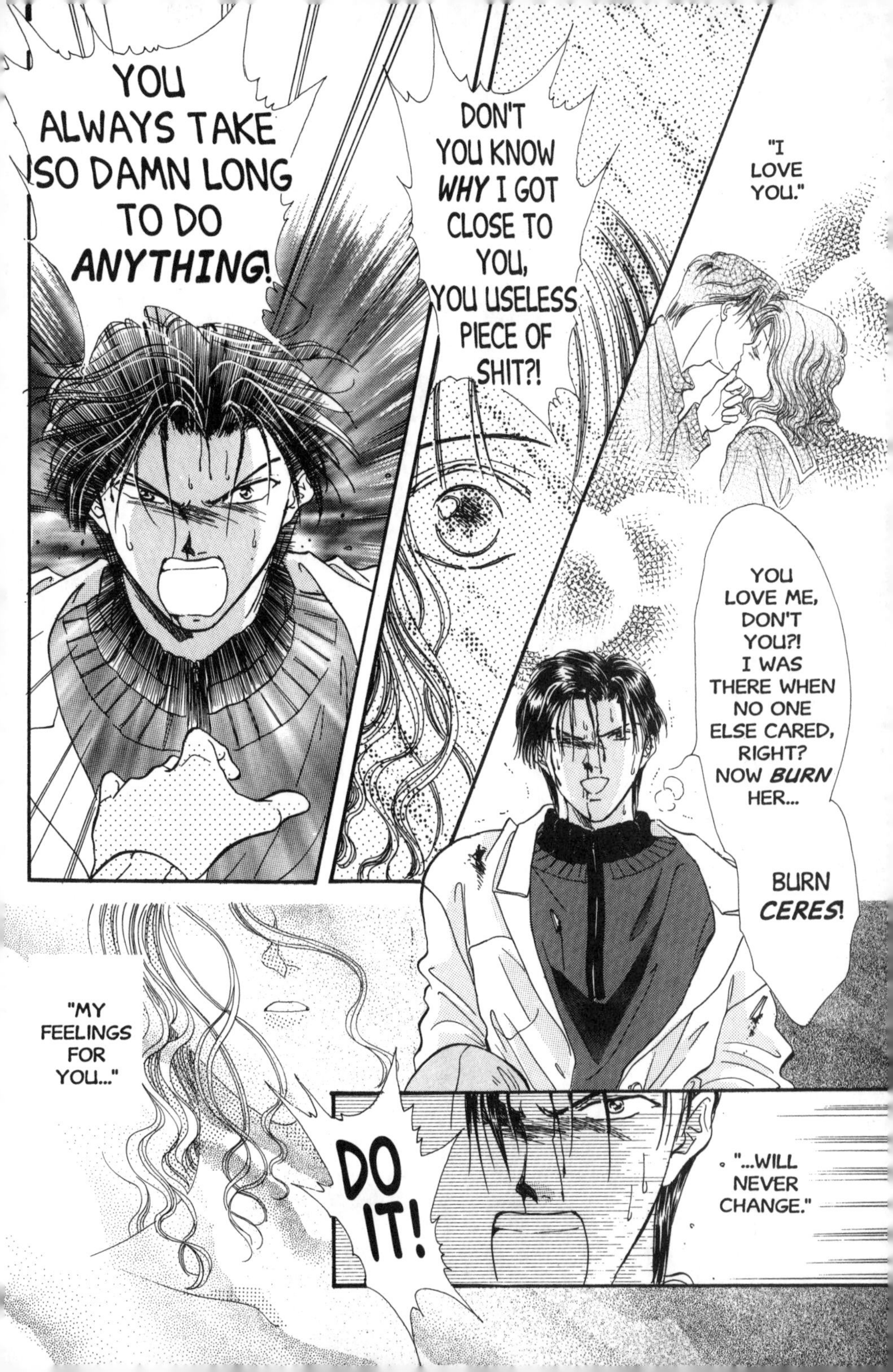
YOU ALWAYS TAKE SO DAMN LONG TO DO ANYTHING!
DON'T YOU KNOW WHY I GOT CLOSE TO YOU, YOU USELESS PIECE OF SHIT?!
"I LOVE YOU."
YOU LOVE ME, DON'T YOU?! I WAS THERE WHEN NO ONE ELSE CARED, RIGHT? NOW BURN HER...
BURN CERES!
"MY FEELINGS FOR YOU..."
DO IT!
"...WILL NEVER CHANGE."

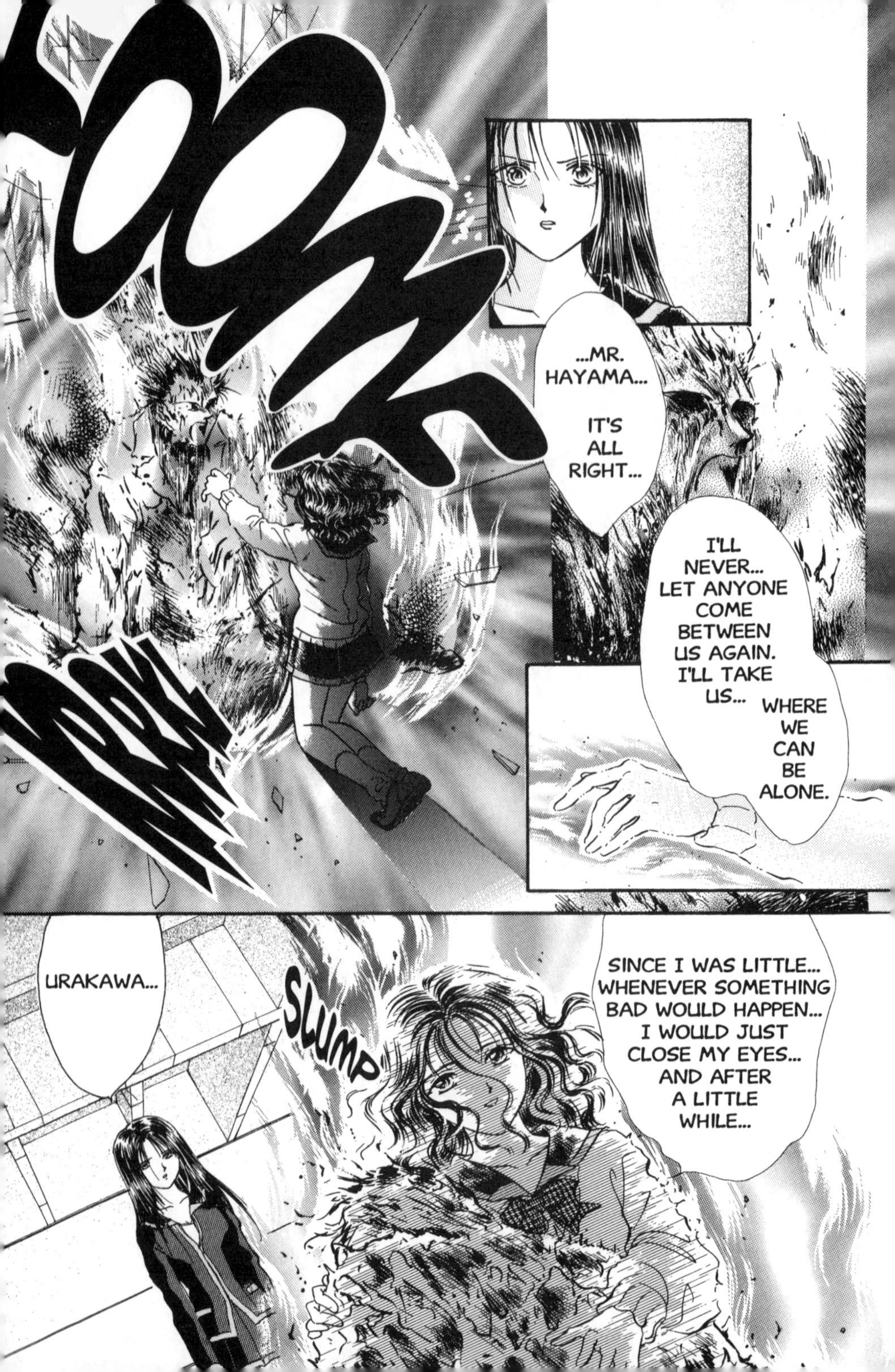
...MR. HAYAMA...
IT'S ALL RIGHT...
I'LL NEVER... LET ANYONE COME BETWEEN US AGAIN. I'LL TAKE US...
WHERE WE CAN BE ALONE.
URAKAWA...
SLUMP
SINCE I WAS LITTLE... WHENEVER SOMETHING BAD WOULD HAPPEN... I WOULD JUST CLOSE MY EYES... AND AFTER A LITTLE WHILE...

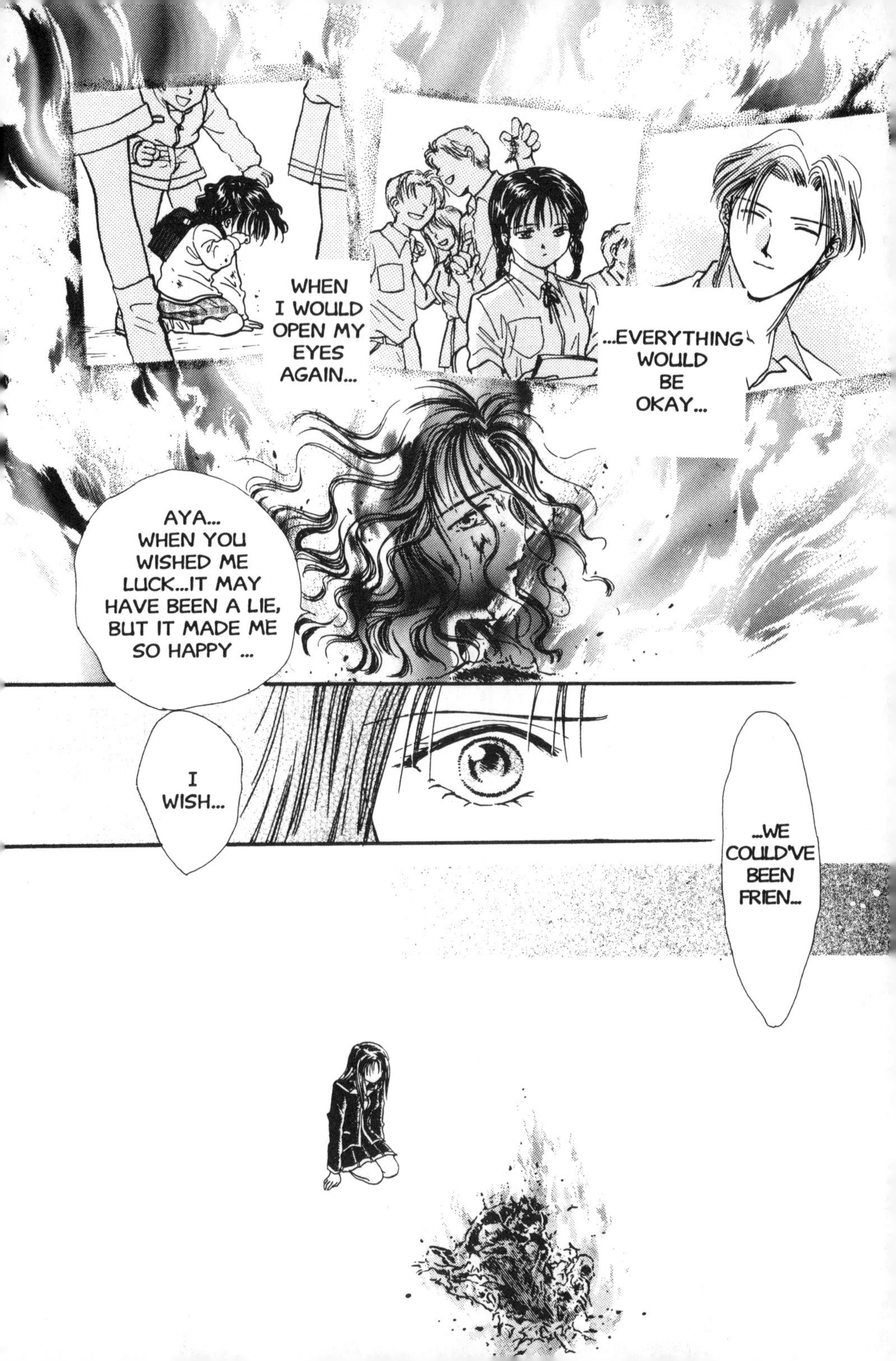
WHEN I WOULD OPEN MY EYES AGAIN...
...EVERYTHING WOULD BE OKAY...
AYA... WHEN YOU WISHED ME LUCK...IT MAY HAVE BEEN A LIE, BUT IT MADE ME SO HAPPY ...
I WISH...
...WE COULD'VE BEEN FRIEN...

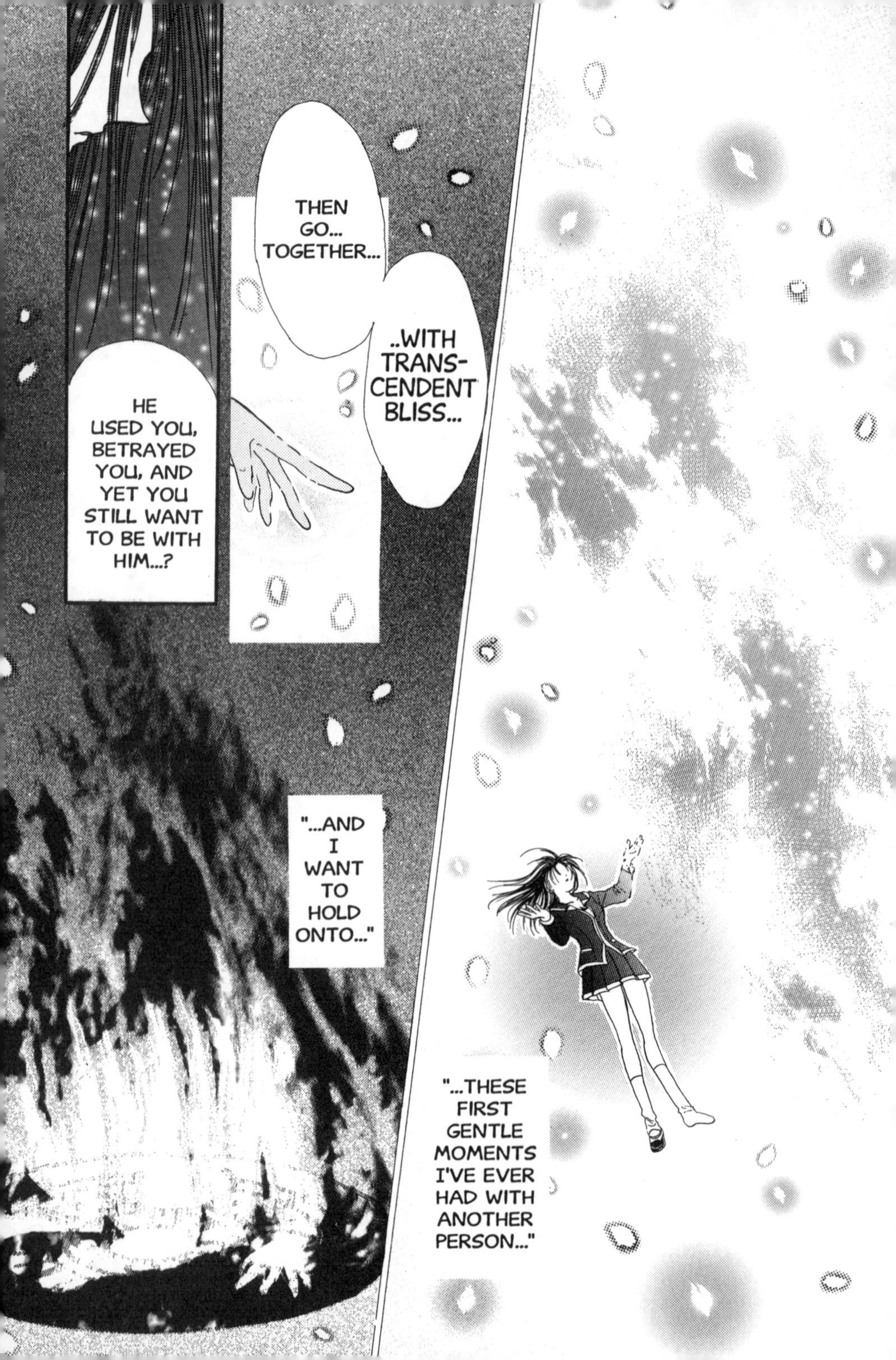
HE USED YOU, BETRAYED YOU, AND YET YOU STILL WANT TO BE WITH HIM...?
THEN GO... TOGETHER...
..WITH TRANS-CENDENT BLISS...
"...AND I WANT TO HOLD ONTO..."
"...THESE FIRST GENTLE MOMENTS I'VE EVER HAD WITH ANOTHER PERSON..."

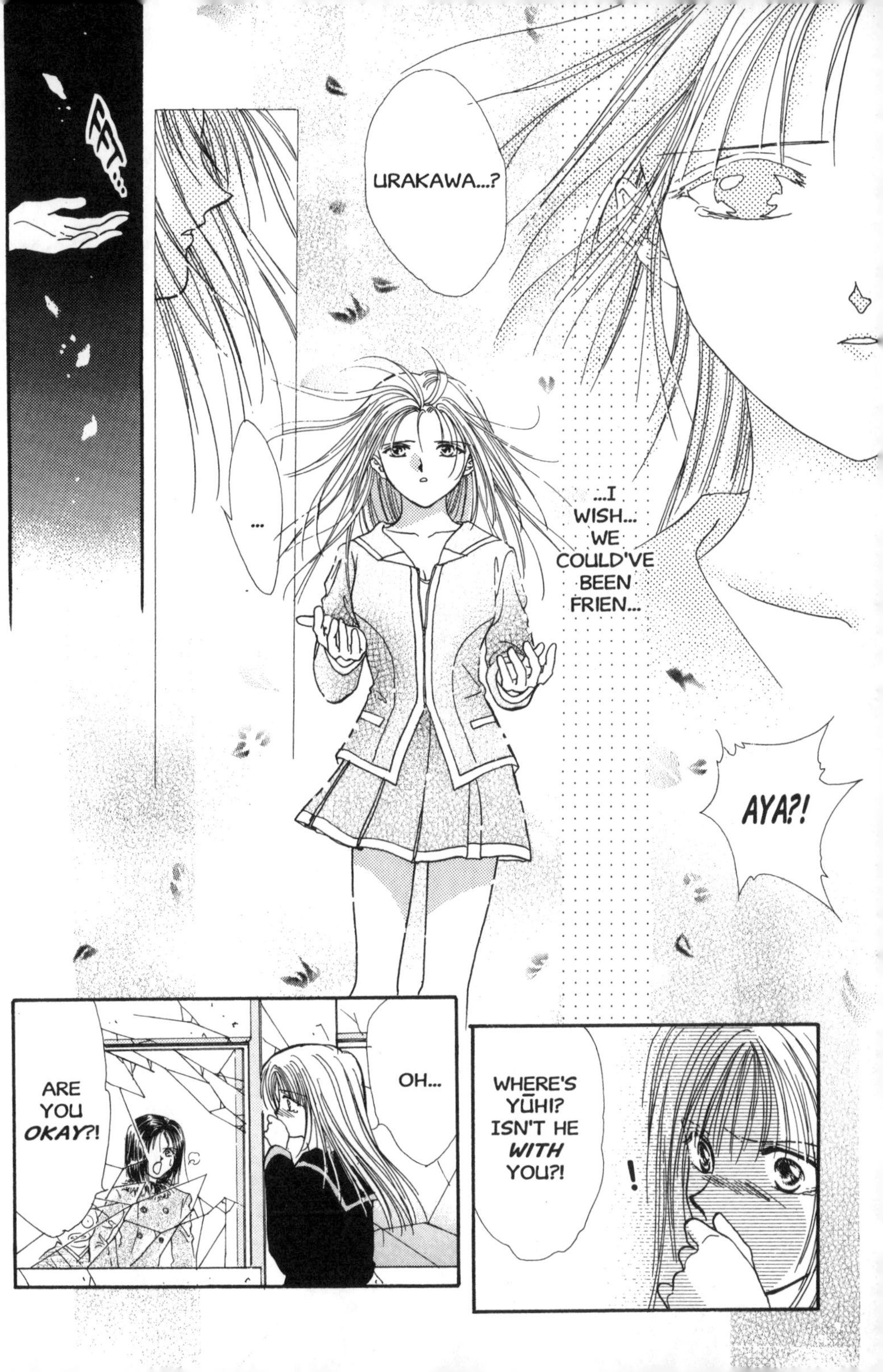
FFT...
URAKAWA...?
...
...I WISH... WE COULD'VE BEEN FRIEN...
AYA?!
ARE YOU OKAY?!
OH...
WHERE'S YŪHI? ISN'T HE WITH YOU?!
!

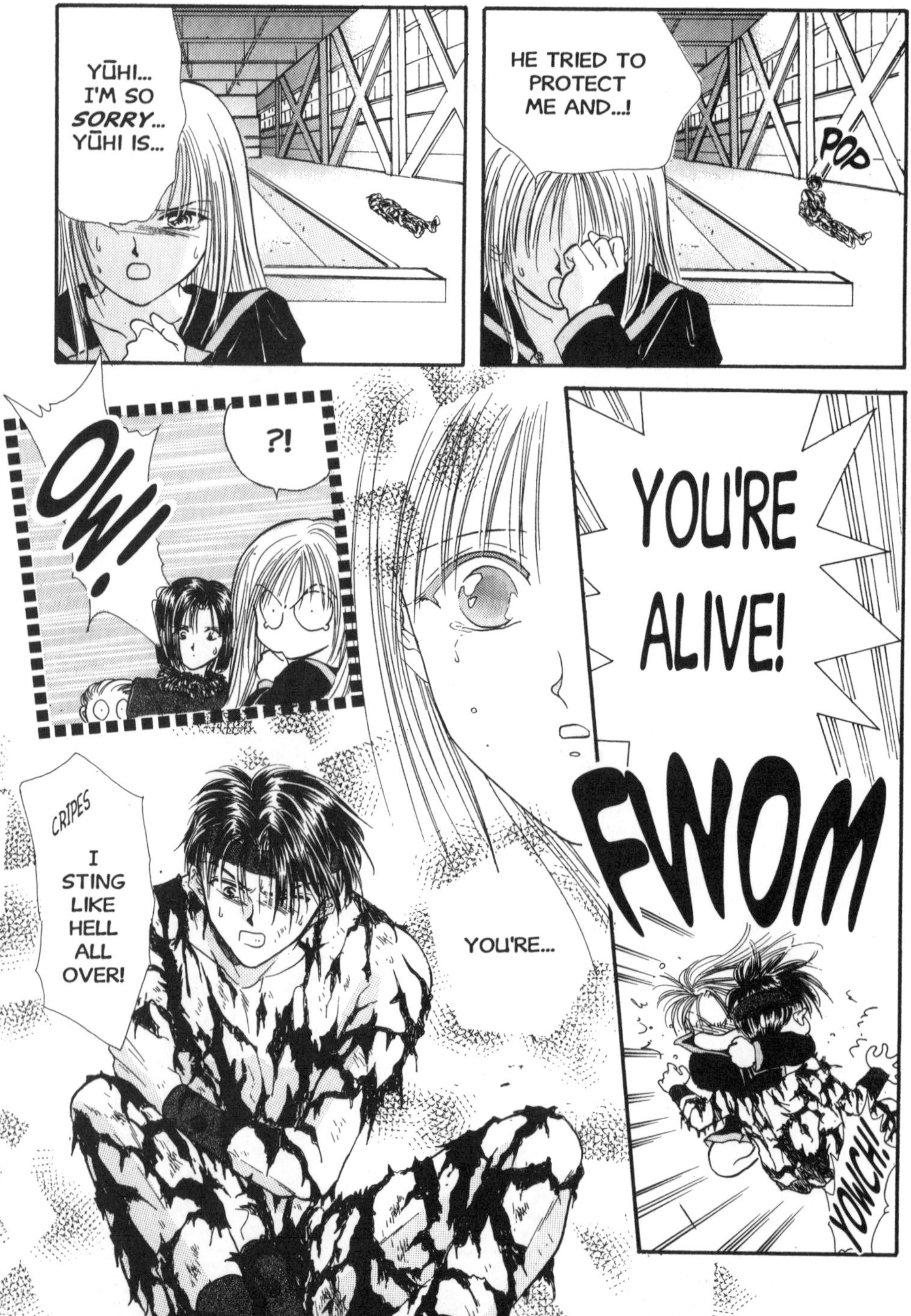
YŪHI... I'M SO *SORRY*... YŪHI IS...
HE TRIED TO PROTECT ME AND...!
POP
OW!
?!
CRIPES
I STING LIKE HELL ALL OVER!
YOU'RE...
YOU'RE ALIVE!
FWOM
YOWCH!

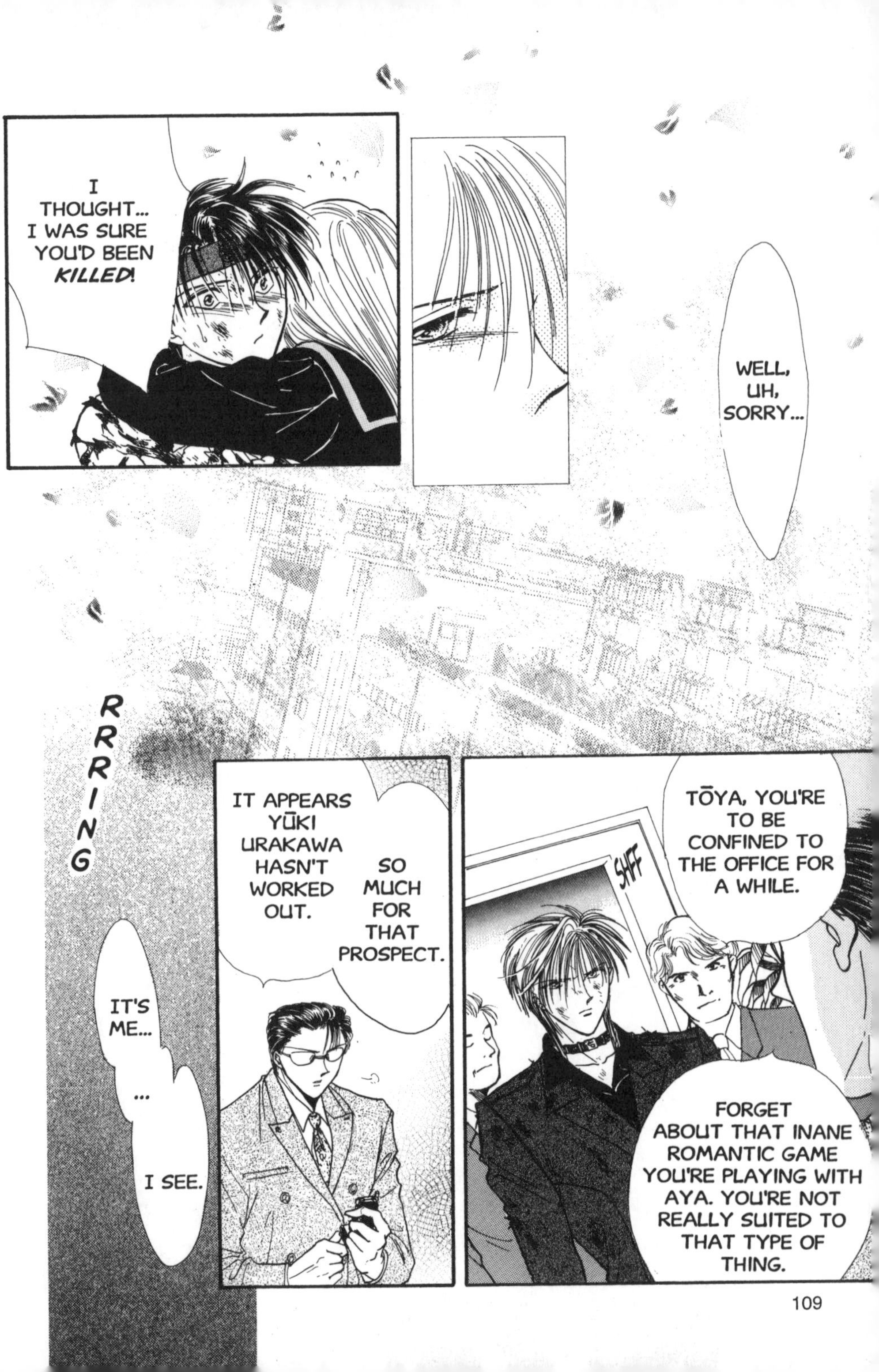

I THOUGHT... I WAS SURE YOU'D BEEN *KILLED*!
WELL, UH, SORRY...
RRRING
IT'S ME...
...
I SEE.
IT APPEARS YŪKI URAKAWA HASN'T WORKED OUT.
SO MUCH FOR THAT PROSPECT.
TŌYA, YOU'RE TO BE CONFINED TO THE OFFICE FOR A WHILE.
SHFF
FORGET ABOUT THAT INANE ROMANTIC GAME YOU'RE PLAYING WITH AYA. YOU'RE NOT REALLY SUITED TO THAT TYPE OF THING.

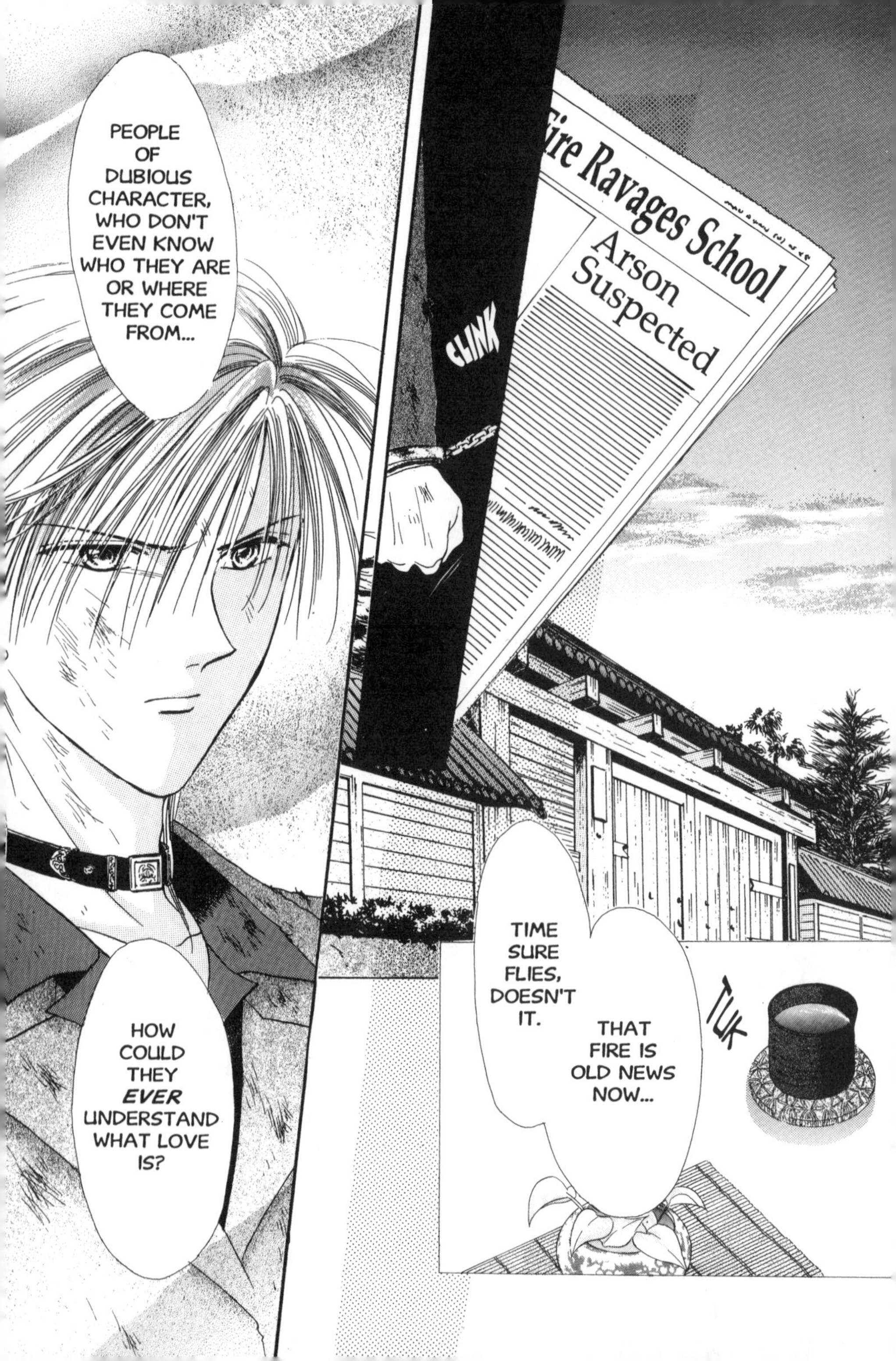
PEOPLE OF DUBIOUS CHARACTER, WHO DON'T EVEN KNOW WHO THEY ARE OR WHERE THEY COME FROM...
HOW COULD THEY *EVER* UNDERSTAND WHAT LOVE IS?
Fire Ravages School
Arson Suspected
CLINK
TIME SURE FLIES, DOESN'T IT.
THAT FIRE IS OLD NEWS NOW...
TUK

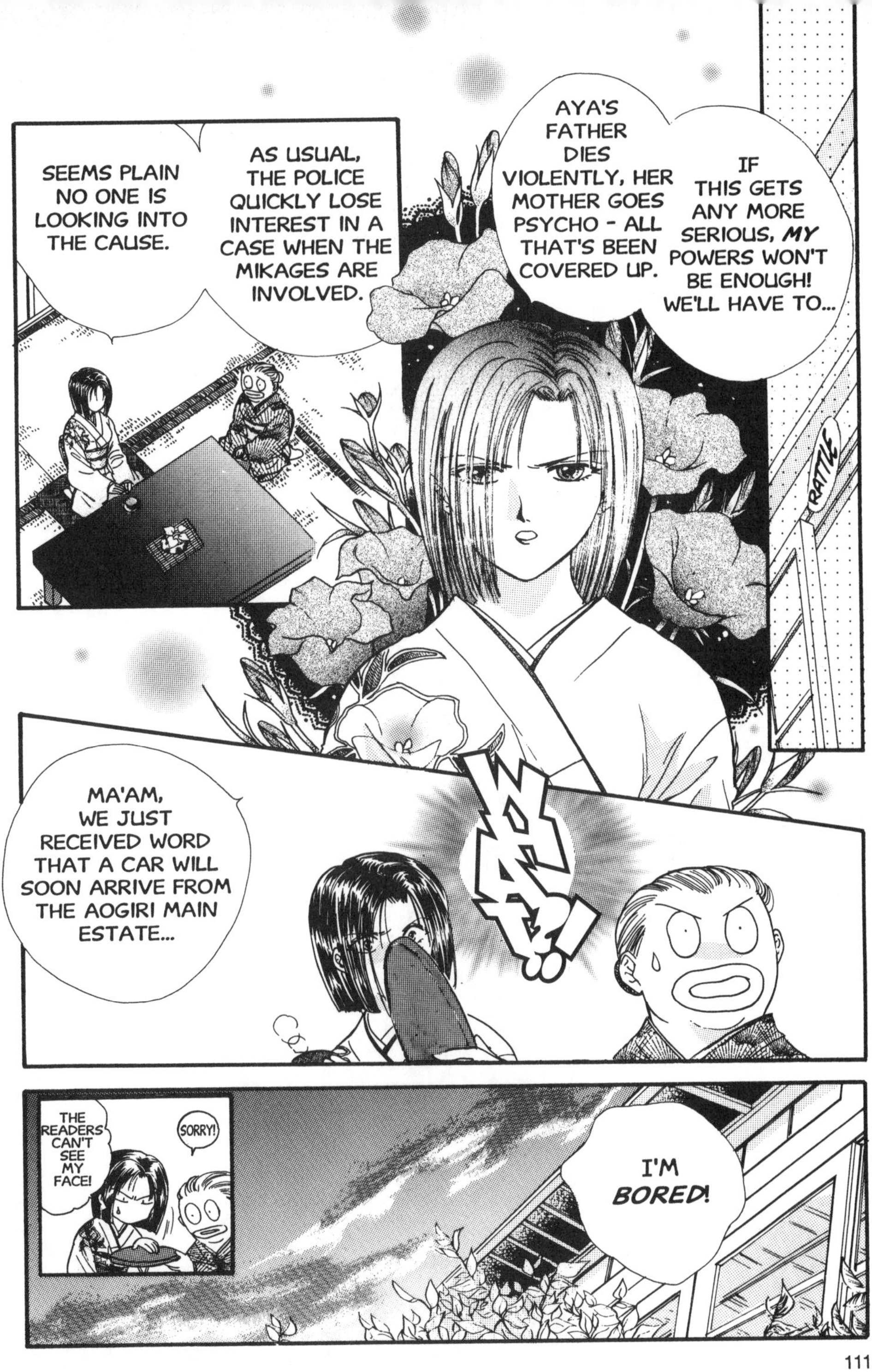
SEEMS PLAIN NO ONE IS LOOKING INTO THE CAUSE.
AS USUAL, THE POLICE QUICKLY LOSE INTEREST IN A CASE WHEN THE MIKAGES ARE INVOLVED.
AYA'S FATHER DIES VIOLENTLY, HER MOTHER GOES PSYCHO - ALL THAT'S BEEN COVERED UP.
IF THIS GETS ANY MORE SERIOUS, *MY* POWERS WON'T BE ENOUGH! WE'LL HAVE TO...
RATTLE
MA'AM, WE JUST RECEIVED WORD THAT A CAR WILL SOON ARRIVE FROM THE AOGIRI MAIN ESTATE...
THE READERS CAN'T SEE MY FACE!
SORRY!
I'M *BORED*!

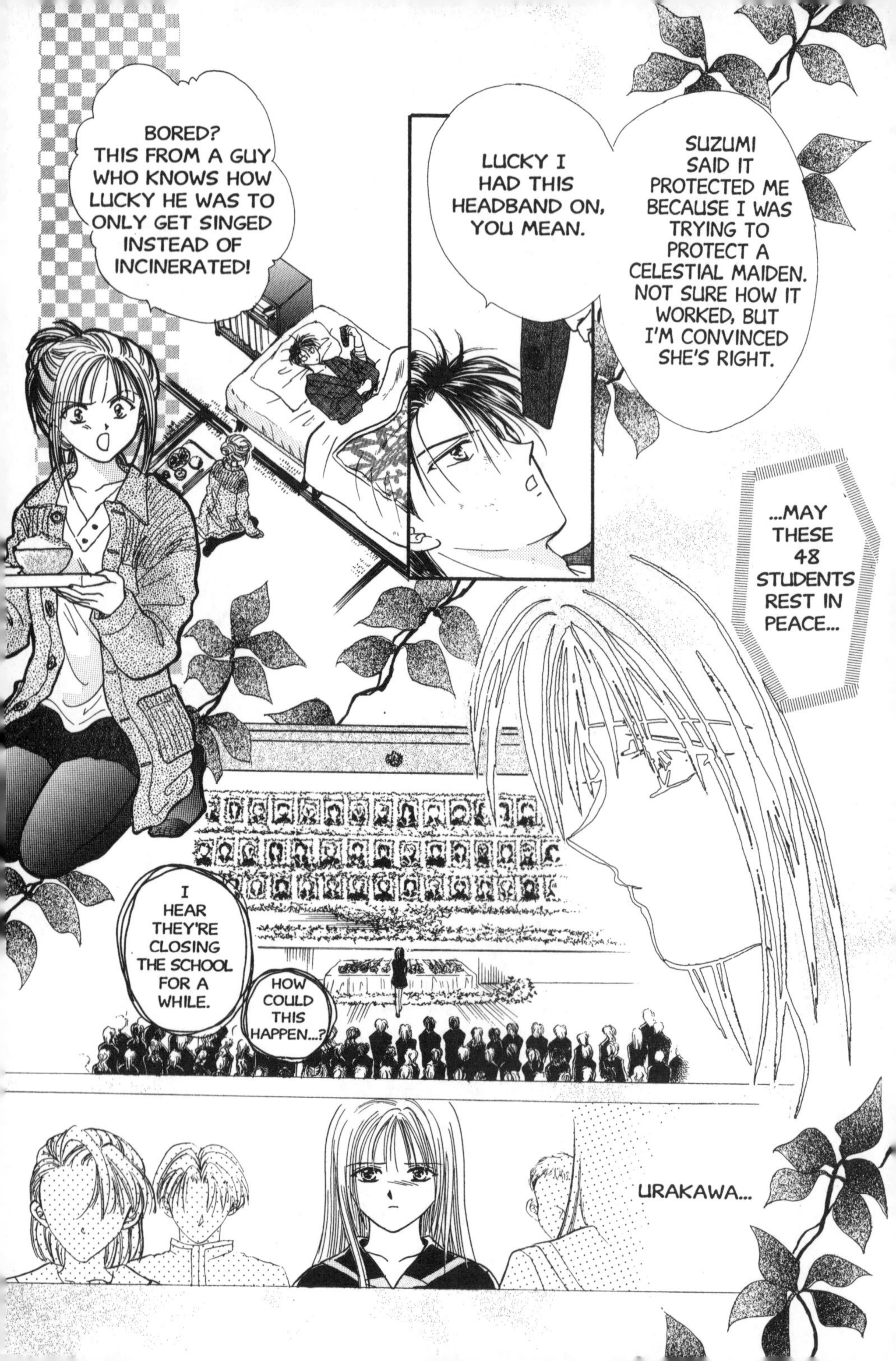
BORED? THIS FROM A GUY WHO KNOWS HOW LUCKY HE WAS TO ONLY GET SINGED INSTEAD OF INCINERATED!
LUCKY I HAD THIS HEADBAND ON, YOU MEAN.
SUZUMI SAID IT PROTECTED ME BECAUSE I WAS TRYING TO PROTECT A CELESTIAL MAIDEN. NOT SURE HOW IT WORKED, BUT I'M CONVINCED SHE'S RIGHT.
...MAY THESE 48 STUDENTS REST IN PEACE...
I HEAR THEY'RE CLOSING THE SCHOOL FOR A WHILE.
HOW COULD THIS HAPPEN...?
URAKAWA...

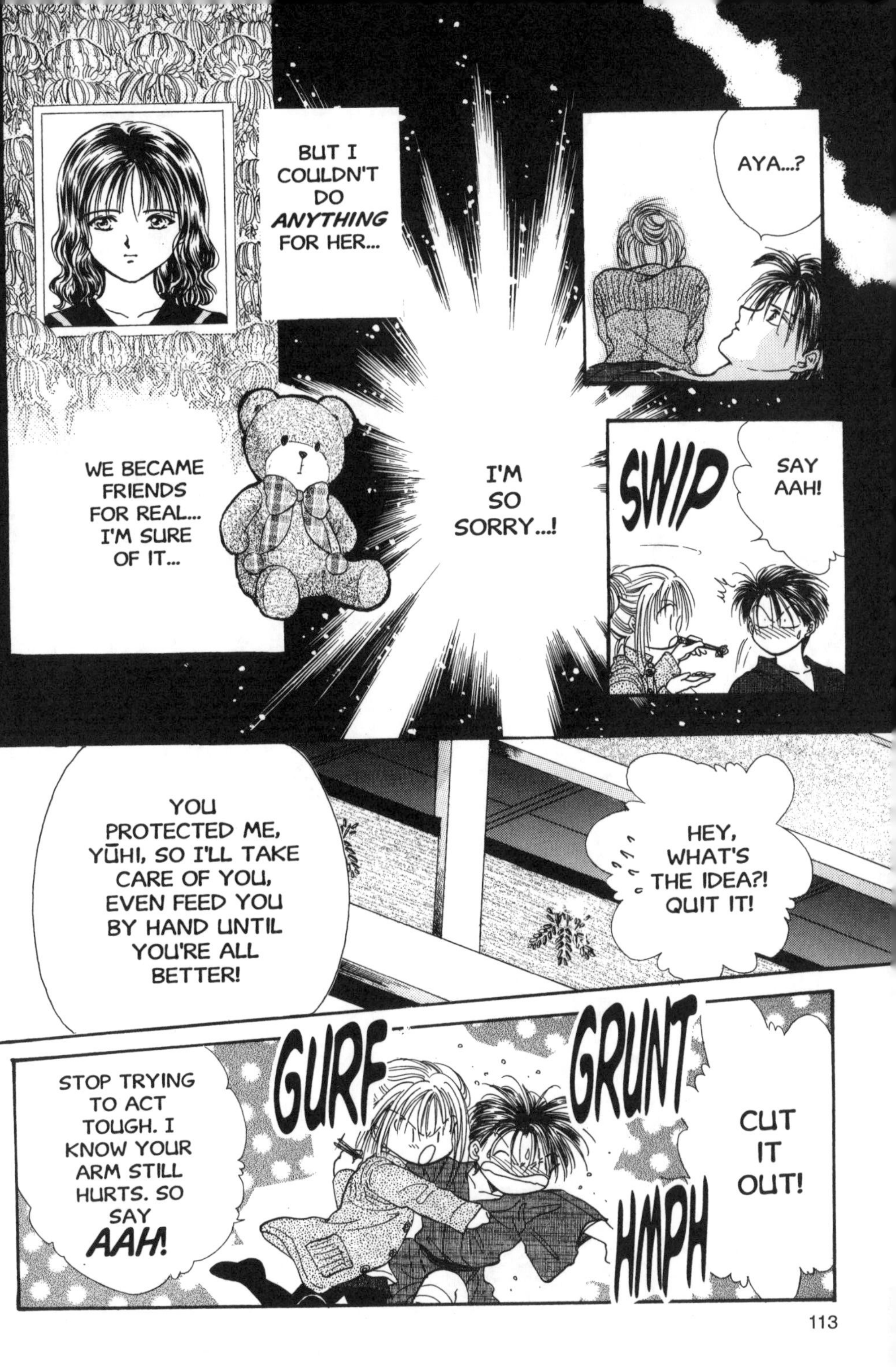
BUT I COULDN'T DO *ANYTHING* FOR HER...
WE BECAME FRIENDS FOR REAL... I'M SURE OF IT...
I'M SO SORRY...!
AYA...?
SWIP
SAY AAH!
YOU PROTECTED ME, YŪHI, SO I'LL TAKE CARE OF YOU, EVEN FEED YOU BY HAND UNTIL YOU'RE ALL BETTER!
HEY, WHAT'S THE IDEA?! QUIT IT!
STOP TRYING TO ACT TOUGH. I KNOW YOUR ARM STILL HURTS. SO SAY *AAH!*
GURF
GRUNT
HMPH
CUT IT OUT!

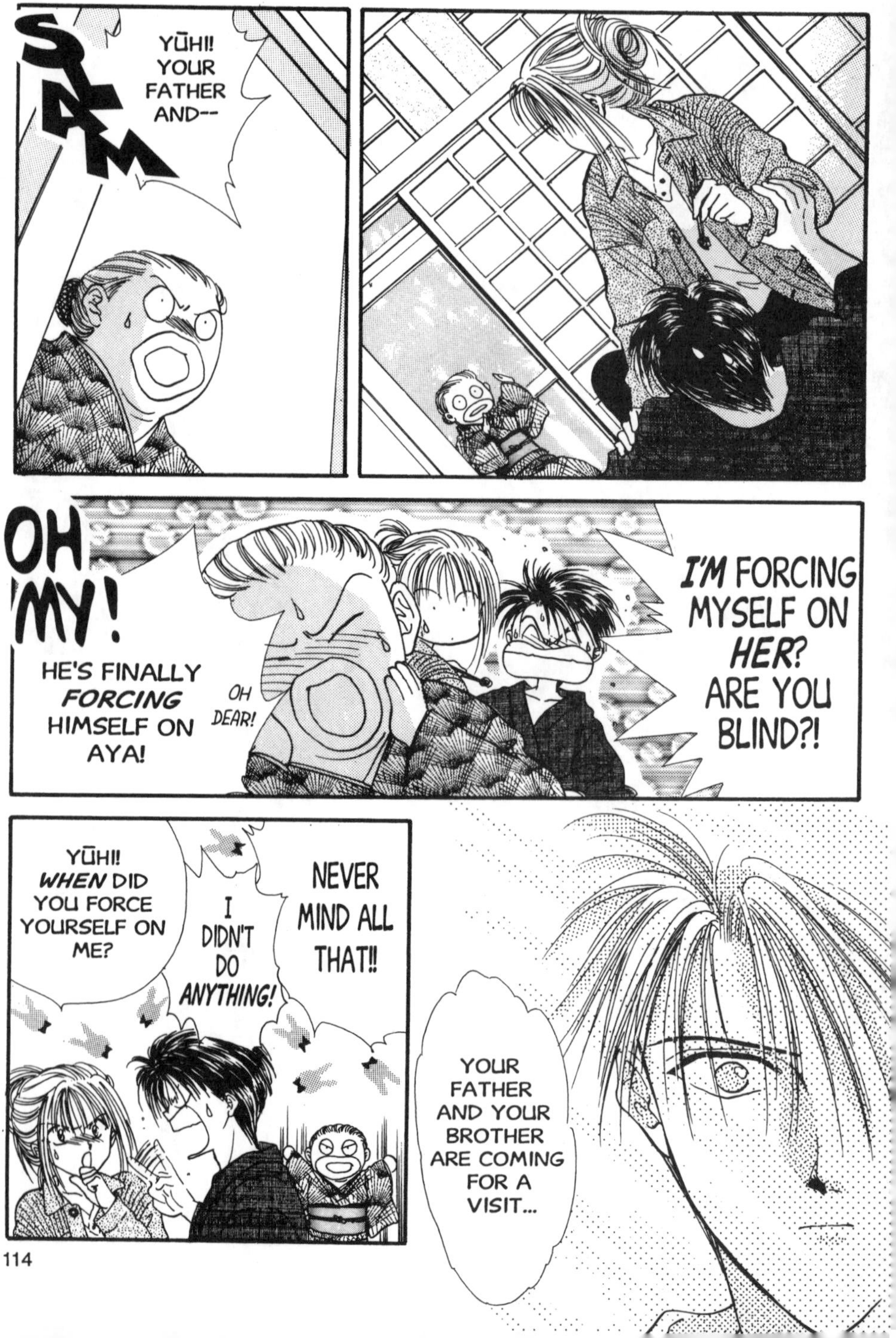
SLAM
YŪHI! YOUR FATHER AND--
OH MY!
HE'S FINALLY *FORCING* HIMSELF ON AYA!
OH DEAR!
I'M FORCING MYSELF ON *HER*? ARE YOU BLIND?!
YŪHI! *WHEN* DID YOU FORCE YOURSELF ON ME?
I DIDN'T DO *ANYTHING!*
NEVER MIND ALL THAT!!
YOUR FATHER AND YOUR BROTHER ARE COMING FOR A VISIT...

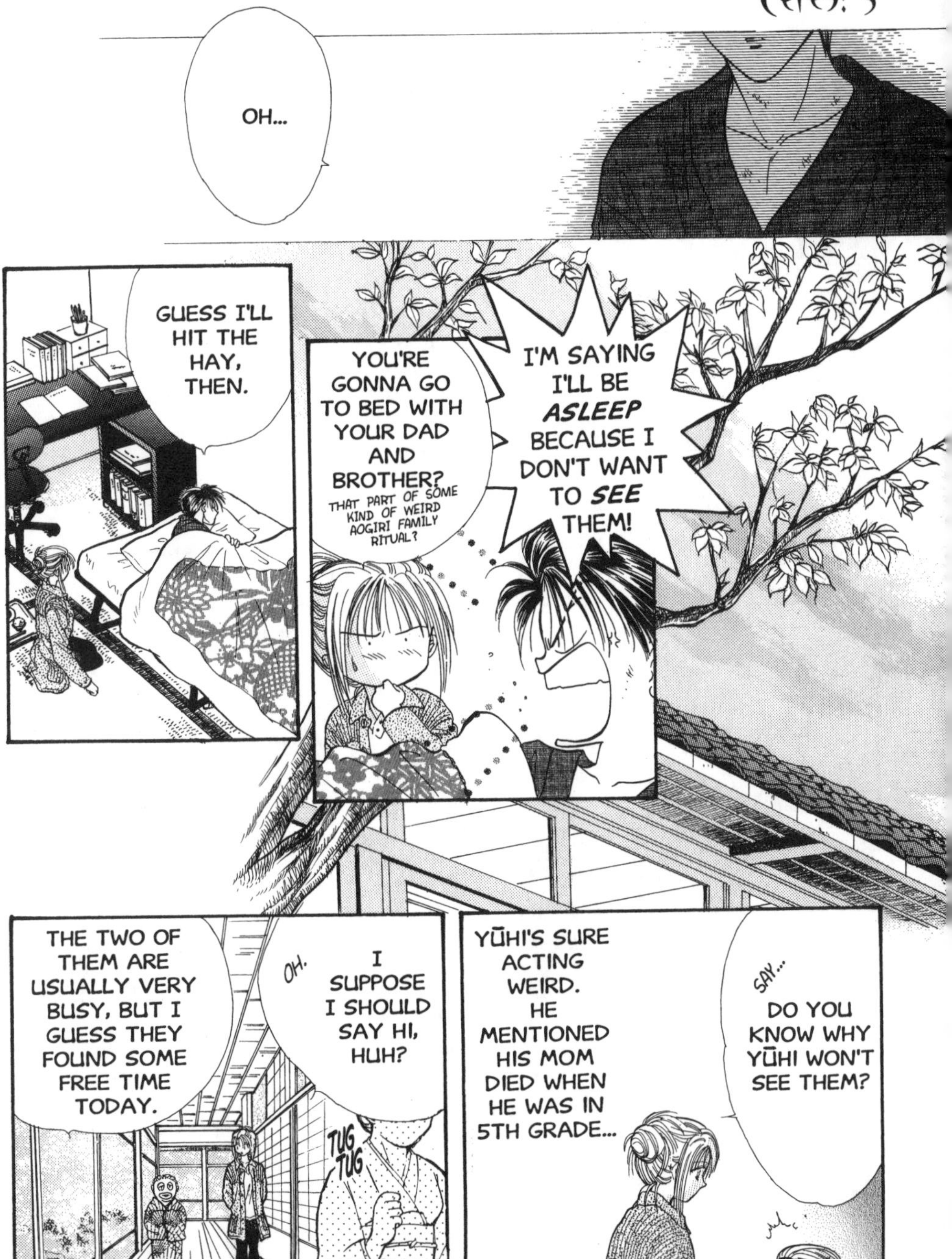
OH...
GUESS I'LL HIT THE HAY, THEN.
YOU'RE GONNA GO TO BED WITH YOUR DAD AND BROTHER? THAT PART OF SOME KIND OF WEIRD AOGIRI FAMILY RITUAL?
I'M SAYING I'LL BE ASLEEP BECAUSE I DON'T WANT TO SEE THEM!
THE TWO OF THEM ARE USUALLY VERY BUSY, BUT I GUESS THEY FOUND SOME FREE TIME TODAY.
OH. I SUPPOSE I SHOULD SAY HI, HUH?
TUG TUG
YŪHI'S SURE ACTING WEIRD. HE MENTIONED HIS MOM DIED WHEN HE WAS IN 5TH GRADE...
SAY... DO YOU KNOW WHY YŪHI WON'T SEE THEM?

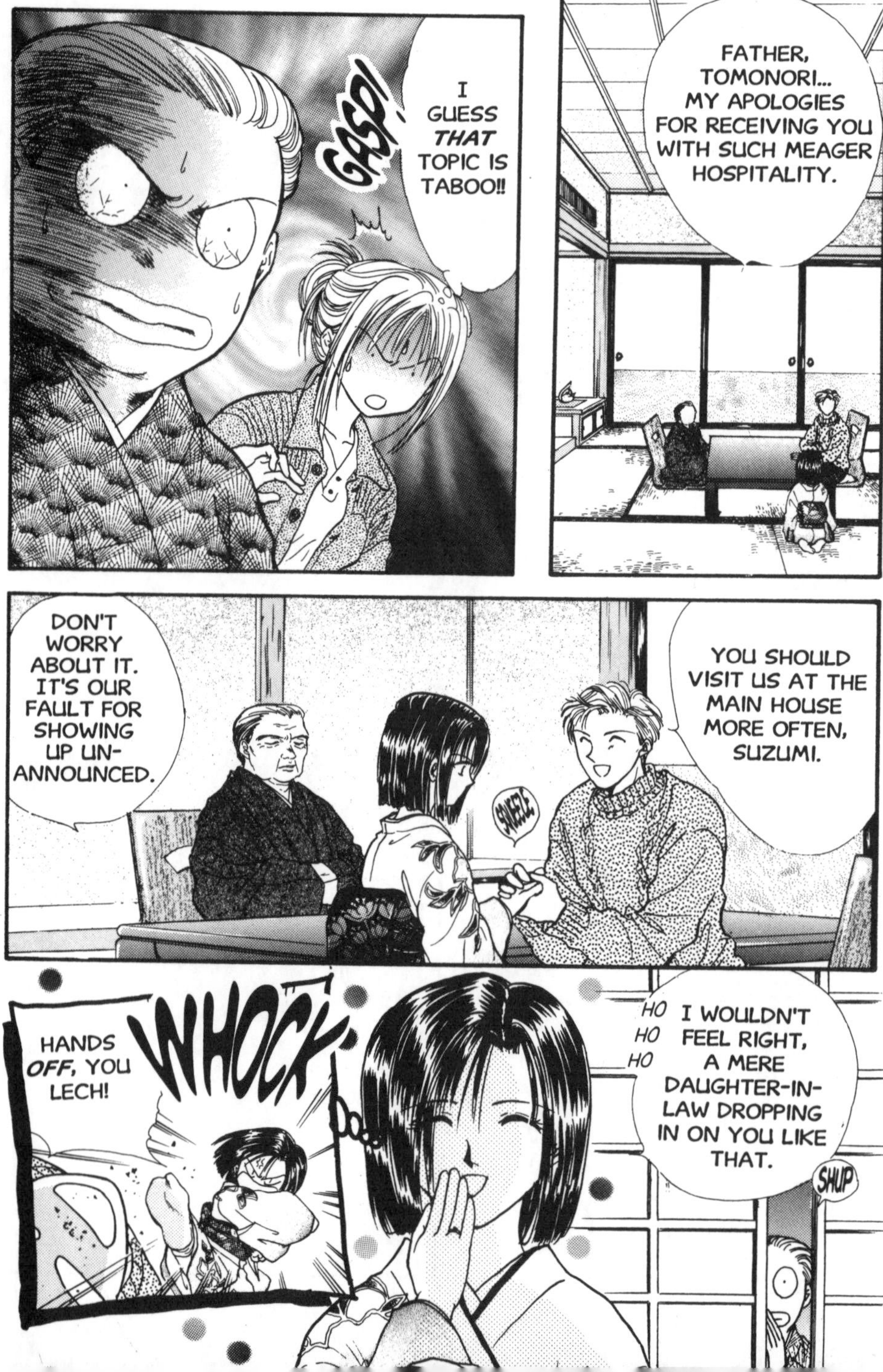
GASP!
I GUESS *THAT* TOPIC IS TABOO!!
FATHER, TOMONORI... MY APOLOGIES FOR RECEIVING YOU WITH SUCH MEAGER HOSPITALITY.
DON'T WORRY ABOUT IT. IT'S OUR FAULT FOR SHOWING UP UN-ANNOUNCED.
SQUEEZE
YOU SHOULD VISIT US AT THE MAIN HOUSE MORE OFTEN, SUZUMI.
HANDS *OFF*, YOU LECH!
WHOCK
HO HO HO
I WOULDN'T FEEL RIGHT, A MERE DAUGHTER-IN-LAW DROPPING IN ON YOU LIKE THAT.
SHUP

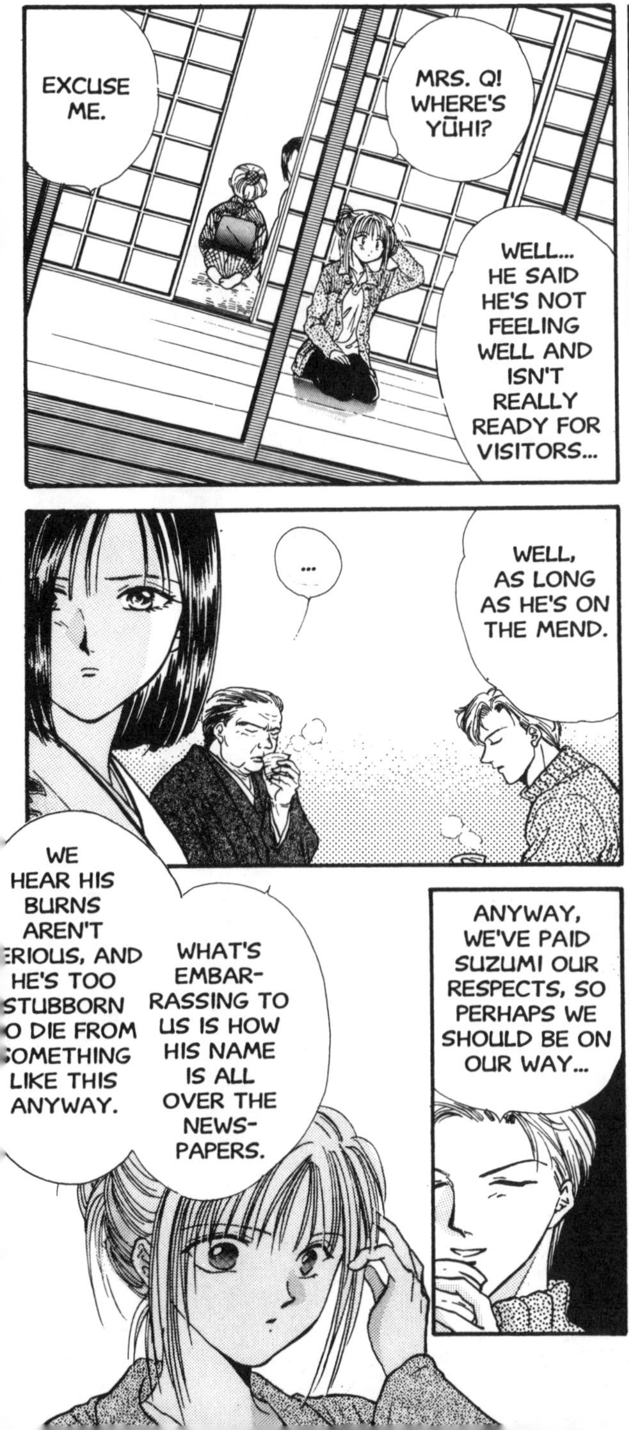
EXCUSE ME.
MRS. Q! WHERE'S YŪHI?
WELL... HE SAID HE'S NOT FEELING WELL AND ISN'T REALLY READY FOR VISITORS...
...
WELL, AS LONG AS HE'S ON THE MEND.
WE HEAR HIS BURNS AREN'T ERIOUS, AND HE'S TOO STUBBORN O DIE FROM OMETHING LIKE THIS ANYWAY.
WHAT'S EMBARRASSING TO US IS HOW HIS NAME IS ALL OVER THE NEWSPAPERS.
ANYWAY, WE'VE PAID SUZUMI OUR RESPECTS, SO PERHAPS WE SHOULD BE ON OUR WAY...

Although I only have a superficial understanding, maybe I can do a simple explanation of all the scientific terms when the tankōbon comes out. (Do I know enough to do that?) *Hmm...*

As for those clones I mentioned in the last sidebar, "monkey clones" came up on the news the other day. It's a huge controversy and people are protesting and saying, "Stop this now! Wouldn't it be terrible if they did this kind of research on humans!?"

So I asked the people at the laboratory about it, and they said, "It's like having your identical twin get born later." That wasn't how I had imagined it to be, so I was surprised.

A clone is "a copy," in other words, kind of like the robots in **Perman** a manga by Fujiko Fujio where kids have robots that look exactly like them, so that they can go off to save the world while their look-a-like robots attend school for them. (*what kind of example is that?*). You take one of your cells, and artificially create your clone from it... You know, it's like in old manga stories where they always show a person with an an exact duplicate of themselves. But when you think about it, you realize it's not possible...

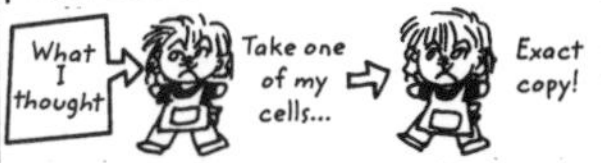
What I thought
Take one of my cells...
Exact copy!

When I get real busy, I complain that I need a clone of myself. But the life that would begin with that single cell has to start over from infancy. And furthermore, the cell would be as old as I am, so it's been used for 20-odd years and a little aged (cells die, and genes get worn out) so that's the kind of baby you'd get...

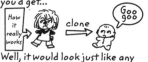

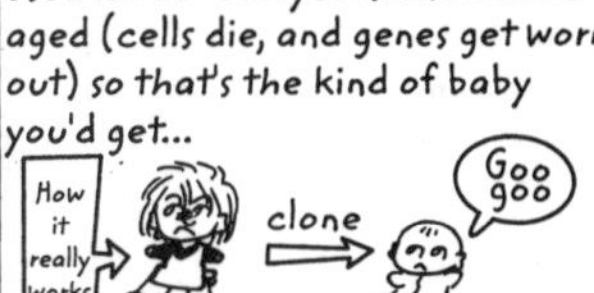
How it really works
clone
Goo goo

Well, it would look just like any other baby though.

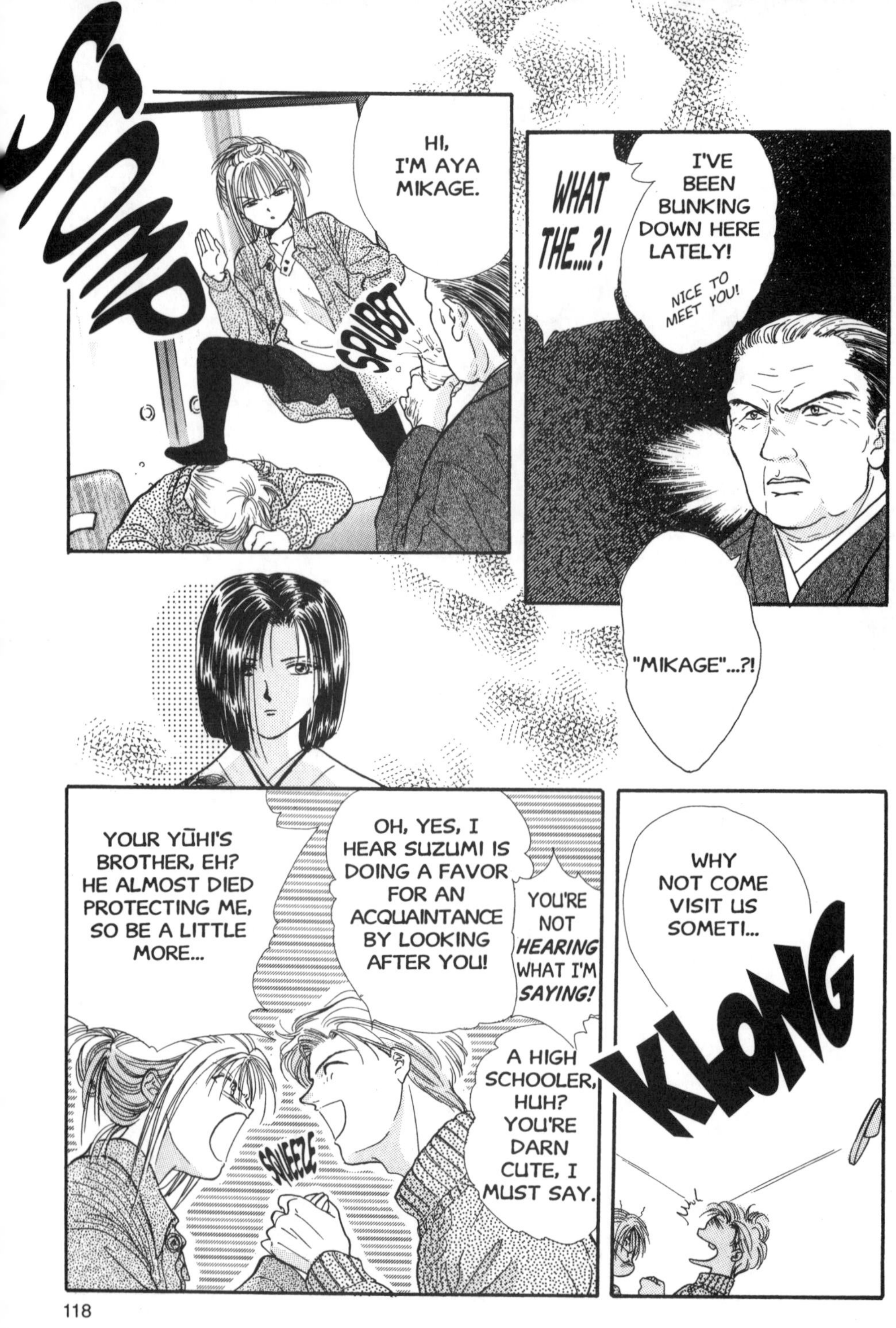
STOMP
HI, I'M AYA MIKAGE.
SPUBBT
WHAT THE...?!
I'VE BEEN BUNKING DOWN HERE LATELY!
NICE TO MEET YOU!
"MIKAGE"...?!
YOUR YŪHI'S BROTHER, EH? HE ALMOST DIED PROTECTING ME, SO BE A LITTLE MORE...
OH, YES, I HEAR SUZUMI IS DOING A FAVOR FOR AN ACQUAINTANCE BY LOOKING AFTER YOU!
YOU'RE NOT *HEARING* WHAT I'M *SAYING!*
A HIGH SCHOOLER, HUH? YOU'RE DARN CUTE, I MUST SAY.
SQUEEZE
WHY NOT COME VISIT US SOMETI...
KLONG

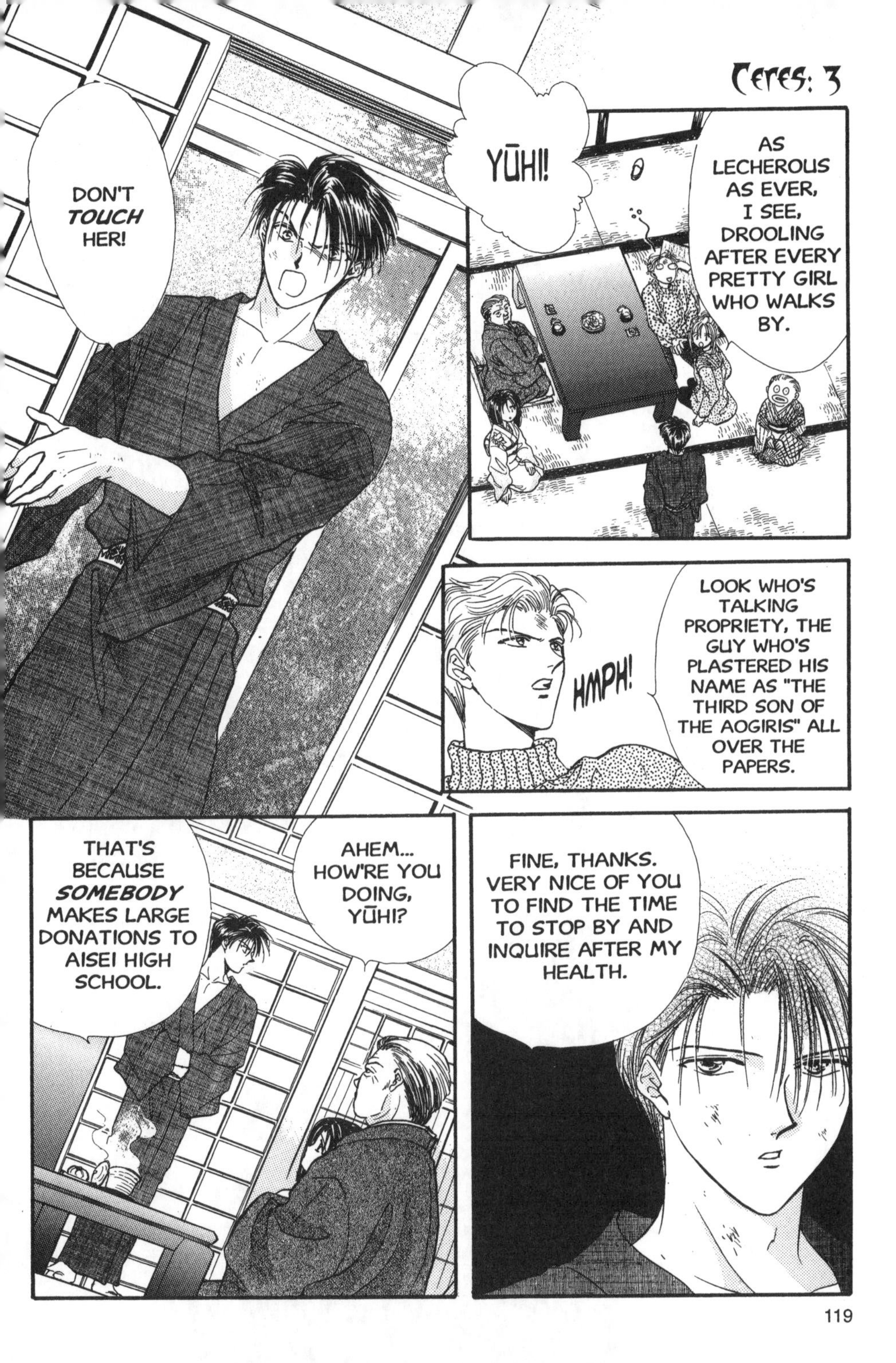
DON'T *TOUCH* HER!
YŪHI!
AS LECHEROUS AS EVER, I SEE, DROOLING AFTER EVERY PRETTY GIRL WHO WALKS BY.
HMPH!
LOOK WHO'S TALKING PROPRIETY, THE GUY WHO'S PLASTERED HIS NAME AS "THE THIRD SON OF THE AOGIRIS" ALL OVER THE PAPERS.
THAT'S BECAUSE *SOMEBODY* MAKES LARGE DONATIONS TO AISEI HIGH SCHOOL.
AHEM... HOW'RE YOU DOING, YŪHI?
FINE, THANKS. VERY NICE OF YOU TO FIND THE TIME TO STOP BY AND INQUIRE AFTER MY HEALTH.

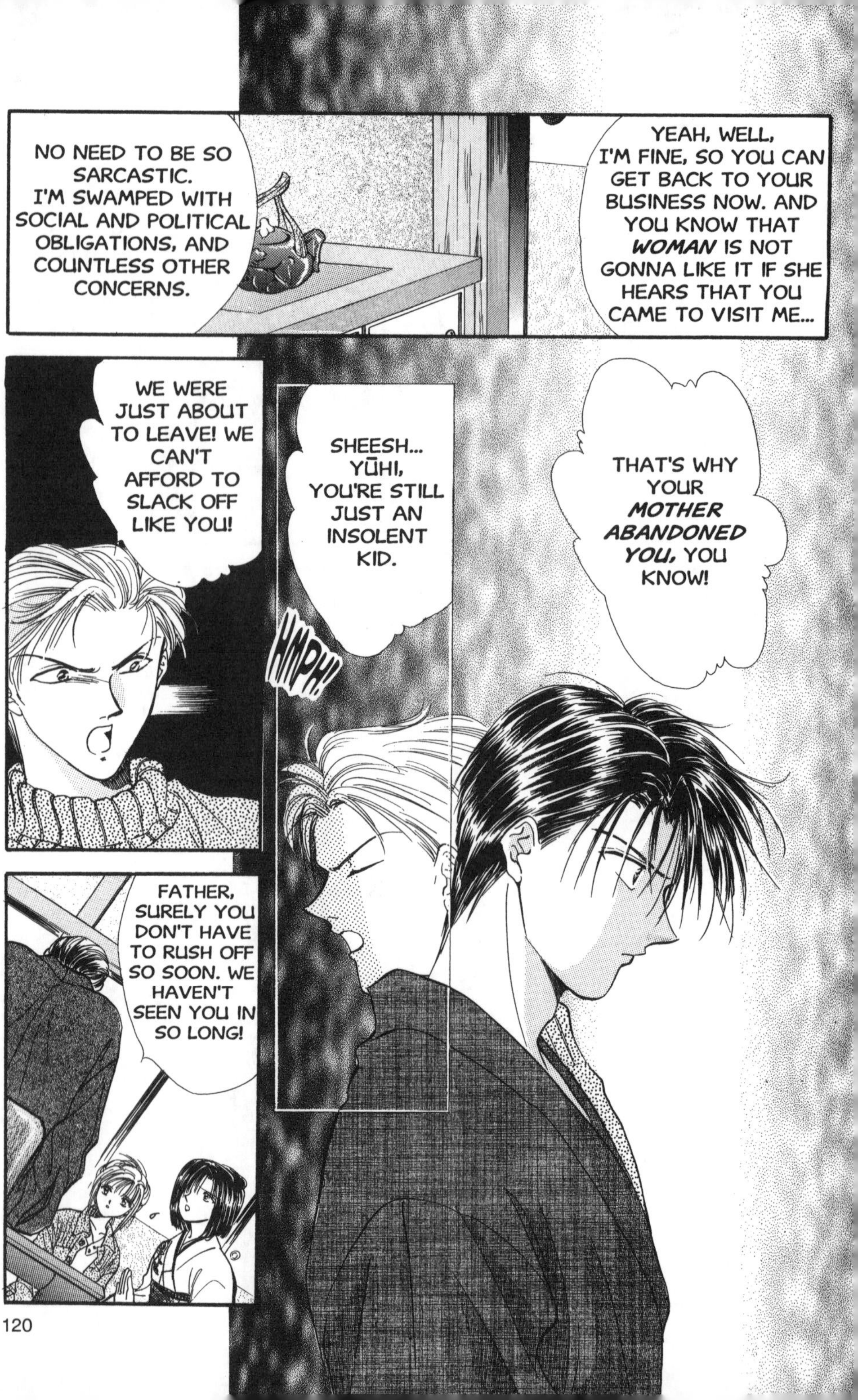
NO NEED TO BE SO SARCASTIC. I'M SWAMPED WITH SOCIAL AND POLITICAL OBLIGATIONS, AND COUNTLESS OTHER CONCERNS.
YEAH, WELL, I'M FINE, SO YOU CAN GET BACK TO YOUR BUSINESS NOW. AND YOU KNOW THAT *WOMAN* IS NOT GONNA LIKE IT IF SHE HEARS THAT YOU CAME TO VISIT ME...
WE WERE JUST ABOUT TO LEAVE! WE CAN'T AFFORD TO SLACK OFF LIKE YOU!
FATHER, SURELY YOU DON'T HAVE TO RUSH OFF SO SOON. WE HAVEN'T SEEN YOU IN SO LONG!
SHEESH... YŪHI, YOU'RE STILL JUST AN INSOLENT KID.
HMPH!
THAT'S WHY YOUR *MOTHER ABANDONED YOU,* YOU KNOW!

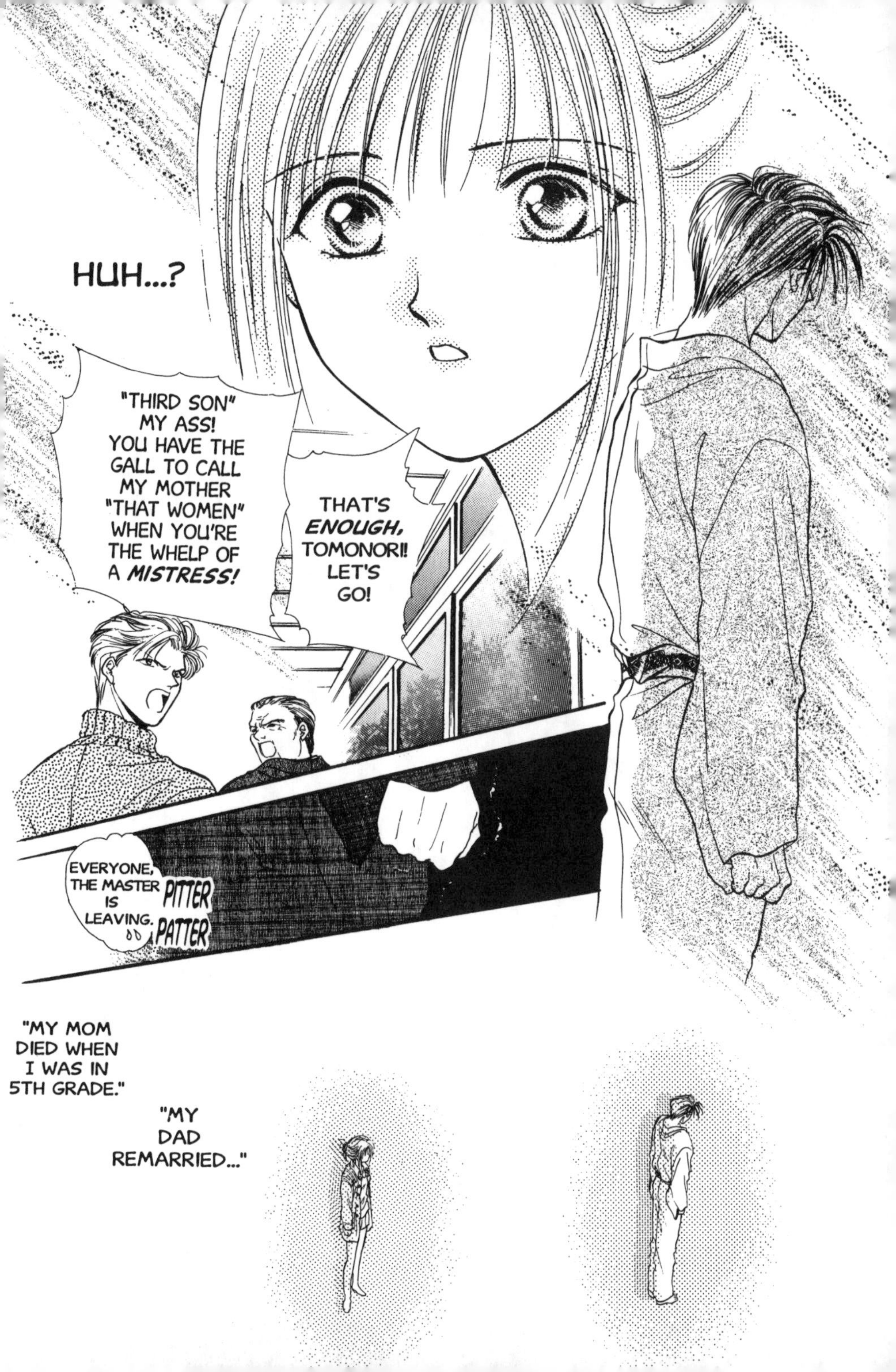
HUH...?
"THIRD SON" MY ASS! YOU HAVE THE GALL TO CALL MY MOTHER "THAT WOMEN" WHEN YOU'RE THE WHELP OF A MISTRESS!
THAT'S ENOUGH, TOMONORI!! LET'S GO!
EVERYONE, THE MASTER IS LEAVING.
PITTER PATTER
"MY MOM DIED WHEN I WAS IN 5TH GRADE."
"MY DAD REMARRIED..."

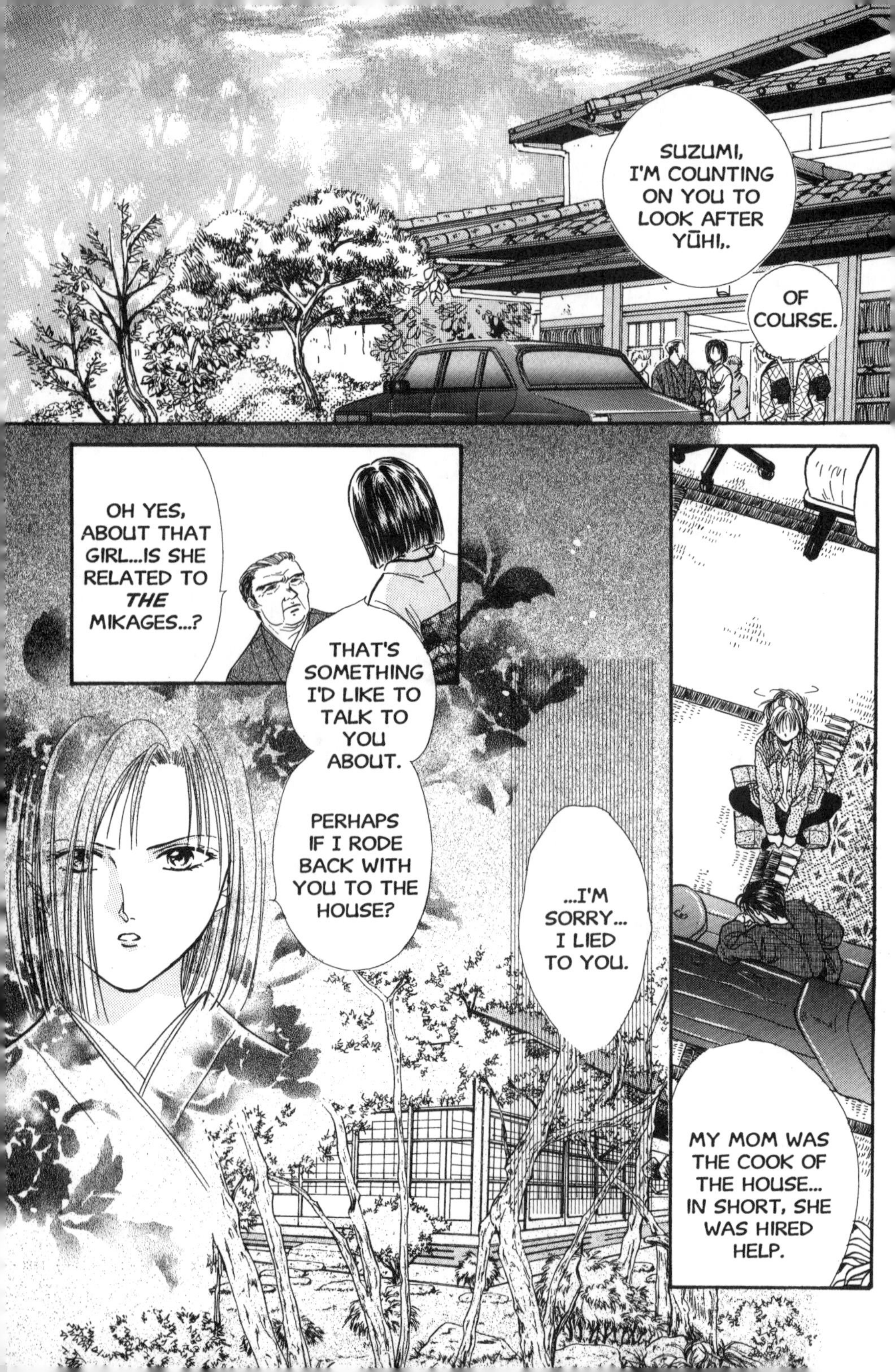
SUZUMI, I'M COUNTING ON YOU TO LOOK AFTER YŪHI,.
OF COURSE.
OH YES, ABOUT THAT GIRL...IS SHE RELATED TO *THE* MIKAGES...?
THAT'S SOMETHING I'D LIKE TO TALK TO YOU ABOUT.
PERHAPS IF I RODE BACK WITH YOU TO THE HOUSE?
...I'M SORRY... I LIED TO YOU.
MY MOM WAS THE COOK OF THE HOUSE... IN SHORT, SHE WAS HIRED HELP.

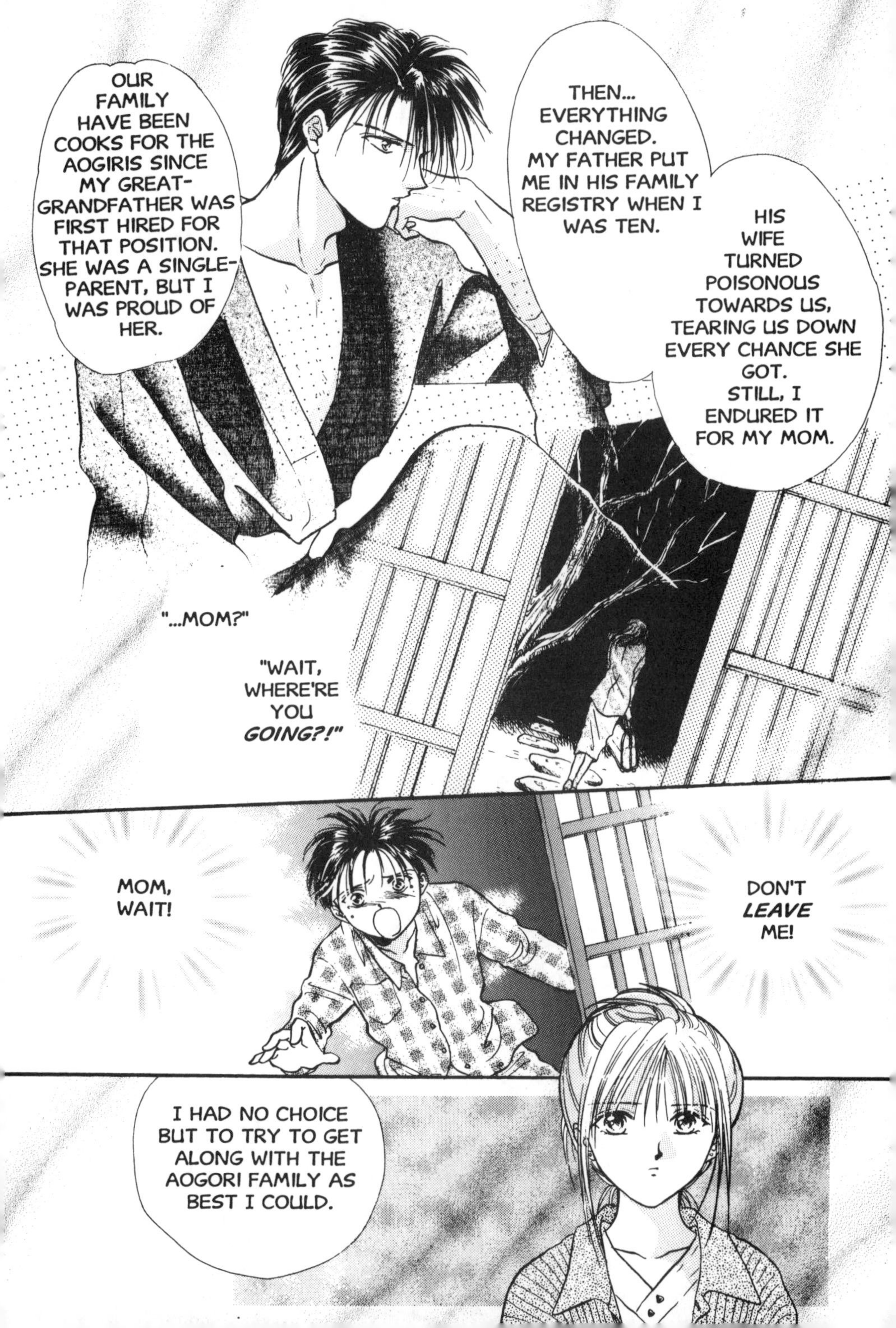
OUR FAMILY HAVE BEEN COOKS FOR THE AOGIRIS SINCE MY GREAT-GRANDFATHER WAS FIRST HIRED FOR THAT POSITION. SHE WAS A SINGLE-PARENT, BUT I WAS PROUD OF HER.
THEN... EVERYTHING CHANGED. MY FATHER PUT ME IN HIS FAMILY REGISTRY WHEN I WAS TEN.
HIS WIFE TURNED POISONOUS TOWARDS US, TEARING US DOWN EVERY CHANCE SHE GOT. STILL, I ENDURED IT FOR MY MOM.
"...MOM?"
"WAIT, WHERE'RE YOU *GOING?!*"
MOM, WAIT!
DON'T *LEAVE* ME!
I HAD NO CHOICE BUT TO TRY TO GET ALONG WITH THE AOGORI FAMILY AS BEST I COULD.

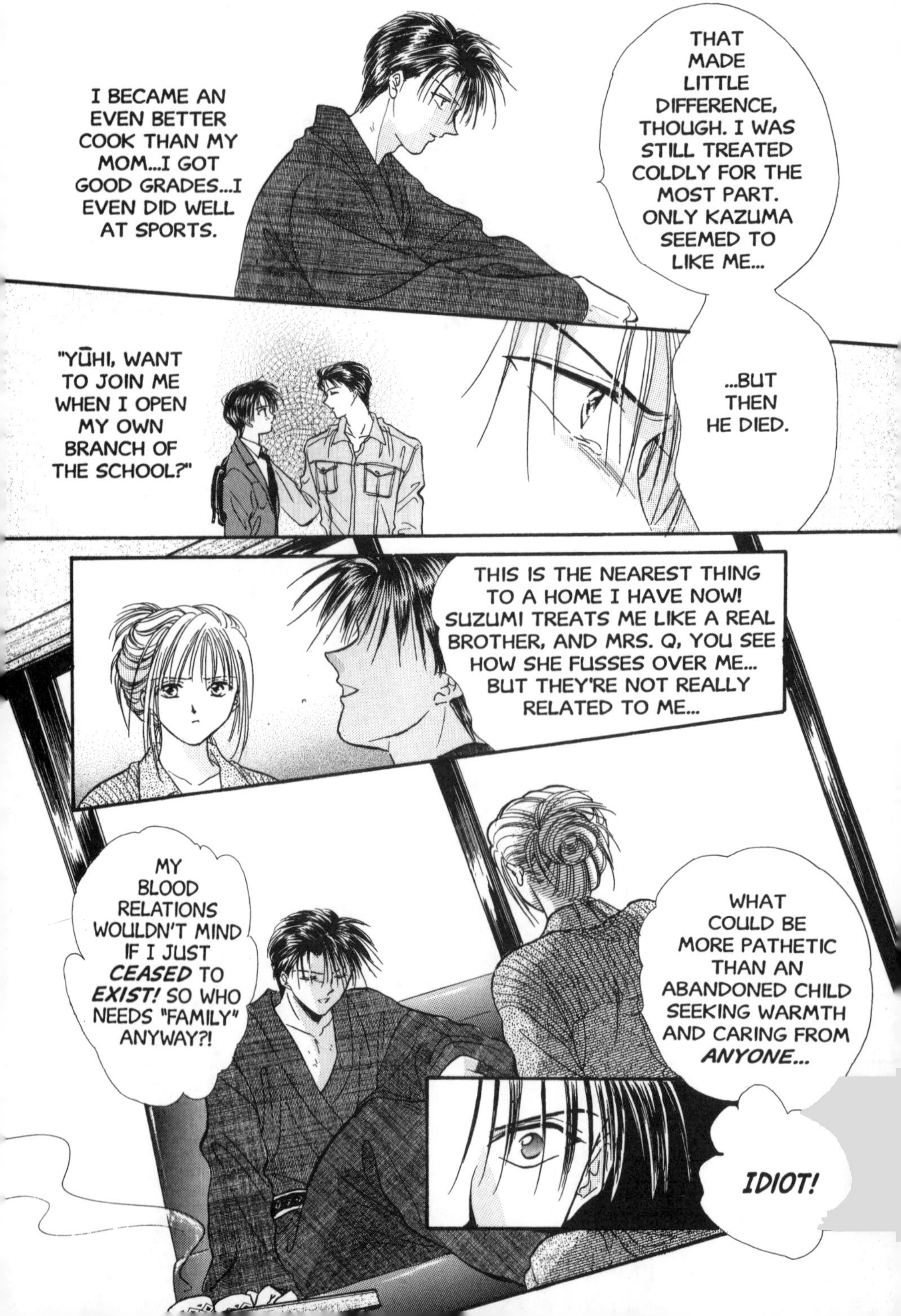
I BECAME AN EVEN BETTER COOK THAN MY MOM...I GOT GOOD GRADES...I EVEN DID WELL AT SPORTS.
THAT MADE LITTLE DIFFERENCE, THOUGH. I WAS STILL TREATED COLDLY FOR THE MOST PART. ONLY KAZUMA SEEMED TO LIKE ME...
"YŪHI, WANT TO JOIN ME WHEN I OPEN MY OWN BRANCH OF THE SCHOOL?"
...BUT THEN HE DIED.
THIS IS THE NEAREST THING TO A HOME I HAVE NOW! SUZUMI TREATS ME LIKE A REAL BROTHER, AND MRS. Q, YOU SEE HOW SHE FUSSES OVER ME... BUT THEY'RE NOT REALLY RELATED TO ME...
MY BLOOD RELATIONS WOULDN'T MIND IF I JUST *CEASED* TO *EXIST!* SO WHO NEEDS "FAMILY" ANYWAY?!
WHAT COULD BE MORE PATHETIC THAN AN ABANDONED CHILD SEEKING WARMTH AND CARING FROM *ANYONE*...
IDIOT!

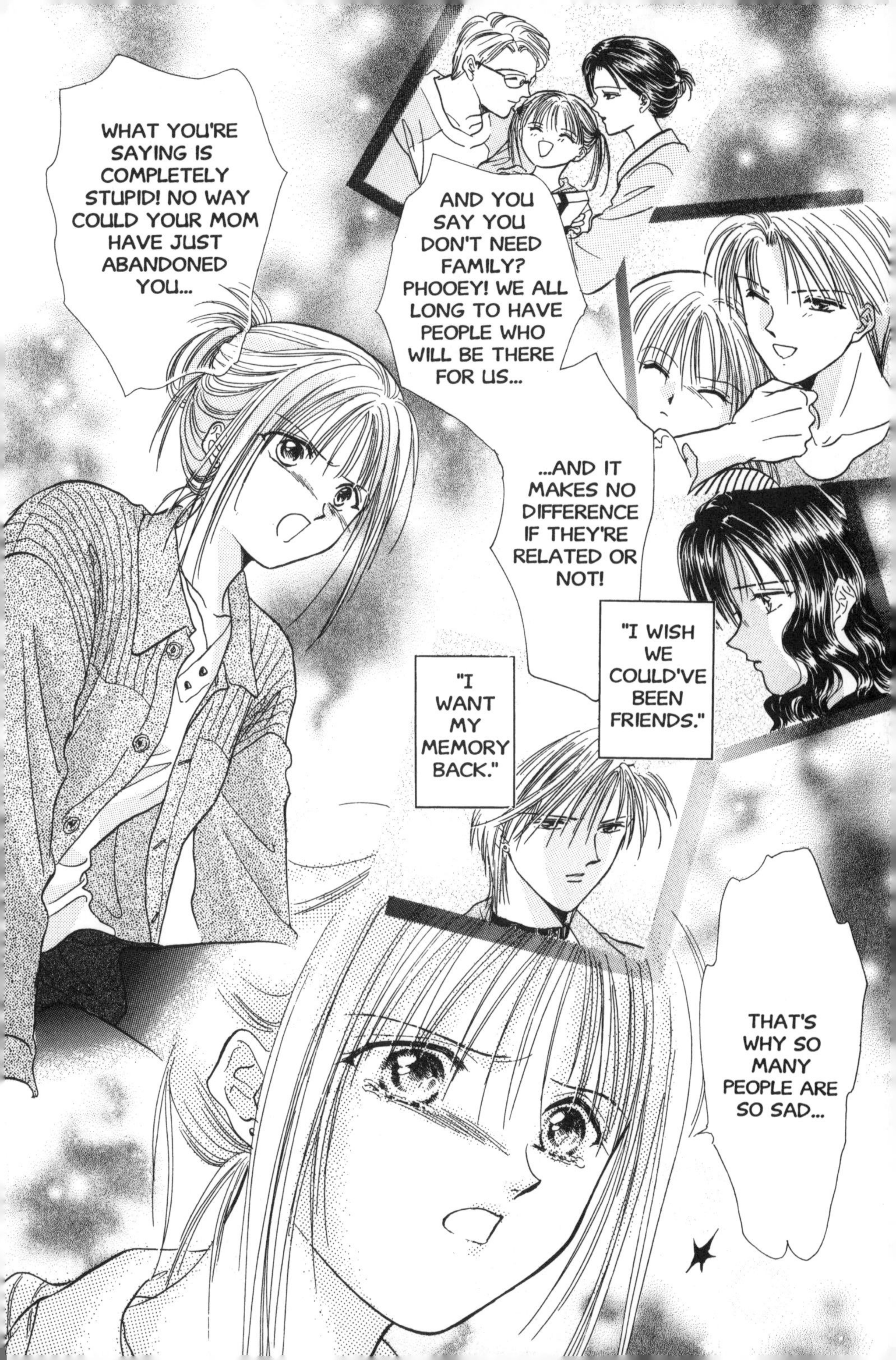
WHAT YOU'RE SAYING IS COMPLETELY STUPID! NO WAY COULD YOUR MOM HAVE JUST ABANDONED YOU...
AND YOU SAY YOU DON'T NEED FAMILY? PHOOEY! WE ALL LONG TO HAVE PEOPLE WHO WILL BE THERE FOR US...
...AND IT MAKES NO DIFFERENCE IF THEY'RE RELATED OR NOT!
"I WISH WE COULD'VE BEEN FRIENDS."
"I WANT MY MEMORY BACK."
THAT'S WHY SO MANY PEOPLE ARE SO SAD...

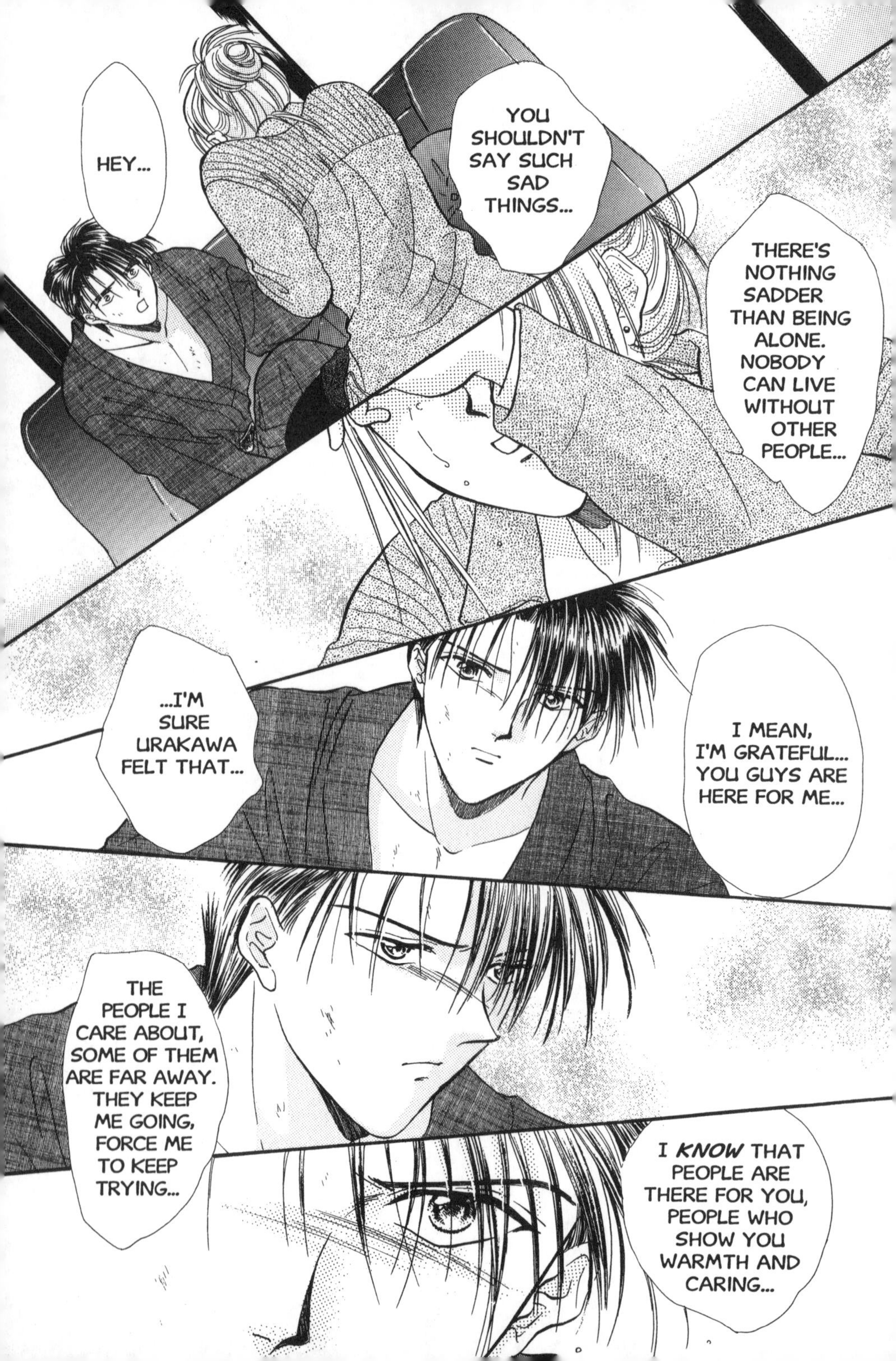
HEY...
YOU SHOULDN'T SAY SUCH SAD THINGS...
THERE'S NOTHING SADDER THAN BEING ALONE. NOBODY CAN LIVE WITHOUT OTHER PEOPLE...
...I'M SURE URAKAWA FELT THAT...
I MEAN, I'M GRATEFUL... YOU GUYS ARE HERE FOR ME...
THE PEOPLE I CARE ABOUT, SOME OF THEM ARE FAR AWAY. THEY KEEP ME GOING, FORCE ME TO KEEP TRYING...
I *KNOW* THAT PEOPLE ARE THERE FOR YOU, PEOPLE WHO SHOW YOU WARMTH AND CARING...

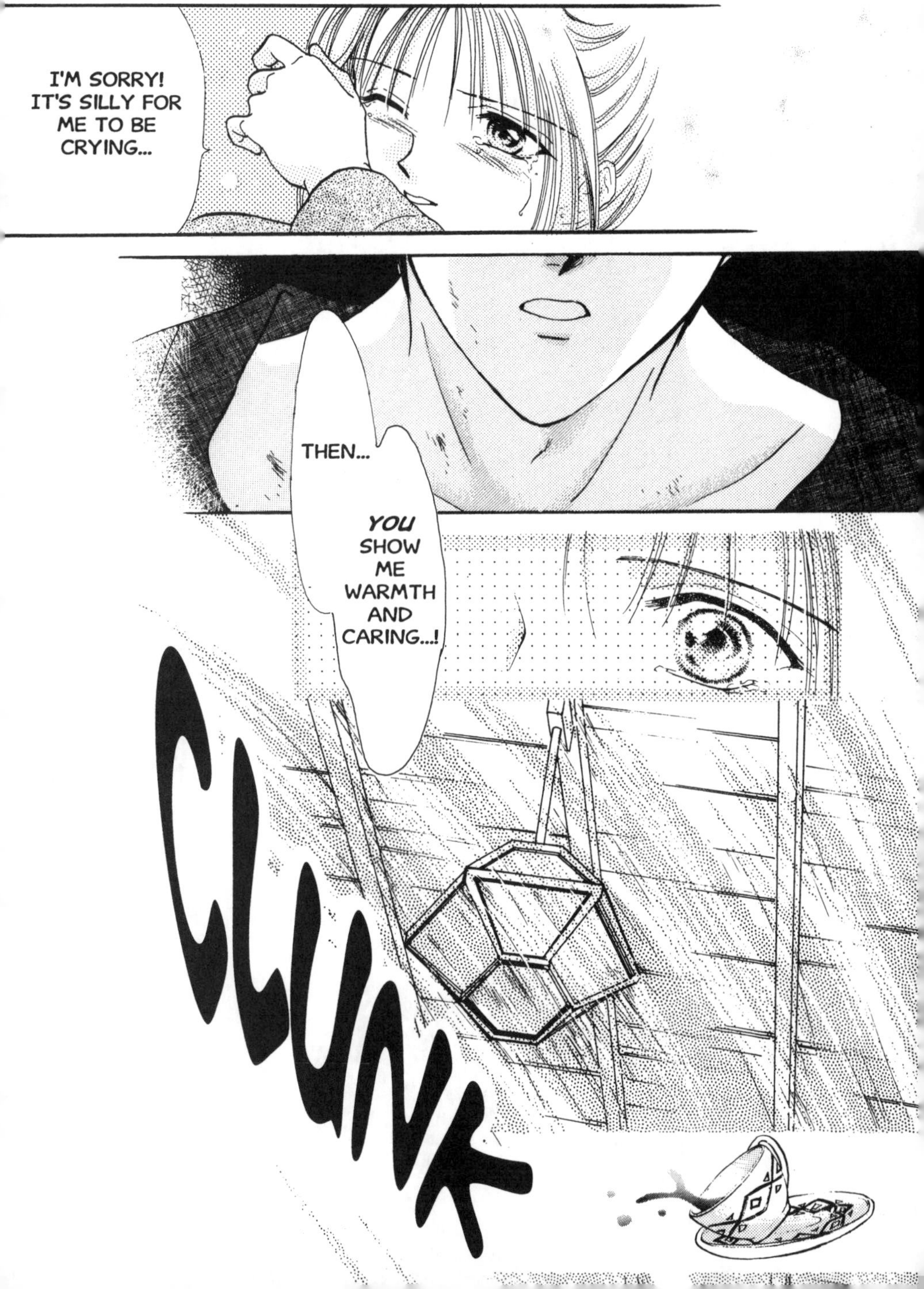
I'M SORRY! IT'S SILLY FOR ME TO BE CRYING...
THEN...
YOU SHOW ME WARMTH AND CARING...!
CLUNK

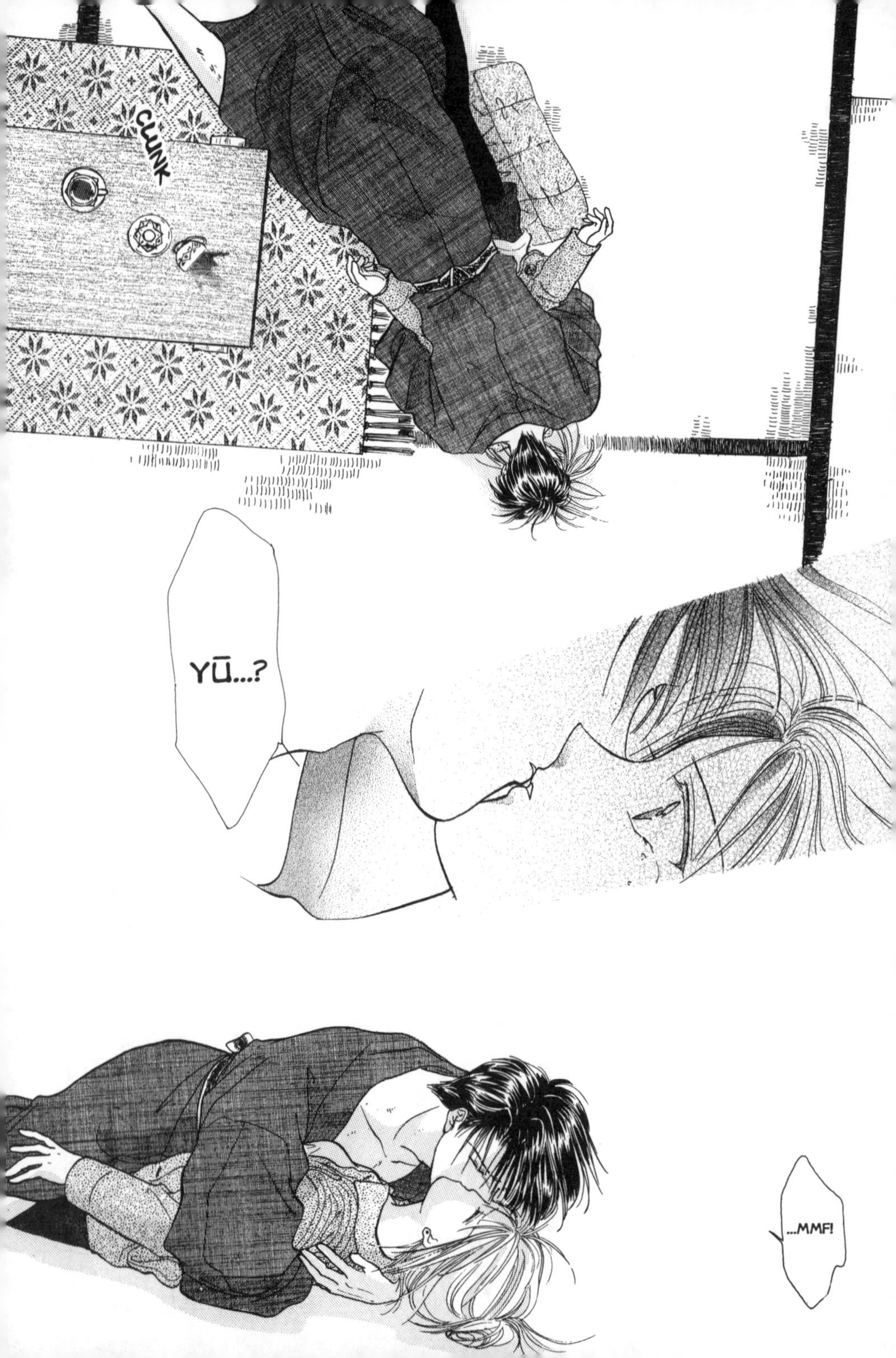
CLUNK
YŪ...?
...MMF!

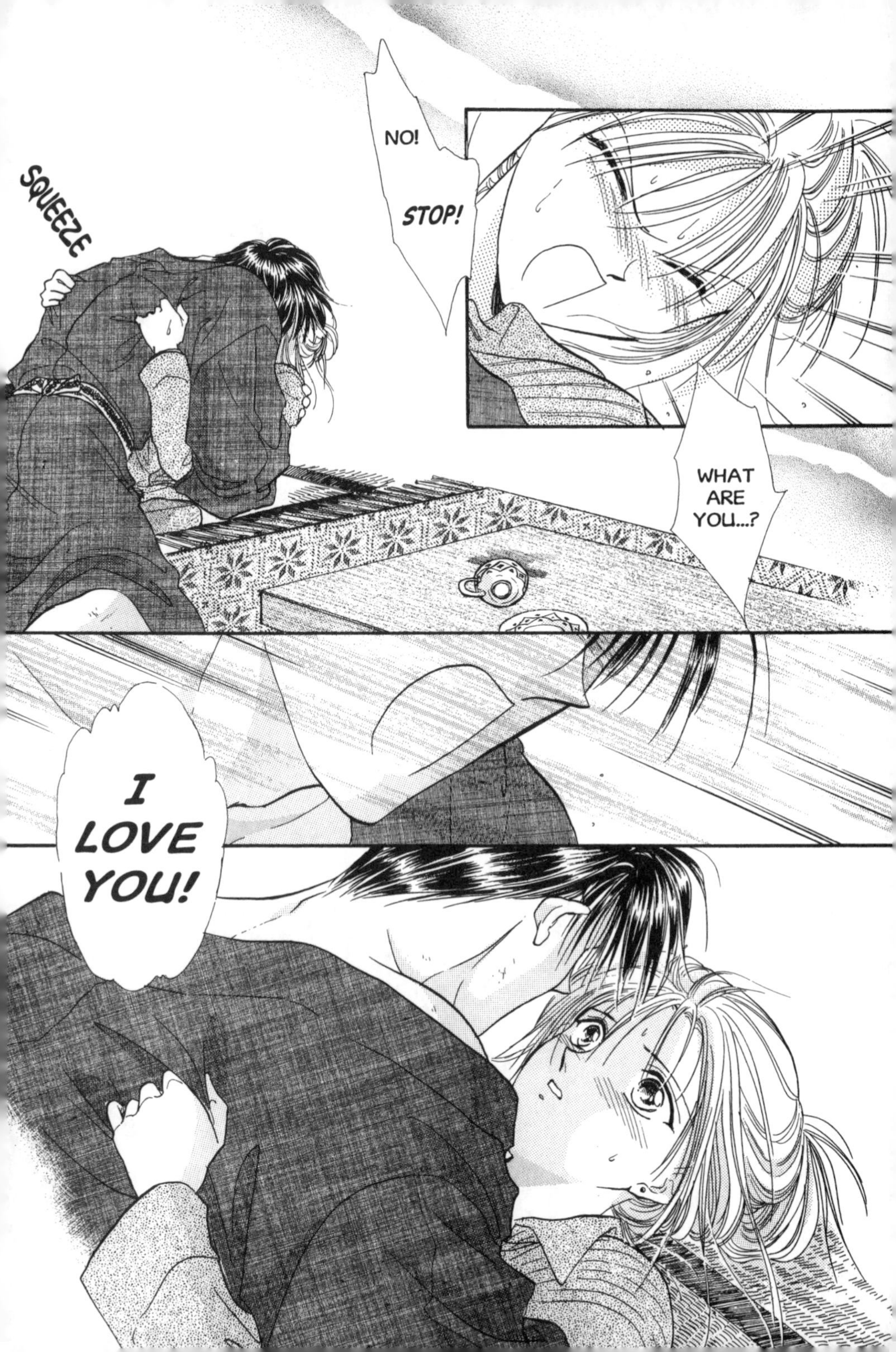
SQUEEZE
NO!
STOP!
WHAT ARE YOU...?
I LOVE YOU!

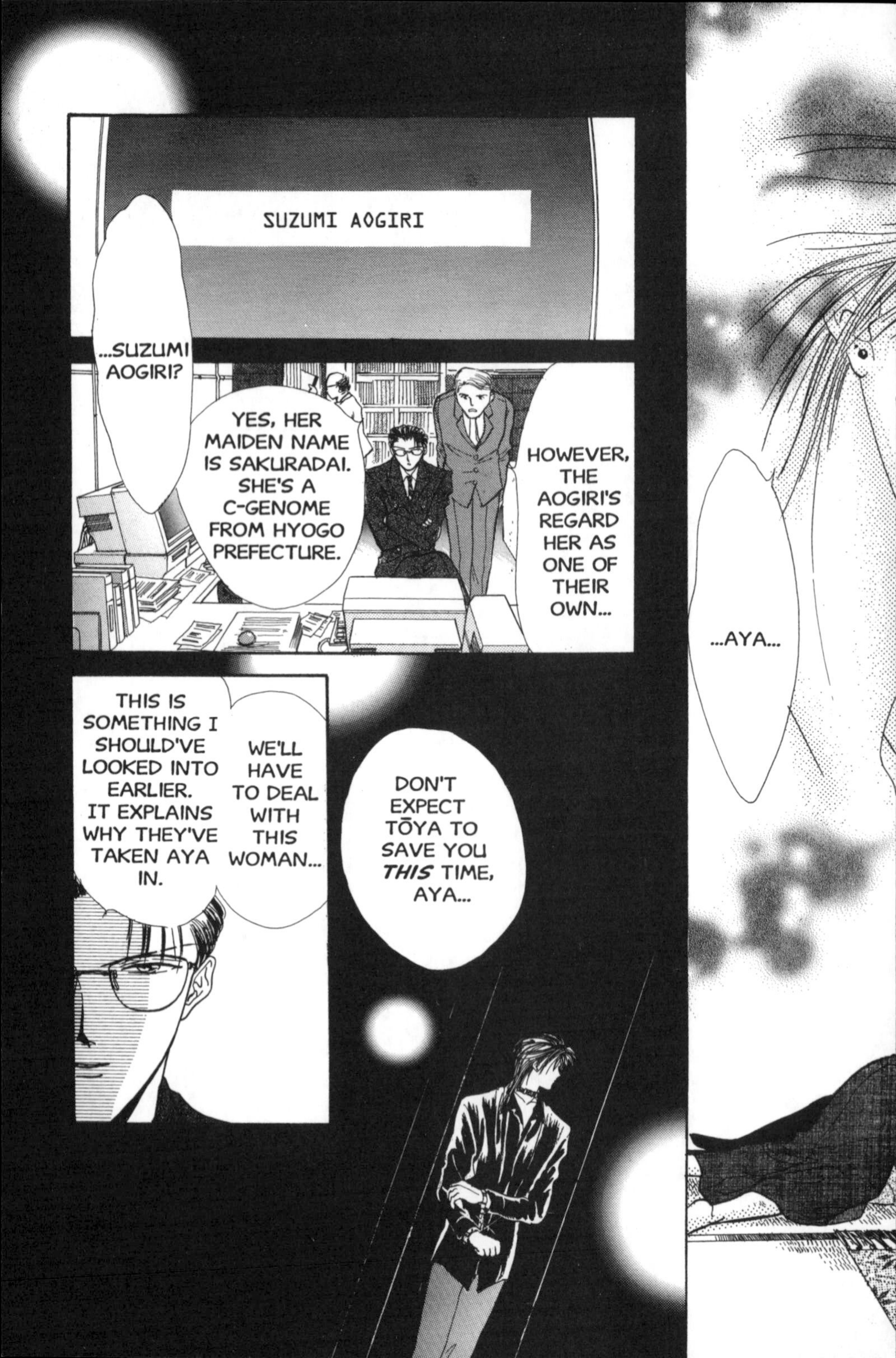
SUZUMI AOGIRI
...SUZUMI AOGIRI?
YES, HER MAIDEN NAME IS SAKURADAI. SHE'S A C-GENOME FROM HYOGO PREFECTURE.
HOWEVER, THE AOGIRI'S REGARD HER AS ONE OF THEIR OWN...
THIS IS SOMETHING I SHOULD'VE LOOKED INTO EARLIER. IT EXPLAINS WHY THEY'VE TAKEN AYA IN.
WE'LL HAVE TO DEAL WITH THIS WOMAN...
DON'T EXPECT TŌYA TO SAVE YOU *THIS* TIME, AYA...
...AYA...

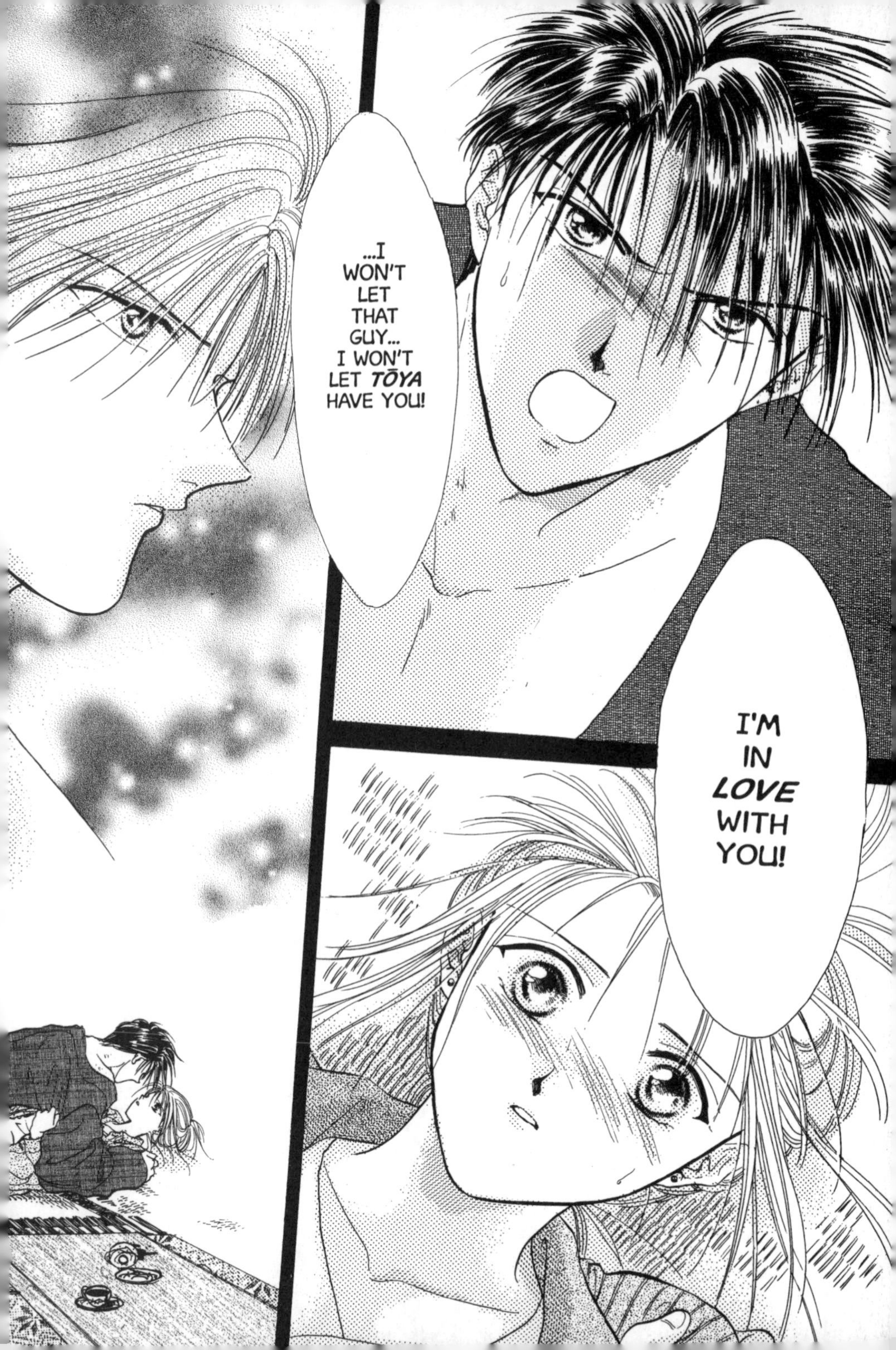
...I WON'T LET THAT GUY... I WON'T LET *TŌYA* HAVE YOU!
I'M IN ***LOVE*** WITH YOU!

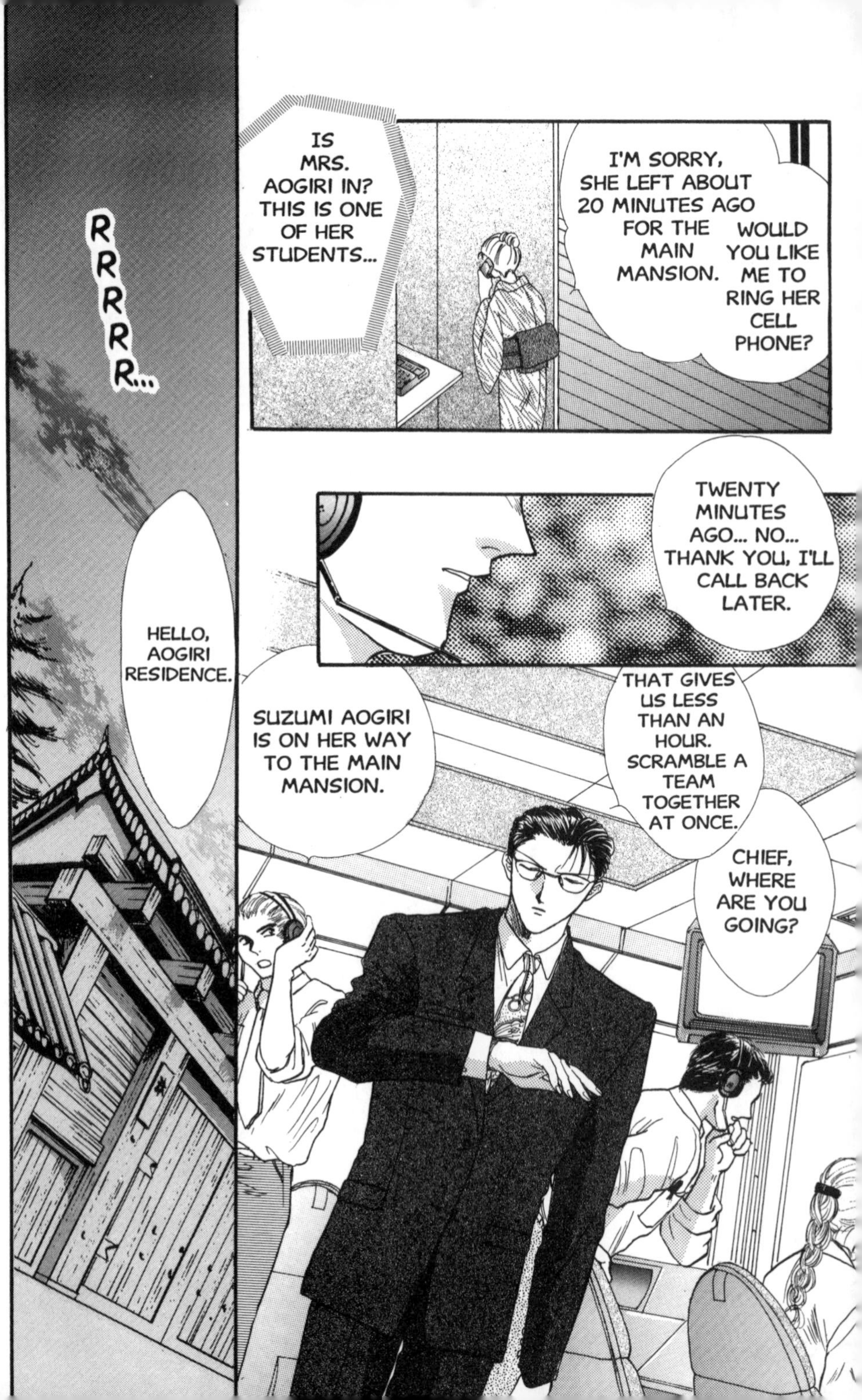
RRRRR...
HELLO, AOGIRI RESIDENCE.
IS MRS. AOGIRI IN? THIS IS ONE OF HER STUDENTS...
I'M SORRY, SHE LEFT ABOUT 20 MINUTES AGO FOR THE MAIN MANSION.
WOULD YOU LIKE ME TO RING HER CELL PHONE?
TWENTY MINUTES AGO... NO... THANK YOU, I'LL CALL BACK LATER.
SUZUMI AOGIRI IS ON HER WAY TO THE MAIN MANSION.
THAT GIVES US LESS THAN AN HOUR. SCRAMBLE A TEAM TOGETHER AT ONCE.
CHIEF, WHERE ARE YOU GOING?

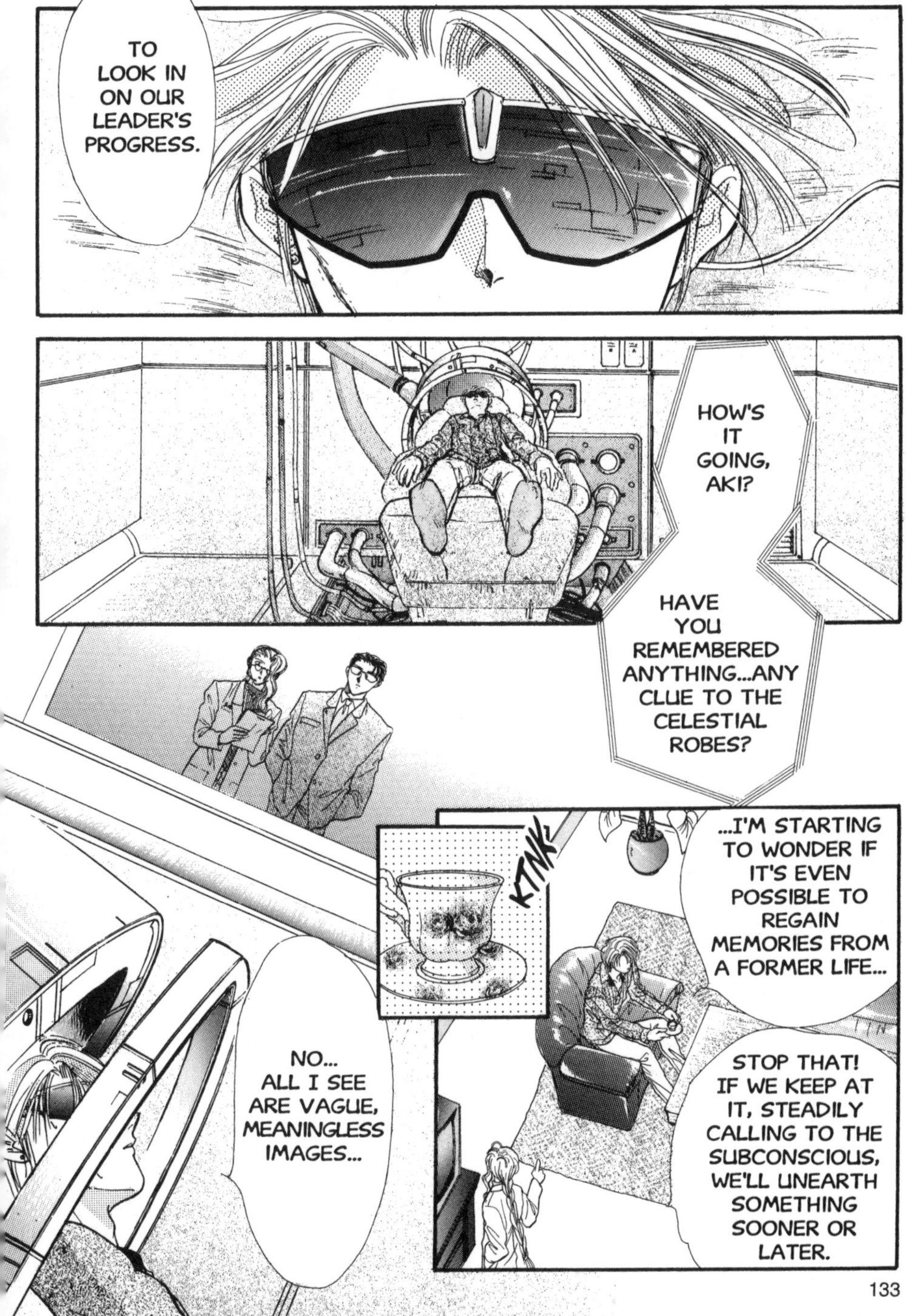
TO LOOK IN ON OUR LEADER'S PROGRESS.
HOW'S IT GOING, AKI?
HAVE YOU REMEMBERED ANYTHING...ANY CLUE TO THE CELESTIAL ROBES?
NO... ALL I SEE ARE VAGUE, MEANINGLESS IMAGES...
KTNK
...I'M STARTING TO WONDER IF IT'S EVEN POSSIBLE TO REGAIN MEMORIES FROM A FORMER LIFE...
STOP THAT! IF WE KEEP AT IT, STEADILY CALLING TO THE SUBCONSCIOUS, WE'LL UNEARTH SOMETHING SOONER OR LATER.

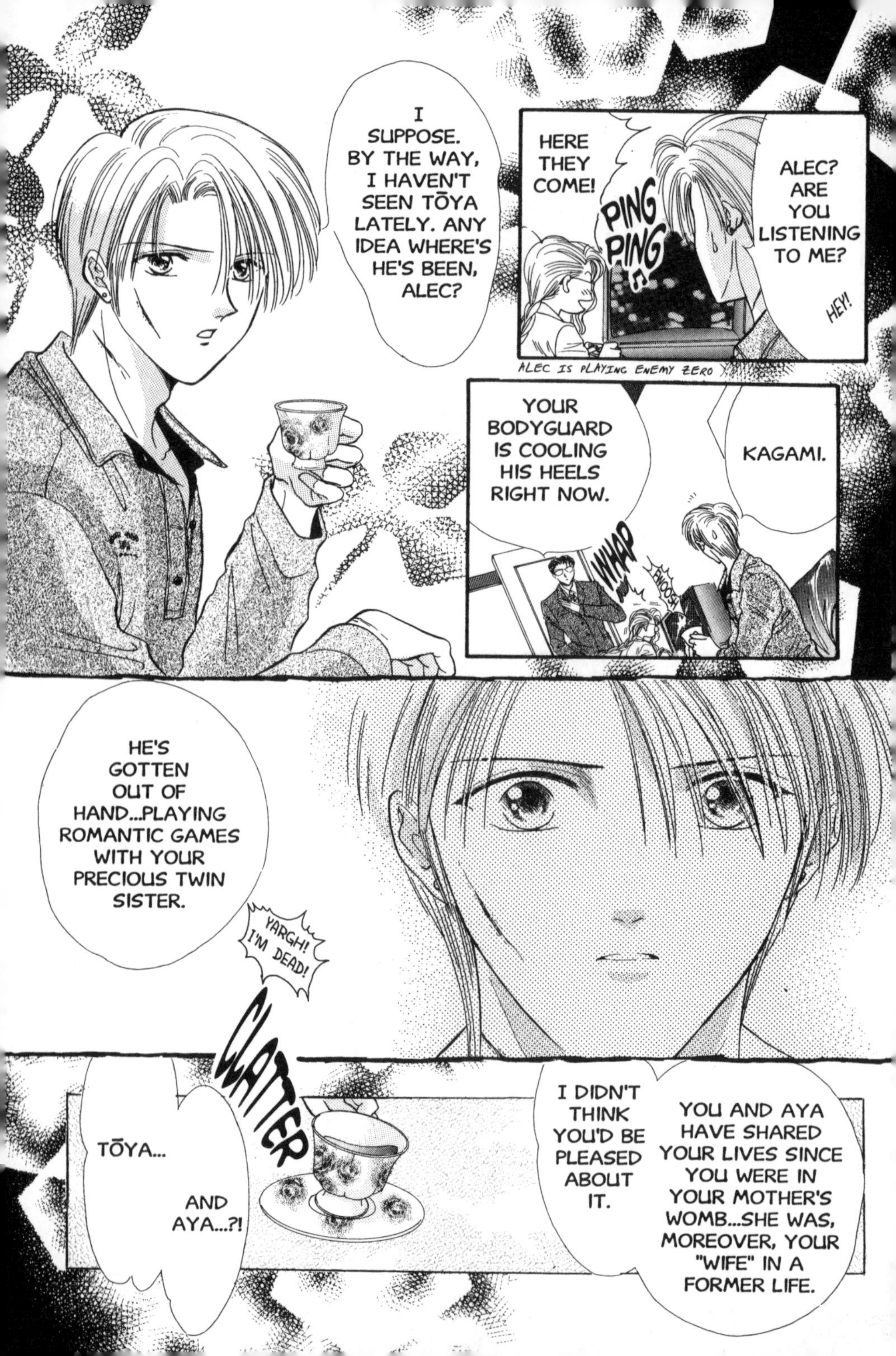
I SUPPOSE. BY THE WAY, I HAVEN'T SEEN TŌYA LATELY. ANY IDEA WHERE'S HE'S BEEN, ALEC?
HERE THEY COME!
PING PING
ALEC? ARE YOU LISTENING TO ME?
HEY!
ALEC IS PLAYING ENEMY ZERO
YOUR BODYGUARD IS COOLING HIS HEELS RIGHT NOW.
KAGAMI.
WHAP
FWOOSH
HE'S GOTTEN OUT OF HAND...PLAYING ROMANTIC GAMES WITH YOUR PRECIOUS TWIN SISTER.
YARGH! I'M DEAD!
CLATTER
TŌYA...
AND AYA...?!
I DIDN'T THINK YOU'D BE PLEASED ABOUT IT.
YOU AND AYA HAVE SHARED YOUR LIVES SINCE YOU WERE IN YOUR MOTHER'S WOMB...SHE WAS, MOREOVER, YOUR "WIFE" IN A FORMER LIFE.

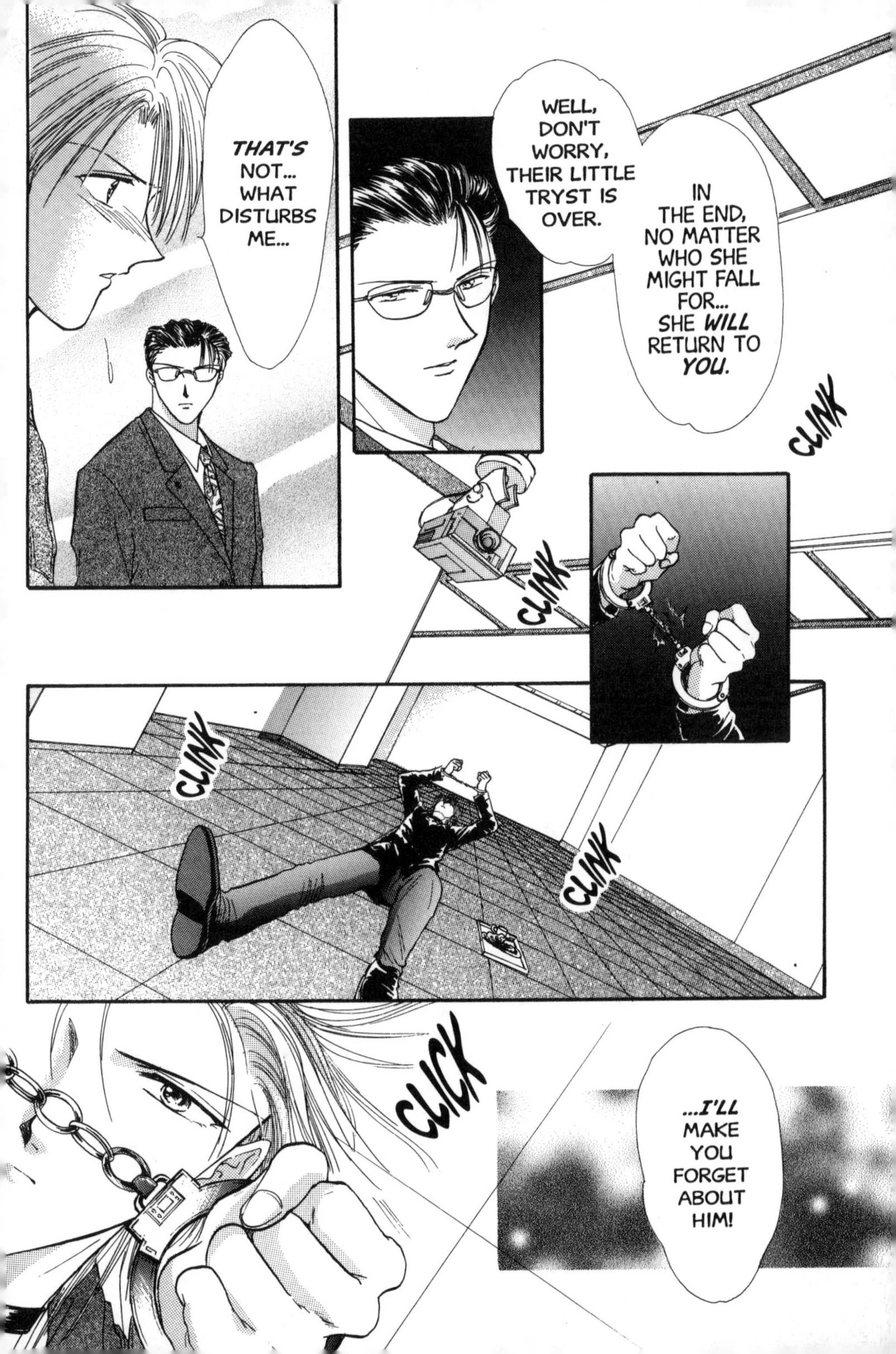
THAT'S NOT... WHAT DISTURBS ME...
WELL, DON'T WORRY, THEIR LITTLE TRYST IS OVER.
IN THE END, NO MATTER WHO SHE MIGHT FALL FOR... SHE WILL RETURN TO YOU.
CLINK
CLINK
CLINK
CLINK
CLICK
...I'LL MAKE YOU FORGET ABOUT HIM!

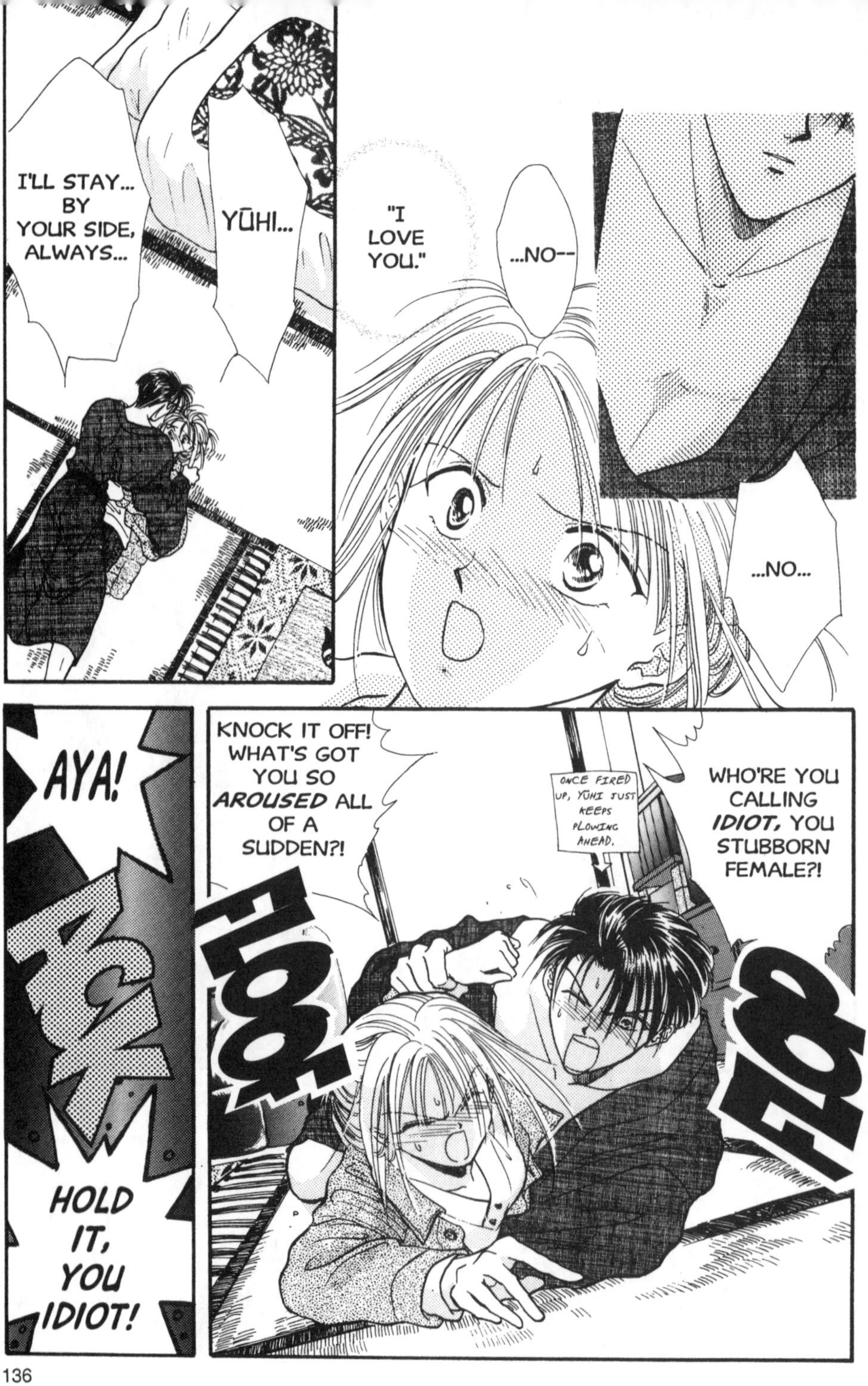
I'LL STAY... BY YOUR SIDE, ALWAYS...
YŪHI...
"I LOVE YOU."
...NO--
...NO...
AYA!
ACK!
HOLD IT, YOU IDIOT!
KNOCK IT OFF! WHAT'S GOT YOU SO AROUSED ALL OF A SUDDEN?!
ONCE FIRED UP, YŪHI JUST KEEPS PLOWING AHEAD.
WHO'RE YOU CALLING IDIOT, YOU STUBBORN FEMALE?!
FLOP!
FLOP!

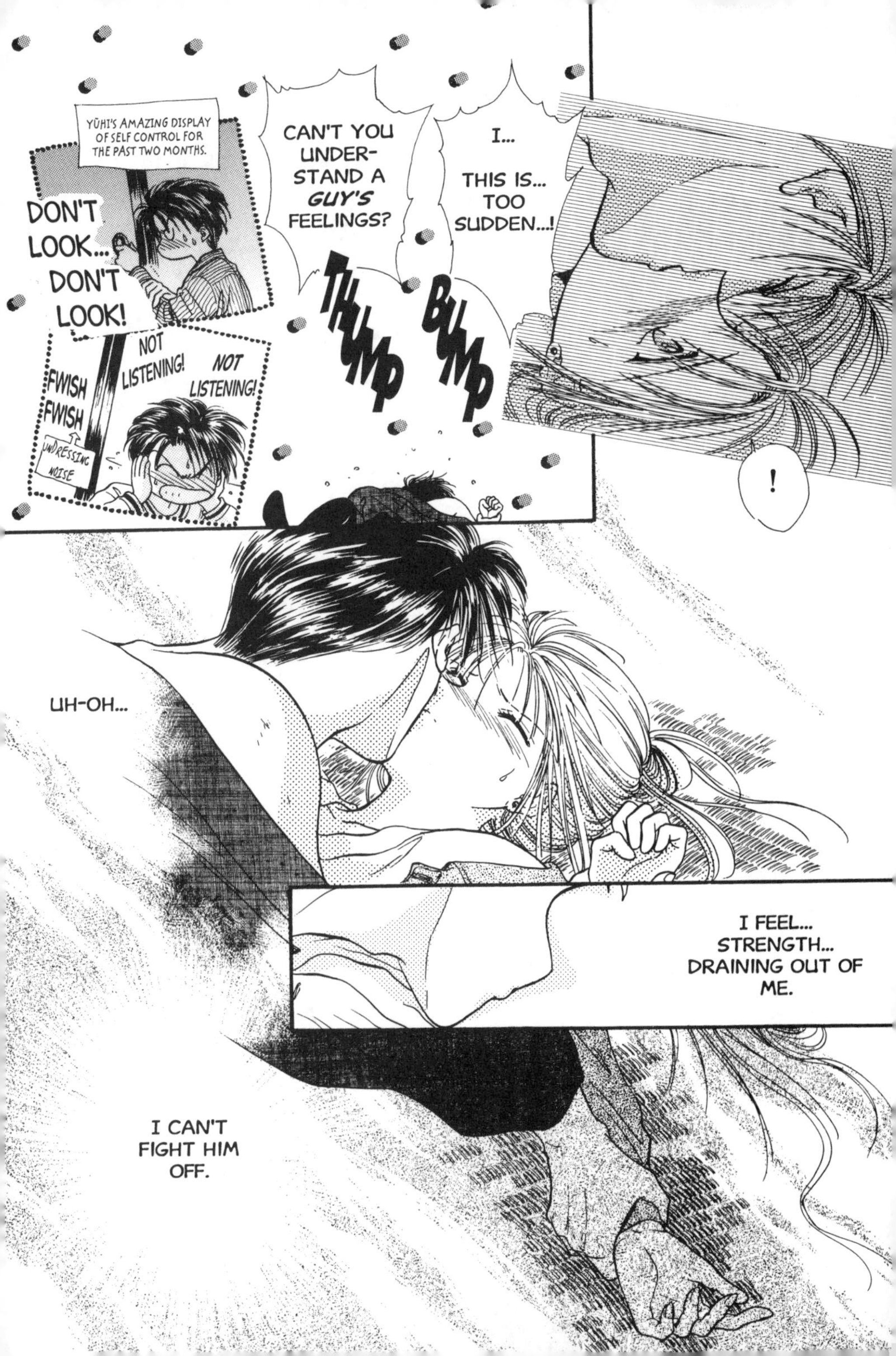
YŪHI'S AMAZING DISPLAY OF SELF CONTROL FOR THE PAST TWO MONTHS.
DON'T LOOK... DON'T LOOK!
FWISH FWISH
UNDRESSING NOISE
NOT LISTENING!
NOT LISTENING!
CAN'T YOU UNDER-STAND A GUY'S FEELINGS?
I...
THIS IS... TOO SUDDEN...!
THUMP
BUMP
!
UH-OH...
I FEEL... STRENGTH... DRAINING OUT OF ME.
I CAN'T FIGHT HIM OFF.

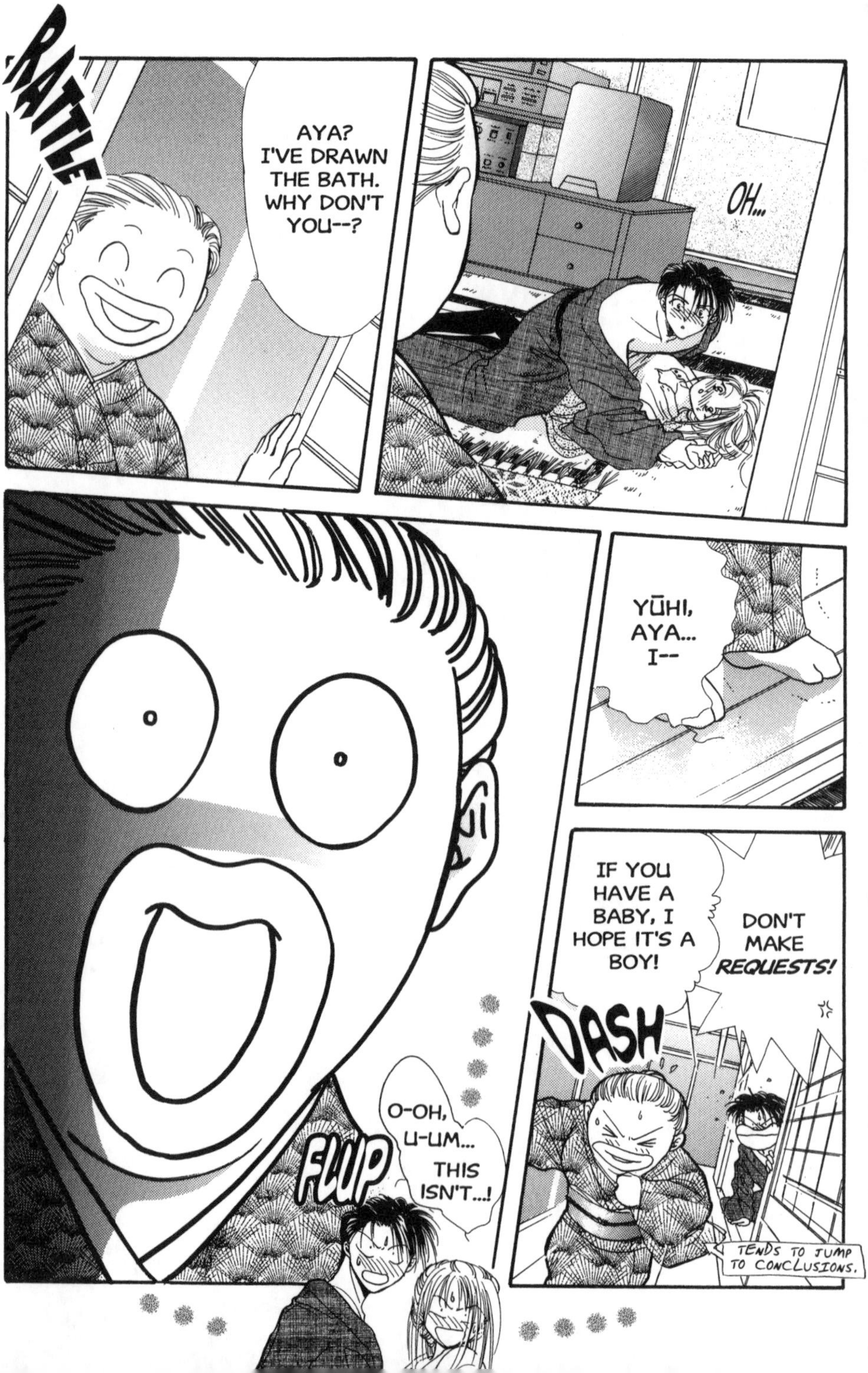
RATTLE
AYA? I'VE DRAWN THE BATH. WHY DON'T YOU--?
OH...
FLUP
O-OH, U-UM... THIS ISN'T...!
YŪHI, AYA... I--
IF YOU HAVE A BABY, I HOPE IT'S A BOY!
DON'T MAKE *REQUESTS!*
DASH
TENDS TO JUMP TO CONCLUSIONS.

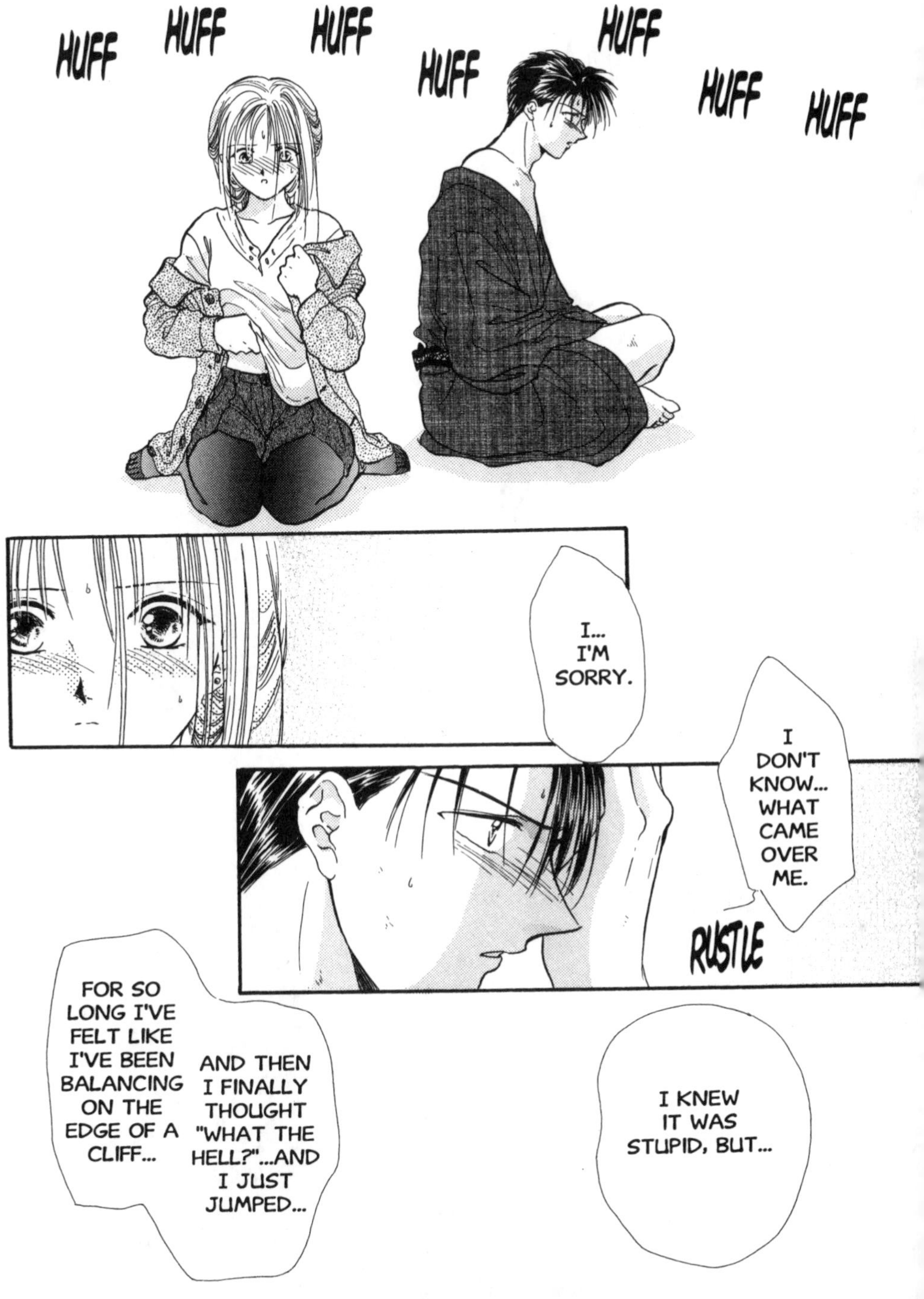
HUFF
HUFF
HUFF
HUFF
HUFF
HUFF
HUFF
I... I'M SORRY.
I DON'T KNOW... WHAT CAME OVER ME.
RUSTLE
FOR SO LONG I'VE FELT LIKE I'VE BEEN BALANCING ON THE EDGE OF A CLIFF...
AND THEN I FINALLY THOUGHT "WHAT THE HELL?"...AND I JUST JUMPED...
I KNEW IT WAS STUPID, BUT...

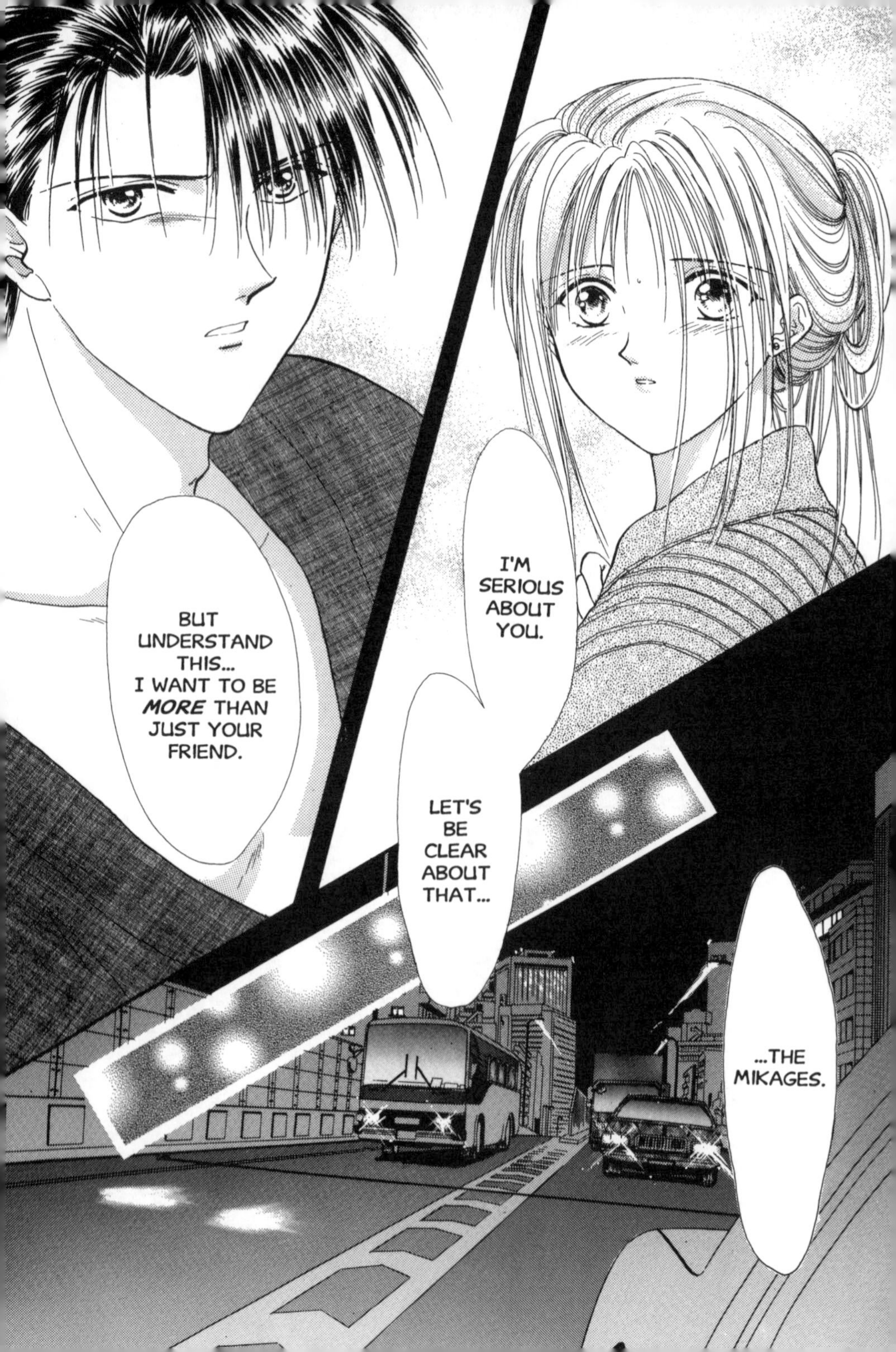
BUT UNDERSTAND THIS... I WANT TO BE ***MORE*** THAN JUST YOUR FRIEND.
I'M SERIOUS ABOUT YOU.
LET'S BE CLEAR ABOUT THAT...
...THE MIKAGES.

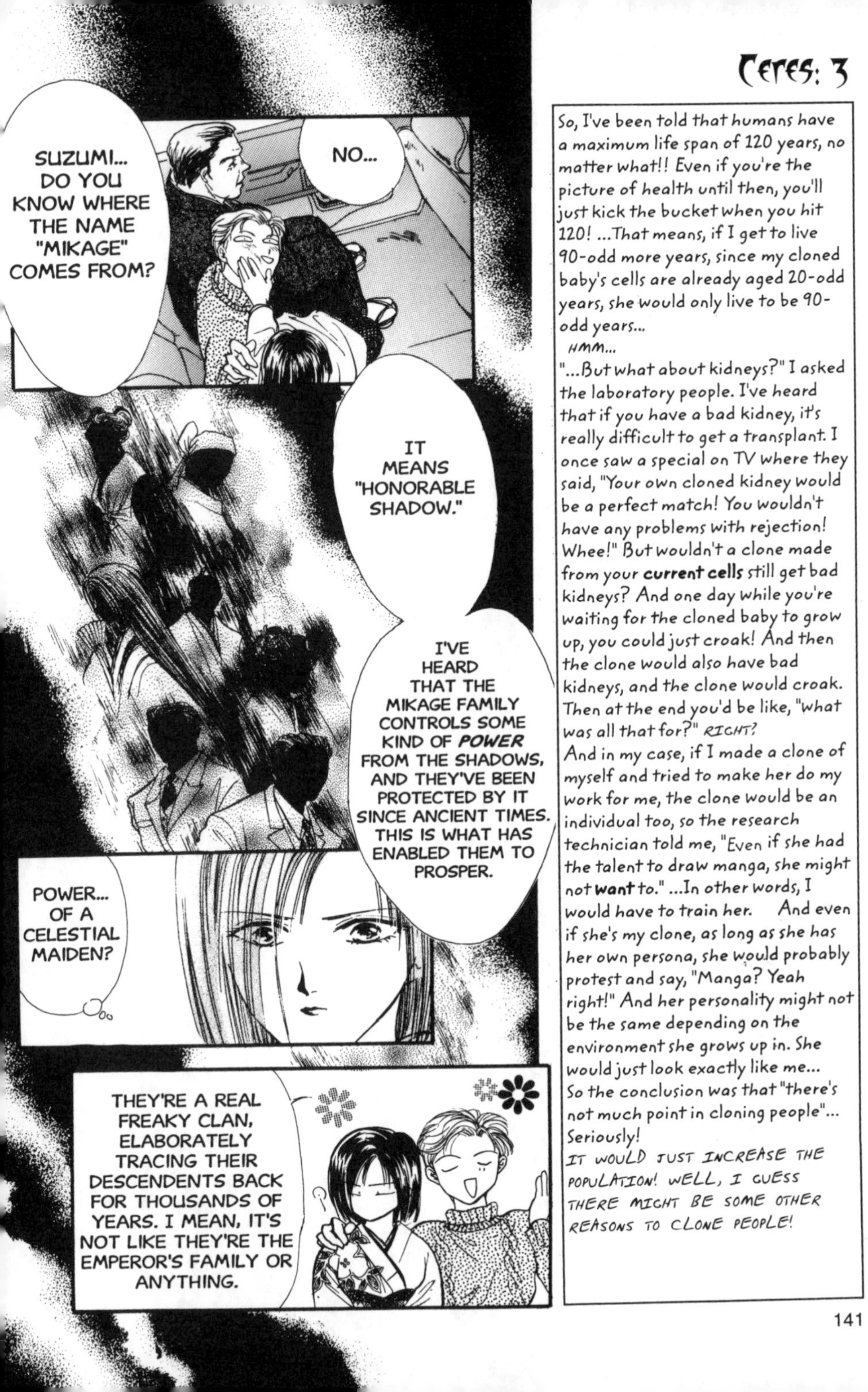
SUZUMI... DO YOU KNOW WHERE THE NAME "MIKAGE" COMES FROM?
NO...
IT MEANS "HONORABLE SHADOW."
I'VE HEARD THAT THE MIKAGE FAMILY CONTROLS SOME KIND OF *POWER* FROM THE SHADOWS, AND THEY'VE BEEN PROTECTED BY IT SINCE ANCIENT TIMES. THIS IS WHAT HAS ENABLED THEM TO PROSPER.
POWER... OF A CELESTIAL MAIDEN?
THEY'RE A REAL FREAKY CLAN, ELABORATELY TRACING THEIR DESCENDENTS BACK FOR THOUSANDS OF YEARS. I MEAN, IT'S NOT LIKE THEY'RE THE EMPEROR'S FAMILY OR ANYTHING.

Ceres: 3

So, I've been told that humans have a maximum life span of 120 years, no matter what!! Even if you're the picture of health until then, you'll just kick the bucket when you hit 120! ...That means, if I get to live 90-odd more years, since my cloned baby's cells are already aged 20-odd years, she would only live to be 90-odd years...

HMM...

"...But what about kidneys?" I asked the laboratory people. I've heard that if you have a bad kidney, it's really difficult to get a transplant. I once saw a special on TV where they said, "Your own cloned kidney would be a perfect match! You wouldn't have any problems with rejection! Whee!" But wouldn't a clone made from your **current cells** still get bad kidneys? And one day while you're waiting for the cloned baby to grow up, you could just croak! And then the clone would also have bad kidneys, and the clone would croak. Then at the end you'd be like, "what was all that for?" RIGHT?

And in my case, if I made a clone of myself and tried to make her do my work for me, the clone would be an individual too, so the research technician told me, "Even if she had the talent to draw manga, she might not **want** to." ...In other words, I would have to train her. And even if she's my clone, as long as she has her own persona, she would probably protest and say, "Manga? Yeah right!" And her personality might not be the same depending on the environment she grows up in. She would just look exactly like me... So the conclusion was that "there's not much point in cloning people"... Seriously!

IT WOULD JUST INCREASE THE POPULATION! WELL, I GUESS THERE MIGHT BE SOME OTHER REASONS TO CLONE PEOPLE!

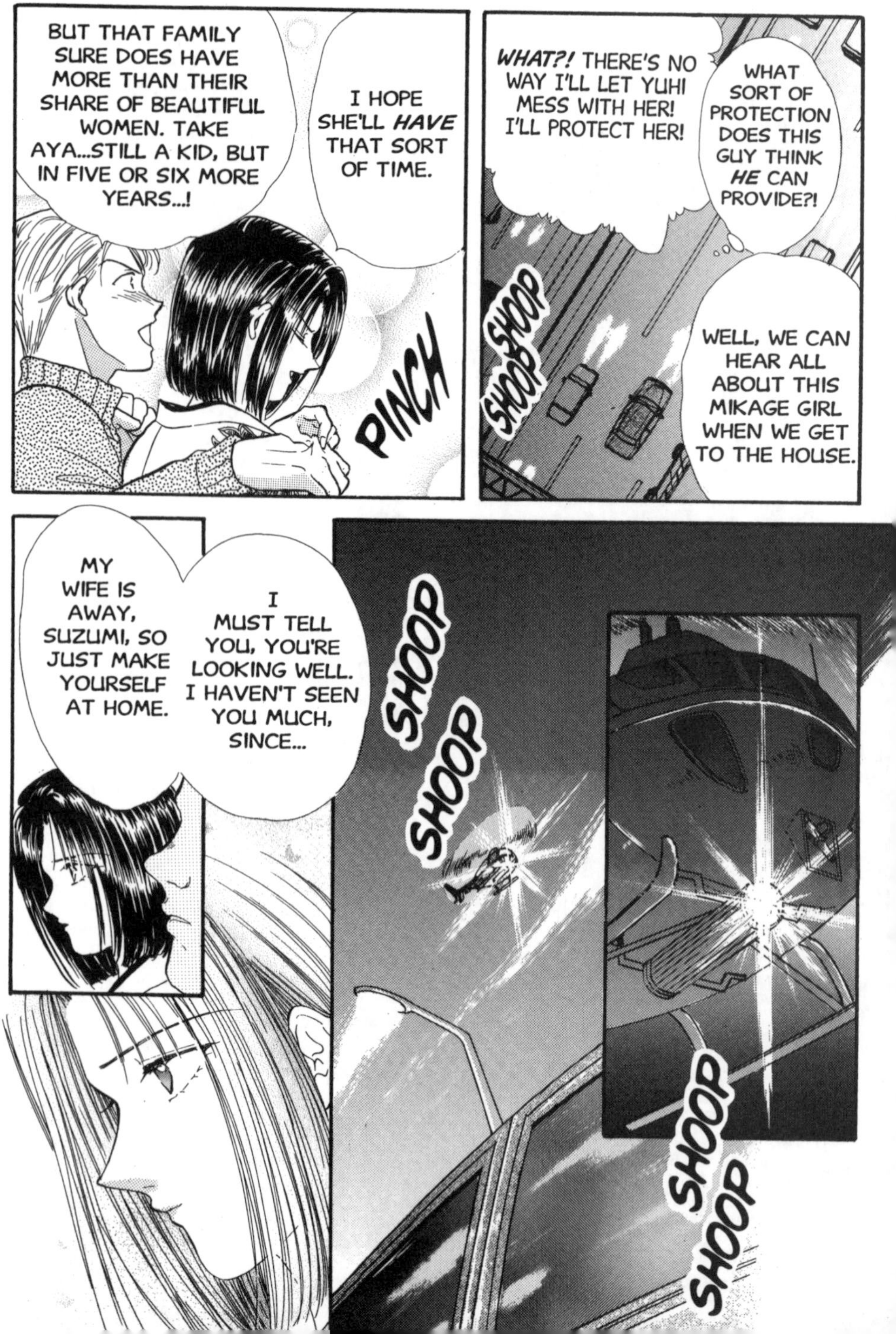
BUT THAT FAMILY SURE DOES HAVE MORE THAN THEIR SHARE OF BEAUTIFUL WOMEN. TAKE AYA...STILL A KID, BUT IN FIVE OR SIX MORE YEARS...!
I HOPE SHE'LL *HAVE* THAT SORT OF TIME.
PINCH
WHAT?! THERE'S NO WAY I'LL LET YUHI MESS WITH HER! I'LL PROTECT HER!
WHAT SORT OF PROTECTION DOES THIS GUY THINK *HE* CAN PROVIDE?!
SHOOP SHOOP
WELL, WE CAN HEAR ALL ABOUT THIS MIKAGE GIRL WHEN WE GET TO THE HOUSE.
MY WIFE IS AWAY, SUZUMI, SO JUST MAKE YOURSELF AT HOME.
I MUST TELL YOU, YOU'RE LOOKING WELL. I HAVEN'T SEEN YOU MUCH, SINCE...
SHOOP
SHOOP
SHOOP
SHOOP

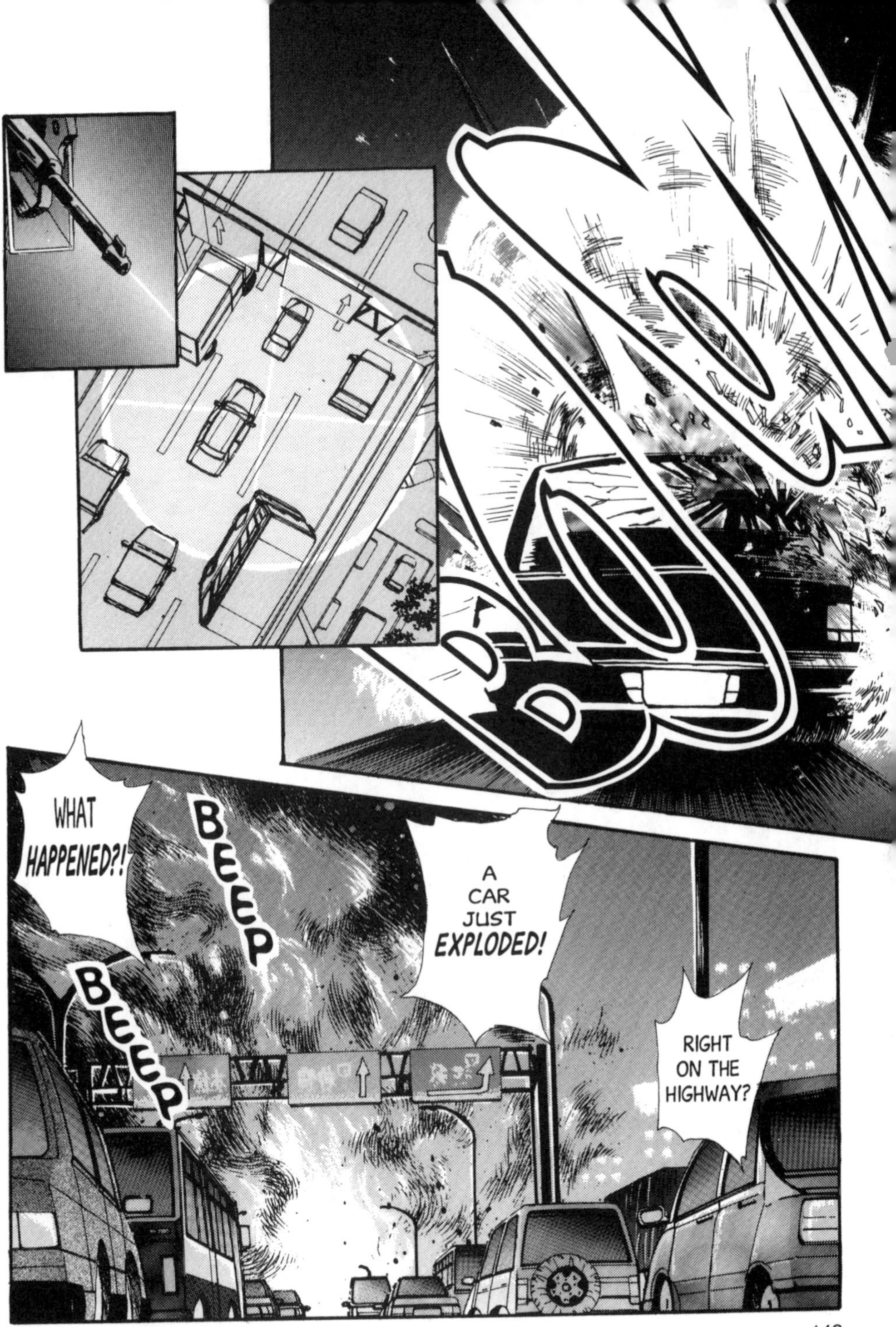
WHAT HAPPENED?!
BEEP
BEEP
A CAR JUST EXPLODED!
RIGHT ON THE HIGHWAY?

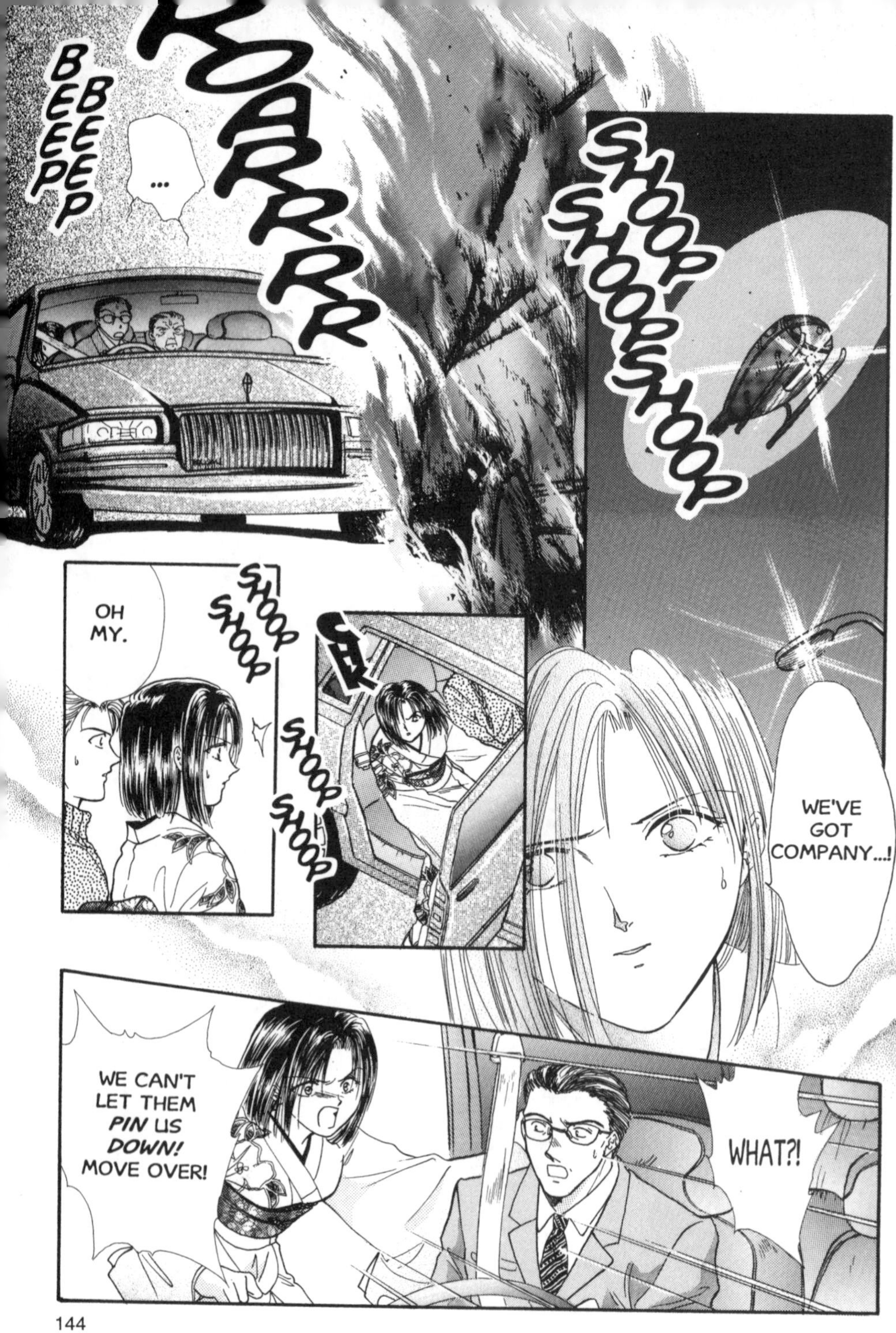
BEEEP BEEEP
...
KOARRRR
SHOOP SHOOP SHOOP
OH MY.
SHOOP SHOOP
SHOOP SHOOP
WE'VE GOT COMPANY...!
WE CAN'T LET THEM *PIN* US *DOWN!* MOVE OVER!
WHAT?!

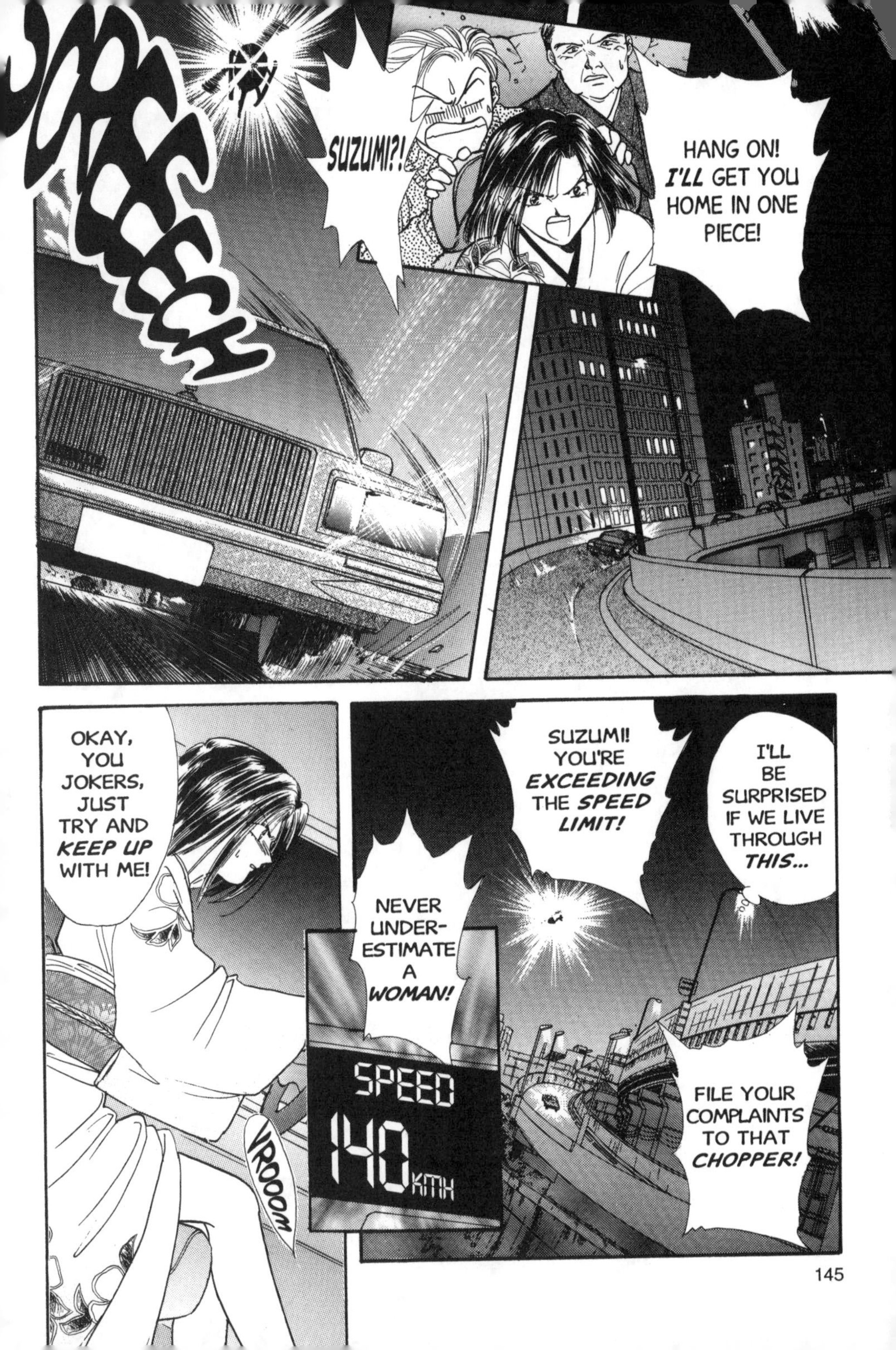
SCREECH
SUZUMI?!
HANG ON! I'LL GET YOU HOME IN ONE PIECE!
OKAY, YOU JOKERS, JUST TRY AND KEEP UP WITH ME!
VROOOOM
SUZUMI! YOU'RE EXCEEDING THE SPEED LIMIT!
I'LL BE SURPRISED IF WE LIVE THROUGH THIS...
NEVER UNDER-ESTIMATE A WOMAN!
SPEED
140 KMH
FILE YOUR COMPLAINTS TO THAT CHOPPER!

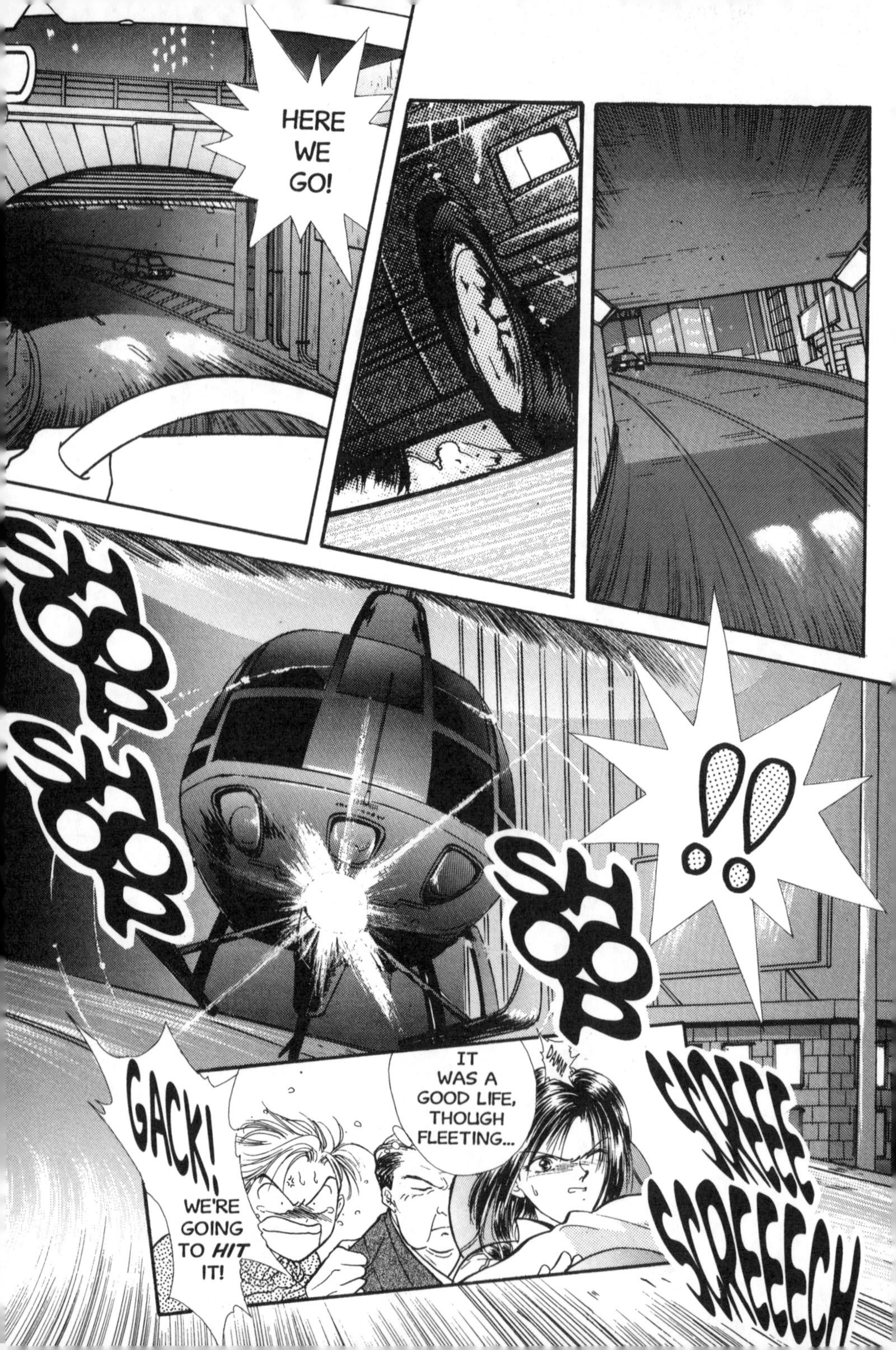
HERE WE GO!
!!
GACK! WE'RE GOING TO *HIT* IT!
IT WAS A GOOD LIFE, THOUGH FLEETING...
DAMN!
SCREEE SCREEECH

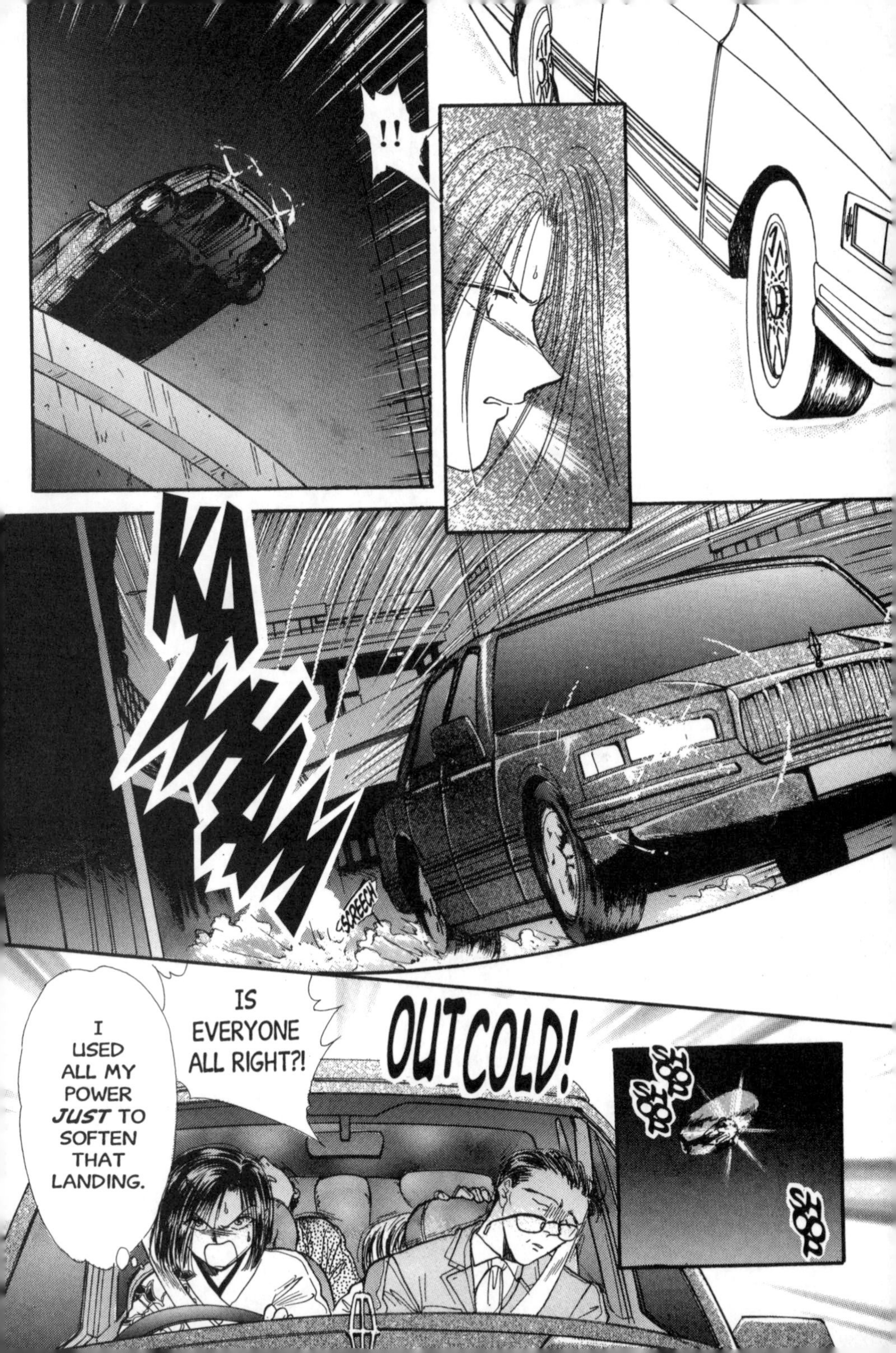
!!
KA-WHAM
SCREECH
I USED ALL MY POWER *JUST* TO SOFTEN THAT LANDING.
IS EVERYONE ALL RIGHT?!
OUT COLD!

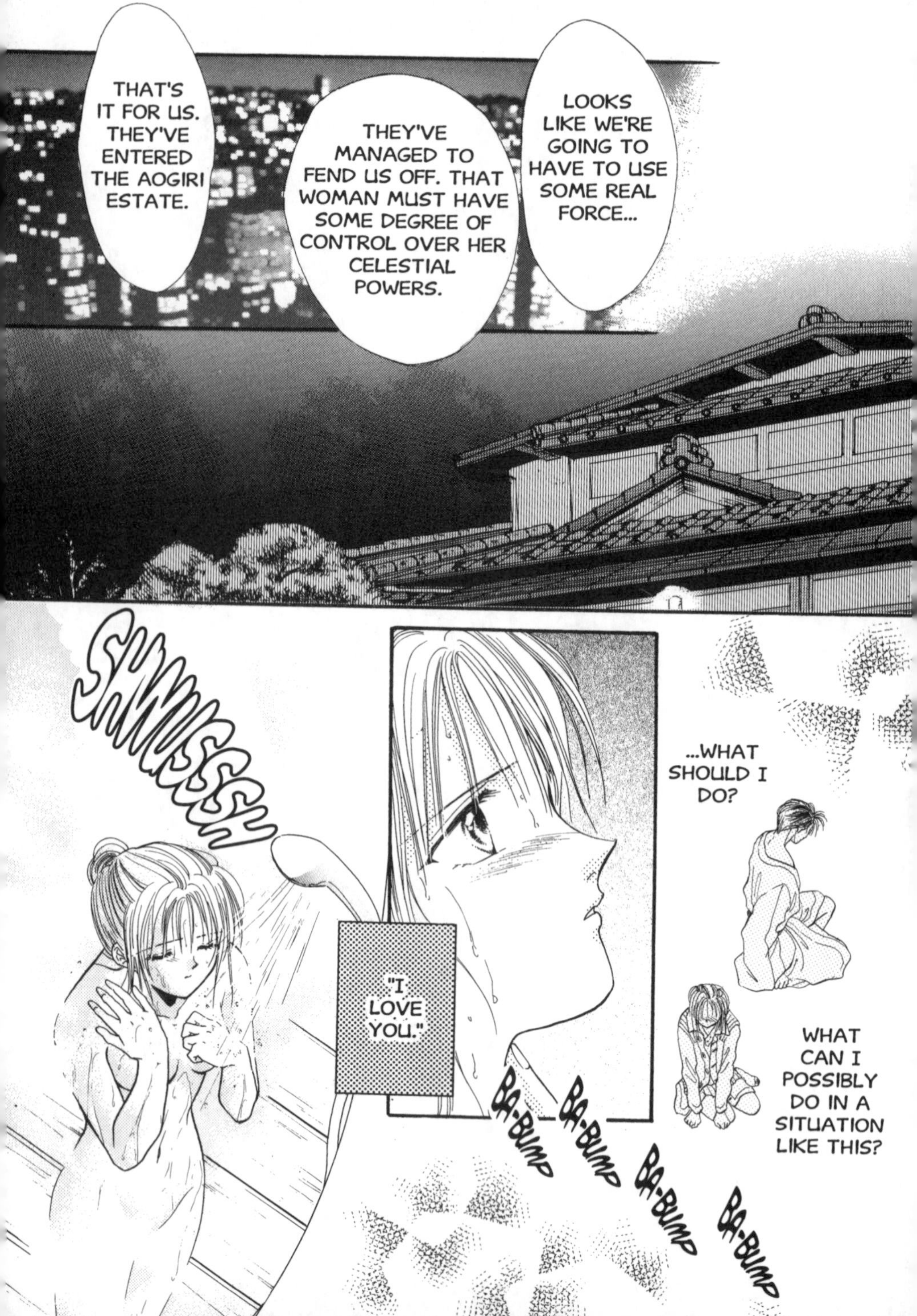
THAT'S IT FOR US. THEY'VE ENTERED THE AOGIRI ESTATE.
THEY'VE MANAGED TO FEND US OFF. THAT WOMAN MUST HAVE SOME DEGREE OF CONTROL OVER HER CELESTIAL POWERS.
LOOKS LIKE WE'RE GOING TO HAVE TO USE SOME REAL FORCE...
SHWISSSH
"I LOVE YOU."
BA-BUMP
BA-BUMP
BA-BUMP
BA-BUMP
...WHAT SHOULD I DO?
WHAT CAN I POSSIBLY DO IN A SITUATION LIKE THIS?

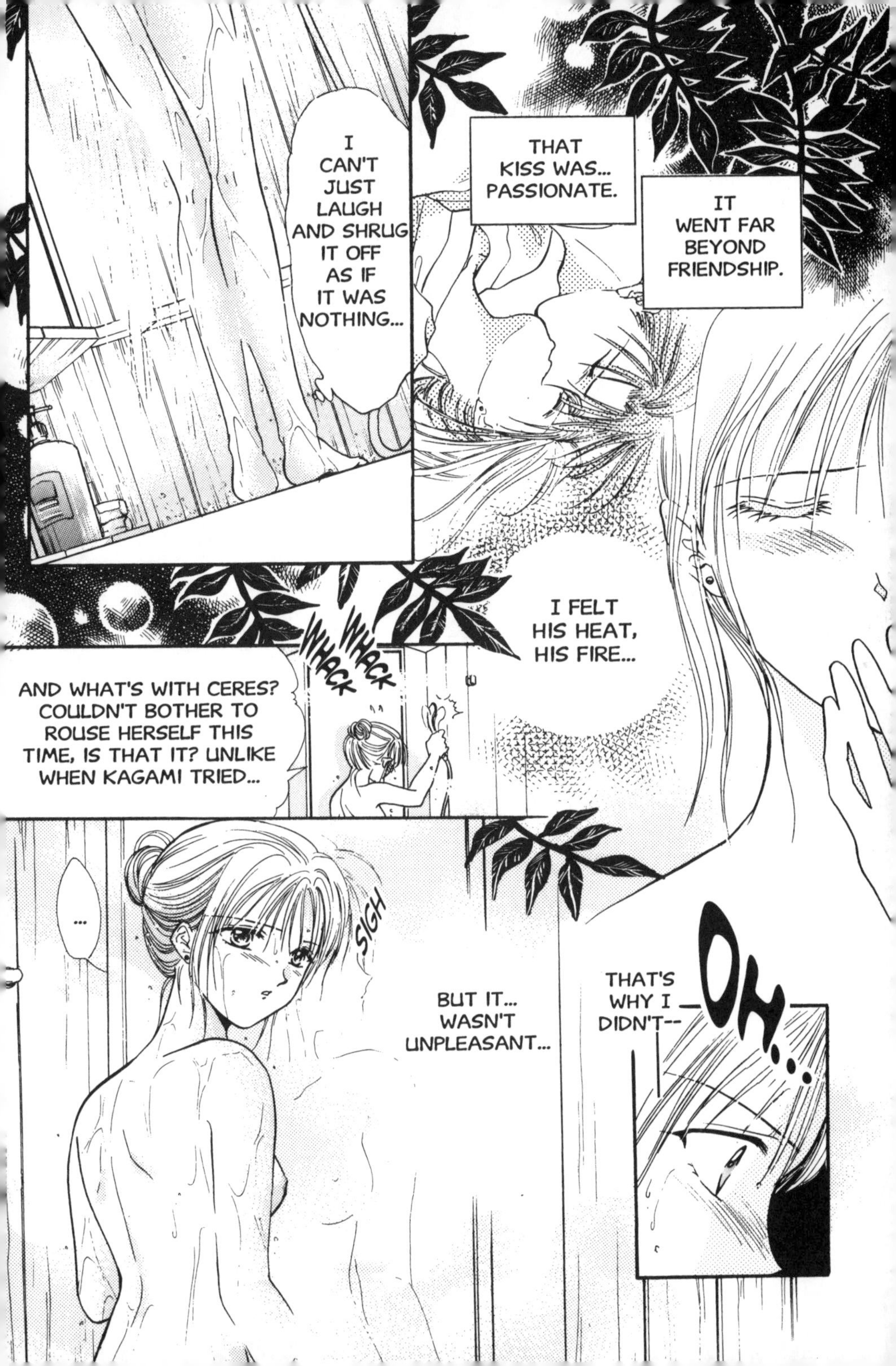
THAT KISS WAS... PASSIONATE.
IT WENT FAR BEYOND FRIENDSHIP.
I FELT HIS HEAT, HIS FIRE...
I CAN'T JUST LAUGH AND SHRUG IT OFF AS IF IT WAS NOTHING...
WHACK
WHACK
AND WHAT'S WITH CERES? COULDN'T BOTHER TO ROUSE HERSELF THIS TIME, IS THAT IT? UNLIKE WHEN KAGAMI TRIED...
THAT'S WHY I DIDN'T--
OH...
BUT IT... WASN'T UNPLEASANT...
SIGH
...

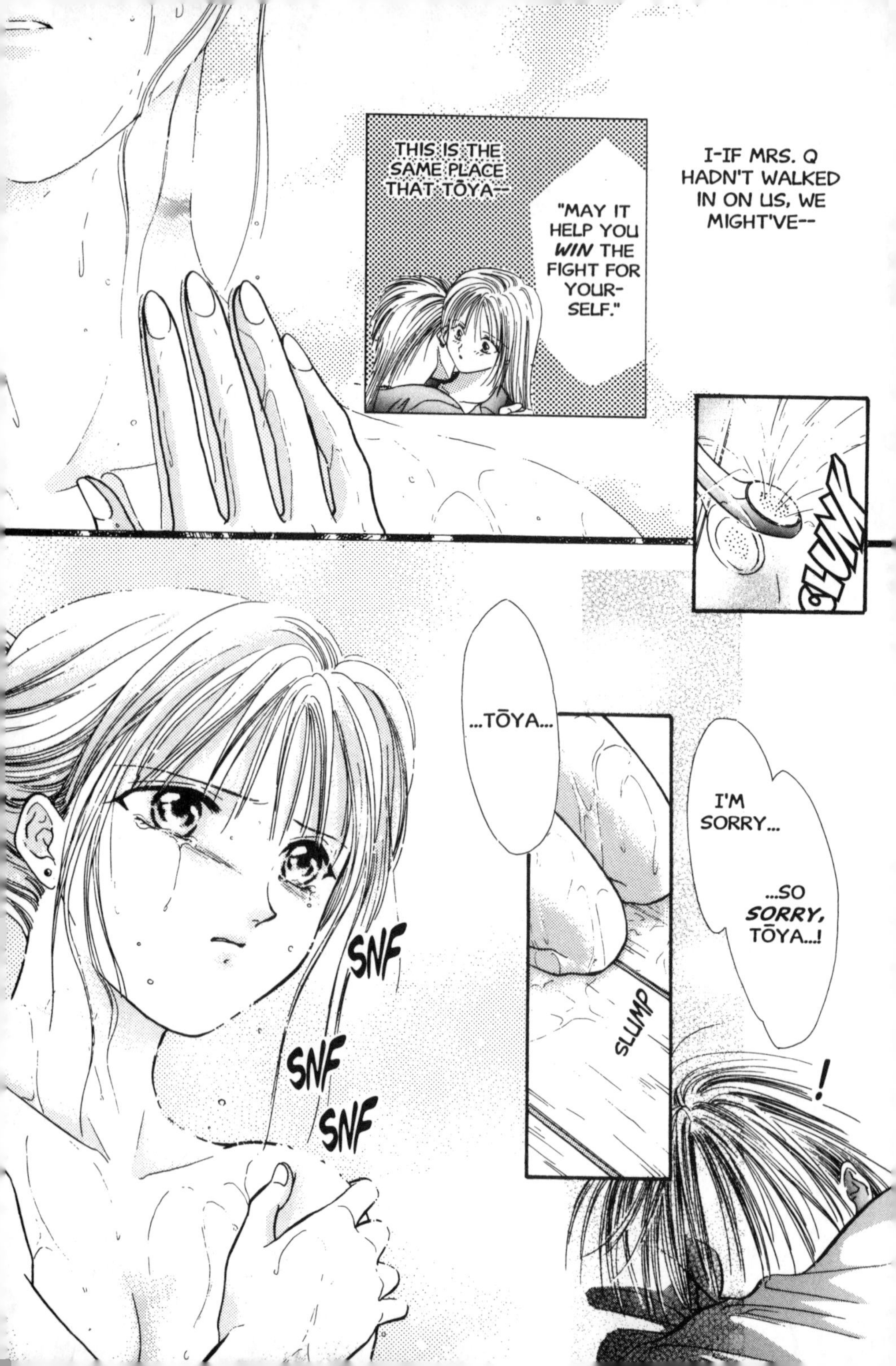
THIS IS THE SAME PLACE THAT TŌYA--
"MAY IT HELP YOU ***WIN*** THE FIGHT FOR YOUR-SELF."
I-IF MRS. Q HADN'T WALKED IN ON US, WE MIGHT'VE--
GLUNK
SNF
SNF
SNF
...TŌYA...
SLUMP
I'M SORRY...
...SO ***SORRY,*** TŌYA...!
!

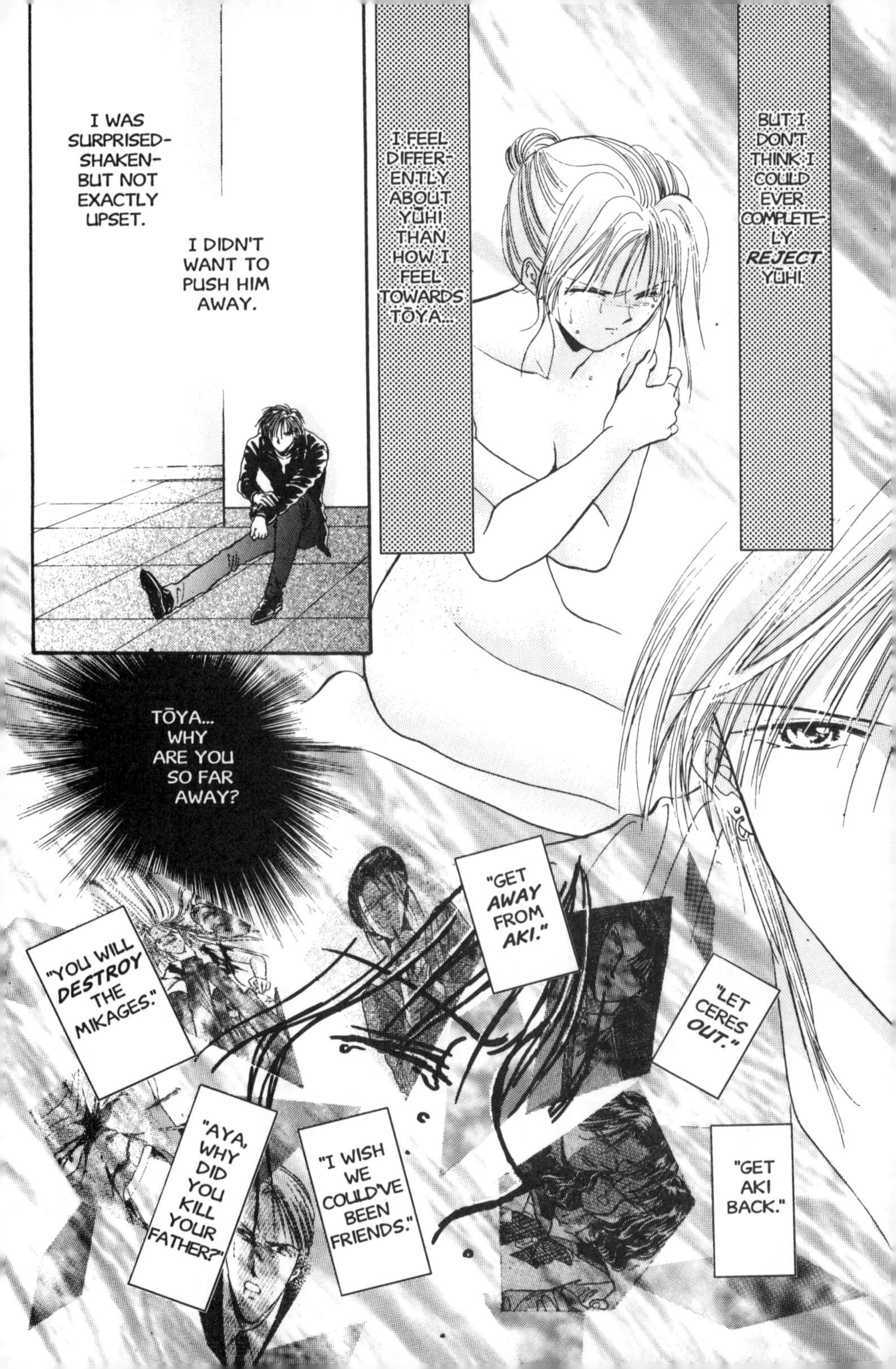
I WAS SURPRISED- SHAKEN- BUT NOT EXACTLY UPSET.
I DIDN'T WANT TO PUSH HIM AWAY.
I FEEL DIFFERENTLY ABOUT YŪHI THAN HOW I FEEL TOWARDS TŌYA...
BUT I DON'T THINK I COULD EVER COMPLETELY *REJECT* YŪHI.
TŌYA... WHY ARE YOU SO FAR AWAY?
"YOU WILL *DESTROY* THE MIKAGES."
"GET *AWAY* FROM *AKI*."
"LET CERES *OUT*."
"AYA, WHY DID YOU KILL YOUR FATHER?"
"I WISH WE COULD'VE BEEN FRIENDS."
"GET AKI BACK."

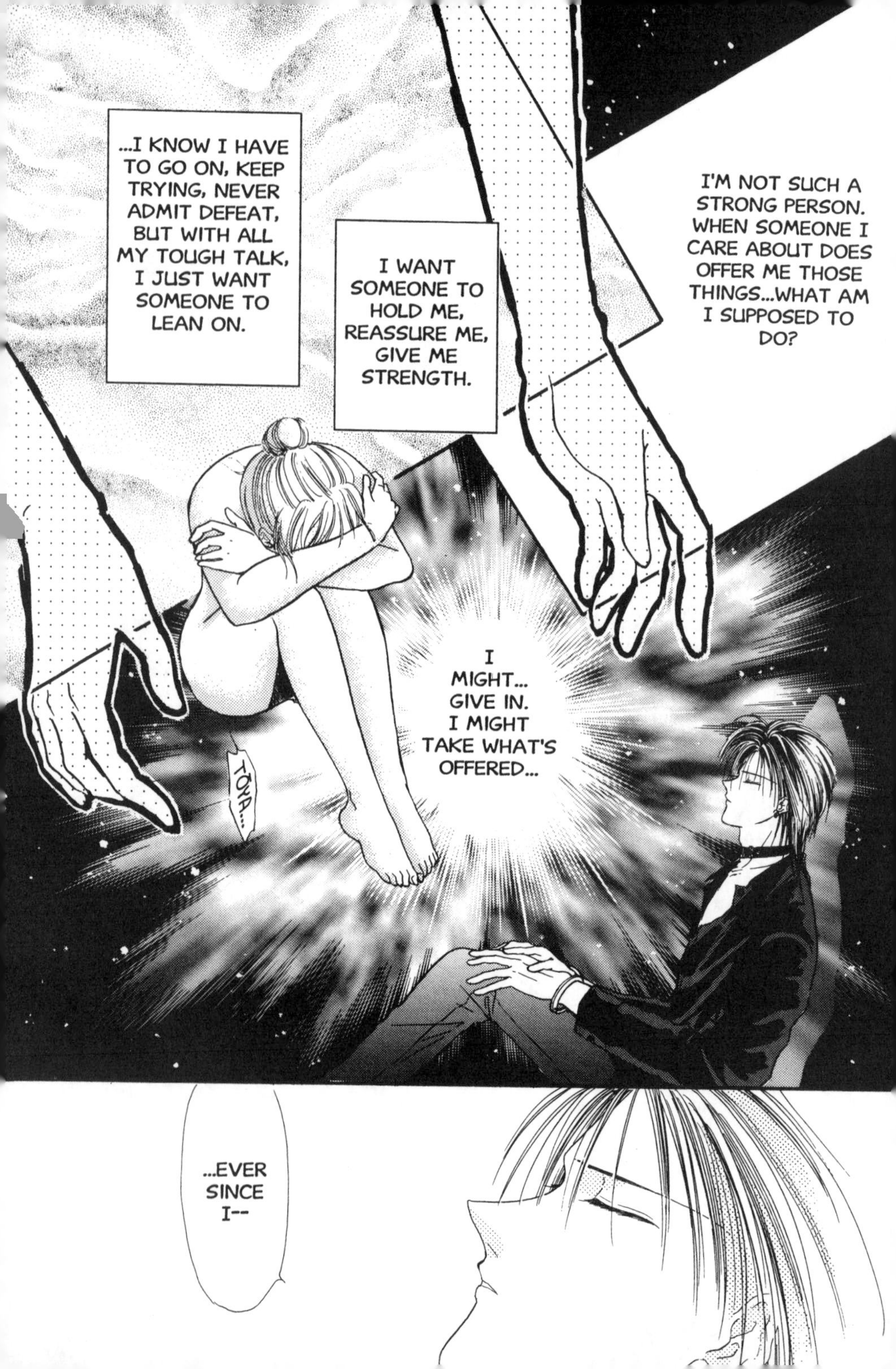
...I KNOW I HAVE TO GO ON, KEEP TRYING, NEVER ADMIT DEFEAT, BUT WITH ALL MY TOUGH TALK, I JUST WANT SOMEONE TO LEAN ON.
I WANT SOMEONE TO HOLD ME, REASSURE ME, GIVE ME STRENGTH.
I'M NOT SUCH A STRONG PERSON. WHEN SOMEONE I CARE ABOUT DOES OFFER ME THOSE THINGS...WHAT AM I SUPPOSED TO DO?
I MIGHT... GIVE IN. I MIGHT TAKE WHAT'S OFFERED...
TŌYA...
...EVER SINCE I--

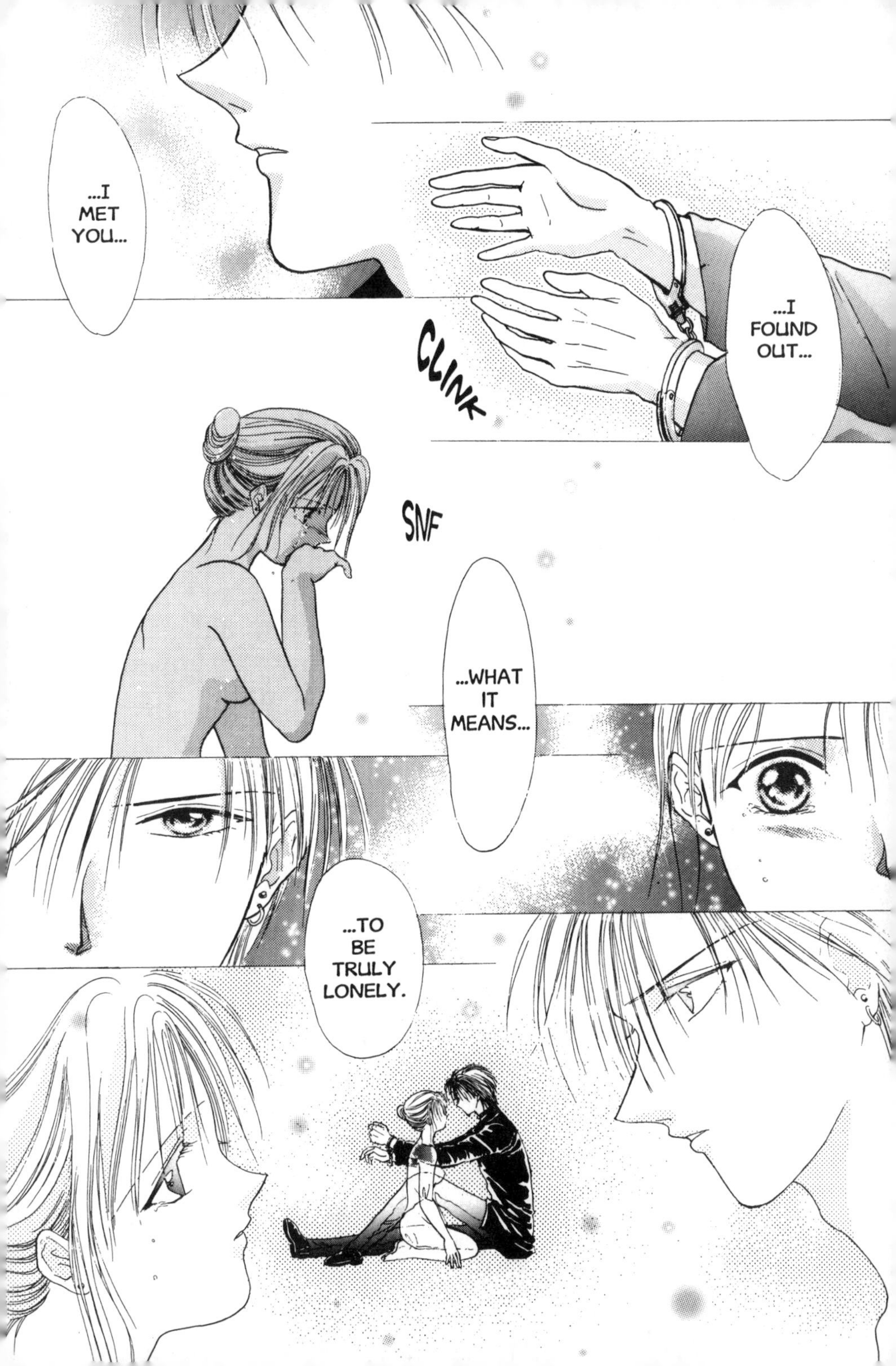
...I MET YOU...
CLINK
...I FOUND OUT...
SNF
...WHAT IT MEANS...
...TO BE TRULY LONELY.

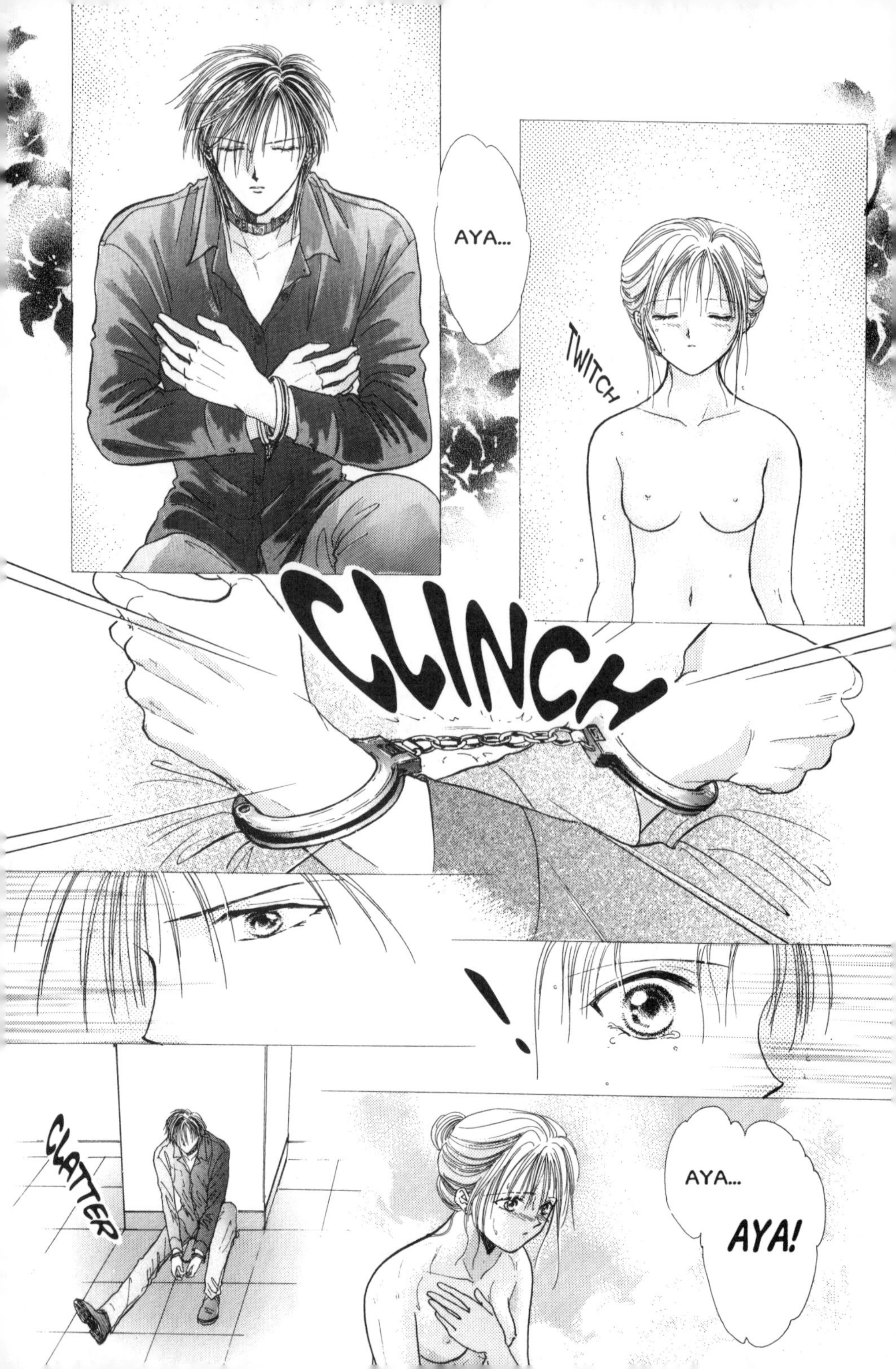
AYA...
TWITCH
CLINCH
!
CLATTER
AYA...
AYA!

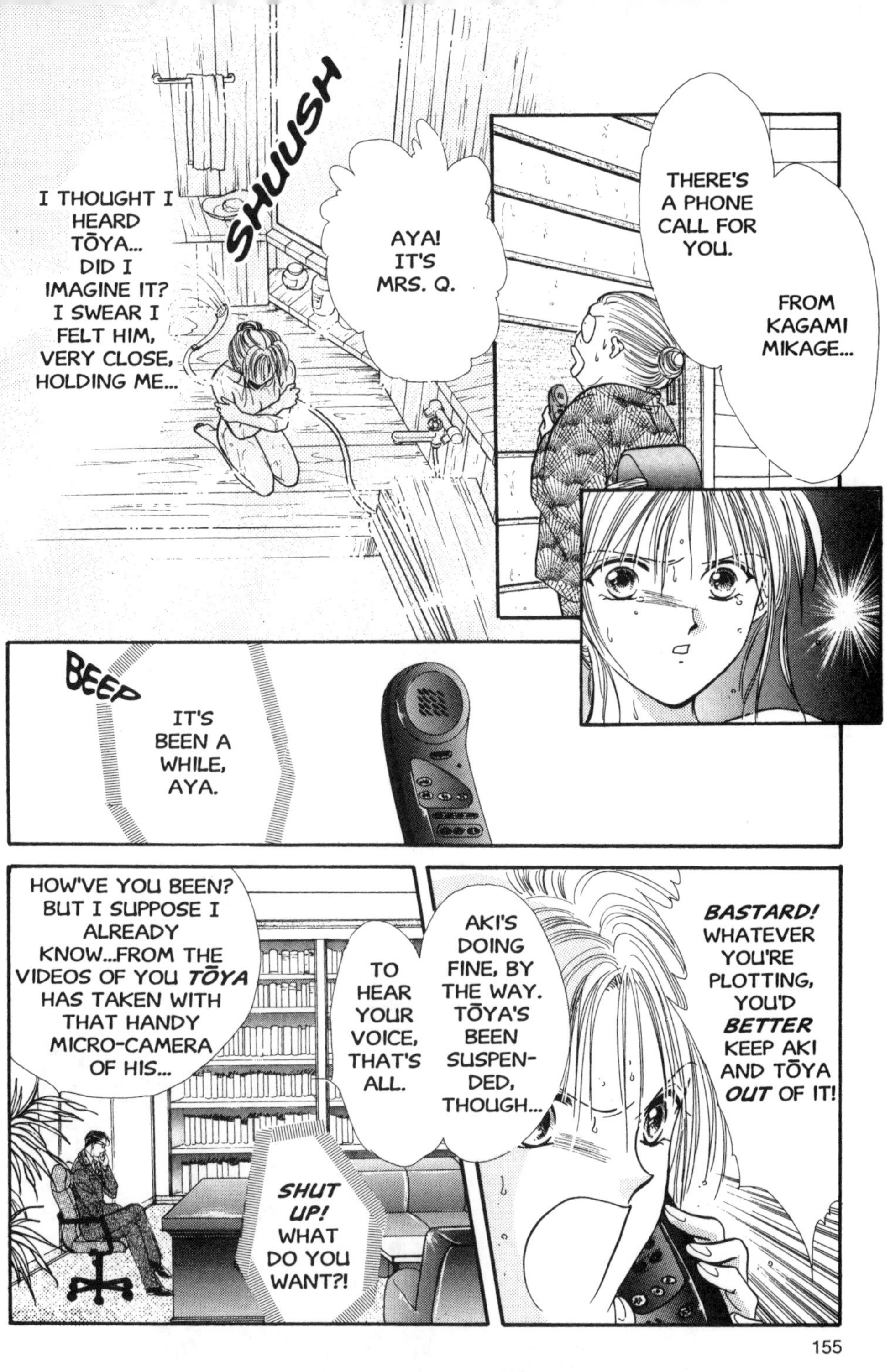
I THOUGHT I HEARD TŌYA... DID I IMAGINE IT? I SWEAR I FELT HIM, VERY CLOSE, HOLDING ME...
SHUUSH
AYA! IT'S MRS. Q.
THERE'S A PHONE CALL FOR YOU.
FROM KAGAMI MIKAGE...
BEEP
IT'S BEEN A WHILE, AYA.
HOW'VE YOU BEEN? BUT I SUPPOSE I ALREADY KNOW...FROM THE VIDEOS OF YOU *TŌYA* HAS TAKEN WITH THAT HANDY MICRO-CAMERA OF HIS...
TO HEAR YOUR VOICE, THAT'S ALL.
SHUT UP! WHAT DO YOU WANT?!
AKI'S DOING FINE, BY THE WAY. TŌYA'S BEEN SUSPEN-DED, THOUGH...
BASTARD! WHATEVER YOU'RE PLOTTING, YOU'D *BETTER* KEEP AKI AND TŌYA *OUT* OF IT!

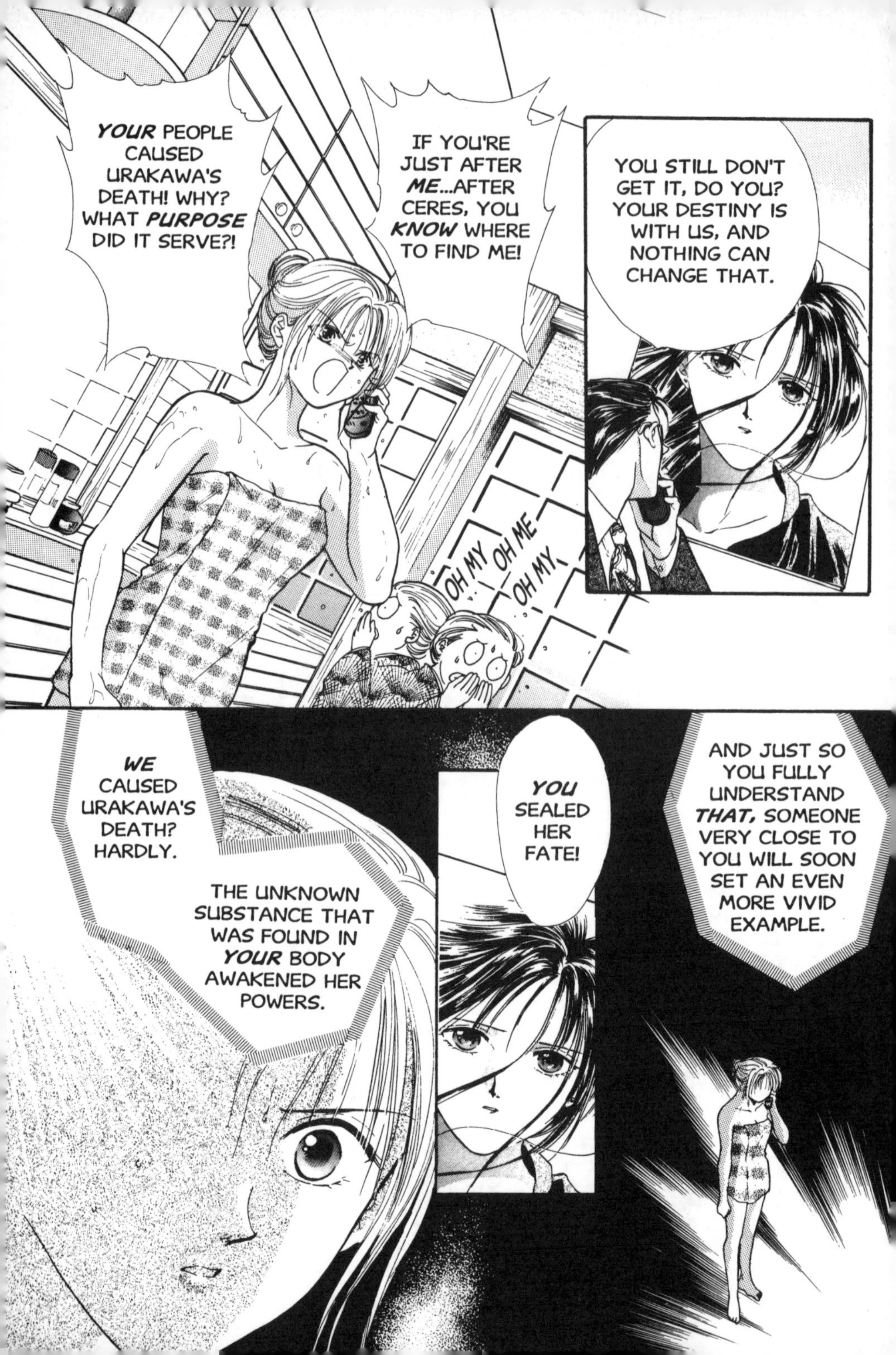
YOUR PEOPLE CAUSED URAKAWA'S DEATH! WHY? WHAT PURPOSE DID IT SERVE?!
IF YOU'RE JUST AFTER ME...AFTER CERES, YOU KNOW WHERE TO FIND ME!
OH MY OH ME OH MY
YOU STILL DON'T GET IT, DO YOU? YOUR DESTINY IS WITH US, AND NOTHING CAN CHANGE THAT.
WE CAUSED URAKAWA'S DEATH? HARDLY.
THE UNKNOWN SUBSTANCE THAT WAS FOUND IN YOUR BODY AWAKENED HER POWERS.
YOU SEALED HER FATE!
AND JUST SO YOU FULLY UNDERSTAND THAT, SOMEONE VERY CLOSE TO YOU WILL SOON SET AN EVEN MORE VIVID EXAMPLE.

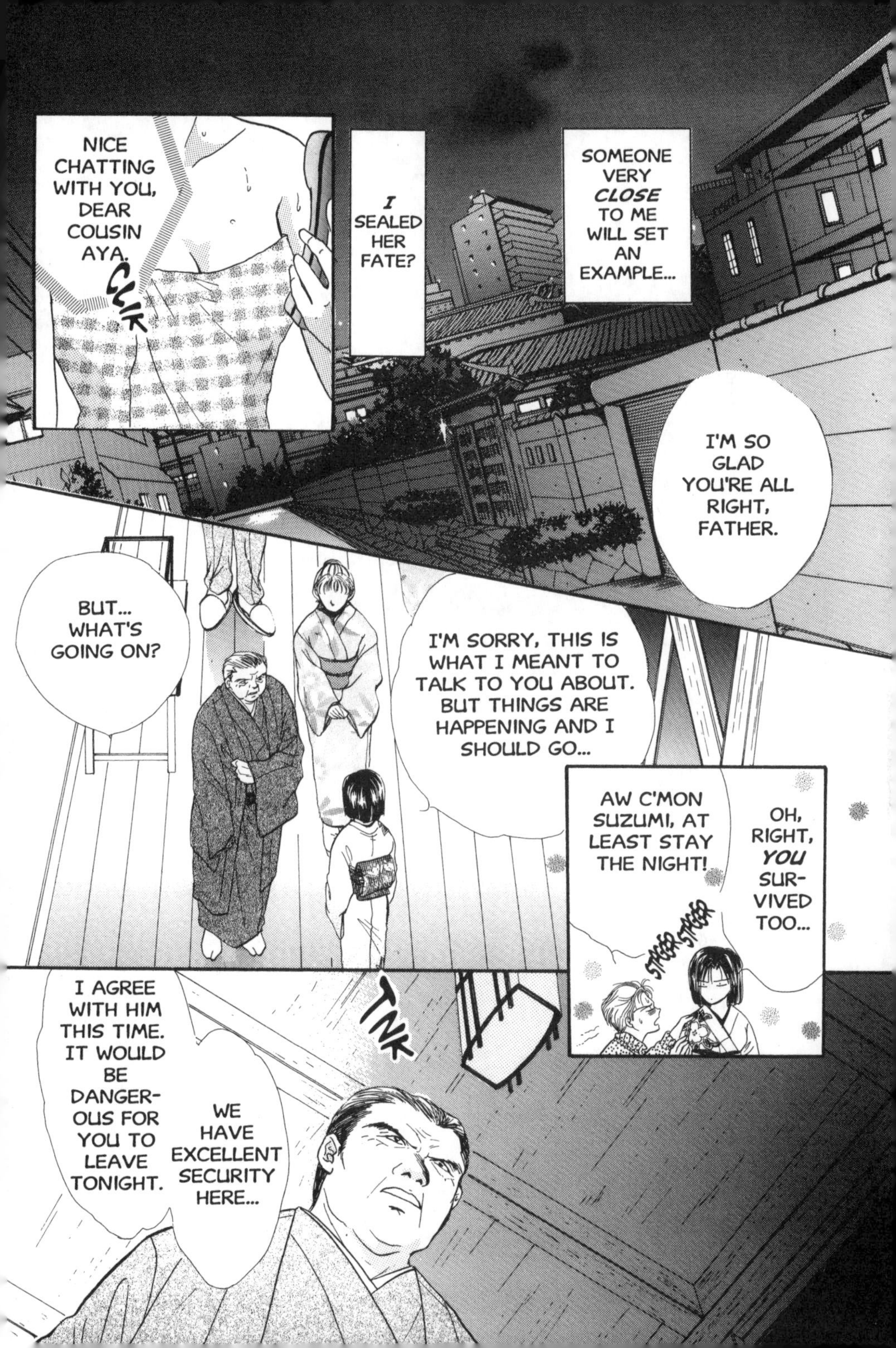
NICE CHATTING WITH YOU, DEAR COUSIN AYA.
CLIK
I SEALED HER FATE?
SOMEONE VERY CLOSE TO ME WILL SET AN EXAMPLE...
I'M SO GLAD YOU'RE ALL RIGHT, FATHER.
BUT... WHAT'S GOING ON?
I'M SORRY, THIS IS WHAT I MEANT TO TALK TO YOU ABOUT. BUT THINGS ARE HAPPENING AND I SHOULD GO...
AW C'MON SUZUMI, AT LEAST STAY THE NIGHT!
OH, RIGHT, YOU SUR-VIVED TOO...
STAGGER STAGGER
I AGREE WITH HIM THIS TIME. IT WOULD BE DANGER-OUS FOR YOU TO LEAVE TONIGHT.
WE HAVE EXCELLENT SECURITY HERE...
TNK

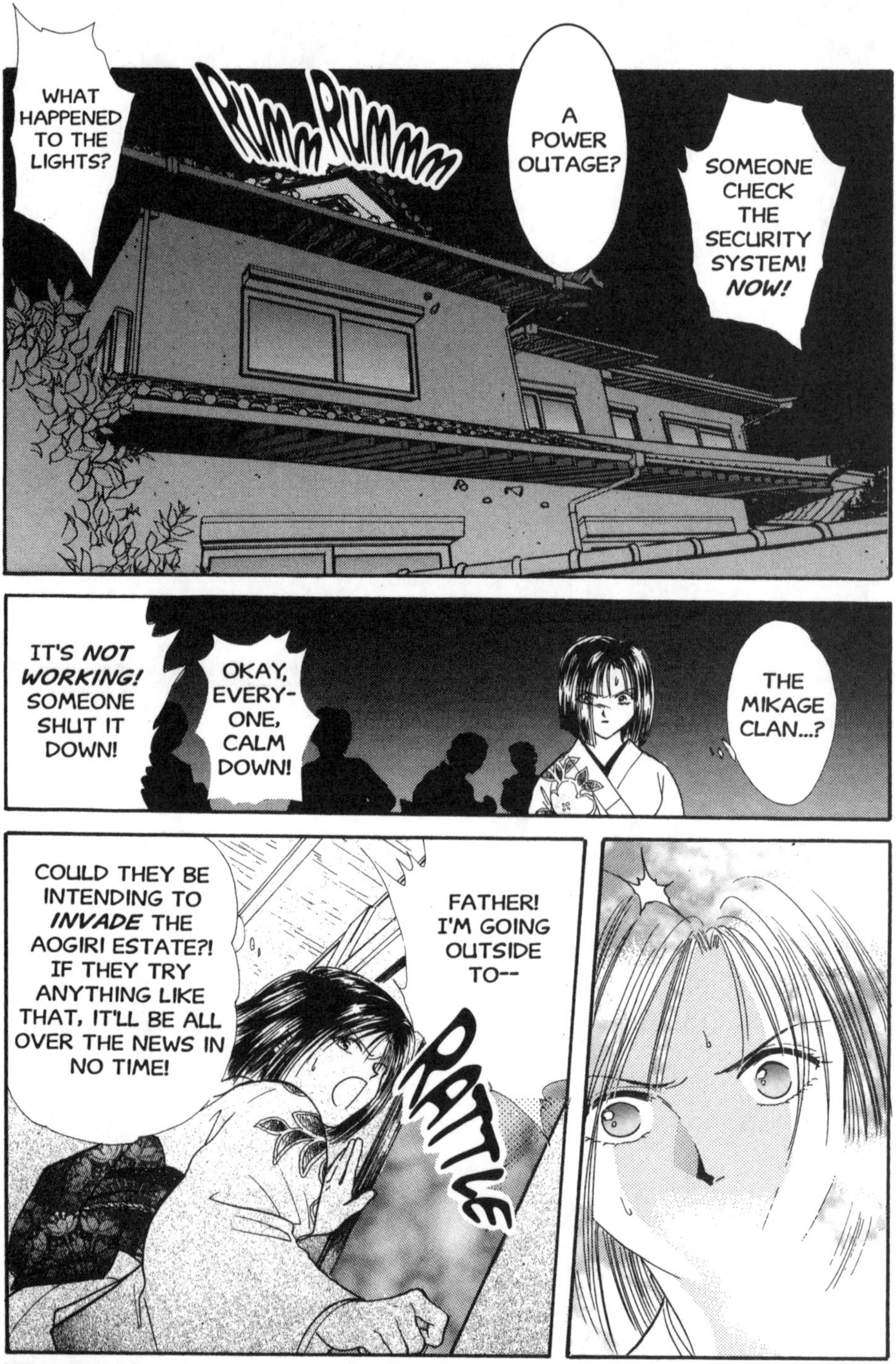
WHAT HAPPENED TO THE LIGHTS?
RUMMM RUMMMM
A POWER OUTAGE?
SOMEONE CHECK THE SECURITY SYSTEM! NOW!
IT'S NOT WORKING! SOMEONE SHUT IT DOWN!
OKAY, EVERY-ONE, CALM DOWN!
THE MIKAGE CLAN...?
COULD THEY BE INTENDING TO INVADE THE AOGIRI ESTATE?! IF THEY TRY ANYTHING LIKE THAT, IT'LL BE ALL OVER THE NEWS IN NO TIME!
FATHER! I'M GOING OUTSIDE TO--
RATTLE

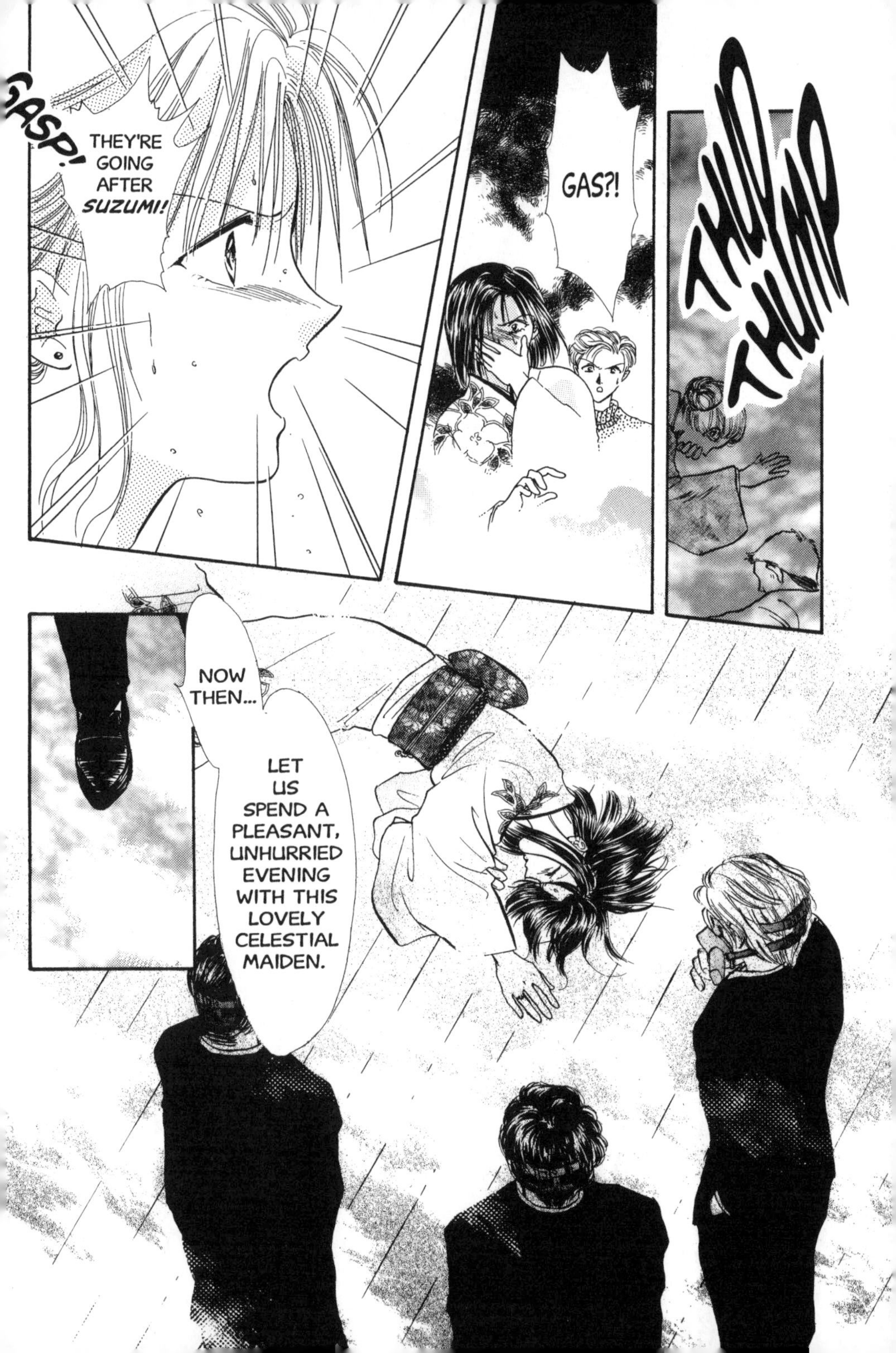
GASP!
THEY'RE GOING AFTER *SUZUMI!*
GAS?!
THUD THUMP
NOW THEN...
LET US SPEND A PLEASANT, UNHURRIED EVENING WITH THIS LOVELY CELESTIAL MAIDEN.

BIRTHDAY: August 8

BLOODTYPE: B

HEIGHT: 5' 10" and still growing

HOBBIES: Cooking! Specializing in Japanese cuisine.

SPECIAL TALENT: Marital arts. Proficient in the use of metal chopsticks as a deadly weapon.

YŪHI AOGIRI

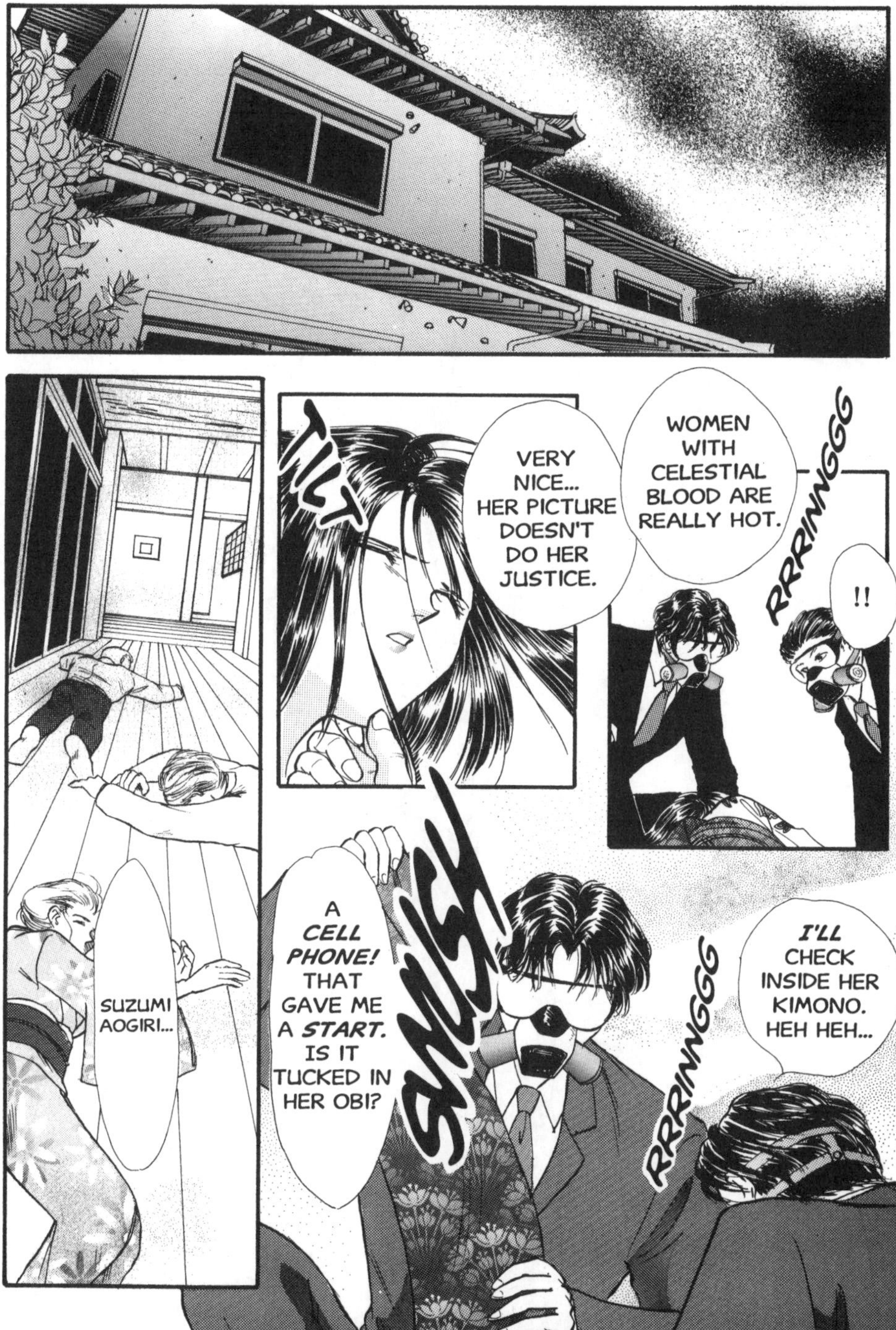
SUZUMI AOGIRI...
TILT
VERY NICE... HER PICTURE DOESN'T DO HER JUSTICE.
WOMEN WITH CELESTIAL BLOOD ARE REALLY HOT.
RRRINNGGG
!!
A *CELL PHONE!* THAT GAVE ME A *START.* IS IT TUCKED IN HER OBI?
SHWISH
RRRINNGGG
I'LL CHECK INSIDE HER KIMONO. HEH HEH...

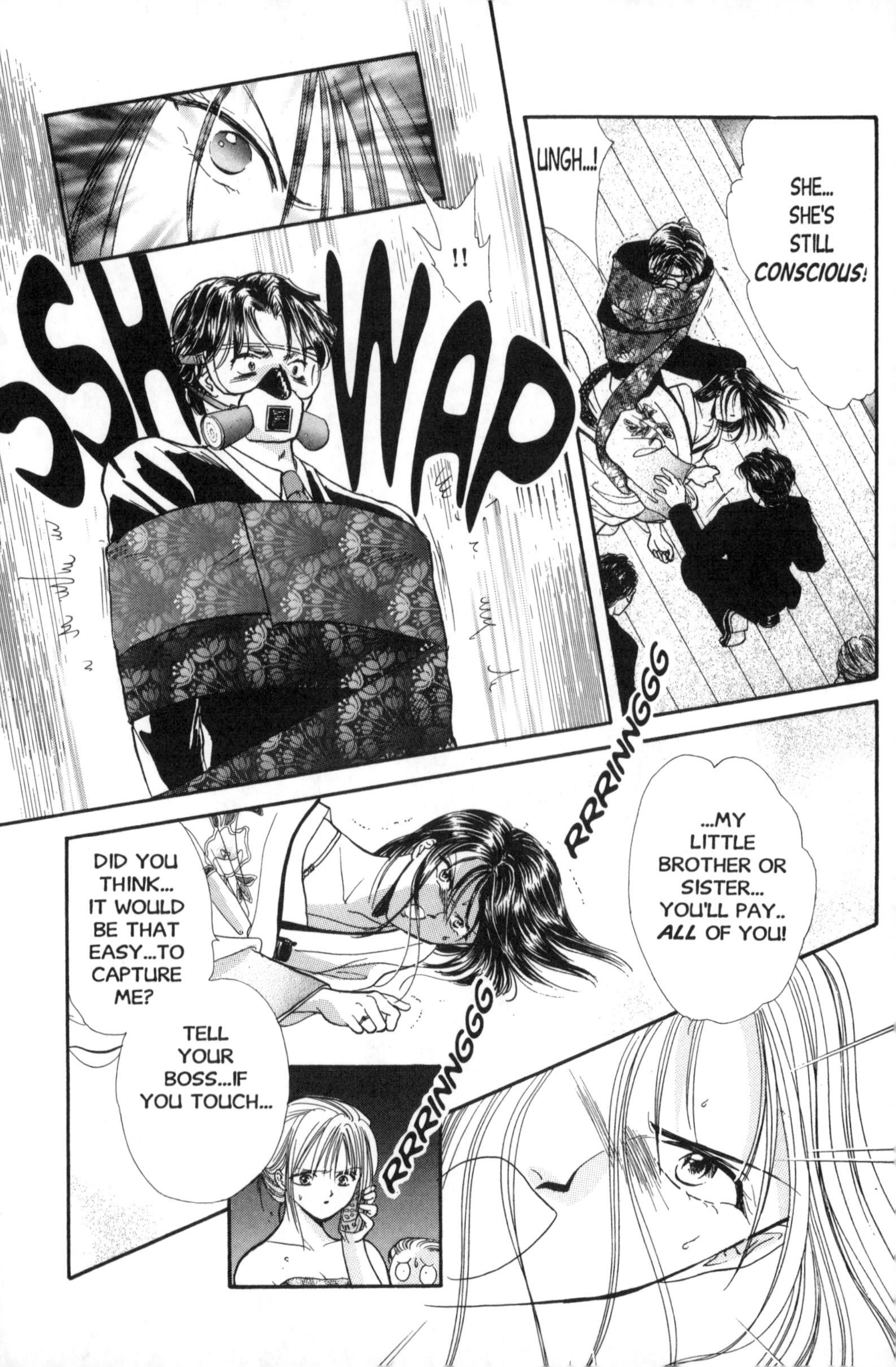
SHWAP
!!
UNGH...!
SHE... SHE'S STILL CONSCIOUS!
RRRINNGGG
DID YOU THINK... IT WOULD BE THAT EASY...TO CAPTURE ME?
RRRINNGGG
TELL YOUR BOSS...IF YOU TOUCH...
...MY LITTLE BROTHER OR SISTER... YOU'LL PAY.. ALL OF YOU!
RRRINNGGG

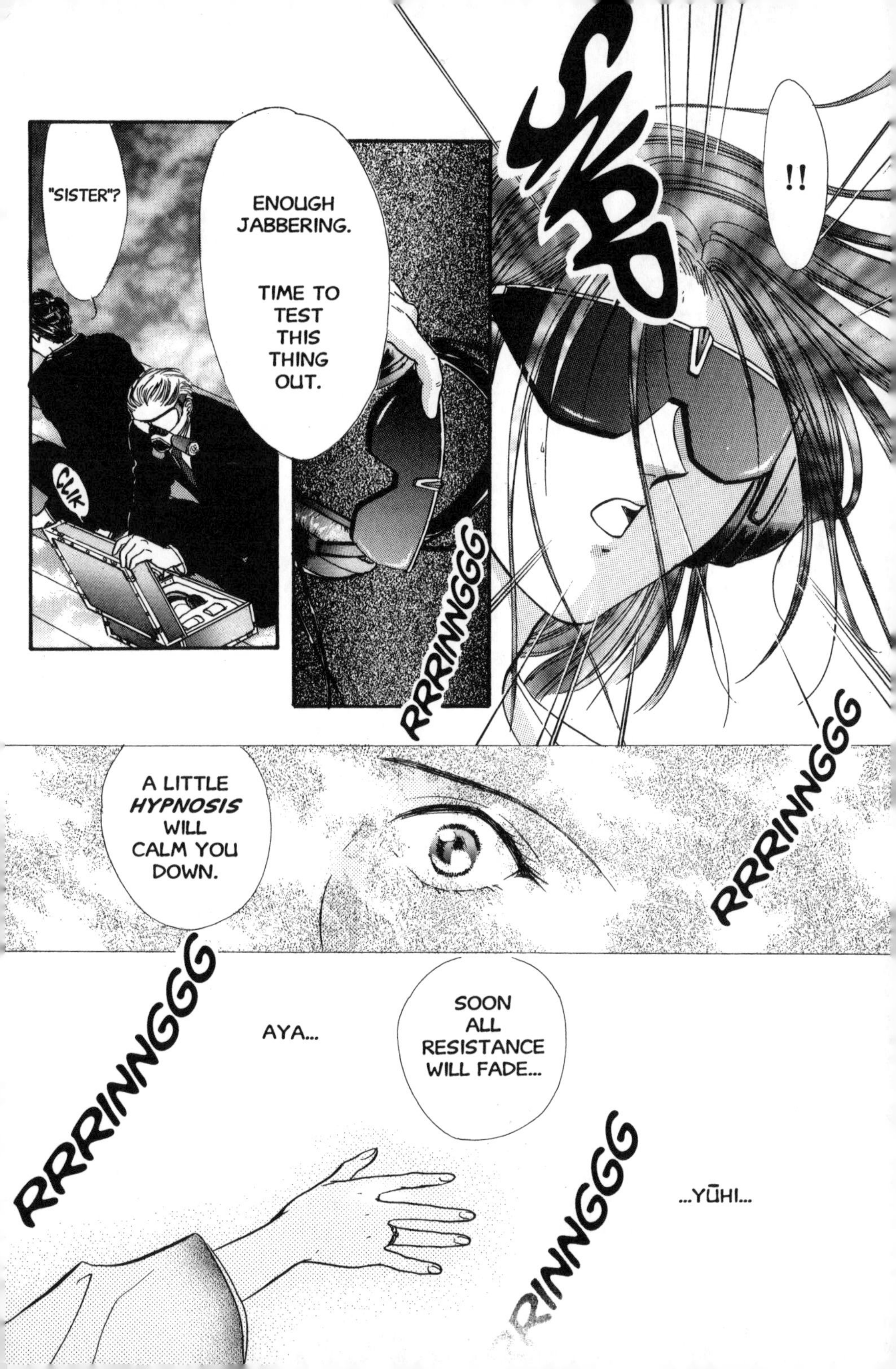
"SISTER"?
CLIK
ENOUGH JABBERING.
TIME TO TEST THIS THING OUT.
RRRINNGGG
SNAP
!!
RRRINNGGG
A LITTLE *HYPNOSIS* WILL CALM YOU DOWN.
RRRINNGGG
RRRINNGGG
AYA...
SOON ALL RESISTANCE WILL FADE...
RRINNGGG
...YŪHI...

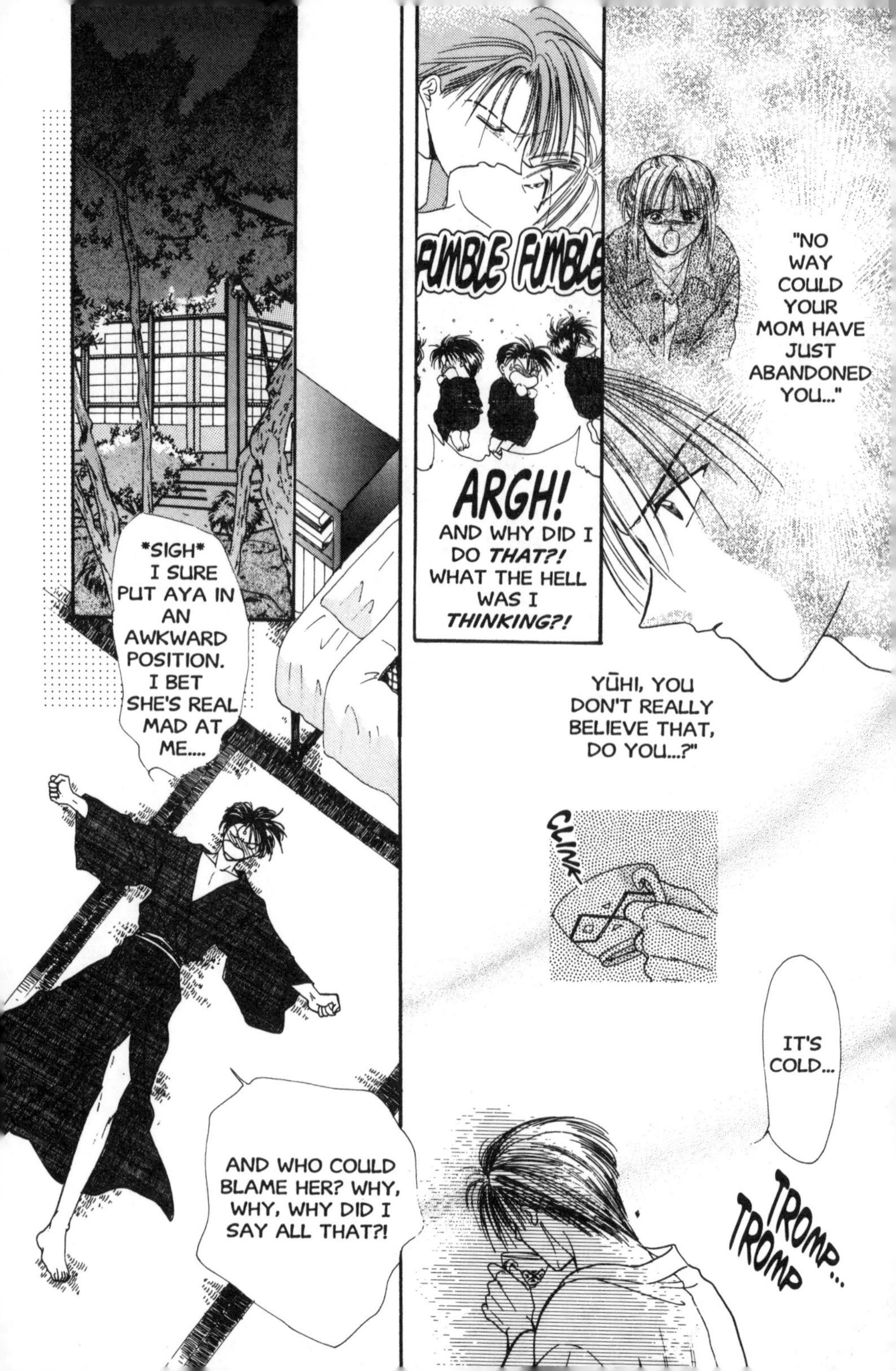
SIGH I SURE PUT AYA IN AN AWKWARD POSITION. I BET SHE'S REAL MAD AT ME....
AND WHO COULD BLAME HER? WHY, WHY, WHY DID I SAY ALL THAT?!
FUMBLE FUMBLE
ARGH!
AND WHY DID I DO THAT?! WHAT THE HELL WAS I THINKING?!
"NO WAY COULD YOUR MOM HAVE JUST ABANDONED YOU..."
YŪHI, YOU DON'T REALLY BELIEVE THAT, DO YOU...?"
CLINK
IT'S COLD...
TROMP... TROMP

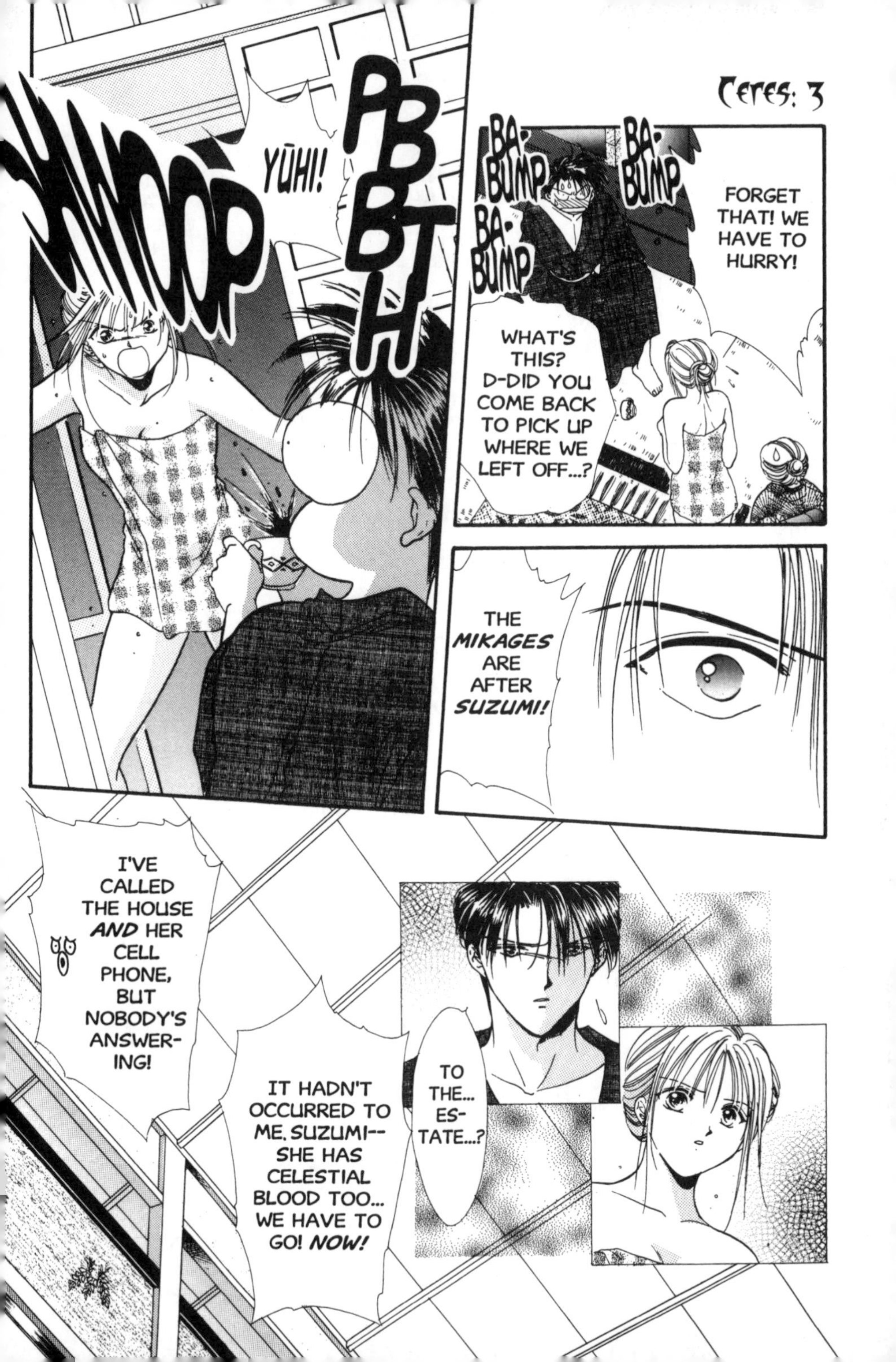
WHOOP
YŪHI!
PBBTH
BA-BUMP
BA-BUMP
BA-BUMP
FORGET THAT! WE HAVE TO HURRY!
WHAT'S THIS? D-DID YOU COME BACK TO PICK UP WHERE WE LEFT OFF...?
THE *MIKAGES* ARE AFTER *SUZUMI!*
I'VE CALLED THE HOUSE *AND* HER CELL PHONE, BUT NOBODY'S ANSWER-ING!
IT HADN'T OCCURRED TO ME. SUZUMI-- SHE HAS CELESTIAL BLOOD TOO... WE HAVE TO GO! *NOW!*
TO THE... ES-TATE...?

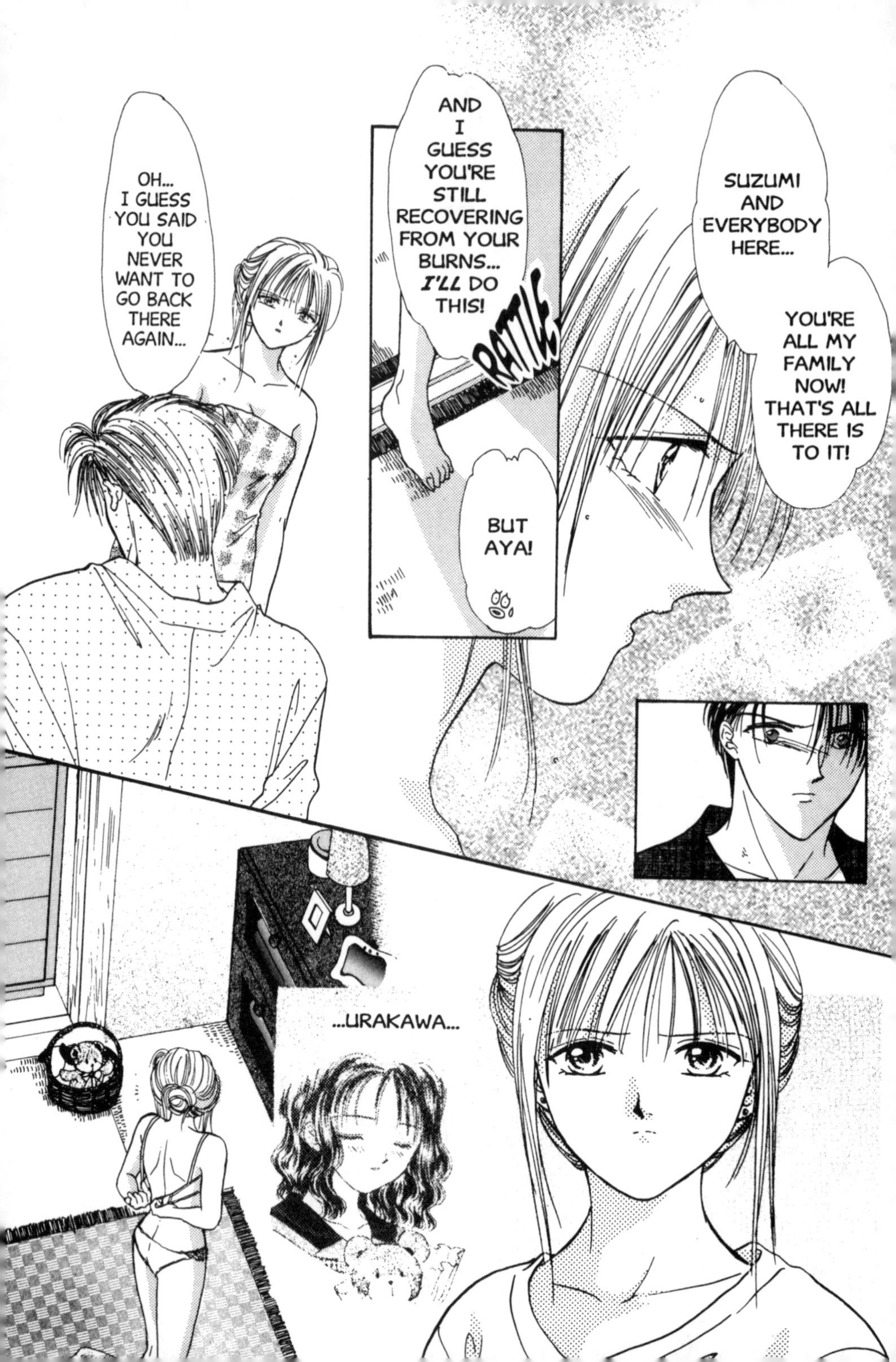
OH... I GUESS YOU SAID YOU NEVER WANT TO GO BACK THERE AGAIN...
AND I GUESS YOU'RE STILL RECOVERING FROM YOUR BURNS... *I'LL* DO THIS!
RATTLE
BUT AYA!
SUZUMI AND EVERYBODY HERE...
YOU'RE ALL MY FAMILY NOW! THAT'S ALL THERE IS TO IT!
...URAKAWA...

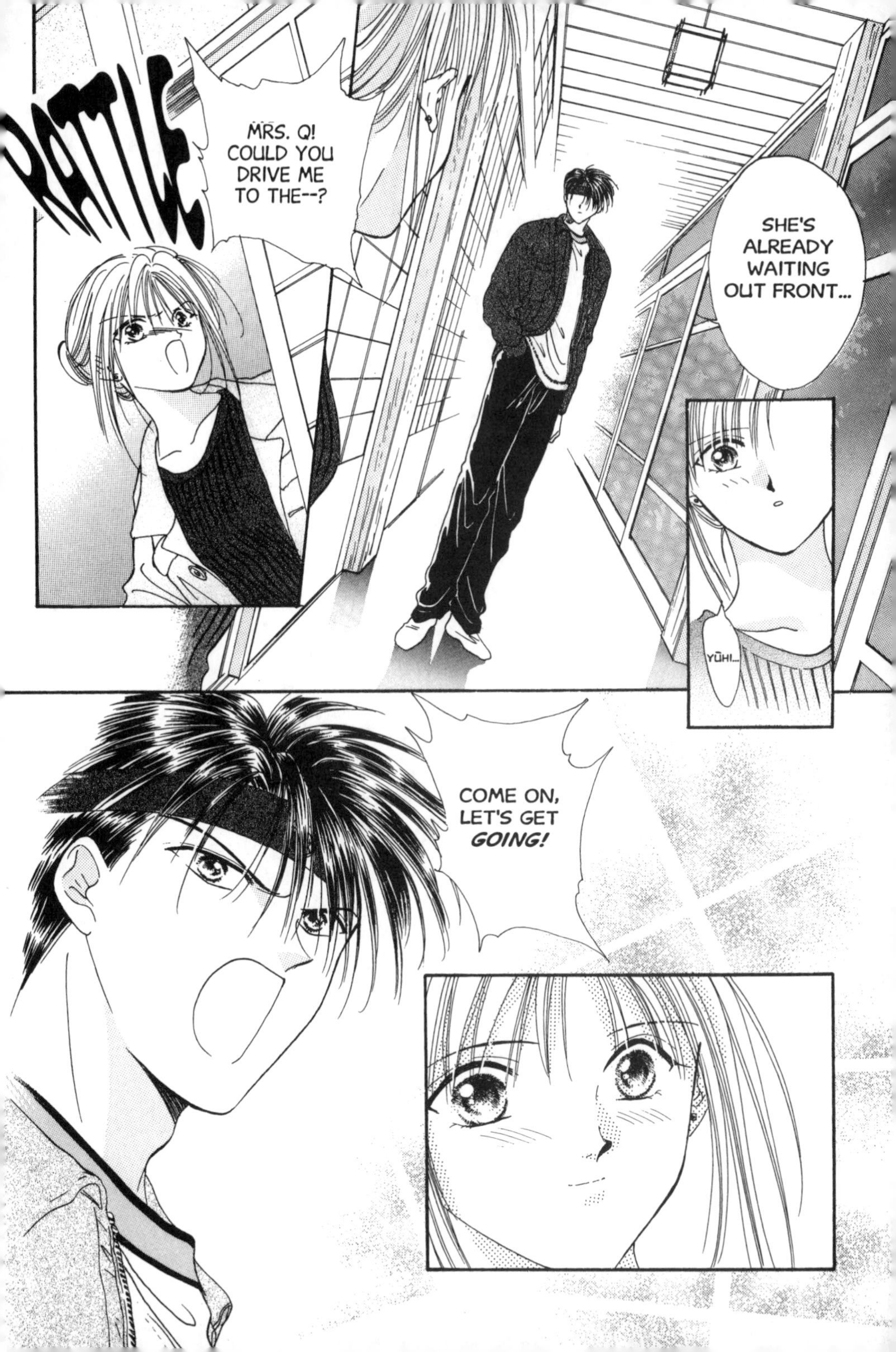
RATTLE
MRS. Q! COULD YOU DRIVE ME TO THE--?
SHE'S ALREADY WAITING OUT FRONT...
YŪHI...
COME ON, LET'S GET *GOING!*

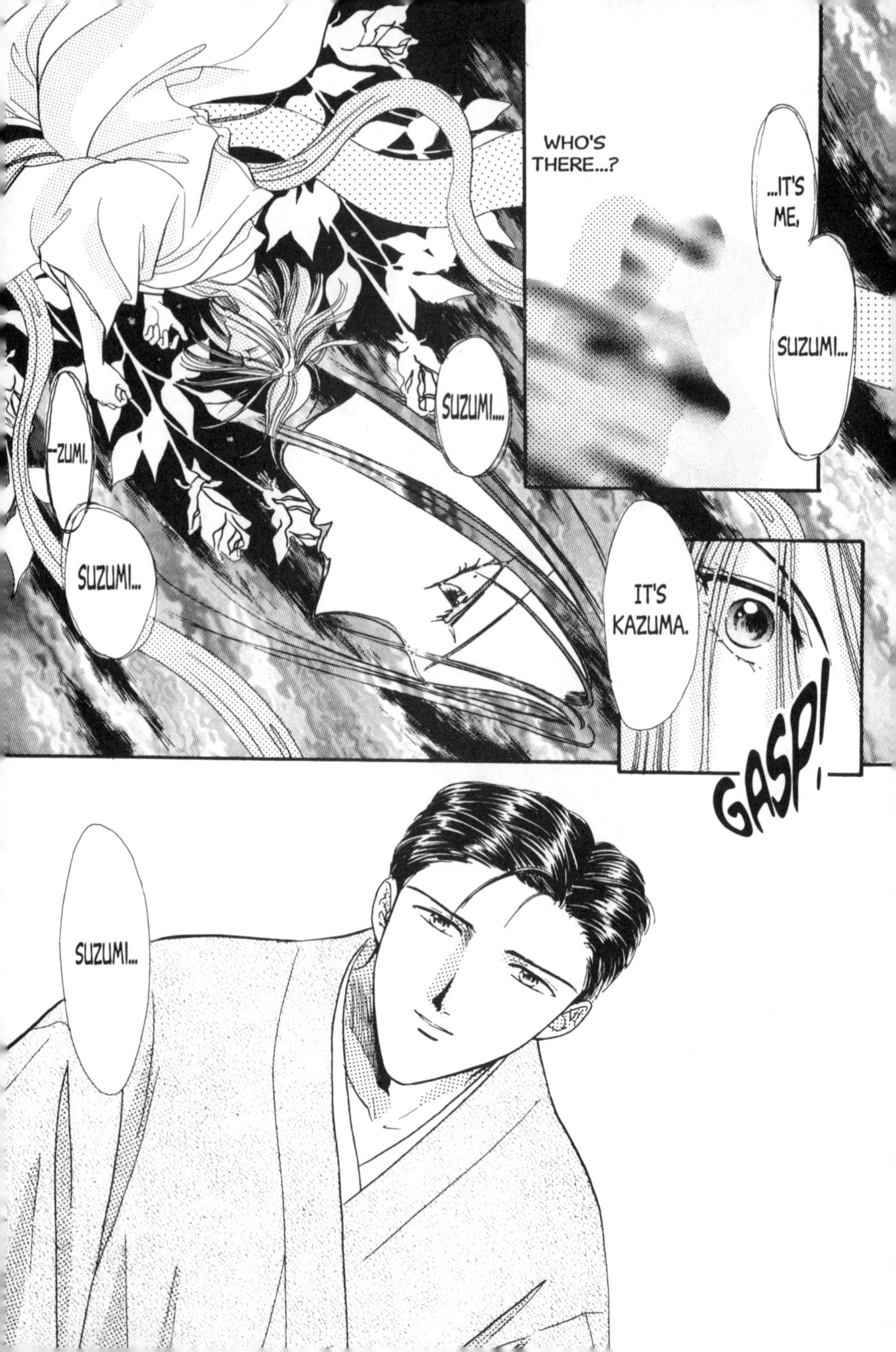
SUZUMI....
-ZUMI.
SUZUMI...
WHO'S THERE...?
...IT'S ME,
SUZUMI...
IT'S KAZUMA.
GASP!
SUZUMI...

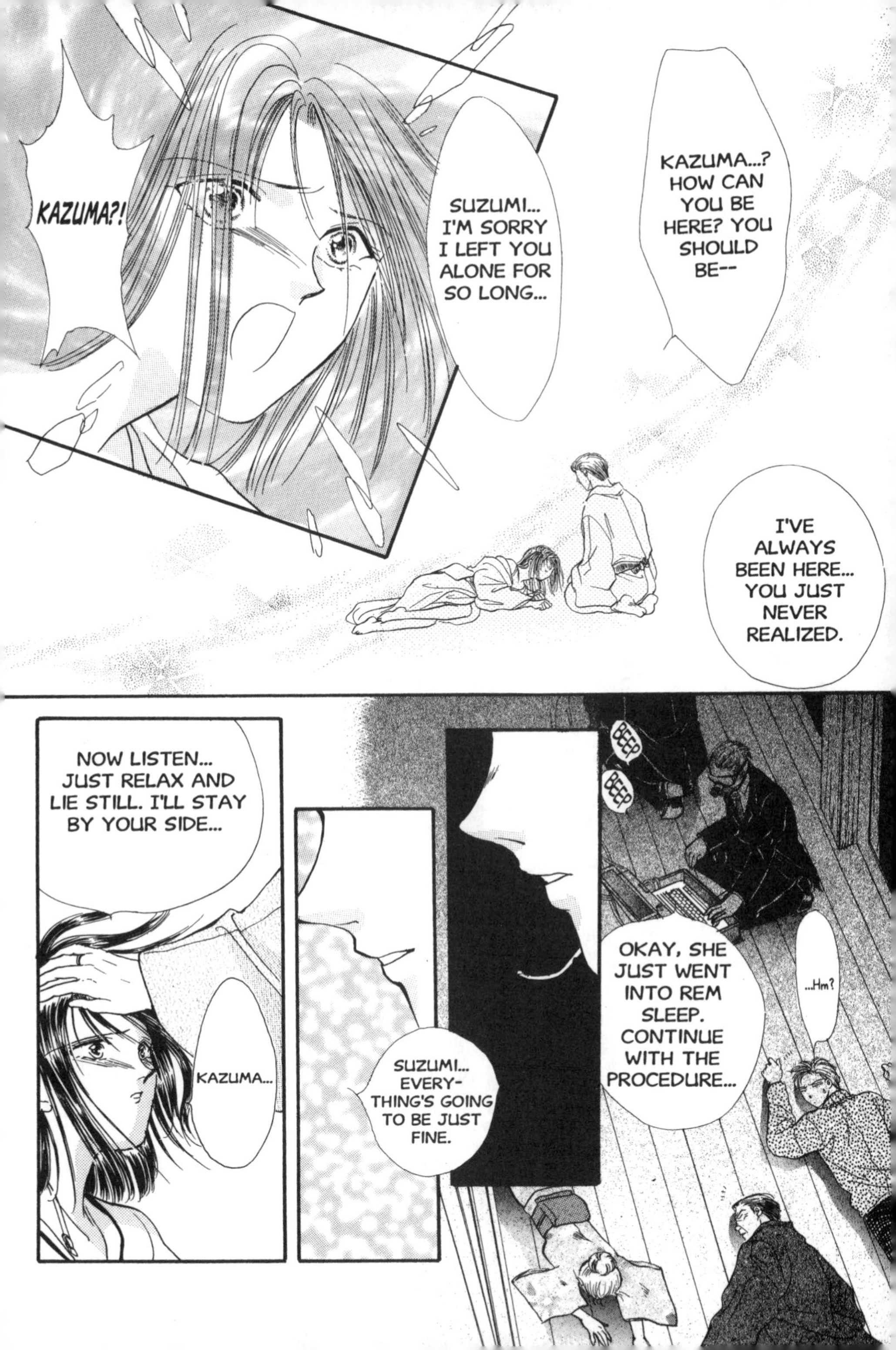
KAZUMA?!
SUZUMI... I'M SORRY I LEFT YOU ALONE FOR SO LONG...
KAZUMA...? HOW CAN YOU BE HERE? YOU SHOULD BE--
I'VE ALWAYS BEEN HERE... YOU JUST NEVER REALIZED.
NOW LISTEN... JUST RELAX AND LIE STILL. I'LL STAY BY YOUR SIDE...
KAZUMA...
SUZUMI... EVERY-THING'S GOING TO BE JUST FINE.
BEEP
BEEP
OKAY, SHE JUST WENT INTO REM SLEEP. CONTINUE WITH THE PROCEDURE...
...Hm?

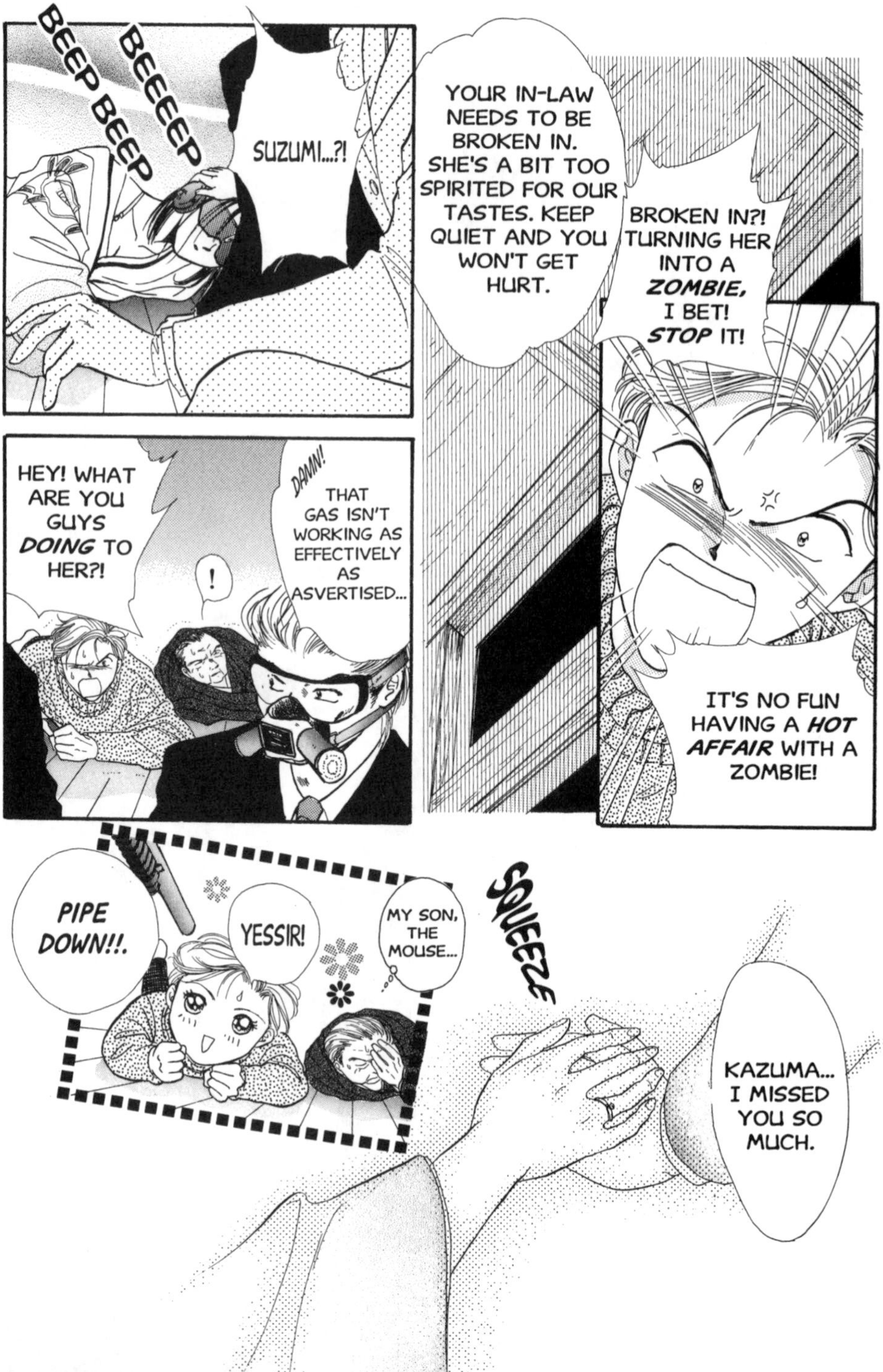
BEEEEEEP
BEEP BEEP
SUZUMI...?!
HEY! WHAT ARE YOU GUYS *DOING* TO HER?!
DAMN!
THAT GAS ISN'T WORKING AS EFFECTIVELY AS ASVERTISED...
!
YOUR IN-LAW NEEDS TO BE BROKEN IN. SHE'S A BIT TOO SPIRITED FOR OUR TASTES. KEEP QUIET AND YOU WON'T GET HURT.
BROKEN IN?! TURNING HER INTO A *ZOMBIE,* I BET! *STOP* IT!
IT'S NO FUN HAVING A *HOT AFFAIR* WITH A ZOMBIE!
PIPE DOWN!!.
YESSIR!
MY SON, THE MOUSE...
SQUEEZE
KAZUMA... I MISSED YOU SO MUCH.

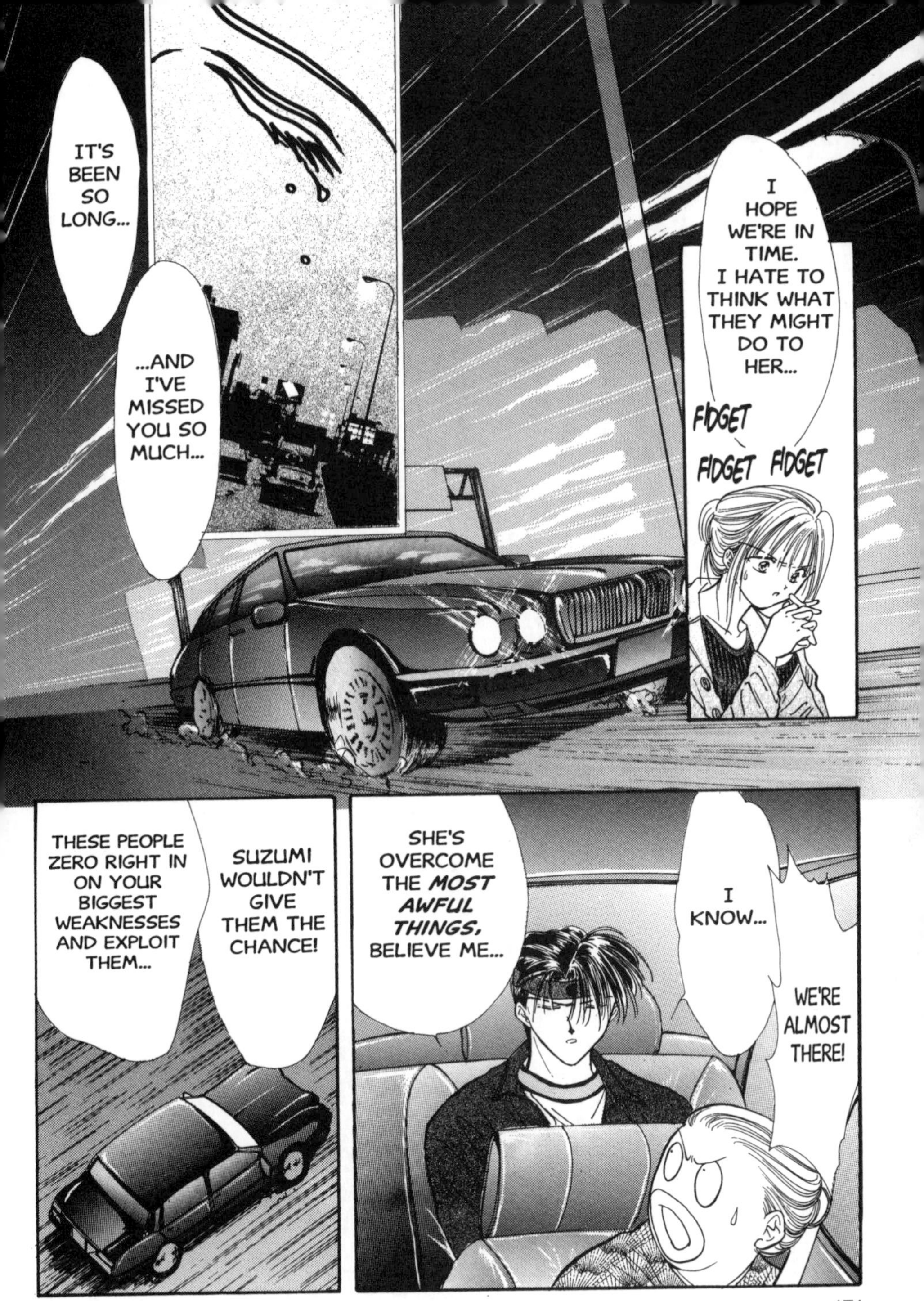
IT'S BEEN SO LONG...
...AND I'VE MISSED YOU SO MUCH...
I HOPE WE'RE IN TIME. I HATE TO THINK WHAT THEY MIGHT DO TO HER...
FIDGET
FIDGET FIDGET
THESE PEOPLE ZERO RIGHT IN ON YOUR BIGGEST WEAKNESSES AND EXPLOIT THEM...
SUZUMI WOULDN'T GIVE THEM THE CHANCE!
SHE'S OVERCOME THE ***MOST AWFUL THINGS,*** BELIEVE ME...
I KNOW...
WE'RE ALMOST THERE!

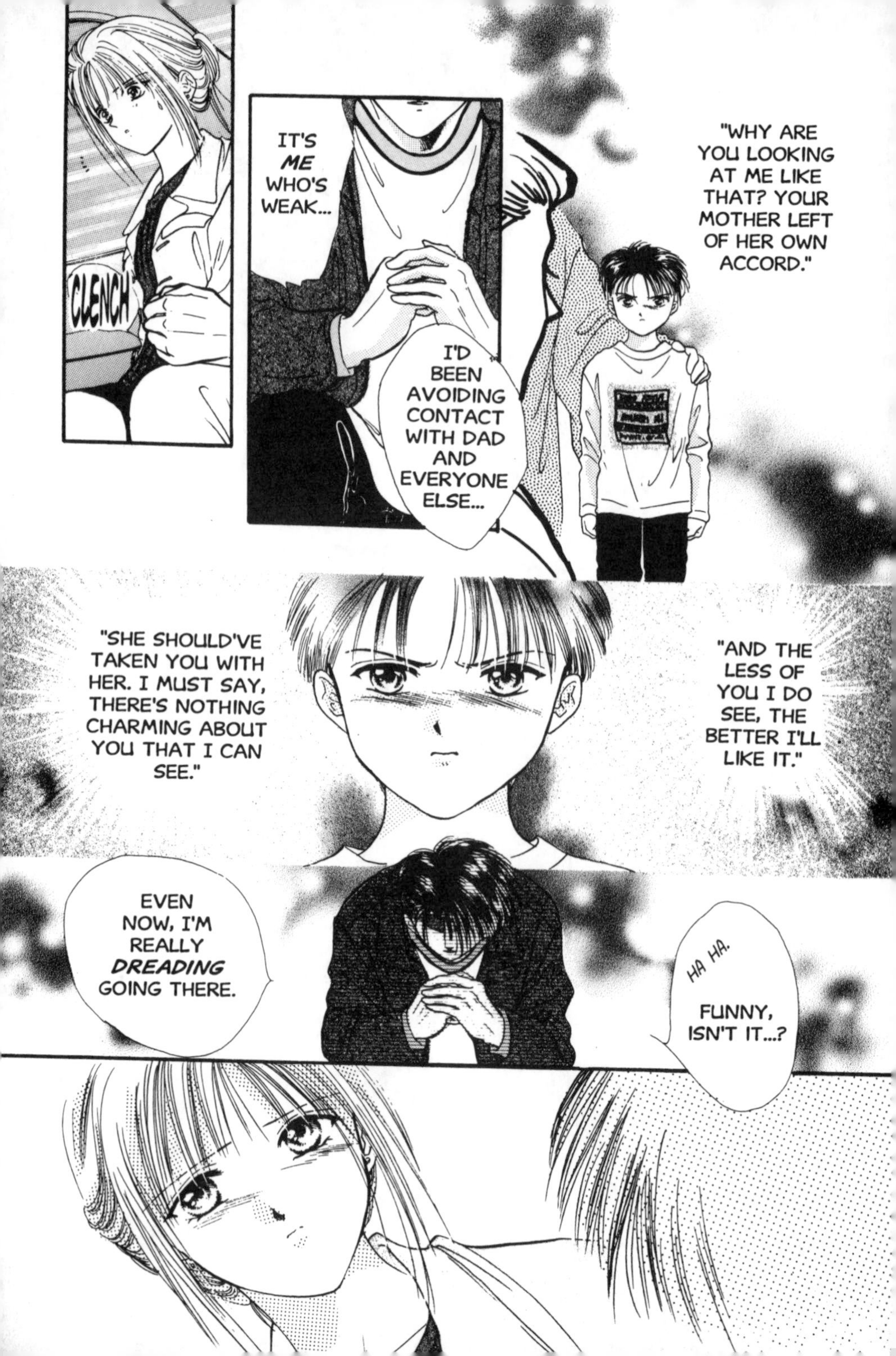
CLENCH
IT'S *ME* WHO'S WEAK...
I'D BEEN AVOIDING CONTACT WITH DAD AND EVERYONE ELSE...
"WHY ARE YOU LOOKING AT ME LIKE THAT? YOUR MOTHER LEFT OF HER OWN ACCORD."
"SHE SHOULD'VE TAKEN YOU WITH HER. I MUST SAY, THERE'S NOTHING CHARMING ABOUT YOU THAT I CAN SEE."
"AND THE LESS OF YOU I DO SEE, THE BETTER I'LL LIKE IT."
EVEN NOW, I'M REALLY ***DREADING*** GOING THERE.
HA HA.
FUNNY, ISN'T IT...?

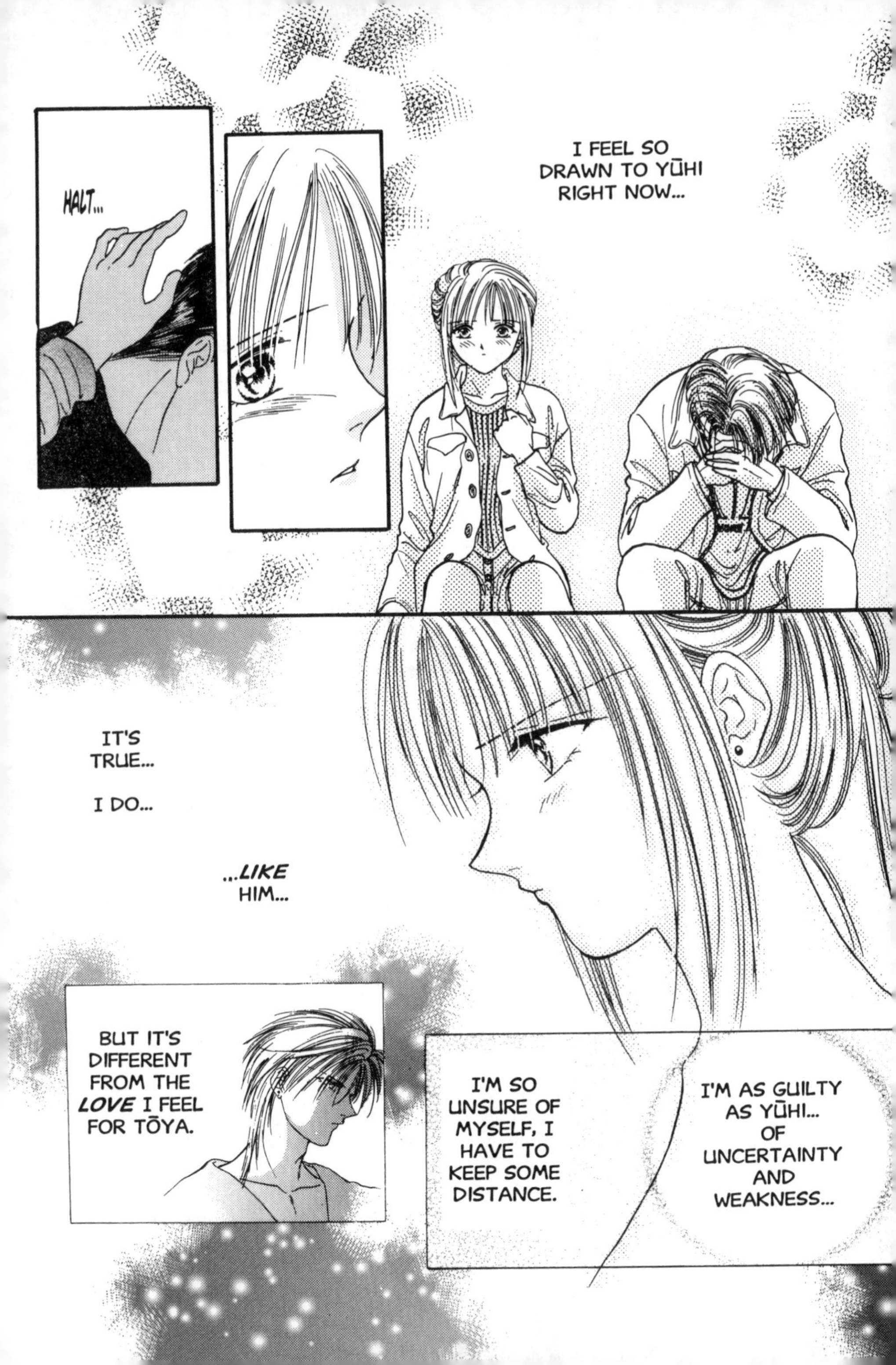
HALT...
I FEEL SO DRAWN TO YŪHI RIGHT NOW...
IT'S TRUE...
I DO...
...*LIKE* HIM...
BUT IT'S DIFFERENT FROM THE *LOVE* I FEEL FOR TŌYA.
I'M SO UNSURE OF MYSELF, I HAVE TO KEEP SOME DISTANCE.
I'M AS GUILTY AS YŪHI... OF UNCERTAINTY AND WEAKNESS...

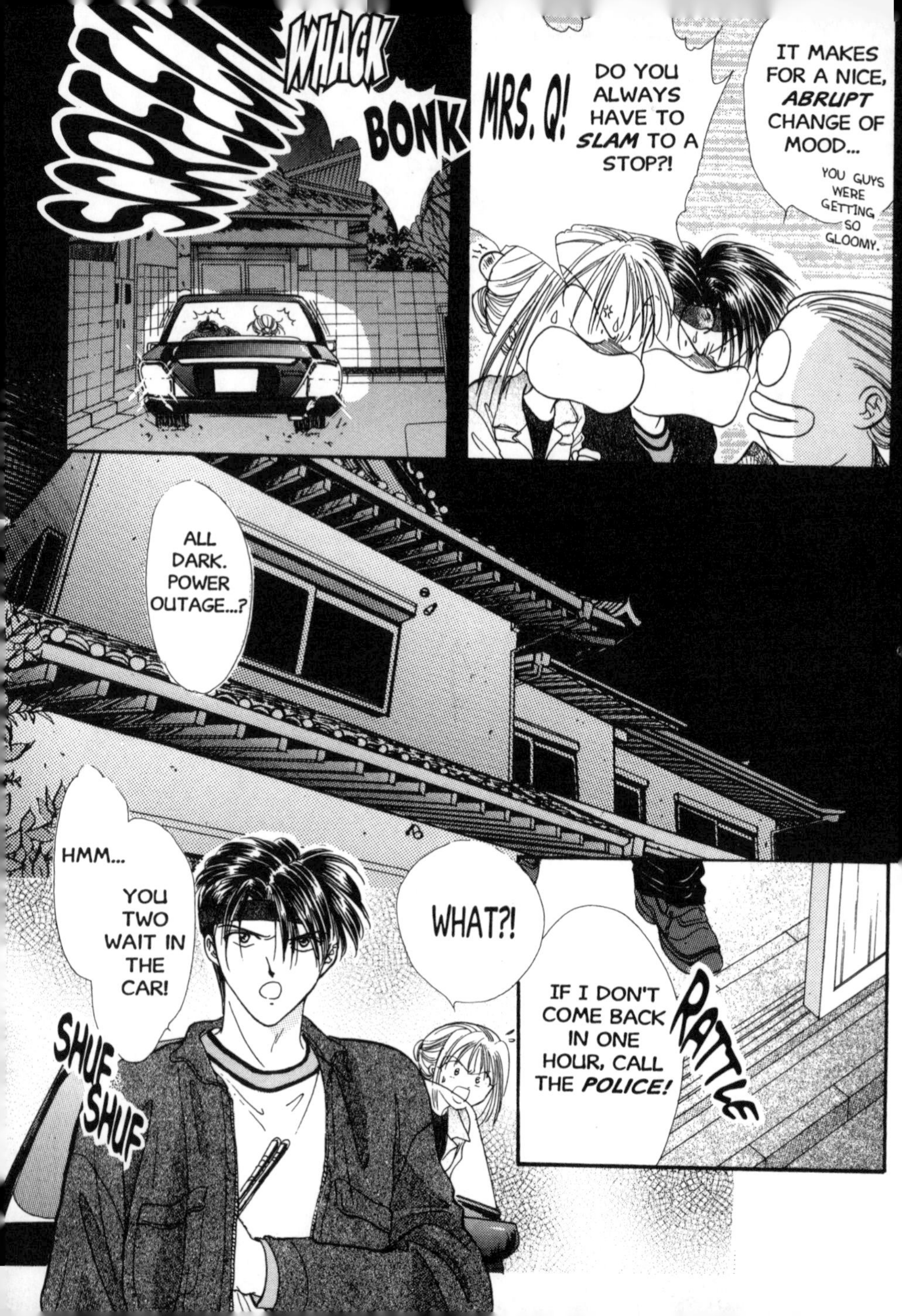
WHACK
BONK
MRS. Q!
DO YOU ALWAYS HAVE TO SLAM TO A STOP?!
IT MAKES FOR A NICE, ABRUPT CHANGE OF MOOD...
YOU GUYS WERE GETTING SO GLOOMY.
ALL DARK. POWER OUTAGE...?
HMM...
YOU TWO WAIT IN THE CAR!
SHUF SHUF
WHAT?!
IF I DON'T COME BACK IN ONE HOUR, CALL THE POLICE!
RATTLE

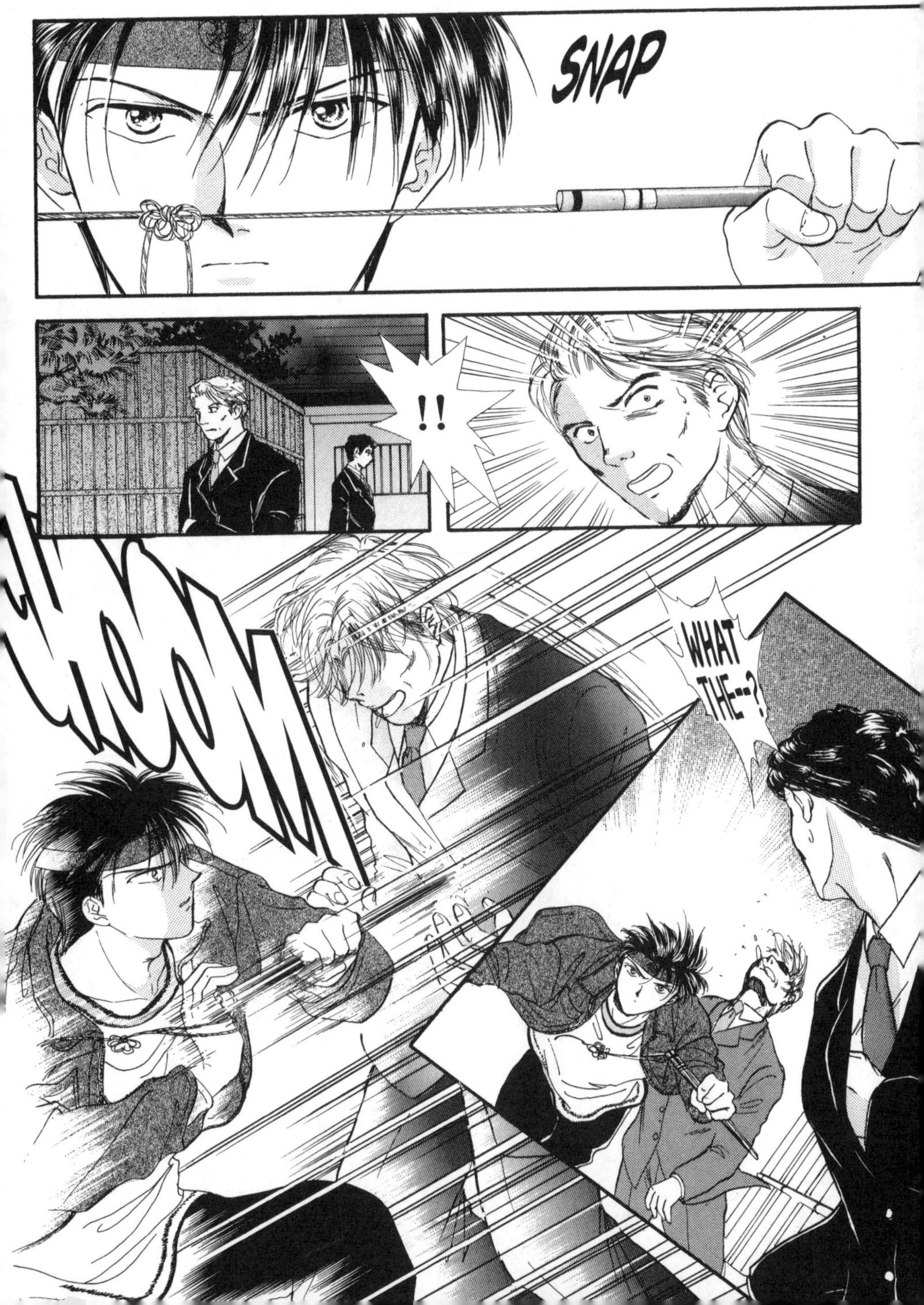
SNAP
!!
WHOOM
WHAT THE--?

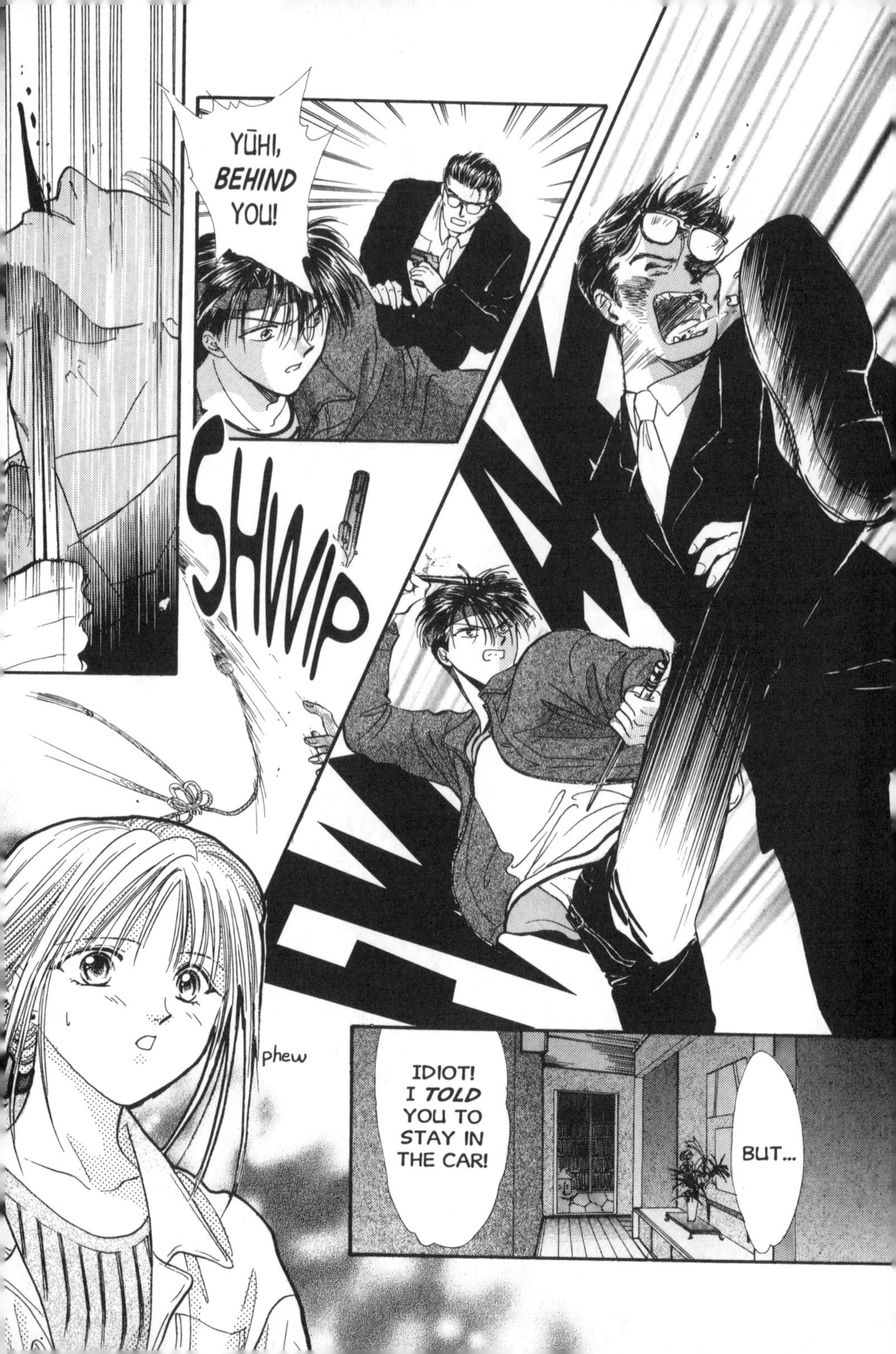
YŪHI, BEHIND YOU!
SHWIP
phew
IDIOT! I TOLD YOU TO STAY IN THE CAR!
BUT...

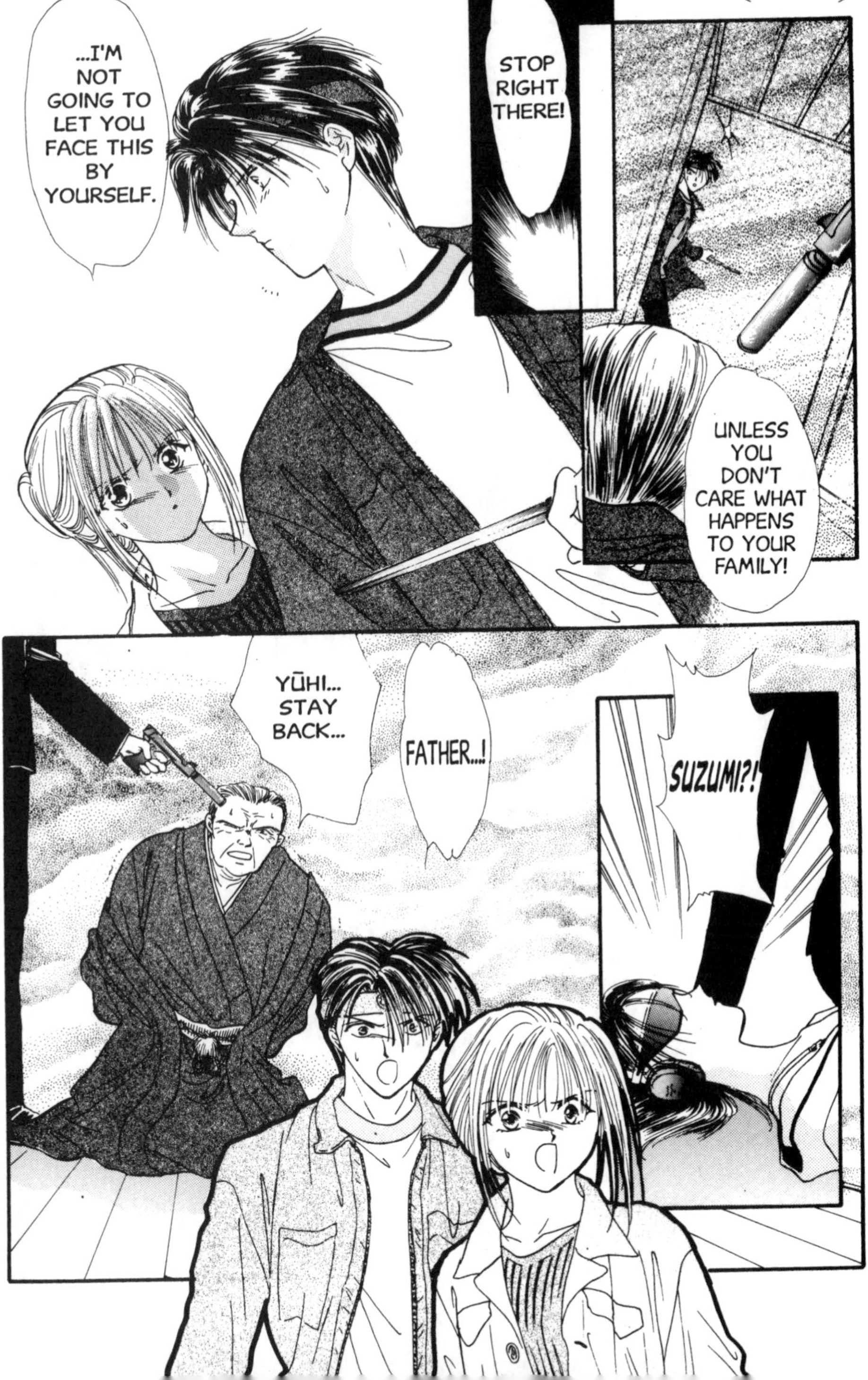
...I'M NOT GOING TO LET YOU FACE THIS BY YOURSELF.
STOP RIGHT THERE!
UNLESS YOU DON'T CARE WHAT HAPPENS TO YOUR FAMILY!
YŪHI... STAY BACK...
FATHER...!
SUZUMI?!

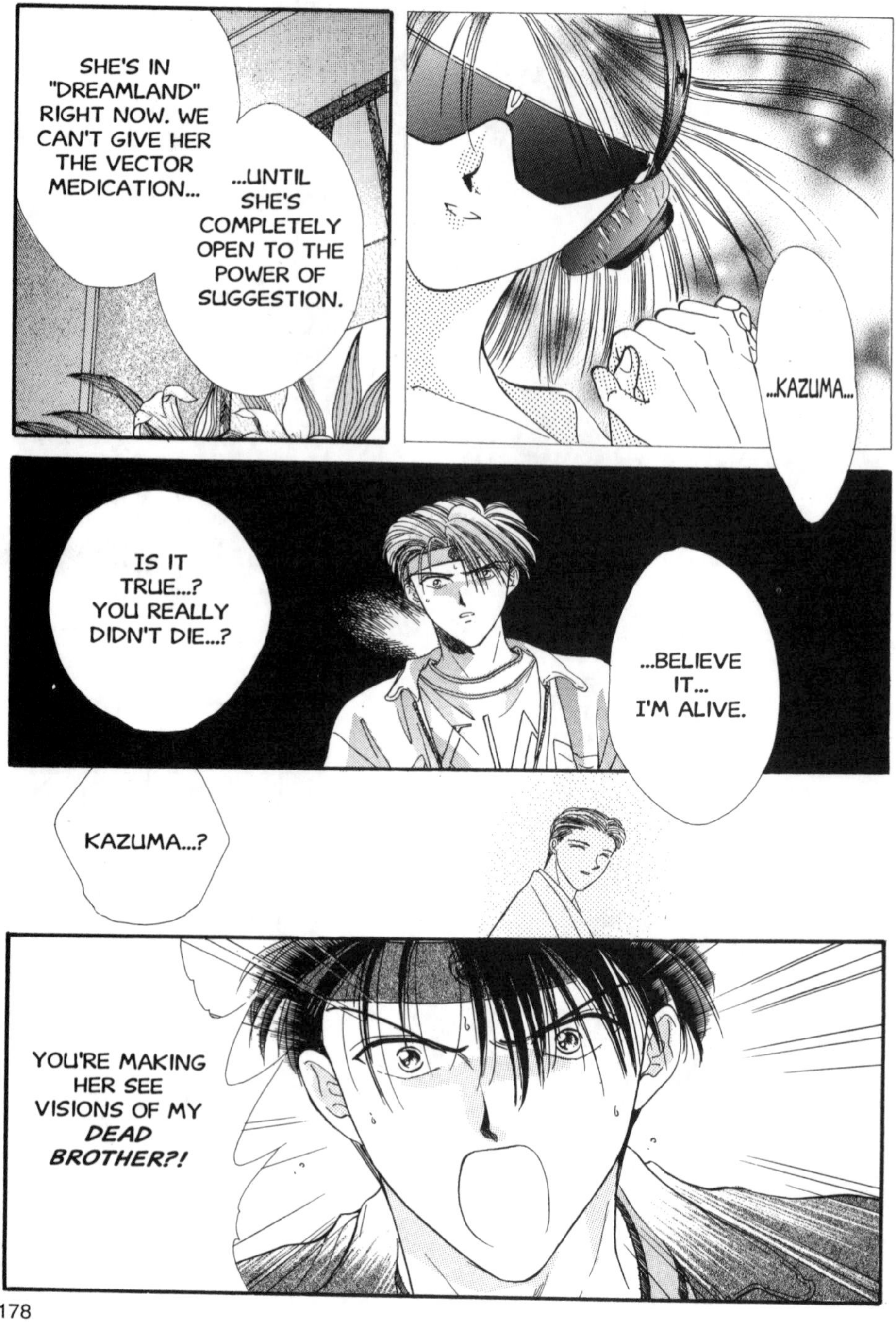
SHE'S IN "DREAMLAND" RIGHT NOW. WE CAN'T GIVE HER THE VECTOR MEDICATION...
...UNTIL SHE'S COMPLETELY OPEN TO THE POWER OF SUGGESTION.
...KAZUMA...
IS IT TRUE...? YOU REALLY DIDN'T DIE...?
...BELIEVE IT... I'M ALIVE.
KAZUMA...?
YOU'RE MAKING HER SEE VISIONS OF MY *DEAD BROTHER?!*

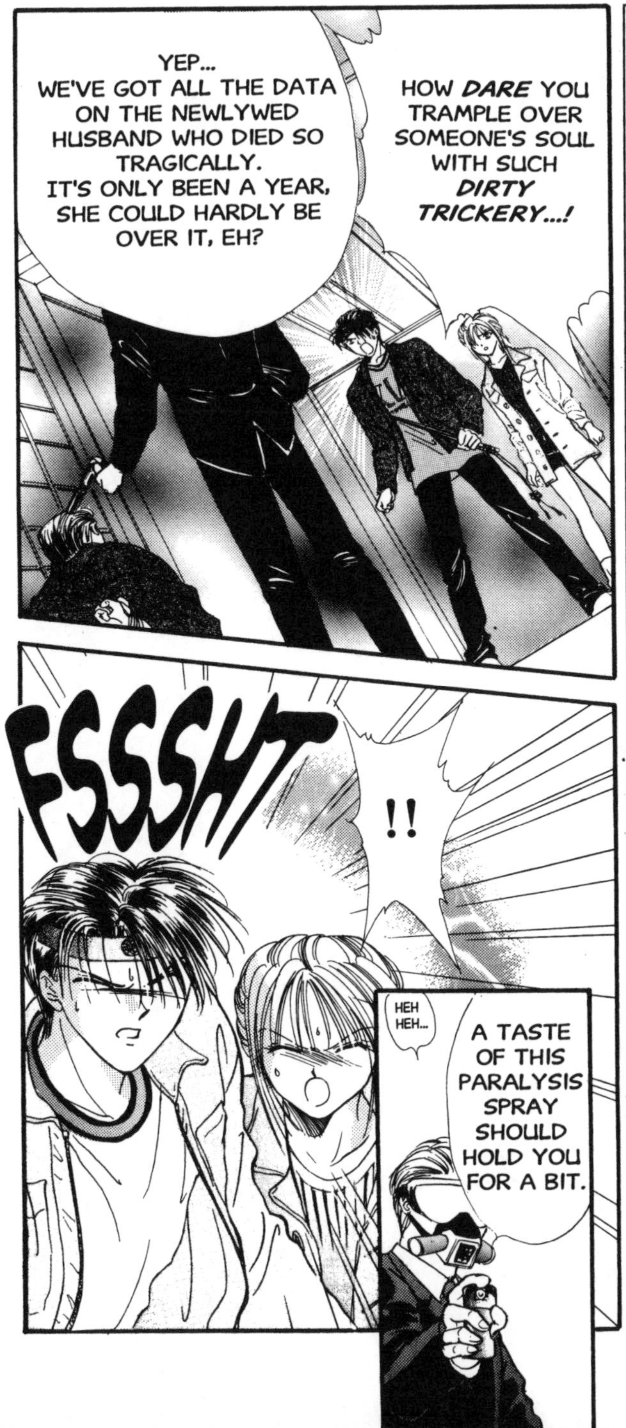
YEP... WE'VE GOT ALL THE DATA ON THE NEWLYWED HUSBAND WHO DIED SO TRAGICALLY. IT'S ONLY BEEN A YEAR, SHE COULD HARDLY BE OVER IT, EH?
HOW *DARE* YOU TRAMPLE OVER SOMEONE'S SOUL WITH SUCH *DIRTY TRICKERY...!*
FSSSHT
!!
HEH HEH...
A TASTE OF THIS PARALYSIS SPRAY SHOULD HOLD YOU FOR A BIT.

Last time I wrote about genes wearing out...and it's true! It wears all the way down and then you die. And you know how people always tell you to "read lots of books in your teens" and "do your homework"? That's because that's when the brain is the most active, and has the best capacity for memory.

Once you're over 20, a hundred million brain cells die each and every day (I **think** that's the right number), so your memory gets worse and worse. And alcohol! If you drink too much, it kills even more of your brain cells, so you become even more stupid than the average person. It's hard to believe people still drink. I didn't like to study when I was younger. My parents didn't force me to do my homework, but they told me, "if you don't study now, **you're** the one who's going to regret it later." ...At the time, I just said, "Yeah right!" and stuck my tongue out at them, but let me tell you - I **do** regret not studying. Trust me, read lots of books. Especially if you want to be a writer or a manga artist. Do your homework. You **will** have a tough time if you're not well-read. Textbooks are written so that everybody can understand them. I should've read them more. I wish I could go back to school again. Students really have it easy.

Hmm, this volume's column has turned out to be pretty educational. (Really?) Hopefully bio class won't be so intimidating anymore. Come to think of it, Mikage's company is so mysterious. The full picture isn't clear. The official name of the company is "Mikage International." But people will probably be more concerned about whether Aya ends up with Tōya or Yūhi. It's no wonder she's wavering, especially under the current circumstances... See you in the next volume!.
—Z

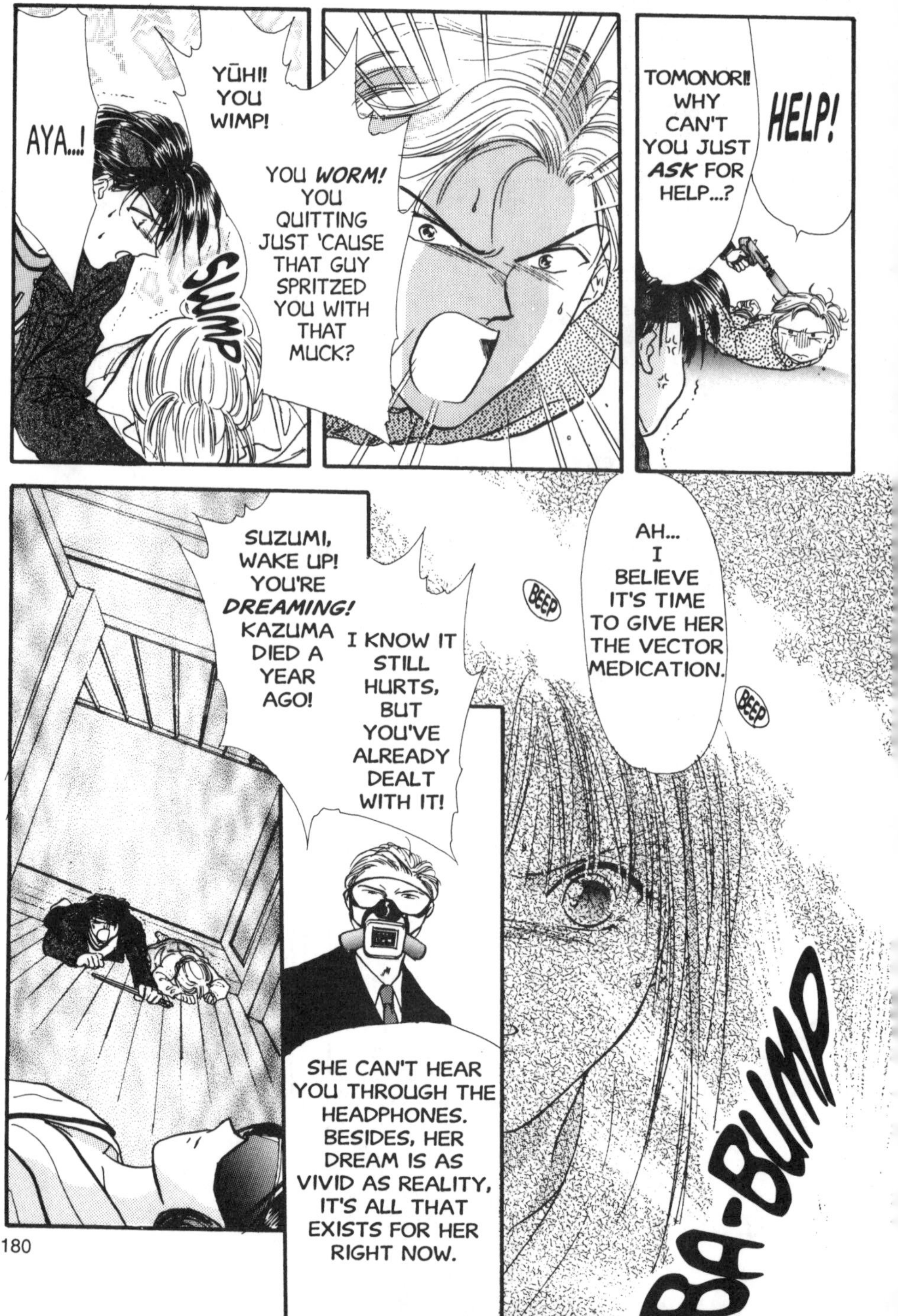
AYA...!
YŪHI! YOU WIMP!
SWUMP
YOU WORM! YOU QUITTING JUST 'CAUSE THAT GUY SPRITZED YOU WITH THAT MUCK?
TOMONORI!! WHY CAN'T YOU JUST ASK FOR HELP...?
HELP!
SUZUMI, WAKE UP! YOU'RE DREAMING! KAZUMA DIED A YEAR AGO!
I KNOW IT STILL HURTS, BUT YOU'VE ALREADY DEALT WITH IT!
SHE CAN'T HEAR YOU THROUGH THE HEADPHONES. BESIDES, HER DREAM IS AS VIVID AS REALITY, IT'S ALL THAT EXISTS FOR HER RIGHT NOW.
AH... I BELIEVE IT'S TIME TO GIVE HER THE VECTOR MEDICATION.
BEEP
BEEP
BA-BUMP

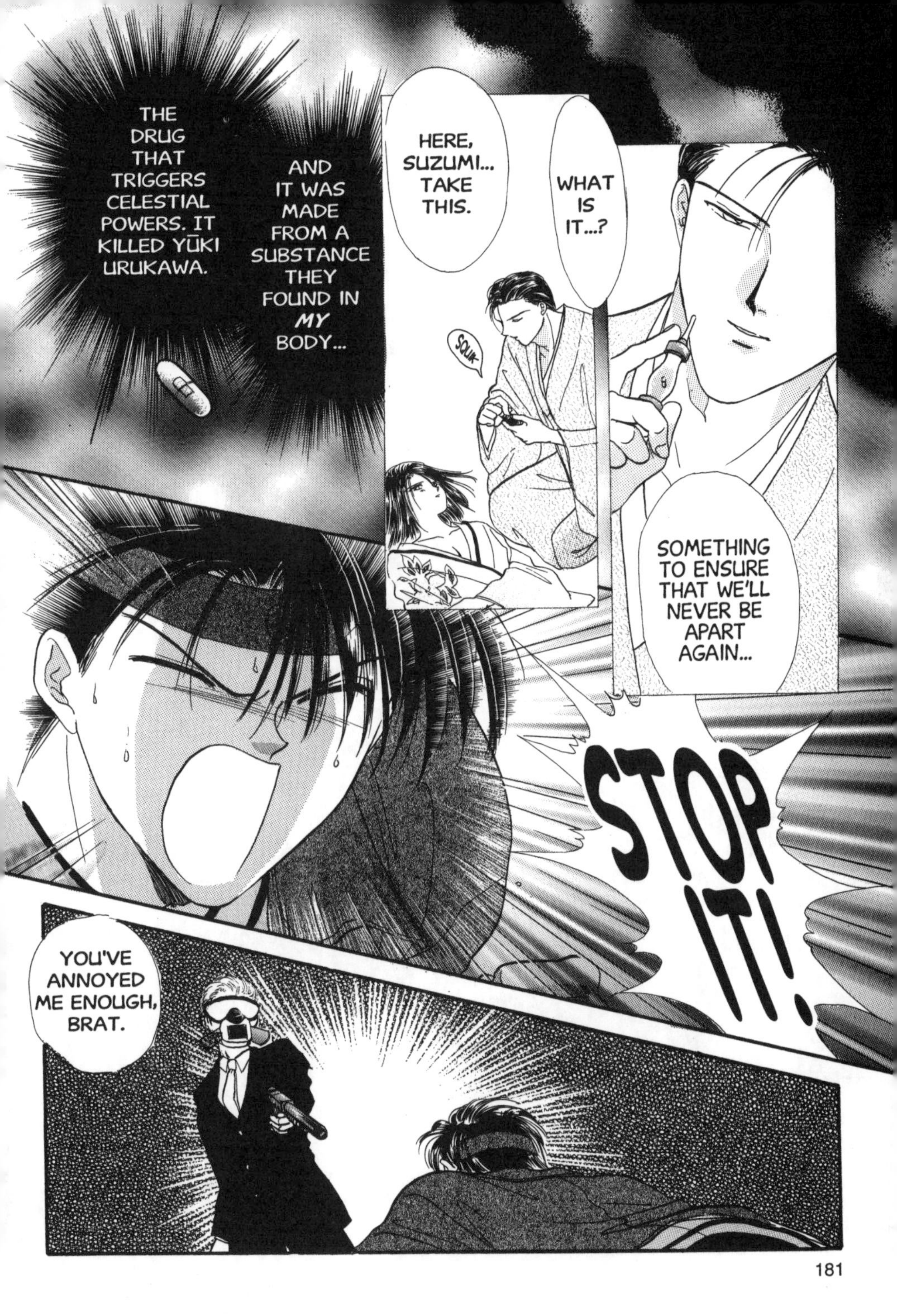
THE DRUG THAT TRIGGERS CELESTIAL POWERS. IT KILLED YŪKI URUKAWA.
AND IT WAS MADE FROM A SUBSTANCE THEY FOUND IN *MY* BODY...
HERE, SUZUMI... TAKE THIS.
WHAT IS IT...?
SQUK
SOMETHING TO ENSURE THAT WE'LL NEVER BE APART AGAIN...
STOP IT!!
YOU'VE ANNOYED ME ENOUGH, BRAT.

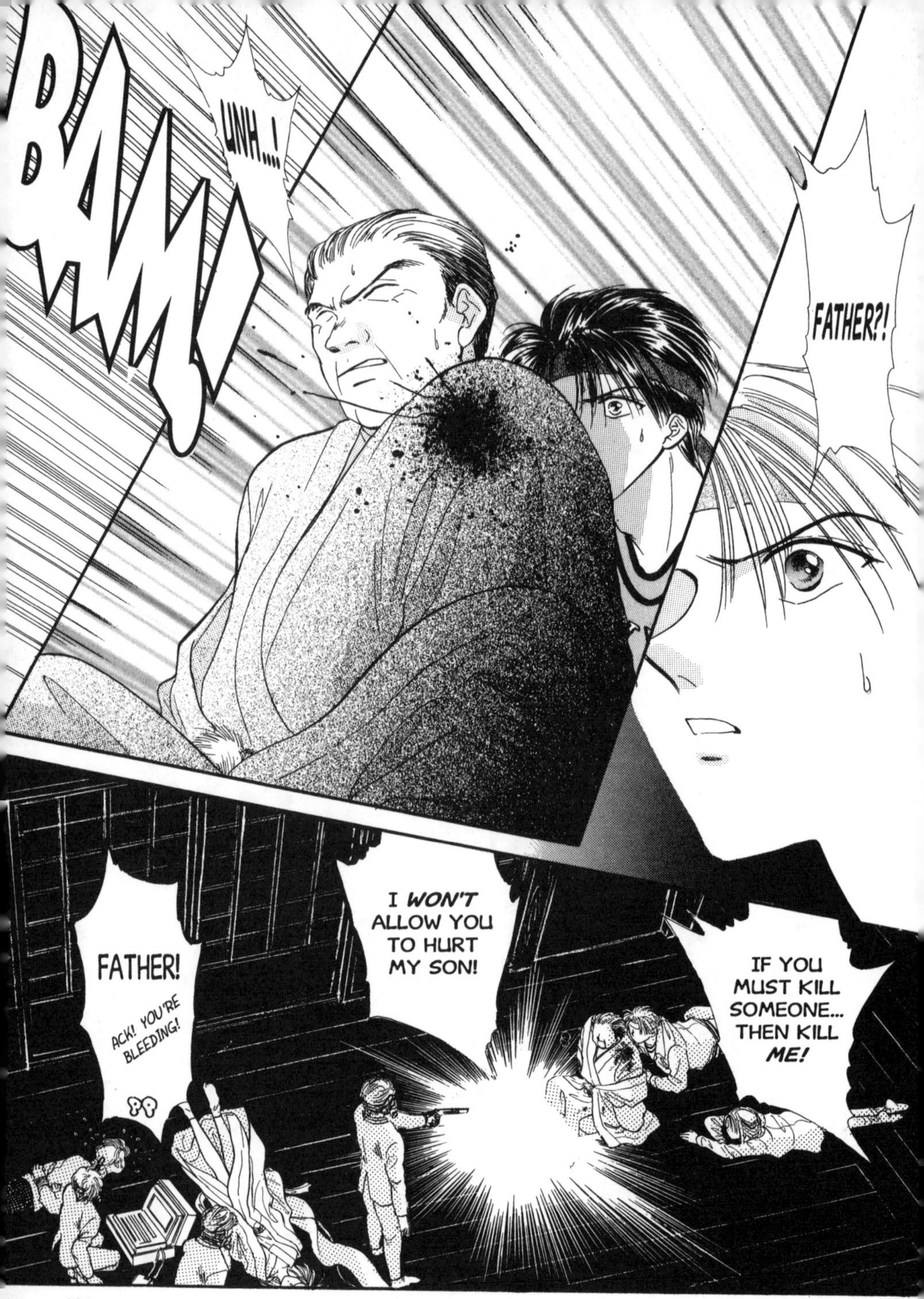
BAM!
UNH...!
FATHER?!
FATHER!
ACK! YOU'RE BLEEDING!
PP
I *WON'T* ALLOW YOU TO HURT MY SON!
IF YOU MUST KILL SOMEONE... THEN KILL *ME!*

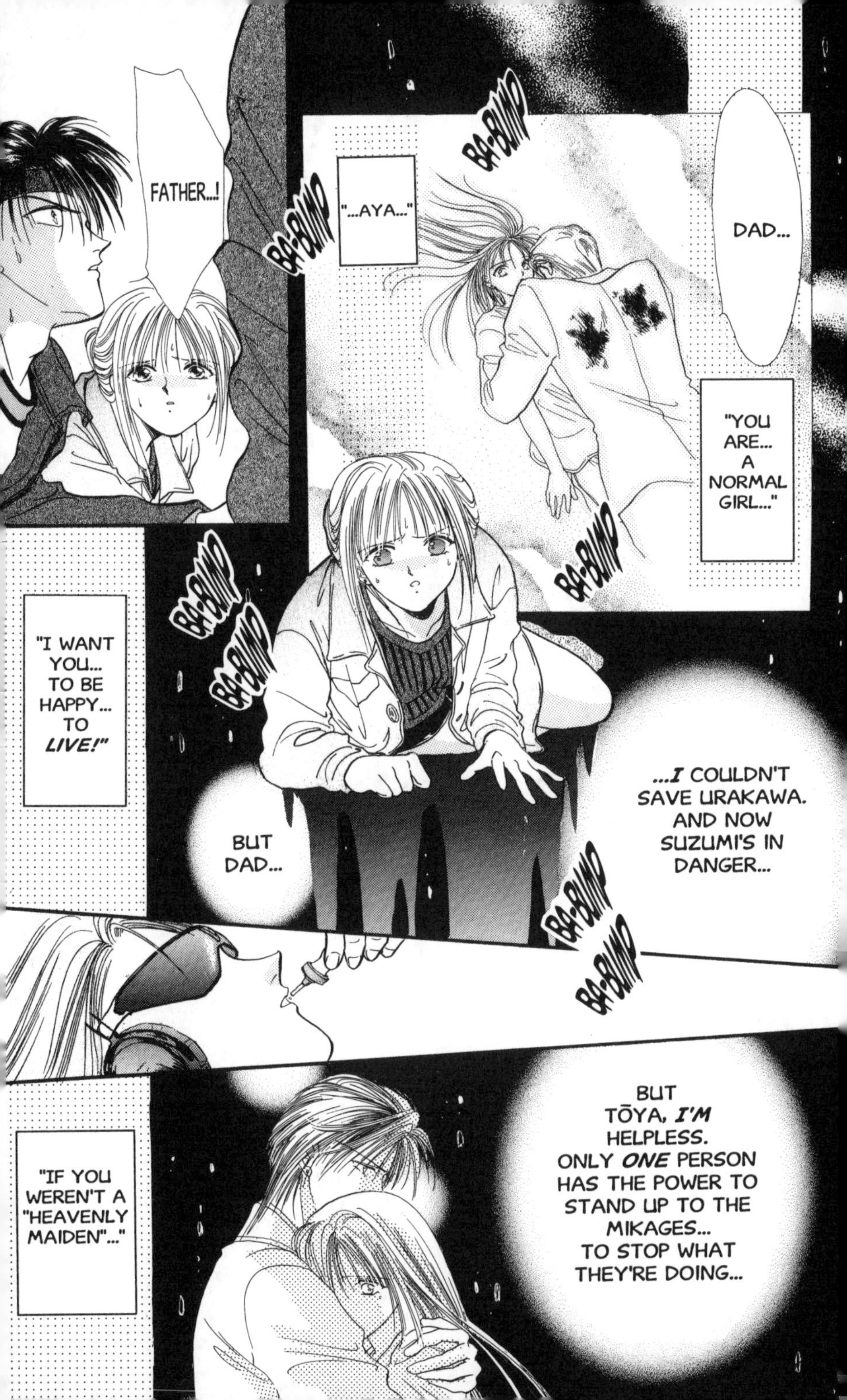
FATHER...!
BA-BUMP
"...AYA..."
BA-BUMP
DAD...
"YOU ARE... A NORMAL GIRL..."
BA-BUMP
"I WANT YOU... TO BE HAPPY... TO *LIVE!*"
BA-BUMP
BA-BUMP
BUT DAD...
...*I* COULDN'T SAVE URAKAWA. AND NOW SUZUMI'S IN DANGER...
BA-BUMP
BA-BUMP
"IF YOU WEREN'T A "HEAVENLY MAIDEN"..."
BUT TŌYA, *I'M* HELPLESS. ONLY *ONE* PERSON HAS THE POWER TO STAND UP TO THE MIKAGES... TO STOP WHAT THEY'RE DOING...

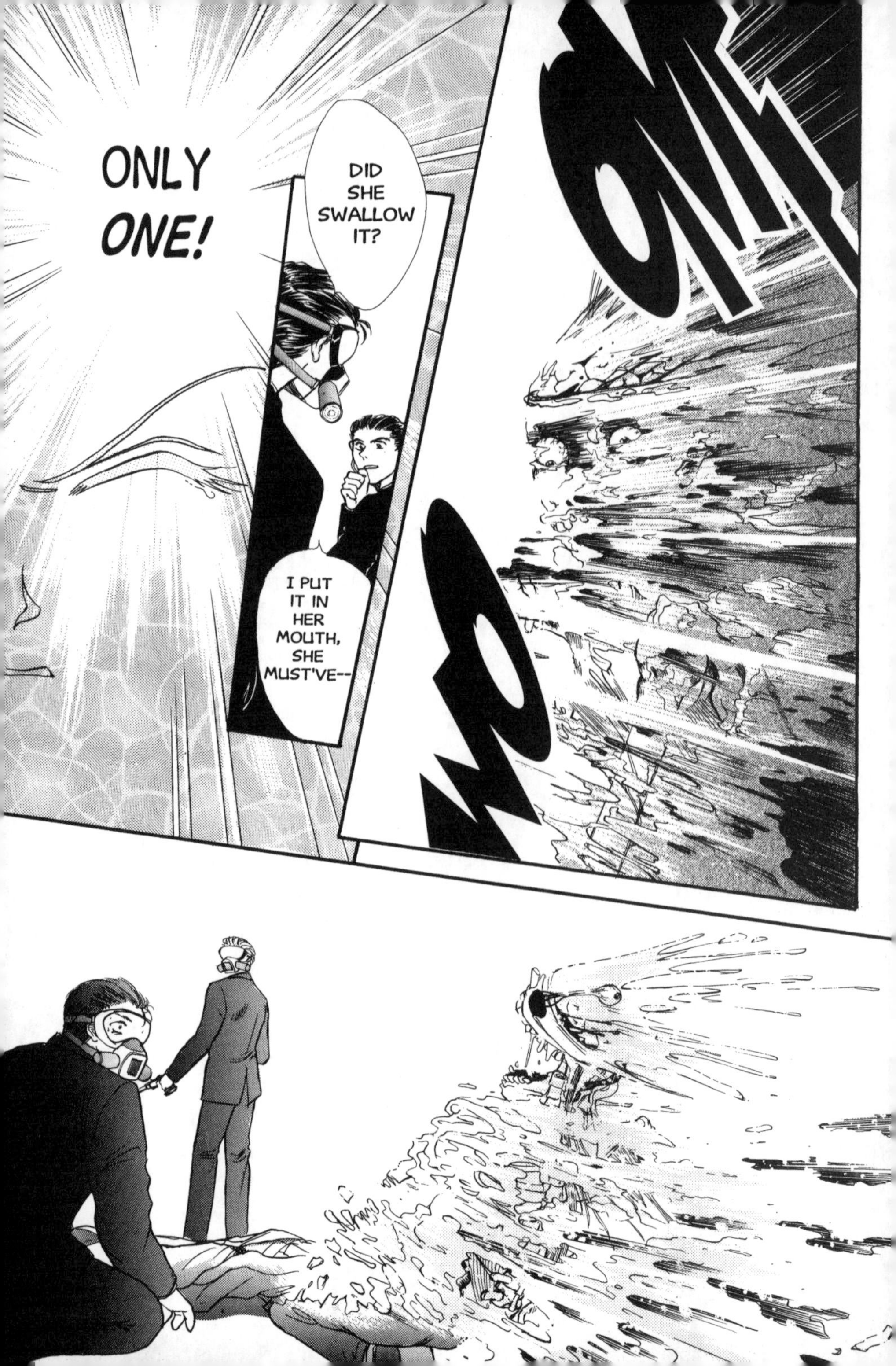
ONLY ONE!
DID SHE SWALLOW IT?
I PUT IT IN HER MOUTH, SHE MUST'VE--

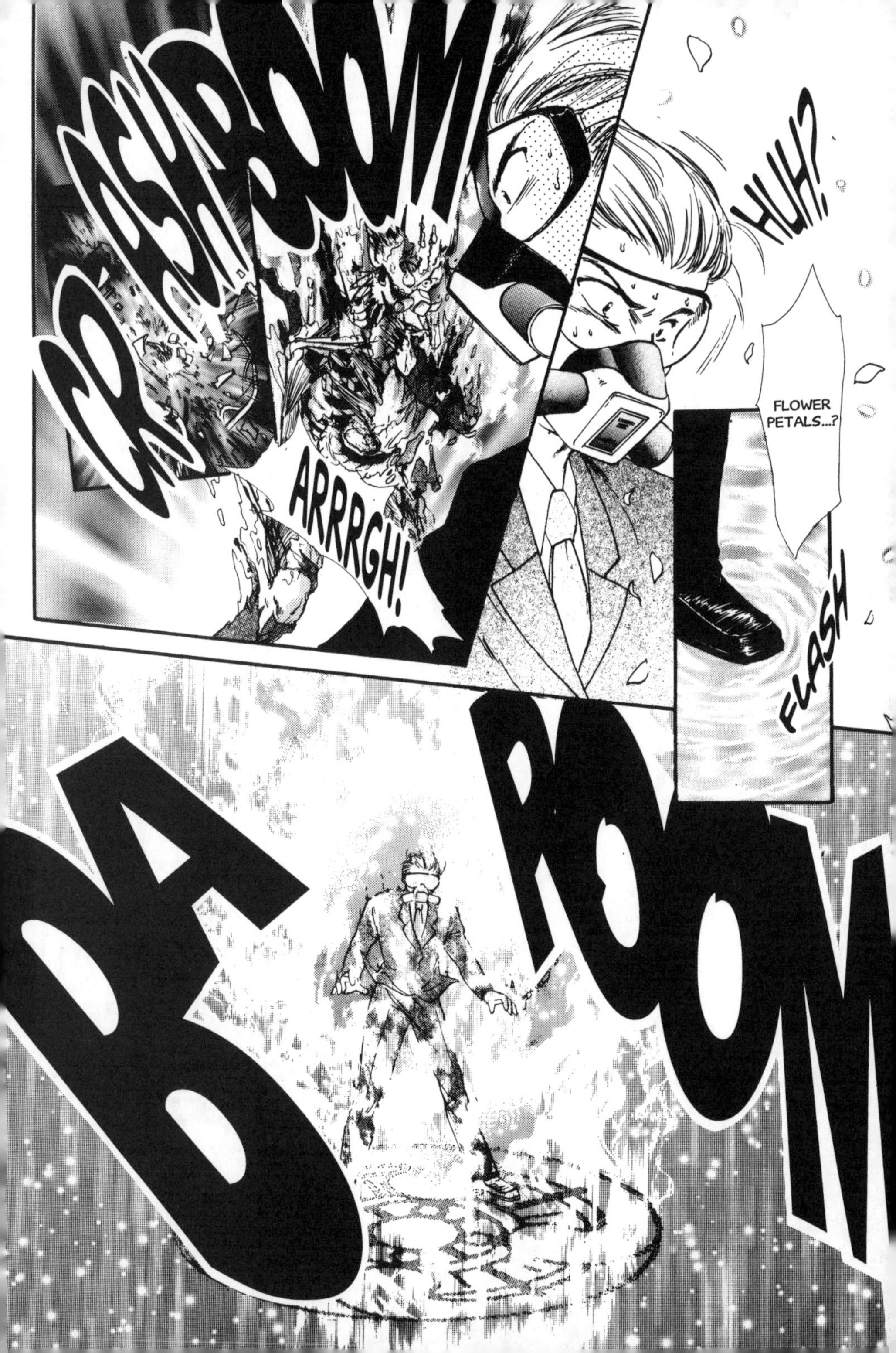
CRASH!
BOOM!
ARRRGH!
HUH?!
FLOWER PETALS...?
FLASH
BA
ROOM

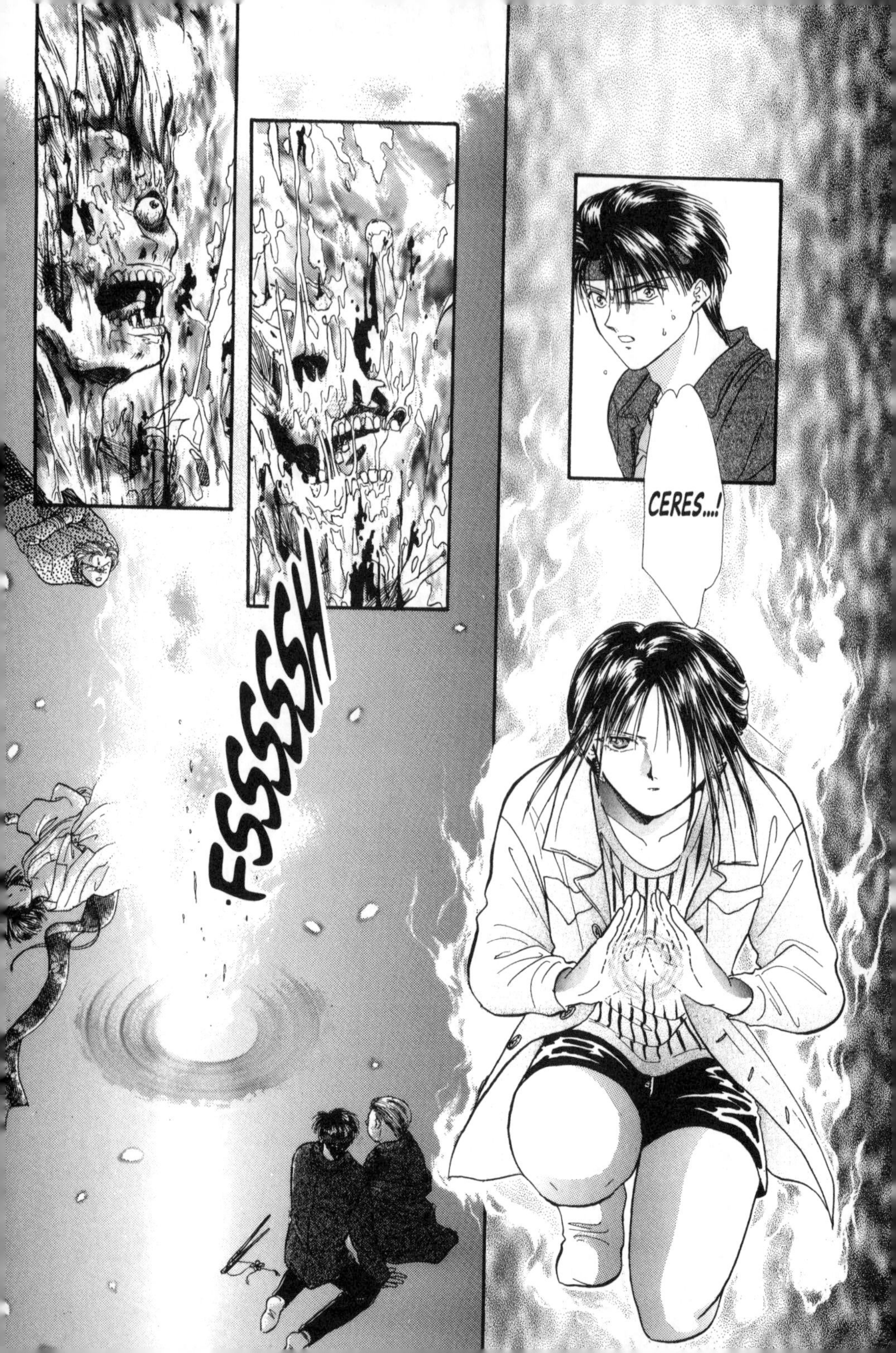
FSSSSSH
CERES...!

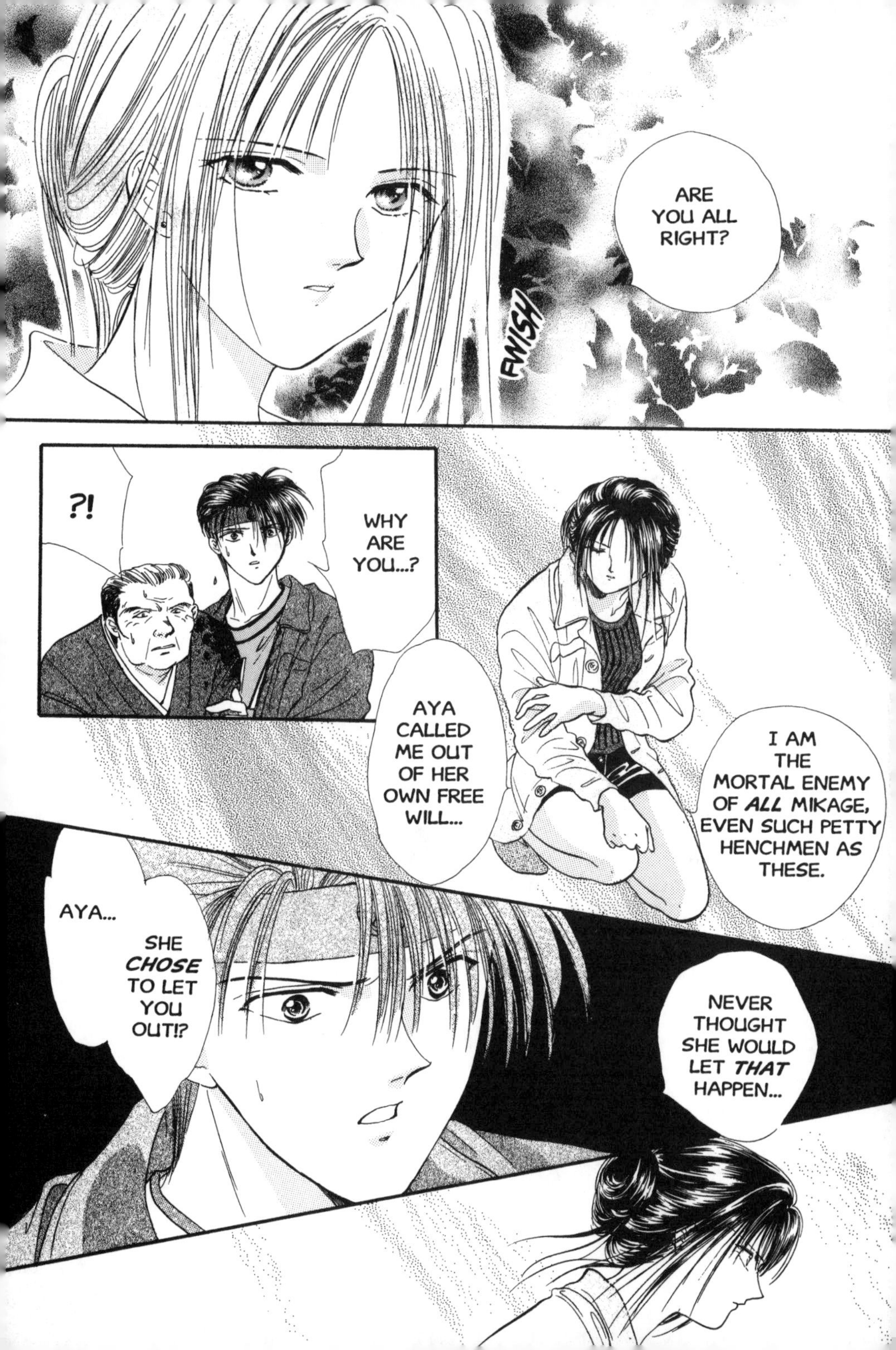
ARE YOU ALL RIGHT?
FWISH
?!
WHY ARE YOU...?
AYA CALLED ME OUT OF HER OWN FREE WILL...
I AM THE MORTAL ENEMY OF *ALL* MIKAGE, EVEN SUCH PETTY HENCHMEN AS THESE.
AYA...
SHE *CHOSE* TO LET YOU OUT!?
NEVER THOUGHT SHE WOULD LET *THAT* HAPPEN...

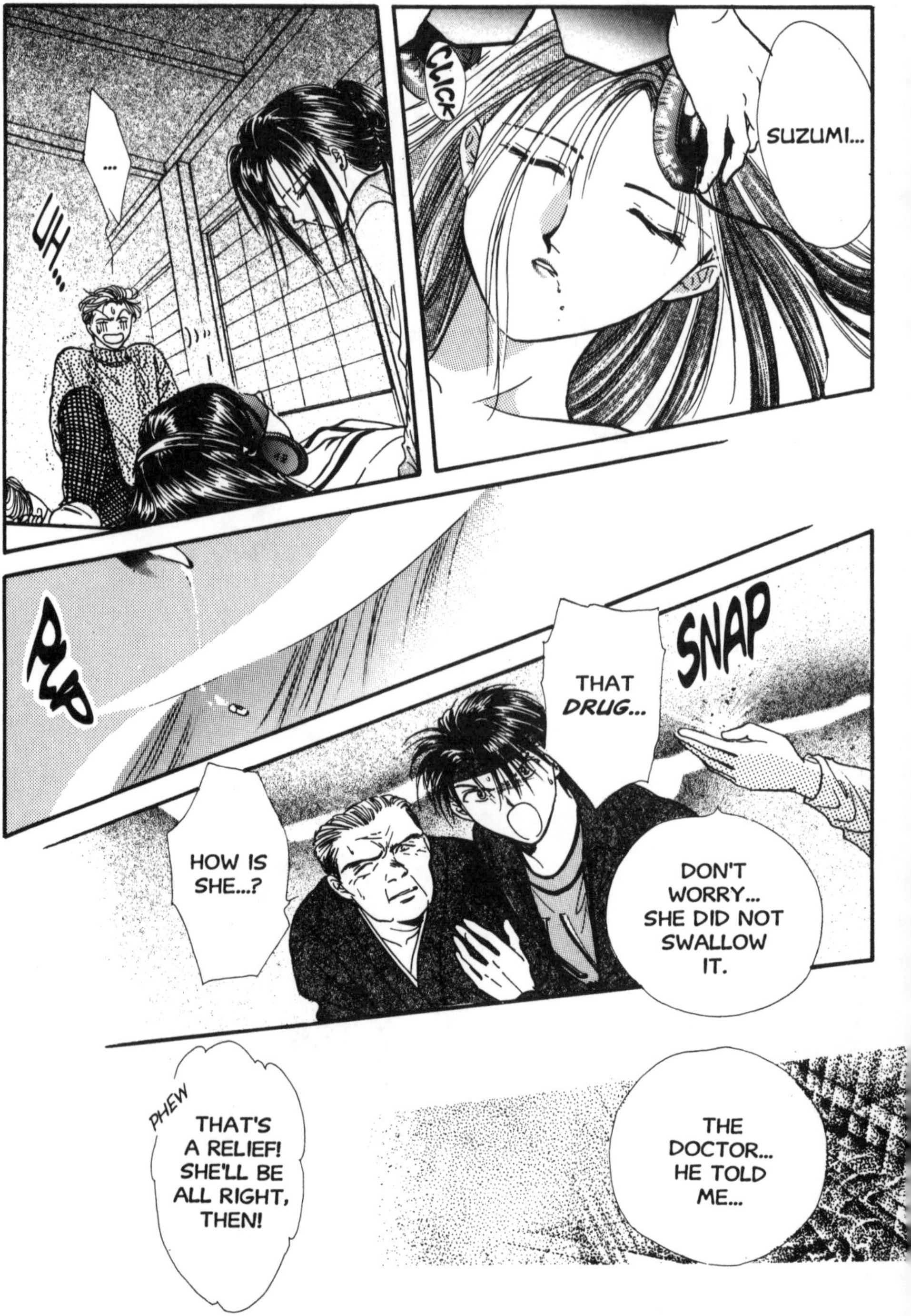
...
UH...
CLICK
SUZUMI...
PLIP
THAT DRUG...
SNAP
HOW IS SHE...?
DON'T WORRY... SHE DID NOT SWALLOW IT.
PHEW
THAT'S A RELIEF! SHE'LL BE ALL RIGHT, THEN!
THE DOCTOR... HE TOLD ME...

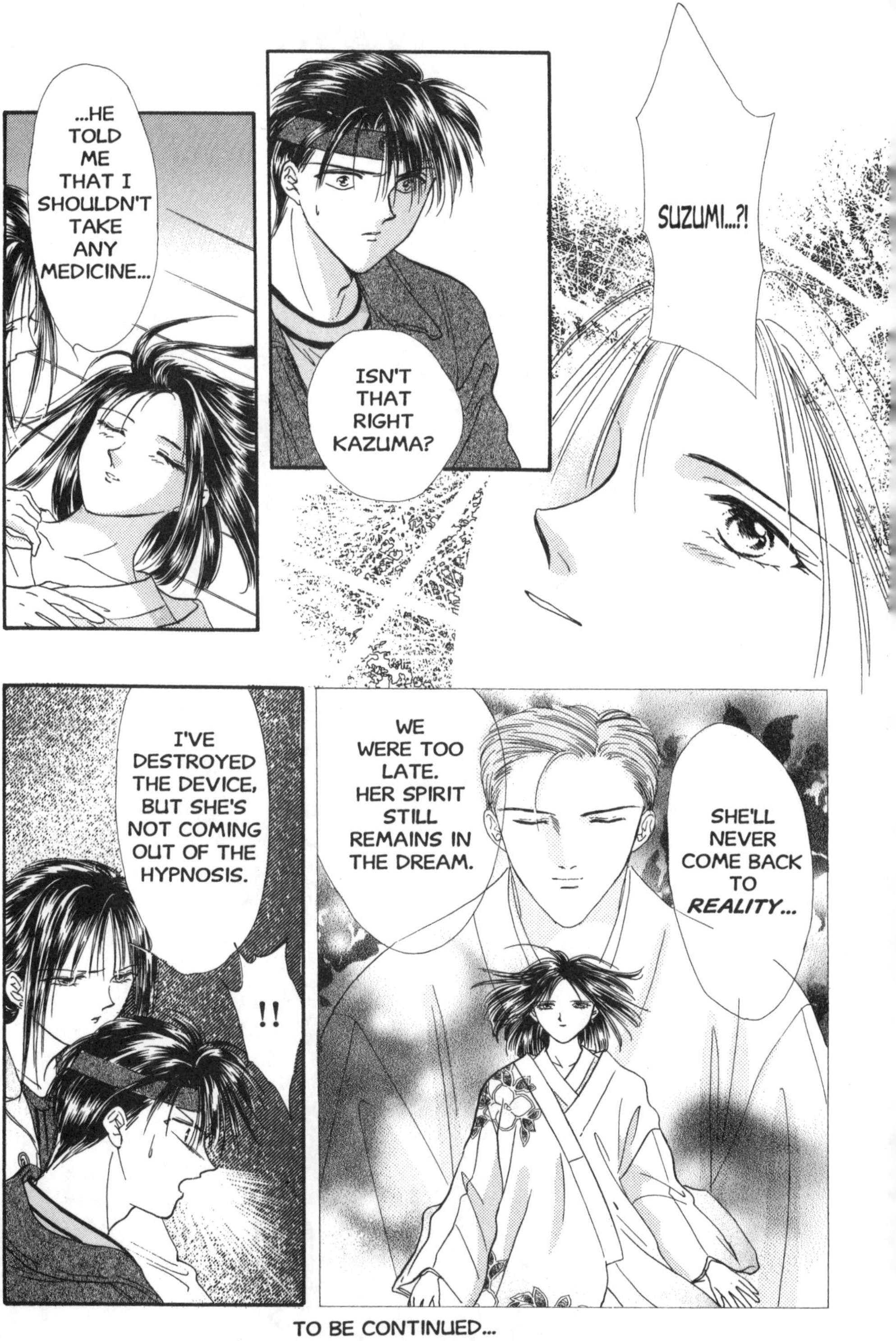
...HE TOLD ME THAT I SHOULDN'T TAKE ANY MEDICINE...
ISN'T THAT RIGHT KAZUMA?
SUZUMI...?!
I'VE DESTROYED THE DEVICE, BUT SHE'S NOT COMING OUT OF THE HYPNOSIS.
!!
WE WERE TOO LATE. HER SPIRIT STILL REMAINS IN THE DREAM.
SHE'LL NEVER COME BACK TO *REALITY*...

TO BE CONTINUED...

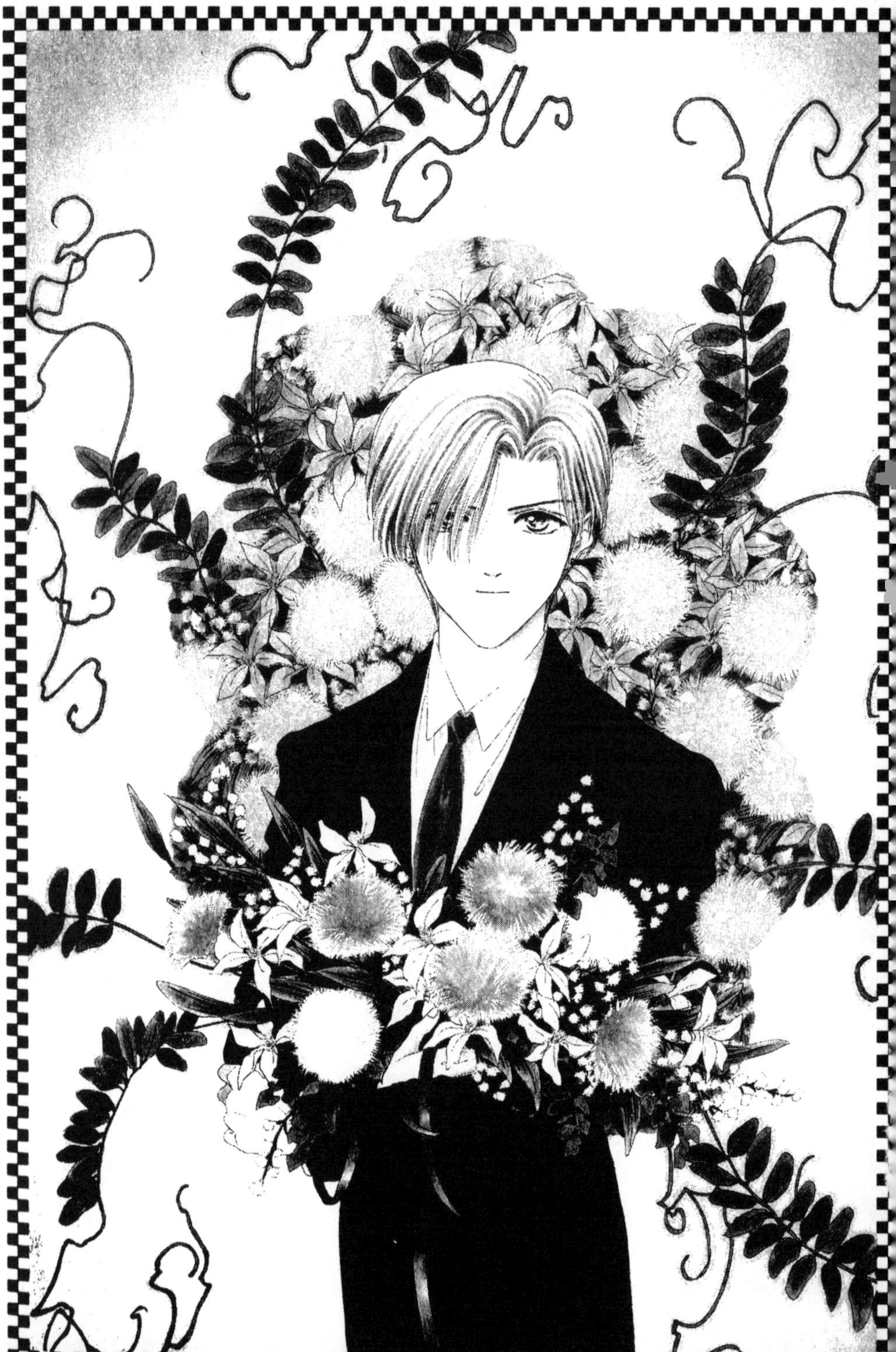

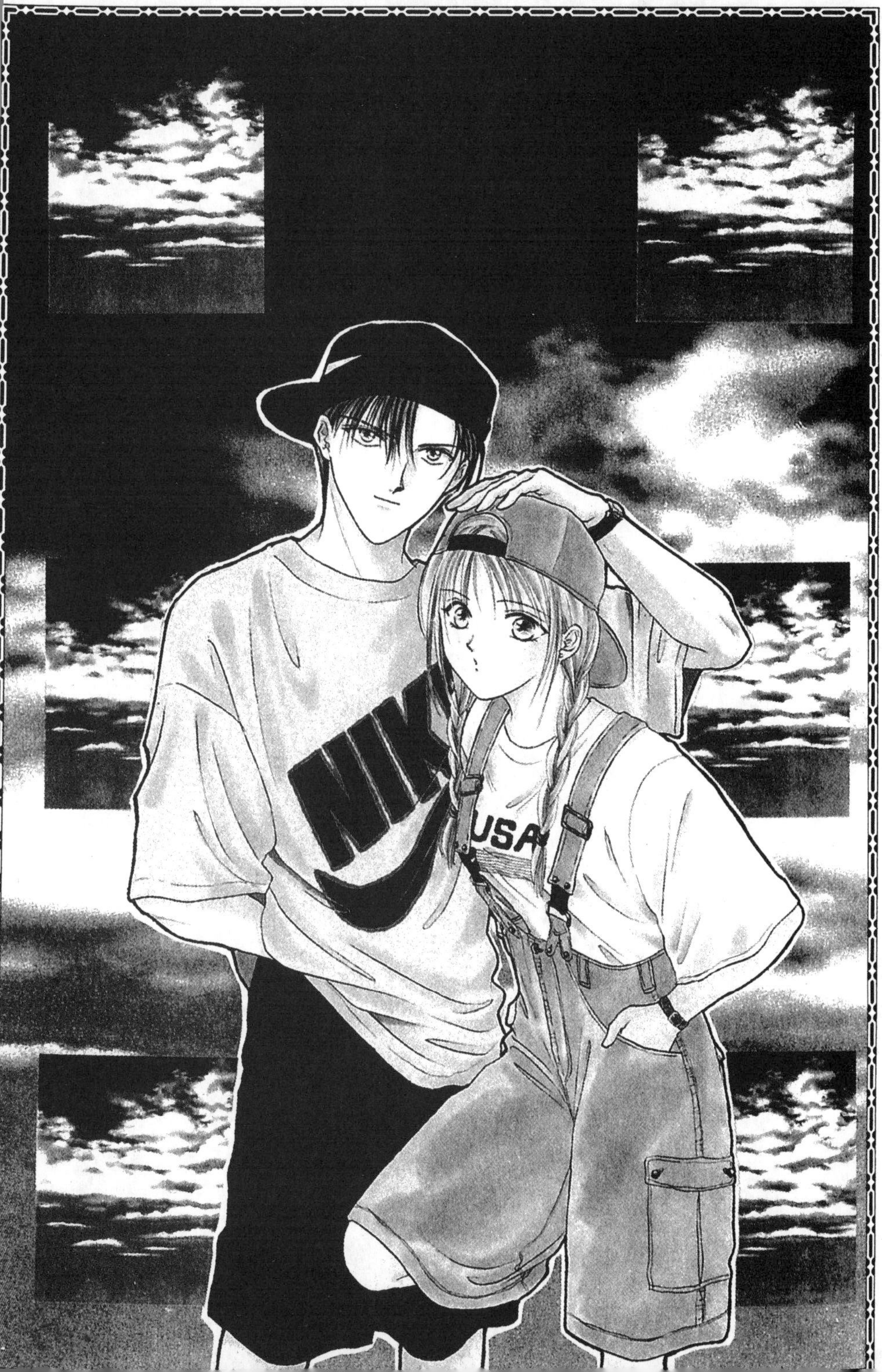
NIK
USA

Yû Watase was born on March 5 in a town near Osaka, and she was raised there before moving to Tokyo to follow the dream of creating manga. In the decade since her debut short story, PAJAMA DE OJAMA ("An Intrusion in Pajamas"), she has produced more than 50 compiled volumes of short stories and continuing series. Her latest series, ALICE 19TH, is currently running in the anthology magazine SHŌJO COMIC. Her smash-hit fantasy/romance story FUSHIGI YÛGI: THE MYSTERIOUS PLAY is available in North America with manga published by Viz, LLC and videos produced by Pioneer. Ms. Watase loves science fiction, fantasy and comedy.